A
MAN CALLED
BLESSED

teddekker.com

A
MAN CALLED
BLESSED

TED
DEKKER
AND BILL BRIGHT

THOMAS NELSON
Since 1798

NASHVILLE   DALLAS   MEXICO CITY   RIO DE JANEIRO

Published in Nashville, Tennessee, by Thomas Nelson. Thomas Nelson is a registered trademark of Thomas Nelson, Inc.

Thomas Nelson, Inc., titles may be purchased in bulk for educational, business, fund-raising, or sales promotional use. For information, please e-mail SpecialMarkets@ThomasNelson.com.

All Scripture quotations used in this book are from the New King James Version (NKJV®), © 1979, 1980, 1982, Thomas Nelson, Inc., Publishers.

ISBN: 978-1-4016-8879-0 (2013 repackage)

Library of Congress Cataloging-in-Publication Data

Bright, Bill.
    A man called blessed / by Bill Bright and Ted Dekker.
      p. cm.
    ISBN 978-0-8499-4514-4 (repak)
    1. Zionists—Fiction. 2. Ethiopia—Fiction. 3. Ark of the Covenant—Fiction.
  I. Dekker, Ted, 1962– II. Title.
    PS3552.R4623 M36 2002
    813'.54—dc21   2002007255

13 14 15 16 17 RRD 5 4 3 2 1

AUTHOR'S NOTE

The novel you are about to read is a message spun from my heart and that of my coauthor, Ted Dekker.

The story and the writing are primarily Ted's. He is a marvelous wordsmith. What a pleasure it has been to work with a man whom I consider to be perhaps the best storyteller on the market today for the simple reason that his stories are not only thrilling reads, but they speak volumes. If you read only a few novels this year, I strongly recommend they be novels written by Ted Dekker. You will be both thrilled and deeply enriched by reading Ted's books.

DR. BILL BRIGHT

PROLOGUE

DAVID BEN SOLOMON, LEADER OF THE Temple Mount Advocates, stood among the smoldering bodies, glued to the ground. Or maybe he wasn't standing. Maybe he was lying there on the asphalt, among the scattered dead. But he was breathing, wasn't he? Breathing heavy. So no, he wasn't dead.

The bus had been ripped into three large chunks by the Hamas bomb, each lay toppled, burning in flames. Sirens wailed and people were running around, yelling, frantic. But none of these details made any impression on David.

The bodies were all he saw.

The bodies and the number 9 on the section of bus that lay on its back, billowing oily smoke.

Most of the bodies were blackened; many were broken; a few still moved. David shoved a numb leg forward. His breath came in ragged gasps, drowning out the wails around him.

Hush, hush. It will be okay. There's been a mix-up.

But there was no mix-up, was there? This hadn't been just any bus working its way through busy Jerusalem streets on a Tuesday morning. This was bus number 9. And today David had kissed his wife, Hannah, and hugged his five-year-old daughter, Ruthie, and put them on bus number 9. It was Ruthie's first day of kindergarten, and Hannah had made a great fuss over the event. They'd climbed aboard the bus beaming and waving. The last thing David remembered seeing was the pink backpack little Ruthie herself had picked out a month earlier in anticipation of this day.

Someone was screaming behind him, screaming his name. "Papaaa!"

David staggered forward, tearing his eyes from the bubbling black paint that made the 9. *My God! Oh, my dear God, please!* The bodies were everywhere and he stumbled over them like a man possessed now, pulling them to see their faces. His hands shook and a soft whimper followed him—his own.

The scream from the sidewalk had taken on a guttural tone. "Papaaaaaa . . ."

David leapt around the bodies, frantic. *I beg you, dear God. I beg—*

He was in midstride when the pink backpack materialized under his right leg. Three facts crashed in on his mind, like bricks tossed from heaven. The first was that he was straddling little Ruthie. The second was that Ruthie had been burned to death. The third was that Ruthie was still in her mother's arms. And Hannah wasn't in one piece.

Something snapped in David's mind then. No man could see what he was seeing and remain whole. Air would never enter his lungs easily again; his heart would never beat with the same rhythm it had. Nothing would ever be the same.

"Papaaa . . ."

The two bodies lay still, dead and unfeeling, and he stared at them in utter horror. He clamped his eyes shut, dropped trembling arms to his side, and lifted his chin to the sky. His breathing settled to long pulls. His muscles quivered from head to toe.

Dear God, what have you done?

"Papaaa . . ."

David's hands knotted to fists and he began to sob, open mouthed.

"Papaaaa . . ."

The call cut through his mind for the first time, a bloodcurdling scream. Papa. Papa.

"Papaaaaaa!"

Rebecca! Oh, dear God, Rebecca!

David caught his breath and jerked his head to the sound. She stood on the sidewalk, face wrinkled with terror, arms spread to fists, screaming at him.

"Papaaaaaa!"

Her name was Rebecca and she was ten years old and she was his older daughter. For an endless moment he just stared at her. Rebecca's face was stained with soot, mixed with tears. She was staring at his legs, screaming. No, not at his legs . . .

David Ben Solomon tore his feet from the concrete and ran for his daughter. He leapt over the bodies, desperate now. This young girl who stood melting on the sidewalk was his child. His only child, now. He wasn't sure what he was doing—he only knew that he had to hold her and take her away from this.

"Rebecca . . ."

David cleared the last of the carnage and swept his daughter from her feet. They latched onto each other in a fierce embrace. Rebecca wrapped her legs around his belly and buried her face in his neck, sobbing bitterly.

David began to walk, holding her as if he were holding his own heart. He stumbled into a run.

He wanted to tell her it would be all right. That he loved her. That everything would be the same. But he couldn't speak past the fire in his throat. And the truth was that nothing would ever be the same.

Nothing. Ever.

1

D AVID BEN SOLOMON TURNED FROM THE window overlooking the Old City's night skyline and faced the old man.

"So you have a tale that will change the life of every Jew. Every Jew has a tale that will change the life of every Jew. In the end they never do." He paused, studying the man. "We don't have all night. Get on with it."

The hunched Falasha Jew bit off a reply in his foreign tongue, Amharic, and then sat unsteadily on the chair, favoring his shiny brass cane for support. A large white candle at his elbow cast amber hues on the mud walls, but he could see neither the light nor the five faces watching him from its shadows.

His blind eyes had frozen to slits many years ago.

Rebecca thought the Ethiopian Falasha Jew must have passed the hundred-year mark judging by the wrinkled flesh hanging off his skeleton. Solomon just stared at him. If the Falasha priest hadn't been blind, Rebecca imagined he'd be drilling her father with an indignant stare.

The servant boy who had guided the man here spoke beside the door. "He says that he won't speak to a man who does not show proper respect," the boy said nervously. "He is a keeper of truth—a great elder in Ethiopia."

In the shadows, Avraham Shlush, her father's rugged bodyguard, stood with arms crossed, peering at the old man past a frown. Next to him Professor Zakkai stood with hands in pockets, leaning against the wall. The archaeologist had a one-track mind and, as of yet, this meeting clearly wasn't on it.

They were here because her father, David Ben Solomon, had been told that the old Falasha priest had information critical to the Temple Mount, and any information critical to the Temple Mount was, in one way or another, lifeblood to the leader of the Temple Mount Advocates.

"Forgive me, Rabbi," Solomon said, using the respectful title. "But I have been told many things before. I'm growing tired of stories."

The Falasha priest didn't move. His jaw was covered in a ragged gray beard. A tan tunic badly in need of a good scrub wrapped his frail body. The bright red beads around his neck and the shiny golden cane in his hand stood in contrast to everything else about him. But then the Falasha Jews, better known as the *Black Jews of Ethiopia,* had always been an enigma. A throwback to ancient Judaism. Unlike other Jews scattered to the four corners, the Falasha were the only living Jews who still practiced blood sacrifice among other ancient Jewish customs. Very few historians could agree on how Judaism first made its way into Ethiopia, but it had appeared suddenly, remarkably intact. In the remote Falasha villages of Ethiopia, Judaism had remained virtually unchanged for at least a thousand years. Perhaps two thousand or longer. Like a fly frozen in amber.

An enigma.

The old priest looked as though he had just pried himself out of that amber and made his way back to Jerusalem to find God like so many of his countrymen. Perhaps to find the Messiah.

Rebecca blinked in the dim light. *But the Messiah isn't here, is he, Rabbi? You have come back to a bankrupt nation which refuses to make room for God, much less the Messiah.*

Her father spoke again, his voice gentle now. "I beg your forgiveness, Rabbi." He regarded the old Jew with amusement now. "Thirty years ago I would have spared no effort to hear your story. But I've given my life to the fruitless pursuit of rebuilding the Temple and these days I find myself wrestling more with doubt than dancing with hope. Surely you understand."

Her father stood tall, dressed in black slacks and a white shirt. He'd always favored casual clothes, and his latest obsession in archaeology suited it well, Rebecca thought. His hair was white and his firm jaw line clean shaven.

"I don't doubt the prophecies," he continued. "You'll have a hard time finding a Jew with as much passion to see the prophecies of the Temple's rebuilding and the Messiah's coming fulfilled. These will happen, in my lifetime if I'm so fortunate. However, I am beginning to doubt that mere talk will have much bearing on the prophecies. Stories feed the mind, but they don't remove the Muslim soldiers who guard the Temple Mount."

"I, too, believe in the prophecies," the priest said in a soft, scratchy voice. He spoke perfect Hebrew now. "I, too, have decided that the Messiah will come soon. I, too, believe that he will come only when we rebuild his Temple. But unlike you, I believe my story will quicken that coming."

The old Falasha Jew pushed himself to his feet and tapped his cane on the stone floor. "Perhaps I misjudged you."

Her father turned his back on the priest and looked out to the Temple Mount, framed by the rock window. Three hundred meters past the Jewish Quarter, the Dome of the Rock glinted in the rising moon's light.

"Sit, Rabbi," he said. "For heaven's sake sit and tell us your story."

The priest stopped and stood still.

Rebecca saved him. "Please, Rabbi. My father means only good. We wouldn't have invited you if we didn't have the greatest respect for you and your story."

The blind man turned to her. "Rebecca. The beautiful, celebrated hero. Will you kill me if I do not tell my story?" He grinned.

Professor Zakkai now wore an amused grin. Beside him, Avraham still frowned. Her father stared out the window, unmoving. The priest seated himself again. "So now you insist?"

"Yes, we insist," Rebecca said, unable to hold her smile. "Tell us, what does an old Falasha rabbi know that could possibly speed the Messiah's coming?"

"Do you know who I am?"

Solomon didn't respond, so Rebecca did. "You are Raphael Hadane, a Falasha Jew from Ethiopia."

The priest turned his head towards Solomon and then back to Rebecca, as if deciding whether he wanted to continue engaging a woman rather than the great David Ben Solomon.

"There are many kinds of Falasha Jews in Ethiopia. Some hardly know what it means to be Jewish. Do you know from where in Ethiopia I come?"

"No."

"I am from a small island in Lake Tana. Tana Kirkos. Do you know this island?"

"It's known for its priests. According to the Ethiopian legends in the *Kebra Nagast* it was the place to which the Ark of the Covenant was taken," Rebecca said.

The priest waved a hand. "The *Kebra Nagast* is full of inconsistencies and silly stories. But the Falasha Jews from Tana Kirkos are not."

Rebecca glanced at Professor Zakkai who had stepped forward. They had talked of the legend before, but its likelihood was practically zero. The Ethiopian Orthodox Church claimed that the Queen of Sheba had visited King Solomon from Ethiopia and conceived a son born in Ethiopia after her departure. The son, Menelik, later returned and stole the Ark of the Covenant which he returned to his mother's palace in Axum, northern Ethiopia. If this was the old man's tale, her father's skepticism would be justified. The notion that a foreigner could have stolen the Jews' most holy relic without even a notation in the historical biblical record was absurd.

"I know that you are looking for the Ark," the old priest, Hadane, said.

David Ben Solomon turned from the window. "Yes, we are. It's something we'd rather not broadcast."

"Do you know what would happen if the Ark was discovered?"

"A war would happen," Solomon said. Silence held them for a moment. "More importantly, Israel would be forced to rebuild the Temple to house it. Our faith would demand it."

The old man nodded. "And that would prepare the way for the Messiah." Their breathing sounded inordinately loud in the stillness. "I once heard you say that if Israel hadn't given the Temple Mount back to the Muslims after the Six-Day War, the Messiah would have come in 1967. Do you still believe that?"

"Yes," Solomon said. "I was there."

The old man had gotten her father's attention now. Very few knew that the Temple Mount Advocates had shifted their emphasis from protests and legal actions to an all-out effort to discover the Ark.

"It's written in prophecy," Solomon continued. "The Messiah will come to the Temple. So there must be a Temple for him to come to. How do you know about our efforts to find the Ark?"

"It is my business to know about the Ark," the priest said. "It was my father's business to know about the Ark, and his father's."

"We have researched the claims of Ethiopia and concluded that—"

"You have wasted your time. You have not spoken to me. And if it was not for your daughter, Rebecca, you would have lost your chance tonight. I suggest you listen, David Ben Solomon."

Rebecca caught her father's side glance and raised an amused brow. Not too many men spoke to Solomon so directly.

The priest drew a deep breath through his nostrils. "The *Tabotat*—the Ark of the Covenant—in which rests the very presence of God, was brought to Jerusalem by King David 1,006 years before . . . how do you say it in Hebrew?"

Dr. Zakkai spoke for the first time. "1006 B.C.E."

"Yes. 1006 B.C.E. His son, Solomon, built the Temple as the resting place for the Ark. This he did in 955 . . ."

"B.C.E.," Zakkai filled in.

"Yes. 955 and 1006. You probably believe, as do most Jews, that the Ark was taken by the Babylonians in the year 586, four hundred years later, when they destroyed the Temple. But that is your first mistake."

The Falasha priest drew a hand across his lips, wiping some saliva away. "In truth, it was removed from the Temple during the reign of Manasseh by a group of priests in 650 B.C.E."

"No Jewish priest would have ever removed the Ark from the holy place without returning it," Dr. Zakkai said with a slight smile. "Not by choice. It is inconceivable."

"Yes, it is inconceivable. Unless it was the only option. You will recall that Manasseh defiled the Temple by placing an image of Asherah in the most holy place. What priest do you know that would allow a pagan idol to stand next to the Ark in the holy place?"

"The Ark was taken out, but only for a short time," Dr. Zakkai said.

"The idols were not destroyed until many years later. Why does your record not tell us what happened to the Ark during this time? There *is* no definitive record of the Ark being placed back in the holy place. It simply disappears from your history."

"Yes, but King Josiah removed Asherah and ordered—"

"Josiah *ordered* the Ark be returned, but there is no record of it being returned." The old Falasha priest's suddenly strong voice belied his frail stature.

"The Ark never was returned. The priests, fearing that it might be defiled again, kept it hidden. It was a dangerous time. Their decision was justified when the Temple was destroyed by the Babylonians a short time later. But the Ark was not there. It had been taken already."

"Is this possible?" David Ben Solomon asked Dr. Zakkai.

"Unlikely. And even if a group of priests had taken the Ark, they would've left a record of it. They certainly wouldn't have taken the Ark beyond the borders of . . ." He turned to the old man. "Where do you say they took it?"

"Israel was no longer safe. The priests took it south, down the Nile, to Aswan in Egypt."

"Aswan?"

"Has it never puzzled you that very shortly after Manasseh's reign a Jewish temple was built in Aswan, on the island of Elephantine? The only temple outside of Israel ever constructed with the exact dimensions of Solomon's Temple?"

Zakkai hesitated. "Yes. It is . . . strange."

"Yes, strange. Unless you know *why* it existed. It was built by the priests for the same purpose as the only other temple like it in history—to hold the Ark. Jews in Israel ceased blood sacrifice at this time. But not at the temple at Aswan. There the priests continued in the ways of the old law, without compromise. Another coincidence your scholars are pressed to explained."

"I've never heard that," Rebecca said, glancing at the professor. There was no scholar as well versed in Jewish history as Dr. Zakkai, and in her two years with the man, he'd never spoken of the temple at Aswan.

The old man looked at her with blind eyes. "If you had spent as much time with books as you have with a gun, you might have."

Her reputation as a soldier had obviously made an impression on the priest. In many Jewish minds Rebecca Solomon, daughter of David Ben Solomon, was at twenty-five nearly as much a national hero as Ariel Sharon. Not that she had won any wars, like Sharon had, but in the covert war with the Hamas and other PLO groups, she had made her mark. Assassinating a second in command to Arafat tended to make a statement. Doing it twice left a permanent mark.

Rebecca felt divided over her reputation. On one hand, satisfied that she'd personally extracted revenge for her mother's and sister's deaths. On the other hand, sickened by the bloodshed. Underneath her skin she wasn't that sort of person. She was simply a woman who wanted to discover love and life without the terror that had always stalked her.

"A large Jewish community grew up around the temple in Aswan," Hadane continued. "Two hundred years later the temple was destroyed in war and the Jews vanished from the region. Many wonder where they went. I'll tell you. They traveled further down the Nile to Lake Tana in Ethiopia and built a simple tabernacle in which they placed the Ark of the Covenant. The caretakers on the island were my ancestors. We have carefully guarded this secret for two thousand years. And to this day we are the only Jews who still practice blood sacrifice."

"If you have the Ark, why would you hide it?" Rebecca asked. "Why not just bring it back?"

"Did I say I have it? We have guarded the knowledge, not the Ark. And if the Ark's location were known, how many would cross oceans to defile it?"

"So, according to your story, where is the Ark?"

"Today? Yes, I will come to that. For many centuries the Ark remained in obscurity on the remote island. If you go today, you will see many signs of its history. Relics which date back to Solomon's day: candlesticks, incense bowls—only recently have they come into focus among archaeologists. But the Ark was removed once again in 1200 . . . how do you say it?"

"C.E.," Zakkai said.

"Thank you. You know of the Crusades. The Knights Templar besieged and took over Jerusalem in 1099 C.E. For nearly a hundred years the knights lived on the Temple Mount, rarely leaving it. Do you know what they were doing up there?"

"They were digging," Zakkai said.

"Yes. They were looking for the Ark. Their tunnels are still under the Mount today, but the Muslims won't let you explore them. They are sealed."

The room grew still. In reality, Rebecca and Zakkai had examined the

Temple Mount in far more detail than anyone knew. Modern imaging technology was proving itself in their hands. If the Israeli authorities found out, it would be prison. If the Palestinians found out, it would be riots and bloodshed at the least. Either way the explorations hadn't yielded anything of value. Not yet.

"It's not my business if you want to crawl around under the Mount," the priest said. "But you won't find what you're looking for. Neither did the Templars. But they did find artifacts. And they found a letter written by one of the priests during the reign of Manasseh. The letter speaks of the escape route they planned on taking. The route leads south towards Ethiopia."

Rebecca glanced at Zakkai, who stared at Hadane, thoroughly interested now. "You . . . you have this letter?" Zakkai asked.

"No. I don't know where it is. But the Templars understood from the letter that the Ark had gone south, down the Nile, to Ethiopia. They left Jerusalem suddenly, if you recall. What you may not know is that they came to my country and for many years lived in good favor with the king. They built many large monasteries on which they placed their unmistakable crosses. The historians can't understand why the Templars were in Ethiopia," the priest said with a smile. "As I said, many don't even know they *were* in Ethiopia. But we know."

He sighed. "Sadly, the Ark was taken from our island and moved to a church in Axum in 1200."

"Saint Mary's of Zion. So you, too, believe that the Ark is in Saint Mary's as the Ethiopian Orthodox insist?" Zakkai asked.

"No. But it was."

"And how do you know this?"

"Because I am a guardian of the knowledge—a Falasha priest to whom has been entrusted this knowledge. The Orthodox might have taken the Ark, but they could not hide its location from us."

The priest stopped and for a few moments they all just stood there. Solomon finally turned around and stared out to the Temple Mount.

"So now you are going to tell us that the Ark is in such and such a place," he said. "A church in Addis Ababa or in a grave in Lalibela. Either way, it's still nothing but a story from an old man who's telling only what he's heard.

We really can't pick up and travel fifteen hundred kilometers every time an old rabbi tells us another theory."

"You are an impatient man," Hadane said.

"I am a realist." Solomon turned around. "As I said, thirty years ago I would have already packed my bags and would be at the airport, catching the next flight to your country. But after a thousand hopes and a thousand blows, I've become a realist."

"But still, you search for the Ark."

"Because I see no other way," Solomon bit off. "And to be truthful, I'm not sure it makes any sense now. We're no closer to building the Temple today than we were when we started. Meanwhile more secular Jews flood our country, diluting the call for the Messiah's coming. At this rate you won't be able to tell a Jew from an Arab twenty years from now."

"And the Ark would change this?"

"Yes, of course. But you don't have the Ark. You don't even have a candlestick. The last one we spoke to at least had a candlestick. You will forgive my forthrightness, Rabbi, but all you have are words."

"Father—"

"Please, Rebecca. To him, you are nothing but a killer." Solomon's words cut with the kind of resolve built in a man who had battled not only the enemy, but his own people for too long. Rebecca felt heat wash over her face at the rebuke. Behind her father, Avraham, the true killer in this room, now stood with a small grin.

"With a word God created," the old priest said. "Perhaps words are all you need."

"No, Rabbi. I need a gun. A very big gun. Like the Ark. The Ark is a very big gun."

"Then perhaps I did make a mistake in coming here."

"Perhaps."

The priest tapped the floor with his cane and pushed himself to his feet again. His servant boy ran up and took his hand. Together they walked to the door. The old man muttered something in Amharic.

"What did he say, boy?" Zakkai asked.

The servant boy turned back. His eyes darted around the room, nervous, which seemed odd to Rebecca. What reason did the boy have to be nervous? "He said that he will never understand why God chooses such stubborn men. He was right not to show you the letter."

"Letter? I thought you said you didn't have the priest's letter. What letter?" Zakkai demanded.

The priest paused by the door, his back still to them.

Solomon turned from the window. "What letter, Rabbi?"

The priest stepped out of the room.

Solomon spoke in a soft tone. "Do you believe that God has chosen me, Rabbi?"

The priest stopped. For a long time he said nothing. When he spoke, his voice was very quiet. "A letter from the Knight Templar who found the priest's record when the Templars dug under the Temple Mount." The old man turned around.

"The knight left the letter with my ancestors nearly a thousand years ago. That is why we know the legend is true. We have proof. The Ark was taken by the Temple priests to the Nile. If this much is true, the rest surely follows."

"You have this letter?" Zakkai demanded. He stepped forward. "With you?"

"Yes."

Rebecca exchanged a look with Zakkai and her father. Even Avraham had stepped out of the shadows. An actual letter from the Knights Templar that referred to what they had found under the Temple Mount . . . it would be incredible!

"May we see it?" Zakkai asked. His voice had taken on a tremor.

Raphael hesitated, then withdrew a dirty envelope from his tunic. He opened it with unsteady hands and produced a sheet of browned paper, ragged on its edges.

Zakkai stepped forward and took the paper. He studied it for a moment and then looked up at Solomon with wild eyes. He whirled to the table and set the paper down, smoothing it with one hand. Then they were all moving for the table. The atmosphere felt electric.

The letter was in Middle English—faded black letters on very old paper.

I, sir wallace thronburge iii, am a knight in the
service of the holy ark from jerusalem . . .

The letter began to tell the story, precisely as Hadane had just relayed it.

"Is it genuine?" Solomon asked.

Zakkai stroked his beard. "It . . . it appears to be."

Solomon turned around, trembling now. "Where is the Ark today?"

The old man smiled. "*Now* you are ready to listen. Do you wish me to start from the beginning?"

"Forgive me, Rabbi. Surely you understand. Tell me what you know about the Ark's location."

"If I tell you, you will see that the Temple is rebuilt?"

"If I find the Ark, *Israel* will see to it that the Temple is rebuilt! *God* will see to it."

"I will accept that." The old man's lips flattened.

He walked back in, smug and obviously satisfied with himself. He sat once again and lifted his head straight.

"The Ark was taken to Saint Mary's of Zion long ago, as the Orthodox Christians claim, but it was removed whenever war threatened its safety. Often for years at a time, replaced by a *Tabotat* replica—the kind you see throughout Ethiopia today. But then it was decided that the Ark should be removed permanently—too many from the West were beginning to suspect its existence there."

"Where did they take it?" Solomon demanded.

Zakkai stood up from the letter that he still examined. "I . . . I believe it is genuine, David."

"Yes." Her father had evidently decided the same. "Where, Rabbi? Where did they take it?"

"It was taken to an ancient monastery in northern Ethiopia twenty years ago. A very remote monastery named the Debra Damarro, under the care of a Father Matthew."

Rebecca looked up at her father. Not since her last mission with the Mossad two years ago, before she'd given up her gun for a shovel, had she felt the kind of current that now rushed through her nerves.

"Father. We should go—"

"It's not that simple," the Falasha priest said.

"Why?"

"The monastery Debra Damarro was destroyed fifteen years ago during an Eritrean raid. It has since been rebuilt."

"And the Ark wasn't found?"

"No. Father Matthew was a very wise guardian. Before he died, he hid the Ark well and planted the key to its precise location on a pure vessel of God. A young boy. He alone holds the key to the Ark's discovery."

"How do you know all of this?"

The man paused. "My brother was a very good friend to Father Matthew. His name is Joseph Hadane. He lives in the desert near the monastery. Father Matthew told him about the boy."

"And this boy lives?"

"Yes. He is a young man now."

"What is his name?"

"His name is Caleb."

"Caleb," Rebecca said, letting the name linger on her tongue. If the priest was right, one man stood between them and the salvation of Israel, and his name was Caleb.

Avraham spoke for the first time. His eyes were glazed. "Sir, you must allow me to lead a mission to recover the relic immediately."

Solomon spun. "Rebecca, prepare to leave tomorrow. Take Avraham and Zakkai and ten men. Only the very best."

Avraham stepped forward. "Sir, I believe it is a mistake—"

"Yes, Avraham, I know you think you should lead. Not this time."

Solomon picked up the letter from the table and blinked in the candlelight. "If God wills . . ."

He let the statement die. God's will was too ambiguous to predict these days.

2

ISMAEL WALKED BESIDE HIS FATHER, THE Syrian general, on the *Haram al-Sharif*—Noble Sanctuary to most Muslims and Temple Mount to most Jews. Ahead of them the moon's reflection glinted off the Dome of the Rock. Behind them the Al-Aqsa Mosque swept across the southern end of the Mount, high above the Jews' Western Wall.

It was from here, on this flat rock roughly two hundred meters square, that Mohammed had been taken to heaven and given his vision of God. It was here that the Jews erroneously claimed their ancient king, Solomon, had built his Temple to God. It was here that Jesus, the great prophet whom the Christians mistakenly called God's Son, had cried his message of change.

It was here that mankind's destiny would one day be decided.

"The boy should have come by now," Ismael said.

"You hold his mother. He will come," Abu Ismael said.

Father and son walked in slow tandem stride, with hands behind their backs. "You may not appreciate his threat, Father, but I believe David Ben Solomon is the greatest enemy we face. He talks openly about rebuilding the Jewish Temple, and they can't build their Temple without destroying ours first."

Abu Ismael nodded at a *Waqf* guard who loitered against the wall to their right. "Perhaps, but you must choose your battles, Ismael. There is a time to kill and there is a time to live. I believe it was their King Solomon who said that first, wasn't it?"

"Easy to say when you live in Syria, removed from our struggle, surrounded by all the comforts given to Syria's most respected general. Perhaps you should remember that you're a Palestinian by blood. Palestinians live in the ghettos the world forces us to call home. Here there's no time to live. We're dying all the time."

Abu Ismael chuckled. "Of course, you are dying. And sometimes I think you choose to die. Blowing up a few children does not always lead to life."

"Terror's the only legitimate weapon we have. And you think that when the Jews assassinated Hamil, we did not feel terror?"

It was a low blow, referring to his older brother's assassination—Father had loved him dearly. For a few long steps Abu did not respond. He was dressed in civilian clothes, but under the common attire walked a man with as much power as any other in the Arab League. He not only commanded several hundred thousand troops in the Syrian army, he had the ear of the kings. His evenhanded approach to the challenge that Israel presented the Arab nations earned him that much. And his undying allegiance to Palestinian's right to all of Israel earned him the respect of the PLO.

"We are walking on Islam's third most holy site, Ismael, behind only Mecca and Medina," his father said.

Ismael did not respond.

"How is that possible when this same piece of ground is the Jew's Temple Mount? Their most holy place."

"Their claim's illegitimate," Ismael said. "They've manufactured a lie by saying that their Temple was built here. It's always been holy ground for Islam."

"Yes, of course. But it's still their most holy site. And yet whose guards do you see patrolling the Mount? The *Waqf*. Muslim guards patrol Jewish land. The Jews cannot even come up here to pray. Instead, they are confined below, at the Western Wall where they wail. We control their Temple Mount. You don't see our victory in that? The irony? It is like the Jews taking Mecca from us."

"And they have Jerusalem—the legitimate capital of Palestine!"

"Yes, they have Jerusalem. And encircling Jerusalem, we have the West Bank, which is encircled by Israel, which is in turn encircled by the Arab states. Concentric circles of opposing forces, but we rule the heart. This piece of ground we are walking on now. The holy place."

"And the West stands around us all, biding its time," Ismael said.

"The West is more friendly every day. One step at a time, Ismael. Today we make the Jews bow at the foot of our mosque"—he dipped his head at the Western Wall on their right—"and tomorrow we will push them into the sea."

"And what if today we have their Temple Mount but tomorrow the Jews take it? It's here, on this plot of land, that our fate rests. All your other concentric circles will stand or fall with this one. They may not be admitting it, but Jews already have a plan for retaking the Temple Mount, and one day they will overwhelm us with it. We must strike first."

His father stopped and stared westward to the Jewish Quarter. The breeze carried a Muslim prayer call from the north.

"I agree with you, Ismael—we can never allow Israeli control of the Noble Sanctuary. But unlike you I don't think they have a plan for retaking it. In fact, we have their government shaking in its boots. We surround them on all sides, we march our *Waqf* on their Temple site, and we refuse them entrance. If they sincerely believed that the Mount should be theirs, they would have taken it many years ago. If they tried it now, the world of Islam would descend on Jerusalem with a vengeance they could never survive— they know that as well as we do."

Ismael spit to the side. "We should descend on Jerusalem now. We pick away at their skirts but refuse to go for their heart."

His father ignored his disgraceful act. "You think Israel's allies would stand by for an unprovoked attack? Don't be naive."

Ismael walked on and his father followed. They had always disagreed in degrees. Ismael lived his days soaking in the rhetoric of the PLO in Ramallah, and, frankly, hearing his father talk like this sounded odd. As if the mighty Syrian general had turned his back on the intifada and sided with the politicians who talked too much and did too little. A Palestinian state was not enough. The Jews had to be crushed. Both the '73 war and the '67 war could have been different if it weren't for the old guard. They did a fine enough job fighting with words, but when it came to tanks and machine guns they were like women.

His father was not like the old guard, of course. He knew how to use the tanks under his command and his hatred for Israel was as properly motivated as Ismael's. The Jews had forcefully occupied Palestinian territory for many years, forcing millions of women and children from their homes; that was reason enough to hate. But there was more—the Jews' religion was an open affront to Islam and in fact the dispute over the Temple Mount crowned the struggle. And of course they had murdered Hamil, Ismael's older brother, Abu's elder son. Hamil had been the second in command of Arafat's *Fatah* when he took a sniper's bullet.

Ismael looked at his father. "A leader will come to the Jews and will conquer Islam—"

"I know the prophecies of the *al-Massih*," Abu interrupted. "It's also prophesied that the prophet Jesus will then come back to defeat the Jews and establish Islam as the world's only religion. Let us allow prophecy to run its own course. For now we must be careful to play the cards given us by the world. Any unjustified attack on Israel would only erode sympathies, which are now in the Palestinians' favor."

A small wedge of bitterness rose through Ismael's throat. He despised this kind of talk. His father had the power to deliver all of Palestine in one fell swoop with his armies, but instead he talked about world sympathies.

"And if the cards show a plan by the Israelis to retake the Temple Mount? Will you let your tanks sit rusting then?"

Abu shot him a stern glare. They were both soldiers now, but the general was the elder. Ismael held his eyes.

"Don't be a fool! Your patriotism pales next to mine." Abu turned away, and for a brief moment Ismael fought an urge to strike him. He shuddered in the dark.

The impulse surprised him. Maybe the killing had thinned his blood. The little green pin on his collar identified him as a sharpshooter who had killed more Jews than any other since Ramadan—a badge he wore with pride. But his father was not a Jew.

"Believe me, I will never allow the Jews to take the Mount," Abu Ismael said softly. "The *Haram al-Sharif* is to Islam what blood is to the body."

Feet pattered on the stone behind them. It was the boy, Bennie, finally come from his assignment. Ismael took a calming breath.

The boy slowed to a walk. He looked as Jewish as he did Palestinian, a product of a mixed marriage. The plan had been simple. A week earlier, one of their operatives had learned from the boy's mother—a secular Falasha Jew—that Bennie was assisting an old blind rabbi who was meeting with David Ben Solomon. They had taken the mother yesterday and told the boy she would die if he did not report. The Mossad did not corner the market on information.

The boy stopped before them, winded.

"Well?" Ismael demanded.

Bennie glanced nervously at the general.

"You're safe here, boy. I suggest you begin speaking. Did the old bat meet with Solomon?"

"Where is my mother?"

"Waiting to see you. Speak."

"Yes. They talked for a long time."

A ball of hope turned in Ismael's gut. He had wanted to impress his father with this show of intelligence gathering. Who knew, the boy might actually have something.

"And what did they talk about?"

"About the Ark."

"The Ark?"

"The Ark of the Covenant. Rabbi Hadane told them where it is."

At first the boy's words didn't register. They knew that Solomon had taken up an interest in ancient artifacts, working with Zakkai from the Antiquities Society this past year or so. Solomon obviously wanted to construct evidence about the Temple that would help persuade his people to rebuild it. But the Ark?

His father cleared his throat. "What do you mean?"

"The rabbi is from Ethiopia. He says that the Ark from King Solomon's Temple is there. He told them how to find it."

Ismael blinked. His breathing stopped. A stun grenade could have been dropped thirty meters away at that moment and he might not have noticed. He turned slowly to his father who was glaring at the boy.

"You are saying that Solomon actually believed the man?" Abu asked. "They think they know where the Ark is?"

"Yes. They had a letter that showed it. The woman is going tomorrow to get it."

Even in the dim light Ismael could see his father's face go white. "Tomorrow?" He grabbed the boy's shirt. "This is not a time to play with words! The Ark is a myth!"

"Please . . . please, sir! I'm only telling you what I heard." Tears filled the boy's eyes.

"Is this possible?" Ismael asked. "Could they actually find the Ark?"

Abu Ismael released the boy.

The initial shock began to give way to heat, which spread down Ismael's neck. "If they were to find the Ark and bring it to Jerusalem, it would mean—"

"I know what it would mean!" Abu said.

Ismael finished anyway. "They would demand the Temple Mount to rebuild their Temple!" It was something they all knew. According to legend, Solomon's Temple had been built to house the Ark. If the Ark were found, the people of the book would not rest until the Temple was rebuilt.

Abu Ismael studied the boy. "Do you think the Ark is really where the man said it was?"

The boy shifted nervously. "When they read the letter—"

"Father, we have to stop them!" Ismael interrupted.

"We don't even know it exists," Abu said. "We are hearing a boy who's telling of a story told by an old blind rabbi."

"You heard him. *Solomon* believes it!" Ismael turned to the boy. "Who is the woman?"

"Solomon's daughter. Rebecca."

"Rebecca Solomon!" Ismael felt a tremble take to his fingers. "Hamil's killer."

A long unearthly silence seemed to suffocate them. Surely his father would forget his political nonsense now. The Hamas didn't need the general, of course—the Syrian army had no immediate authority here. But one day the Palestinians *would* need the Syrian army.

"If this is true—"

"Please, leave us until we call you," Abu said to the boy.

The boy ran off towards the steps.

"I am with you," Abu said. A familiar tension filled his father's voice. He hadn't become a general by kissing babies. "But it must be done quietly. If even a rumor surfaces that they have found the Ark, true or not, it will become a problem. And not just for the Palestinians. The entire Arab world will be affected."

The words came like honey, and Ismael felt a sudden surge of adrenaline sweep through his bones. The Hamas had failed to kill Rebecca Solomon on three separate occasions. This time he would not fail. *Could* not fail.

"You must find out what she knows before you kill her," Abu said.

"Yes. Of course." Ismael's voice cracked and he cleared his throat.

"I assume you have the people you need for this?"

"I prefer to work alone," Ismael said. "It's something I do well."

Abu looked at him, but Ismael could not judge his expression. Ismael's mind was already gone—after the girl. *You will soon die, Rebecca.* They could never prove her involvement in Hamil's death, but now it didn't matter. She would die either way.

"Take at least two others. The best you have," Abu said. "You can't afford a mistake on this. If I thought it would help, I would send you a couple of my men, but we don't have time for that."

"Yes." *And your men don't know how to kill, Father. Not like I do. They may have big guns and bombs but they carry their knives like women.*

" . . . cannot allow this to spread," his father was saying. "We can't make the same mistake Solomon did with the boy. Find out everything the boy knows and then kill him."

"Of course."

Ismael smiled. He had decided to kill the boy a week ago. Now his father was not only agreeing with the decision, but ordering it.

The sound of music drifted on the breeze. It was going to be a good night, he thought. A glorious night.

3

REBECCA HAD PLANNED THE MISSION WITH her father and Avraham late into the night. She would lead Avraham, Dr. Zakkai, and ten men south to the port city of Eilat where they would board the *Ellipsis,* an Antiquities Society freighter at Zakkai's disposal. Dressed in the common garb of archaeologists and diggers, they would sail sixteen hundred kilometers directly south through the Red Sea, to Massawa, on the coast of Eritrea. The journey would take them two days. From Massawa they would strike west into Ethiopia, to the remote monastery the blind rabbi had told them about, apprehend Caleb and extract the Ark, if it was found, and then immediately return to Jerusalem.

What they would do then was hardly imaginable.

According to the Falasha priest, the monastery Debra Damarro rarely accommodated visitors. Caleb and his parents ran the rebuilt compound and worked among lepers in a nearby village. God willing, no one would even know the monastery had been taken. They would be gone from Ethiopia before an alarm could be raised.

Rebecca kept one hand on the wheel and removed her cap, allowing the wind to stream through her hair. She glanced back at the trailing open-bed truck, an old Nissan, hauling ten men who looked like nothing more than diggers for hire—a common enough sight in these barren hills. But the crates marked with large *Antiquities* labels at their feet didn't hold the clay pots a curious onlooker might imagine. There was enough metal in those crates to take a small armed fort. They had sailed past three Israeli checkpoints with hardly a glance.

Beside her Zakkai sat in the Land Rover staring at the winding blacktop.

"Do you think we will find it, Professor?" she asked.

He shook his head. "I have been over the old man's story a dozen times . . . To be honest I don't know why I ignored the signs. We've always discounted the Ethiopian theory because of the ridiculous inconstancies in the *Kebra Nagast.* But to listen to the old priest, the inconsistencies are not the point at all." He shook his head again. "The circumstantial evidence alone, put as he put it, is daunting."

"After two years of chasing every possible lead in Israel, we're suddenly confronted with the possibility of finding the Ark in Ethiopia. It seems impossible," Rebecca said.

Zakkai stared out his window. "The writers of Jewish history, including the Bible, fell mysteriously silent after the reign of Manasseh. But then, if the priests *had* taken the Ark, they would've remained silent. In a strange way it makes perfect sense. You don't hide something and then tell everyone where you hid it."

"But you're not sure."

He faced her. "Sure? Of course I'm not sure. How could I be sure about finding something that has eluded the world for twenty-six hundred years? But . . ." Zakkai paused and she saw the glimmer in his eyes. "I do believe there is a reasonable chance. Although to be honest, I can hardly imagine what will happen if we do find it."

Avraham spoke from the rear seat. "War will happen. A million Arabs will die in the desert."

Rebecca studied the man in the rearview mirror. His short-cropped hair exposed an ugly scar on his temple, a gift from a knife-wielding PLO assassin who had barely missed his right eye. The cut had sliced into Avraham's heart, Rebecca thought. The IDF major had subsequently been relieved of his command for his repeated use of unnecessary violence in skirmishes. The Israeli Defense Force might seem liberal in its use of force, but even they had their limits.

"You're too eager for blood, Avraham," Rebecca said.

"I am? This from Israel's most celebrated assassin?"

"When I killed, I did so for God, not for blood. And even then with discretion."

The man sneered. "We'll see what happens to your discretion if we return to Jerusalem with the Ark. The Arabs' missiles will be flying, and you won't have time to think about either God or discretion."

"We have no intention of letting Arab missiles fly. If we show restraint, they will as well. It's a lesson you could learn. Either way, as long as you're under my command you'll kill only who I tell you to kill."

"Of course," he replied with a bite of sarcasm.

"Yes, sir, would be adequate. Or have you forgotten how to address your superiors?"

He flushed red and hesitated. "I'm sorry, I wasn't aware that we had joined the army. Army commanders don't stop and cry at their mother's graves before a mission."

Rebecca blinked at his reference to her graveyard visit a few hours earlier, on their way out of Jerusalem. "You may not approve of my leadership, but my record stands on its own. I only know one way to execute a military mission, and as long as I'm in charge, you'll do only what I allow. Are we clear?"

They had tolerated each other since her father had first brought him on, a year earlier, but Rebecca had never cared for his ruthless nature. She'd asked Solomon about him once, and her father had simply shrugged. "Times are changing, Rebecca. We may need his kind one day. Better to win their allegiance now." She hadn't agreed then, and she didn't agree now.

On the other hand, if they ran into a firefight, she would depend on him. He was as good with a weapon as they came.

For a moment Rebecca was back at her mother's grave, kneeling on one knee, praying. It had become a custom for her. There were two white headstones, the larger standing a meter in the grass and the smaller only thirty centimeters. Her mother, Hannah, and her five-year-old sister, Ruthie. Hannah had boarded the bus at seven o'clock with Ruthie on her first day of kindergarten. The bomb had blown the bus to bits four minutes later. Only three of the fifty-four passengers had survived.

That had been fifteen years ago, and it had sent Rebecca into the military and then on to train with the Mossad. But in the last two years since joining her father, a new desire had begun to burn in her belly. The desire to give life rather than to take it. To bear children. She was grown and she ached to be a woman. Not an assassin or an archaeologist or anything except a woman.

Her discourses at the grave began to change. Like the one this morning while the others waited a hundred meters away in the trucks.

"I am tired of the killing, Mother. I want to give life, not take it." She set a lily on her sister's grave, eyes blurred with tears. "Soon I will give life to a dozen children to replace you, little Ruthie."

She imagined her mother's husky voice. *You will have to find a man first, Rebecca. You think children grow on trees?*

"Yes, of course. I will have to find a man first." She smiled. "A beautiful man with brilliant eyes who knows tender words and loves children." The smile faded. "A man who will love me the way Father loved you. Loves you."

She'd paused and closed her eyes. "Dear God, redeem your children."

Beside her Zakkai was talking. ". . . but I would feel better traveling with an army to take the monastery by force," he said. "We would be justified—the Ark *is* Jewish property, after all."

Rebecca looked at him. "And you live in a fantasy world, Professor. You know as well as I that the Knesset sells its soul to keep this madness they call peace intact. They know what the Ark's discovery would do— they would stop at nothing to prevent it. Sometimes I think they're as much the enemy as the Arabs. If the Israeli army follows us to Ethiopia, it'll be to kill . . ."

She stopped. They had come around a bend and two hundred meters ahead a checkpoint crossed the road. Three armed soldiers stood on guard, one on the right, two on the left. They were a hundred kilometers south of the West Bank—fifty kilometers south of Beersheba. Encountering a checkpoint this far south wasn't unknown, but they should have been told about it. Which meant the roadblock was only hours old.

She snatched up the radio. "We have an unscheduled checkpoint ahead, Michael."

"Copy."

"What's this?" Avraham demanded. He leaned forward and studied the nearing post. "We weren't told of this."

Rebecca slowed the Land Rover. "You're right."

Something about the way the checkpoint looked bothered her. She brought the Land Rover to a stop a hundred meters out. Several tires stood in a heap on the right and a long pole rested diagonally across the blacktop. An Israeli flag coiled slowly in the breeze.

Avraham leaned over Rebecca's seat, sweat dripping from his chin. "You can't stop here! They will suspect—"

"Shut up! Sit back. Something isn't right."

Avraham glared at her and sat back. She had to think.

To either side of the road the creamy desert stretched brown in the morning sun. Beyond the three guards in Israeli uniforms, one of which was now waving them forward, the blacktop snaked over the horizon. They sat on the road, like a bull facing the fighter. Why hadn't they been told about this checkpoint? The Palestinians had been known to erect ambushes exactly like this one, waving an Israeli flag.

She keyed the radio again. "We will drive up slowly. Do exactly as I say. If we're lucky it's nothing. Under no circumstances will anyone bring out a weapon."

"Yes, sir."

Rebecca looked at Zakkai. "If anything happens, I want you on the floor. We can't afford to lose *you* to a stray bullet."

She winked at him and smiled. Then she eased the clutch out and rolled for the roadblock.

———

The checkpoint was Ismael's first and most obvious choice.

The boy had given him more detail than he could have hoped for. Smart kid. Too bad. Rebecca was headed south by land, the boy had said. That meant they would take the Red Sea route to Ethiopia. If they were headed to Eilat, they would come down this road, and Ismael intended to stop them here.

Mustaf and Jamil were the only two patriots he knew who hated the Jews more than he. Both had watched their parents die at the hands of Mossad agents before they were ten. Ismael had simply told them that they were going to kill Hamil's assassin. Rebecca.

The white Land Rover drove towards them. "It's them," Ismael said, pulling up his bandanna. "Ready yourselves. Remember, we want the girl dead."

He glanced at the pothole in the middle of the road where they'd placed the explosive. It was now filled with gravel. *We will see how smart you are, Rebecca.*

Two separate images burned in Rebecca's mind, and she slowed their approach to a crawl. The first was the stance of the soldiers. They were unmoving, which meant they were most likely nervous. The second was the small hole in the middle of the road. It appeared to be a repair, but a few chunks of asphalt, roadside, struck her as having just come from that hole. As if it had been freshly dug rather than slowly worn. And it was positioned to be directly under any vehicle that stopped at the pole they had set across the road. Most potholes were worn on the side of roads, where tires pounded. The three soldiers stood twenty meters back, rifles ready.

The PLO needed to learn a few new tricks, she thought. A bead of sweat broke from her brow and snaked past her left eyebrow. She stopped the truck fifty meters from the three men.

"Avraham. They have a bomb in the road. You see it?"

"The pothole."

Zakkai shrunk in his seat. "Dear God! They're not ours?"

"Easy, Professor. If we can lure them up to the hole before we go, they won't detonate the bomb, unless they're interested in blowing themselves to bits as well. Avraham, take a bottle of water and pour it on the engine block when I pop the hood. Yell at them in Hebrew—tell them that our car is acting up. Wait for them to approach the pothole and when they do, slam the hood."

"That's absurd!"

"If you have a better idea, make it quick. We've done this before." She keyed her radio. "Michael, we're running a double blind. Like the Golan Heights. Have Mark put his sights on the guard to the right and wing him when Avraham shuts the hood. No killing. Make sure they don't see the gun."

"Yes, sir."

Rebecca turned to Avraham. "The steam will mask the shots. Move it. And leave the door open—if you miss us, jump in the back of the other truck. Once we go we won't stop, so I suggest you don't miss."

Avraham grabbed a bottle of water and shoved the door open, cursing under his breath. He immediately began to yell their dilemma, holding his hands up in a helpless gesture. He might not like being told what to do, but he was doing it well. Rebecca popped the hood.

The air remained quiet—they weren't firing. Rebecca eased a handgun from under her seat and held her breath. What if she was wrong? Imagine the mess that would result in shooting an Israeli soldier.

Avraham shielded the water bottle from the soldiers and dumped it onto the engine. A cloud of steam swallowed the front of the truck. Unable to see the checkpoint now, Rebecca watched Avraham, who jumped back from the hood, cursing loudly like any surprised motorist might. He waved at the guards, calling for help, then stopped to listen.

Their response sent Avraham into a frenzy. He screamed at them, furious. "Can't you idiots see that I'm stranded here? I don't care if you're manning the checkpoint. I'm the only car that needs checking and I'm smoking like a bomb here!"

Avraham ducked back behind the hood and then pulled out to urge them on. The soldiers weren't taking the bait. Rebecca began to mull through a change in plans when Avraham suddenly cast her a side glance. His hand reached the side of the hood. This was it; they were walking forward.

"Stay down, Professor," Rebecca said. It had been two years since she had killed a man, and now the familiar rush of adrenaline pumped through her veins. She keyed the mic. "Here we go."

Avraham suddenly jerked the hood down and dove for the back.

Rebecca's foot smashed the gas pedal to the floorboards before the hood slammed. A single crack of gunfire rang over the engine's roar, and the soldier on the right staggered back.

The second got off one wild shot before Mark's next shot took him through the shoulder. The force of the bullet spun him to the ground.

The third soldier wasn't in sight.

Avraham managed to roll into the backseat. "The third one! Off the road! Get off!"

Rebecca understood immediately. The third soldier had pulled back and might still detonate the bomb.

She yanked the wheel hard, three meters from the pothole. The Land Rover roared onto the desert sand and Rebecca aimed it directly at a red pickup truck, behind which she assumed the third soldier waited.

The mine detonated then, just as Michael's truck cleared it. She saw the truck swerve badly in her rearview mirror and she knew it had been hit, but for the moment there was still the third soldier to worry about.

In a sudden burst of anger, Rebecca very nearly rammed the red pickup. She saw the soldier crouched behind now, staring directly at her. He made no move to shoot or run; his eyes were black with resolution, not fear.

A small chill of dread ripped up Rebecca's spine at the sight. This was no common Hamas terrorist glaring at her.

At the last moment Rebecca jerked the wheel. They roared to the pickup's left and when they were abreast, she reached out and pumped two slugs into the left rear tire. The soldier had vanished.

Rebecca shot past the disabled vehicle and bounced back onto the blacktop. The second truck followed, swerving ungainly behind.

"Go, go!" Zakkai shouted, straining for a view behind. The sound of automatic weapons fire riddled the air, but no bullets struck. And then they were out of range, leaving a cloud of dust in the desert air.

They stopped three kilometers down the road and changed out a shredded tire. One of the men's cheeks had been cut by a rock, but the tailgate had caught most of the flying debris.

Next time they might not be so lucky.

"Let's move!" Rebecca urged, shoving the old tire off the road. "Our Hamas friend knows how to change tires too."

They filled the trucks and rolled towards the Red Sea, three hours to the south. The day was hot, but Rebecca couldn't shrug the lingering chill in her bones. Something in the man's stare stayed with her. She had not seen the last of him.

———

Ismael watched the trucks disappear over the horizon, seething. Behind him Mustaf and Jamil held their respective wounds, but he hardly noticed them. An image stuck in his mind—the soldier girl, eyes flashing brown, jaw fixed and smooth as she methodically shot his tire out.

Rebecca.

It was the first time he'd looked into her eyes, and with that one look he knew two things with utter clarity, as if Allah had spoken them directly to him. He knew that Rebecca Solomon had indeed killed his brother. And he knew that he would soon kill her. Today she had outwitted him with her clever little stunt. Tomorrow would be different.

The thought stopped him. She was no idiot; it was possible that her reputation was justified. Ismael spit into the sand. Either way it wouldn't matter. He had the advantage. He knew her route and he knew her destination.

He blinked at the horizon. *You may be searching for your precious Ark, pretty Rebecca, but you will find something very different.*

Ismael grinned and reached for the spare tire. He knew what he would do now, of course. In fact, he'd almost anticipated the roadblock's failure. Now that failure only put him on the path he had wanted. Alone this time.

The path of the true hunter.

4

LEIAH MARKER STOOD AT THE KITCHEN door and watched Caleb in the garden, talking to a child no more than ten years old. The boy was jabbing emphatically westward, towards the leper colony. Caleb knelt on one knee and listened for a few minutes, and then he laughed and rubbed the boy's curly hair. He took the child in his arms and hugged him, and although Leiah couldn't hear what Caleb whispered in his ear, it must have been funny because the boy threw his hands to his face and ran off giggling.

She smiled and stepped down into the rear courtyard. The Debra Damarro stood in the midday sun, an anomaly in the desert highland, vacant and bare except for the odd acacia tree and the stubborn knots of grass that peppered the sandy soil during the dry season. The only way to reach the isolated compound was over a barely navigable road which led to Adwa to the south and to the Red Sea northward. Fifteen years ago Leiah and her husband, Jason, whom she then knew only as the hardheaded Peace Corps worker, had raced down that road with a small orphan boy named Caleb huddled in the back of a Jeep as bullets flew over their heads.

Now that boy had grown to become a strapping man nearly two meters tall—twenty-five years old with a smile that never failed to brighten her world. He still wore his hair long, nearly to his shoulders, and on occasion a goatee graced his tanned face, but he was clean shaven now.

Leiah walked towards him and suppressed the impulse to run up and hug him as she had so many days when he was a child. Hug him the way he had hugged the small boy just now skipping off past the three old camels they kept in the corral.

Caleb faced her, still chuckling. His dark wavy hair framed those impossible pools of green God had seen fit to give him for eyes.

"Hello, Mother."

"Morning, Caleb. What is so terribly funny that has Musava in stitches?"

Caleb shrugged. "One of the little leper girls, Maria, is showing interest in him, but she's informed him that he isn't smart enough for her yet. He asked how he could change her mind."

"And what did you tell him?"

"I told him that he should avoid talking to her and focus instead on appearing wise. Women are generally wiser than men."

"And he thought that was funny?"

"No. He wanted to know what to say if she asked him a question. I told him to raise one eyebrow, say nothing, and go *hmmm*."

Leiah laughed. "This from Casanova himself." She looked to the west. "I thought you were going to visit the lepers today."

He put his arm around her shoulders and kissed her hair. "Tomorrow," he said.

He had said that three days running now.

"You said that yesterday. What will you do today?"

He shrugged. "The garden looks like it could use some weeding. God knows we don't have the water to feed the weeds."

Leiah smiled with him, but her heart felt heavy, looking into his face. There was a sadness in his eyes—not the kind many would notice, but one that had softened his face over the last year nonetheless.

"I'm worried for you, Caleb."

He faced away. "Don't be."

Leiah took his arm. "Walk with me." She led him to the same gate the boy had run through, past the three old camels in their corral, and up the path behind the monastery.

Caleb walked in silence. *He knows it as well as I do,* she thought.

"I'm not saying you *are,* but it seems to me that you're changing, Caleb."

"It's called living," he said. "You can't walk down life's path without changing your position on it. Every step changes that."

"Save your wit for your father. He sees it as brilliance. I see it as fear."

"This coming from the queen of wit."

She smiled despite her attempt at sincerity. "And that's why I know how to characterize it. Please, I'm being serious, Son. You can call it your journey down life's road if you want—I just want to know where your journey is headed. What has changed?"

Caleb said nothing.

They had reached the top of a small knoll overlooking the valley and Leiah turned to face the monastery. The brown mortar blended into the landscape—from a highflying plane it might very well look like one more rock outcropping among a thousand in the arid highlands which fell to the Danakil Desert and then to the Red Sea, 150 kilometers east.

They had rebuilt the monastery together, after its destruction fifteen years ago. Caleb had been ten then, a simple boy who wore faith like an eagle wears its feathers.

"Maybe it's time for a change," Leiah said. "Maybe you should spread your wings a little. See the world."

"I've seen the world."

"And you changed the world." She paused. "I just don't want to hold you back—"

"We've had this discussion. This is my home. And if you hadn't noticed, I haven't changed the world much in the last fifteen years. Have you seen a single person healed at my touch since I was ten?"

"A few."

"A few. Yes, three to be exact. The gift God gave me served its purpose—things change." He shrugged. "Now I'm in Ethiopia doing what I was born to do."

She looked at him. Part of her agreed with him—many a monk had lived detached in the desert. But Caleb was no monk. And she couldn't bear to see him waste away out here in obscurity. The vibrancy that had once characterized him had been replaced with something that looked more like defeat.

"And what about your faith, Caleb? Has it changed?"

His hesitation spoke with more volume than his words. "No. I don't think so."

"Lately you've been withdrawing from the lepers. You used to go to the colony every day. A healed heart is more spectacular than a straightened hand—those were your words, remember? You had half the world believing in those words. And now you don't seem as eager to heal hearts as you once were."

"The Spirit of God heals hearts, not me."

"Yes, and he heals using willing vessels."

"I haven't lost my faith, Mother. No one could see what I've seen and lose their faith."

"I know you haven't lost your faith, Caleb. But perhaps you've misplaced it."

Jason's Jeep rumbled over the far hill—he was returning from Adwa with supplies. Leiah felt her heart tighten at the sight.

"Your father's home."

Caleb nodded.

They watched the Jeep roll down the road and disappear behind the monastery.

"You're twenty-five, Caleb. Maybe it's time you discovered life beyond this valley." Saying it she felt a small dread rise through her chest. The thought of living in the monastery without Caleb was like trying to imagine life without skin, and she knew about that, didn't she?

"You might as well ask me to step into the ocean and drown myself," he said.

"And have you ever thought that maybe you're drowning yourself by staying?" She paused. "I'm not crazy about the thought of you leaving either, believe me. But to be perfectly honest, I don't see any eligible females walking around, do you? You should be falling in love, not weeding a garden."

"And here I was thinking of taking a vow of chastity."

She knew he didn't mean it. "If you must, but you'll miss one of God's greatest gifts. Come on, Caleb. You're no more cut out to live your life alone than I'm cut out to live in a city. I left Canada to find my purpose. All I'm suggesting is that you consider leaving this valley to find your purpose."

"My purpose? I thought you wanted me to find a woman."

"Yes, you could find one of those too." Leiah smiled. Caleb did not.

"You're a man of destiny, Caleb—I know it in my heart. It was no accident that you were put on the doorstep of this monastery as a baby. It was no accident that God used you to make his name famous through the signs. And I don't believe that God is finished. You may not want to say it, but you can't hide your struggle—you wear it like a coat, and in the desert heat, that coat is impossible to miss. All I'm saying is that I'm not sure you'll find your answers in this valley."

Caleb turned and faced the distant white salt flats of the Danakil Depression to the east, dubbed by geologists as earth's hellhole. Its reputation as the most forbidding place on the planet wasn't without reason.

"I honestly can't imagine leaving," he said. "I don't like hearing you say this. I have a place here—the people need me. If I go, then who would love them?"

"The fact that you're so terrified of leaving is an argument for it. As for the people, I would love them. Your father would love them."

He faced her, left brow raised. "You're actually suggesting that I leave?"

Their eyes locked for a few seconds. "I don't know, Son. Most of me is horrified by the thought. But my concern for you is greater than my concern for me."

"You've never said it like this." Caleb faced the monastery. "Now you worry *me*."

"And maybe that's enough." She took his arm again. "Let's go see if Jason has brought anything worthwhile."

They walked down the path in momentary silence. "You really think that woman is one of God's greatest gifts?" Caleb said with a smirk.

"Absolutely. Can you imagine your father without me? He would be a shell of himself."

Caleb chuckled. "I see your point. And you? What would you be without him?"

Leiah looked up at the monastery and her smile softened. "Without him I would be like that desert you were looking at."

5

ISMAEL HUDDLED IN THE ENCLAVE he'd carefully selected on the monastery's south side, meticulously scanning the hills to the north, trying desperately to ignore his mounting frustration.

The ambush had taken three days to set up—flying into Addis Ababa, then on to Adwa where he'd rented a Land Rover and driven here over impossible roads in the dark. He had been in place twelve hours, all the while wondering if the boy's information had been wrong. What if it had been another monastery in the region, one that also began with the world Debra— as it turned out there were many in northern Ethiopia.

He turned the binoculars to the monastery. The Christian church was built solidly, using huge squared rocks and brown plaster formed in a large cross. A single brass bell hung still, high over the entrance, in its round perch. It could as easily be a fort as a church.

Light flashed in the corner of his vision and Ismael jerked the binoculars up. His heart froze. Nothing. Only bare boulders, like potatoes piled—

There! A brilliant reflection. Ismael pulled back, afraid they might see him.

They had come! Praise be to Allah.

He snatched up his rifle and shoved it in the space he'd prepared. The silencer struck the rock and he cursed under his breath. "Slow down. Patience."

Ismael eased his eye to the scope, scanned the rocks again, and stopped when he saw them move. The Jews were strung along the hill, like a row of desert rats, hunched behind their rocks.

He had them now.

Rebecca studied the monastery through the glasses one last time. The small valley was vacant except for the odd robed monk or servant walking for the well or plucking tomatoes from a small garden on the north end. Taking the monastery would be like attending a bar mitzvah. Part of her felt sorry for the helpless men who walked down there, unaware of the storm about to blow their way.

After narrowly escaping the roadblock, she had led the team on an uneventful passage aboard the Antiquities freighter, down the length of the Red Sea, to the sleepy port of Massawa in Eritrea. The 150-kilometer trip south to this valley in two rented lorries offered no excitement either. Even the border crossing provided little more than a ten-minute respite from an otherwise monotonous journey. It was as if Ethiopia had fallen asleep and forgotten that there was anything worth protecting within its borders. If indeed there was.

Looking down at the sleepy monastery known as the Debra Damarro that the old blind priest had insisted held the relic, Rebecca fought off a nauseating wave of doubt. The isolated structure, though built like a fort, seemed too inconsequential to hold anything remotely as powerful as the one relic that could change history simply by its discovery.

To think that God's holy Ark was hidden here, in a *Christian* monastery—a monument to that man who had rejected the Jews in his heretical claim to be God—was ironic at least. Blasphemous, more likely.

"The poor dolts will soon be dead," Avraham said beside her.

Rebecca lowered her binoculars and looked down the line of soldiers crouched behind the knoll. They had exchanged their shovels and picks for machine guns and knives. Any one of them could probably take the monastery alone. Professor Daniel Zakkai stood behind them, the only man without a gun.

"There won't be any killing unless we meet resistance," she ordered. "We don't need to draw attention."

Avraham looked at her, taken aback. "You can't be serious. There's not a soul anywhere near. We don't need prisoners."

"No. We won't have the innocent blood of monks on our hands."

"Christian monks aren't any less guilty than the Arabs, or don't you know your history? Wasn't Hitler a Christian? We should kill them—anything less would be a tactical error."

"There's never enough killing for you, is there, Avraham? Give your gun to Moshen."

Avraham blinked.

"You heard me. Please, we don't have all day."

Now the man grew red in the face, but he didn't hand his weapon over.

Rebecca faced the monastery. "Samuel, take Avraham's gun. If he refuses to give it to you, shoot him in the leg."

"You're an insolent little . . ." Avraham stopped short at Rebecca's glare. Samuel took his rifle.

"This is a military exercise," Rebecca said. "I'm your commander. A soldier follows his commander without question. Until you accept that fact, I will keep you in check. We're going in hot; the last thing I need is an unruly man with a gun in hand."

Rebecca ignored his scowl and addressed the others. "Here's how this works. I want three men on the north, three on the west, and two with me on the road to the south. Moshen and Jude will set up a post on the crest of the road. Once we're in the monastery, no one leaves the valley. Unless the monks decide to bring out guns, nobody shoots. The nearest village is five kilometers to the west, but there's no telling how far a shot will carry in these hills."

"What about their radio?" Michael asked.

"If you find one, destroy it."

"Caleb must not be harmed," Zakkai said.

Rebecca nodded. "Yes, of course. Caleb." Before leaving they had learned that, evidently, this Caleb was the same person who as a boy fifteen years ago had sparked a worldwide controversy with his power to heal. Rebecca had been too distracted mourning her mother's death at the time to notice.

"If all goes well, we'll find whatever there is to find and be gone by morn-

ing. If it takes us longer, we should be prepared to hold the monastery for as
long as necessary."

She glanced at her watch. "You have half an hour for positions. Leave the
trucks hidden until we take the monastery."

———

It took Rebecca fifteen minutes to reach the crest of the road from the south
where Jude and Moshen would remain at a post. With Avraham in tow and
two others at her flanks she walked for the monastery. They kept their rifles
shouldered at their backs.

Nothing but the crunching of their boots and the occasional call of a
crow disturbed the silence. The monastery slept in the falling afternoon sun,
a huge monolith, unsuspecting.

Rebecca had searched out a dozen promising sites for the Ark's resting
place with Zakkai. Finding the relic had always seemed like a long shot, but
next to their failing political attempts at gathering support for rebuilding
the Temple, the possibility of actually locating the Ark had inspired them
all. If there was one thing God had said clearly about the future of Israel it
was that the Temple would be rebuilt before the Messiah would come.
There was nothing that could unite Israel behind the Temple's rebuilding
like the discovery of the Ark.

Even so the months of failure had left her pessimistic about their
prospects of success. As if they were children on a treasure hunt, unable to
shake the nagging thought that it was a box full of sand that they would find
rather than a true treasure trove. They had traveled sixteen hundred kilometers over three days since the old man had told his tale and produced his
letter. But now walking up to the monastery Rebecca couldn't shake the
feeling that this place, like so many in its wake, was filled with nothing
more than old men and dust.

They approached to within fifty meters of the gate and still no one
showed. Maybe they'd all gone to bed early, God knew there was little else
to do in such a remote—

Whap!

The unmistakable sound of a bullet smacking into flesh jerked Rebecca from her thoughts. She instinctively threw herself to the ground and rolled to her left. To her right Peter staggered forward with a head wound.

The ground belched dust two meters to the right as a second bullet buried itself. She came up out of her roll in a full run, leaving her hat to the wind. Behind her, Avraham had snatched up Peter's gun and drew abreast.

"No shots!" Rebecca snapped.

"They're shooting at us!"

The shots were from behind, but she didn't have the time to point the fact out at the moment. She ran forward, weaving, as three more projectiles spun passed her. Seven steps rose to the entrance and she took them in two strides.

Then she was inside the monastery. Avraham and Samuel flattened themselves against the wall beside her.

"No shots!" Rebecca repeated. "Samuel, guard the door. The shooter's in the hills; keep him there. Avraham, with me."

Rebecca turned and ran into the sanctuary where a monk stood wide-eyed, dressed in a tan tunic that hung to his ankles.

"Pardon us, Father, but I must speak to a man named Caleb immediately."

Confusion froze the monk's features. With any luck, they would have the monastery before anyone realized they'd been attacked. Speed was now an issue. Whoever had fired on them had done so without warning, which meant they knew too much. She would have to silence the shooter, but not at the expense of their first objective, which was Caleb. The sooner they controlled the monastery, the sooner they could deal with the shooter.

Rebecca snatched up her radio. "Michael, did you get a bearing?"

"No, sir. Peter's down."

"Leave him." She lowered her radio. "Father? Quickly!"

"You are not permitted in the—"

"Listen, you old bag," Avraham's voice rang through the great room. "She asked you where Caleb was, and I suggest you start talking before we—"

"Shut up, Avraham! Forgive us, Father, but we are in a hurry. It's a matter of utmost importance," Rebecca said.

"I . . . yes, of course. He should be in the refectory at the back." The priest lifted a trembling hand to the hall behind him.

"Thank you."

Rebecca hurried for the hall. Avraham hesitated and then followed. She had a notion to put the butt of her rifle between his teeth, but she dismissed the thought. Another took its place.

She would send him after the shooter.

As soon as they had Caleb.

———

Leiah was down the hall from the sanctuary retrieving a can of margarine from the storeroom when she heard Caleb's name echo angrily from the domed room.

"*. . . where Caleb was and I suggest you start talking before we—*"

"*Shut up, Avraham!*"

Heat flashed up Leiah's neck. Bandits! Someone had come for Caleb! For a moment she stood frozen, the can of margarine in her hand.

I've got to get him out! The thought blasted through her mind, and she tore from the room and sprinted down the hall. She nearly tripped, crashing into the study.

"Caleb!" Jason was with him—thank God. "Jason, there are men looking for Caleb. We have to hide him!"

"What? What do you mean, men?"

She looked over her shoulder at the sound of running feet and motioned frantically for the closet. "Hurry!"

"Leiah—"

"Not now, Jason!" She ran into the corner of the table, but she hardly felt it. Jason and Caleb scrambled from their chairs and ran in after her.

"What's happening?" Caleb asked. Outside a voice yelled that the kitchen was empty.

"I don't know! They want you!"

"Then I should talk to them," Caleb said.

"No! I think they have guns. I don't know what they want, but it can't be good."

Jason hesitated only a few seconds. "Okay, Caleb, we have to get you into the tunnel and out."

"You're serious? We don't even know what they want."

"No, Caleb," Leiah whispered. "Please, you have to go. Now!"

Jason was suddenly as urgent as Leiah. "We have to move." He cracked the door, saw that the way was clear, and pushed it open. "The ladder at the back. You too, Leiah. Hurry!"

"No," Leiah said. "I'm staying to hold them."

"Don't be crazy—"

"Go!"

Jason hesitated and then pushed Caleb towards the narrow stairway at the back of the library.

———

They were halfway down the ladder when Leiah's voice drifted to them. "What do you mean, barging in on supper? You'll wait at the front door like anyone else!"

"We are interested only in Caleb," a woman's voice replied. "Only to talk to him."

Another voice rattled off in what sounded to Caleb like Hebrew.

Shots rang out from somewhere above. Caleb stopped, suddenly panicked. "Father?"

"It was from somewhere else," Jason said, but his voice held a tremor. "The radio, maybe. Hurry!"

They ran for the lower tunnel that exited fifty meters beyond the back wall. It had been restored as part of the reconstruction because Caleb insisted. Most of the old tunnels had been collapsed, but several, like this one, were still stable enough to repair.

"I can't leave, Father. Where do I go?"

Jason ran ahead and ducked into the dim tunnel. "To the hills. You know them better than anyone."

"That's crazy! For how long? And if there's danger, I should be here, not running off."

"They want you; you heard them. They have guns and they're asking for you. In my book that means you're in danger, so you get out."

"And when will I come back?" Caleb asked, breathless. His mind spun. This was impossible! He hadn't even seen a gun in fifteen years, and now someone was firing above his head in the church.

"When do I come back?" he asked again.

"I don't know. As soon as it's safe. An hour. Tomorrow." Jason's slapping boots echoed in the long tunnel. "We'll put a white rag on the fence. When you see a white flag, you'll know it's safe."

"And what if you don't put a white flag on the fence?" Caleb asked, unbelieving. "This is crazy, Father. I can't go!"

Jason spun and grabbed Caleb by the arm. "Listen, Caleb! We're not playing around here. Leiah's no fool. If she says get out, it means get out. At the least to be safe. Go into the hills, and if there isn't a white flag on the fence soon, you head for help."

Caleb could hardly believe his ears. "Head for help? Where?"

"I don't know. Just find help." Muffled voices reached them and Jason spun back down the tunnel. "If we don't move, nobody will be going. Hurry!"

They ran. Around a blind corner to a small stairwell that led to the surface. Jason cracked the storm door, looked outside, and then threw it open.

Caleb clambered past him. He glanced around. The afternoon was quiet. "No one's here."

"Run!"

Caleb hesitated, bent in to give his father a hug and quick kiss on the cheek, and then ran for the hills.

He turned once to see the storm door close. Then he crested a hill and the monastery disappeared from sight.

———

Ismael tilted his head back and closed his eyes, still furious that he'd missed the woman. He'd mistaken the one with wider hips to the right for Rebecca and had realized his error only after Rebecca's hat had flown off revealing long black hair. His next three shots had missed, partly from her surprising speed, partly from the slight tremble his own frustration had brought to his hands.

Now they were inside and his element of surprise was gone.

Ismael considered going down to finish the job. But that would only give them the advantage, and if there was one rule he would never break it was that killing must always be done from a position of advantage. He had killed thirty-four Jews from such a position. Unsuspecting squatters not ready for a fight. Civilians mostly, because not only were civilians easier to kill, their deaths caused greater grief than a soldier's. Soldiers were bred to die. Nursing mothers were not. That was his advantage—killing people when they did not expect to be killed.

He'd once blown the head off a woman at three hundred meters as she kissed her husband off to work. The cruelty of the strike played as heavily as the fact that the man was one of Jerusalem's best-known bankers. Not even Israel was prepared for such sudden terror. Terror was the greatest advantage of strong-willed soldiers who understood the will of Allah.

Ismael lowered his head and cursed bitterly. He had to find a way to persuade the Jews that he'd left. That would take time. Time was something he had; it was the patience he wasn't as sure about.

The Jew-witch had escaped him twice—both times by the length of a bullet. The thought made him sick.

"Do you know the English word for the people of the book?" his brother had once asked him.

"No."

"Jewitch," Hamil had said past a wide grin.

"Jewish, yes, that's what I thought."

"No. Jew-witch. Jew-witch. You see, even they know the truth."

It had become a little joke between them.

Ismael spit to the side. It was no longer a joke. He was now hunting the Jew-witch who had killed Hamil.

6

REBECCA'S COMMANDO FORCE SEIZED THE Debra Damarro the way a child might seize a toy. Peter was dead, of course, but the shooter had been kept outside of the monastery, in the hills. Within the compound itself they found an old musket, but nothing capable of shooting live ammunition, much less a silenced sniper rifle. Whoever had shot Peter hadn't done so in cooperation with these monks.

Rebecca walked into the church where her men had gathered six Ethiopian Orthodox monks, five servants, and two westerners dressed in khakis. The sound of her boots echoed through the domed room with each footfall. Above her, the faces of Christianity stared down in large paintings of red and yellow. Around her, three of her soldiers stood at the church's entrances. Four others guarded the doors into the monastery, leaving the last two on the hill to make nine. And one dead. The monastery was sealed; its radio riddled with bullets. They had accomplished their first objective with relative ease.

She keyed her radio and called the post on the hill. "Report, Moshen."

"All clear, sir. From here the valley looks asleep. Still no sign of the shooter."

"Good. Keep glassing those hills. I'm sending Avraham out. Watch his back."

"Yes, sir."

Rebecca faced Avraham. "Go out the back and circle around through the hills to the front side."

He hesitated, eyes squinted.

"It's what you do best, isn't it?" Rebecca said. "We're probably dealing with a lone shooter—someone who followed us. No other scenario makes sense. Our Palestinian friend from the roadblock, if I had to guess."

Avraham grunted and was gone.

Rebecca approached the gathered prisoners. "Forgive our rude entrance, but you must know that we mean you no harm," Rebecca said, looking at the western woman. This was Leiah, Caleb's adoptive mother, if her information was right. And the western man, Jason, his father.

"You must be Leiah."

"Yes." The woman held her jaw fixed. Not exactly the kind to be easily frightened.

"I have no reason to hurt your son, Leiah. I only wish to talk to him." Rebecca looked at the others. "If one of you is Caleb, it would spare us all a lot of misery if you stepped forward now."

"What do you want with him?" Jason demanded.

"And you must be Jason," Rebecca said, turning to him. "I'll be blunt. We believe that Caleb can lead us to the Ark of the Covenant."

They just stared at her.

"Yes, I know that Ethiopia is rich in its traditions about the Ark. You perhaps believe that it's in Saint Mary's Chapel at Axum, but we've come to think otherwise. We believe, in fact, that it's hidden near here, and that Caleb knows its location."

She let the revelation sink in. The dome seemed to amplify their breathing.

"That's absurd," Leiah finally said.

"Well, that's the beauty of our mission, Leiah. One way or another we'll find out just how absurd it is—with or without Caleb's help. With it we can be precise. Without it we may be forced to tear down every wall in this monastery. But believe me when I say that we won't leave this building without exhausting our search."

Jason stepped forward. "You're not understanding this, are you? There's no Ark here. You could torture Caleb for a week and he wouldn't tell you a thing because he doesn't know anything. And you can tear down every wall in the Debra, but all you'll find is rock and mortar. I should know—I helped build it."

Professor Zakkai approached Jason. "You oversaw the monastery's rebuilding after it was destroyed fifteen years ago, yes?"

"That's what I just said."

Zakkai smiled. "Yes . . . And what about the foundation? Did you build on top of the old foundation?"

"Yes, of course. But it was leveled—"

"And the foundation itself, did you leave it intact?"

Jason paused. "Parts of it. Yes."

"So then you did not actually rebuild portions of the monastery that were underground, correct?"

"No, but it's solid rock and concrete down there. There's no hiding place for the Ark. The whole idea's . . . crazy."

Zakkai smiled again. "Evidently Father Matthew did not think it crazy. But I do understand your sentiment. Two weeks ago I myself would have thought it crazy. But today I might use a word more like *brilliant,* rather than *crazy.* Believe me, we're not acting on a whim. The Ark has been hopelessly lost for twenty-six hundred years, and for the first time in modern history, tangible evidence about its location has surfaced. That evidence leads us to this monastery, my friend. I hardly think *crazy* is the word to use."

Jason stood, silenced by Zakkai's proclamation.

"As you can see," Rebecca said, "we really need to speak to Caleb."

"You're Israeli soldiers," Leiah said.

"Yes."

"If you really believe the Ark is here, you'll do anything to find it."

"Yes."

"Including torturing Caleb, if you must?"

Rebecca had shoved the possibility from her mind, but hearing it now she wondered how far they would go.

"We will do only what God wills."

"And you think that maybe God would will you to force knowledge from Caleb? I'm sorry, but Caleb isn't here."

"I didn't say that we would harm your son."

"You didn't say that you wouldn't."

Rebecca considered reassuring the woman that her son would not be harmed. That God was filled with love and kindness, not death and torture. But God had also lifted a sword for Israel's sake before—many times in fact—and he would do it again. Leiah knew it as well; she was no idiot.

Rebecca turned to Zakkai. "Professor, we will begin a search of the lower tunnels immediately. Bring the dynamite." They couldn't actually use explosives, of course—the risk to the Ark would be far too high. She eyed the huddled group. "Please consider yourselves prisoners. You are confined to this room unless given express permission to leave it. We have guards about the compound and a post on the road. No one will be coming or going until we have finished our business. The more cooperative you are, the sooner we leave. It's unfortunate—"

"Sir?" Michael's voice squawked on the radio.

Rebecca keyed it quickly. "Go ahead."

"It looks like one of them may have escaped. I'm in a tunnel that leads from the monastery. It surfaces through a storm door. There are fresh prints in the sand outside."

Rebecca glanced at Leiah's concerned eyes and knew immediately that the prints belonged to her son. So Caleb had escaped after all. She swore softly and turned her back to the others.

Under other circumstances her decision would be quick. Follow him. But the sniper changed the equation. Caleb had the advantage of knowing the hills and any pursuit would be preoccupied with covering its flank.

"Sir?"

Rebecca lifted the radio. "Pull back, Michael. We'll give Avraham time to neutralize the sniper before following. Out."

She strode to the archway that led down the hall towards the kitchen. "Let's begin, Professor. We have work to do."

7

ISMAEL SAW THE LONE SOLDIER ON the northern slope. Actually, he saw his boot, a black smudge on a tan landscape. How the man had managed to get behind the rocks in the first place was reason enough for concern. No ordinary soldier would have made it so far without revealing himself.

So they were sending someone after him—the Israelis had never been short on spine. But he still had the clear advantage, and he would play the game his way. In any other situation he would have already killed the two sentries posted on the road to the west. And at any other time he would probably draw a bead on that boot and shoot the man's foot off—it was only two hundred meters, he could make the shot easily. Like shooting the hand off a Jew as he ate supper in his home.

But this was not any ordinary situation. He hadn't come here to kill Jews. He had come to kill Rebecca Solomon. And to keep her from finding the Ark—although he doubted there was an Ark to find. So really he was here to kill the woman who had killed his brother.

"Jew-witch," he whispered.

A thought suddenly screamed through his mind. He had seen one of the monastery's residents flee out the back and thought nothing of it—a stray Ethiopian was of no concern to him. This soldier had come from the back as well, which only made sense, since he had shot the other soldier by the front gate. But what if the fleeing man had been Caleb? And what if Rebecca decided to go after him? What if she went after him under cover of darkness?

He had to get over there before nightfall. And he had to do so without being spotted by this soldier.

"Allah in heaven, give me grace."

Caleb stumbled over the lumpy ground, fighting panic with each step. He had to get help; he had decided that much minutes after losing sight of the monastery. But he couldn't actually leave before seeing whether his father had put that white flag on the fence or not.

And what if Jason didn't put the flag on the fence? Dread floated through his chest like a hollow bullet. He'd cycled back to the crest two hours earlier and peered over the ledge to the monastery below. There'd been no white flag. Which meant that whoever had fired in the monastery were holding his mother and father. He'd fled back towards the desert.

"Dear God, help me."

Tears blurred his vision and he tripped over a boulder. He stumbled to his right knee and lurched forward. A shaft of pain shot through his femur, but he ignored it.

"Father, I beg you for guidance. Don't let any harm come to Jason and Leiah, I beg you."

And who was *he* to beg? A child who had become a man only to lose his . . . No, he hadn't lost his faith. He had lost the need for it. He had put it in a closet and forgotten about it.

But he still loved God, didn't he? Yes, yes he did. And he loved his neighbor. The lepers might not have seen him as regularly as before, but then everyone had their cycles. He was simply in a downcycle.

"I beg you, Father, forgive me."

Caleb felt as helpless as he could remember feeling. He stumbled over the rocky ground, panting, up one hill and down the next, without having any clue as to where he was going. He stopped and decided that he should circle back one more time. Night was coming. What if he met the soldiers on the way back?

He groaned and headed back.

At least he wore pants, which made movement easier. Beige khakis and a white shirt. His hair had flattened with sweat and stuck to his neck and cheeks. It occurred to him that he was worthless. Weak in his faith and now powerless, stumbling on the hills, bleeding from one knee and covered in dirt.

"Father, I beg you."

God wasn't answering right now.

The sun was setting when Caleb found his way back to the ledge over-looking the monastery from the north. He pulled up and dropped to his belly. He'd been gone hours now—maybe as many as six. If there was no flag down there . . .

He swallowed against a dry mouth and pulled himself forward like a lizard. He peered carefully over the ledge, blinking sweat from his eyes.

The valley lay quiet, no different than on any other summer evening. A gentle breeze pushed through bedsheets that hung out back—the same sheets one of the servants had hung there this morning. The camels sat under an acacia tree in the corner of their corral, but otherwise there was no sign of life.

And the brown fence was bare. No flag.

Caleb dropped his head and clenched his eyes against pinpricks of light that flooded his vision.

"Dear God."

He'd hardly expected otherwise, but still he had hoped. Now the last of his hope was jerked away.

He looked again, just to be sure. The fence stood small, so far away, but it was as bare as the day he and Jason had pounded it into the ground, singing an old Ethiopian nursery rhyme about the desert's beauty.

He had to get help, and waiting for morning would just delay the inevitable. Adwa was the closest town with police and Adwa was a hundred kilometers away. Three days' walk. If he could get to a radio, he could try to raise someone—but not even the leper colony had a radio.

Caleb rolled onto his back and stared at the dimming sky.

The soldiers below had spoken Hebrew. What could Israeli soldiers want with the monastery? Unless it was Falasha . . .

A voice filled his memory. The voice of Father Matthew, speaking to him as a child.

"I want you to promise me something, Caleb."

"Yes, Dada."

"If you are ever in a place where you don't know what to do, or if men ever come to the monastery to hurt you, I want you to find a man for me."

"Find a man where?"

"I want you to go to the desert and ask for a Father Joseph Hadane, a Falasha Jew. He will know what to do."

"Just go to the desert? The Danakil?"

"Yes. Will you promise me?"

"I promise, Dada."

The conversation rang in Caleb's mind as if Father Matthew had come back to life and spoken from the rock. He jerked up and sucked a deep breath.

The desert!

He spun around and stared east. The salt flats shimmered beyond the hills, white and red in the sinking sun. By appearances you might be able to hurl a rock and watch it bounce off the surface, but in reality the flats themselves were thirty kilometers away. Geologists called it the Danakil Depression because much of it was actually well below sea level. Caleb had never known any westerner to cross the wasteland, at least not in his lifetime. Some had tried, but failed.

Fifteen years ago his father had told him to find a Father Hadane in the desert. A Falasha Jew. The soldiers' use of Hebrew in the monastery had triggered the memory.

Caleb turned back to the south, towards the monastery and far beyond, Adwa. He would never make it to Adwa.

And the desert? How could he find a lone Falasha Jew in the desert? These were his options? A known destination a hundred kilometers over rugged terrain, and an unknown destination in the desert, thirty kilometers away.

Caleb blinked and turned back to the desert. "Okay, Dada." He swallowed. "Let's hope fifteen years hasn't washed away Father Hadane."

He stood to his feet, glanced at the monastery one last time, and set off at a jog. Only when he'd run a couple kilometers did it occur to him that he had no water. There was a spring about sixteen kilometers towards the desert. He would need water for the desert. And what about animals at night? Or the Afar tribe? He'd never met the natives of the desert, but he'd heard a hundred stories. The headhunters of the Amazon were like lambs next to these natives. Their tradition which prohibited a male from becoming a man and marrying until he had taken another human's life did nothing to encourage safe passage through their territory. Only their isolation kept the Ethiopian government from stepping in and enforcing some sort of restriction on their ancient practices.

On the other hand, he desperately needed help. Father Matthew's insistence that he find a Falasha Jew named Hadane sounded distant, maybe even impossible at the moment, but only without considering Father Matthew himself. Dada had rarely been wrong. And it seemed as though he'd anticipated this day.

What if Jason or Leiah had been killed already? The thought stopped him midstride on the hillside.

But he couldn't go back. Not now. In fact, avoiding the soldiers might be the only way to keep his parents alive. If they were after him, then once they had him they might have no qualms about killing his parents. Until then, they would keep them as leverage. Hopefully.

Caleb groaned softly in the night and resumed his jog east. The questions flogged him with each footfall.

"Dear God, I beg you. Please I beg you."

8

THEY SCOURED THE MONASTERY'S LOWER LEVELS, inch by inch through the night. There were a hundred nooks and crannies where an Ark might have been tucked away, but the wavering flames of their torches weren't quick to reveal anything except brown rock.

Including the tunnel Caleb had escaped through, only four tunnels remained out of the dozens that had once crisscrossed the subterranean foundation. When they'd rebuilt the monastery they'd covered the rest with concrete, sealing only God knew what. Unfortunately, the old maze of tunnels now acted as the monastery's foundation, and an uncalculated tampering with it might bring down the whole thing.

After their first pass, Zakkai approached Jason and persuaded him to help them search. No one knew the foundation of the monastery like Jason, and after a lengthy retelling of the old Falasha priest's story, Jason reluctantly agreed. If he doubted that the Ark was indeed hidden under the monastery, he seemed persuaded that the sooner the question was resolved, the sooner the Israelis would leave.

The renowned archaeologist led Jason and Rebecca through each chamber, asking very specific questions about the reconstruction project Jason had overseen fifteen years earlier. Most of the questions had to do with distances.

"How far are we from the outer wall?"

"I don't know," Jason answered. "We didn't exactly work off blueprints."

"But roughly. To your best recollection."

"Five, maybe six meters."

Zakkai would jot that down. "And when you laid the floor above, did this wall run parallel to the wall above or was it offset?"

"I'm not sure I see what difference it makes."

"But I am, so please—"

"This was mostly just a large slab of rock, just like you see it today. Any tunnels were buried when the first monastery came down. Caleb knew; he grew up in the old monastery."

"Splendid, but we don't have Caleb, do we? You made sure of that."

Jason nodded. "So you want to know if the wall above is parallel to the old one?"

"Yes. It gives me an indication of whether or not the old wall was load bearing—deduction, the foremost tool used by us moles."

"It was offset," Jason said.

And so on Zakkai went, with the dogged method of a seasoned scientist. He plotted each wall on a grid and shaded areas that he considered able to support a cavern large enough to house the Ark. It was guesswork, deduction as he called it, but the guessing was being done by one of the sharpest archaeological minds on earth.

One tunnel in particular interested Zakkai. It had supposedly led to a chamber deep underground which fed into several small rooms. Caleb had slept there as a young child, Jason told them. He grew up there by the lights of torches most of his early years. Now the tunnel was diverted into the monastery's root cellar, a large damp room with enough potatoes to hold an army for a month. Jason thought the root cellar was directly above Caleb's old room.

"Was he kept there against his will?" Zakkai asked.

"Heavens no. He had the run of the place. But he preferred it, studying by torchlight."

Zakkai spent an hour tapping the floor and walls, searching for any anomaly that might shed light on what lay behind. The effort proved nothing. After mapping the room, Zakkai finally sighed and suggested they move on.

Rebecca knew then that short of resorting to dynamite, finding anything Father Matthew might have hidden would prove hopeless without Caleb. Dynamite was out of the question because of the Ark. They needed Caleb.

They had just left the room when Rebecca's radio squawked. "Avraham has just returned, sir."

She glanced at her watch. Ten o'clock. "I'll be right there."

Rebecca left them and climbed through the now familiar tunnels to the kitchen where they had set up a command post of sorts. Avraham stood alone by the stove, sipping a cup of hot tea.

"Well?"

He frowned. "Nothing." He tossed her four shells: 726 rounds. "I found these behind a rock, but whoever shot them is long gone."

"How do you know they aren't waiting?"

"Because I know. I covered the perimeter."

"They could have moved."

"I just walked across the driveway. If anyone was out there, I wouldn't be standing here drinking tea, would I?"

He wasn't only insolent and proud, he was thickheaded, she thought. But there was some reason to his conclusion.

"He'll show up again," she said. "I want you to sweep the perimeter again at first light. Samuel will be in charge while I'm gone. You do nothing without his permission."

Avraham blinked. "While you're gone where?"

"I'm going after Caleb in the morning. Searching the monastery without him is pointless."

"You're going alone? Perhaps I should come with you," he said through a smile.

"I can handle a farm boy. It's the monastery I'm more concerned about. If Caleb wasn't so critical to our mission, I would send someone else to bring him in. But nine of you should be able to hold this fortress from a dozen unarmed civilians, don't you think?"

"I think that your father would have a few words about your running off after a man by yourself."

"I didn't say I was going alone. I'm taking Michael. And you obviously don't understand my father. One of your problems, Avraham, is that you're trapped in a time when women were considered inferior fighters to men. You'd think my record alone would be enough to help you pull your head from—"

"Your record is overrated," Avraham interrupted. "So you've killed a handful of Palestinians—most of them with a rifle. In a street fight I think you'd be killed before you had the time to pluck your pretty little eyebrows. Frankly, a shovel suits you more than a gun."

Rebecca felt heat wash down her back, and she fought the impulse to slap his face.

"Be careful, Avraham. One day we might have to see if your theory holds true. In the meantime, you will follow my orders, and I'm ordering you to follow Samuel. If you cross him while I'm gone, you'll regret it. Are we clear?"

He scowled, and Rebecca knew that too much had passed between them for Avraham to ignore. The day would come when this man would test her resolve beyond words.

"You're dismissed, Avraham."

He slammed the cup down and ignored the tea that splashed over his hand. "Yes, sir," he said and walked out the back.

Rebecca left the kitchen, frustrated with her own pride. The last thing she needed was a soldier as powerful as Avraham to stand in her way. Or worse, in Samuel's way.

She entered the main sanctuary—the community sat in small groups or slept in corners, placid enough. She scanned them quickly and found who she was looking for. Leiah sat in the far corner, staring at her.

Rebecca strode towards her.

———

Leiah watched the woman they called "sir" walk towards her and made no attempt to hide the frown that twisted her face.

The Jewish zealot was a beautiful woman with her jet-black hair and pouting lips, a fact which bothered her. The disparity between her feminine demeanor and the fact that she was not only a soldier, but an accomplished soldier, was unnerving. The whole idea of being invaded by these zealots angered her. Marching around with guns, taking a monastery by force—that wasn't what Christ had in mind. Of course, Rebecca probably didn't care what Christ had in mind. She was too busy looking for her own Messiah.

"Hello, Leiah." Rebecca smiled.

"What? No Ark?"

"We didn't expect to walk in and find it sitting on the coffee table."
Rebecca looked carefully into her eyes. "If you didn't know that this
monastery existed, hidden away from the world in this remote valley, you
might scour the hills for years without finding it, yes? Yet here it is, existing
in obscurity, beyond the eyes of the world. Like the Ark. It's remained hidden from the world for twenty-five hundred years, in an obscure location
unknown to even those who walk near it every day. There are a hundred
walls below us that could hide the Ark."

"These walls don't belong to you."

"No, but the Ark does."

"Then I'm sure your government is capable of making arrangements to
find it in an orderly fashion."

"My government? The Knesset's terrified of the Ark's discovery. And
even if they weren't, we both know that Ethiopia would never allow its
removal. It has become part of this nation's religion."

"If you aren't supported by the Israeli government, then why are you
here? You're treasure hunters?"

"We're here on behalf of Israel. You're a Christian—even the Christian
knows this. If our people don't turn back to God, our nation will inevitably
fracture and pull apart at the seams. Without a Temple, our people will
never turn back to God. Without the Ark, we will never rebuild the
Temple. And now, it seems we won't find the Ark. Not without your son.
We need him, Leiah."

Rebecca's eyes momentarily flashed with a conviction that made Leiah
wonder what she was really thinking.

"Even if Caleb possessed the key to the Ark, I would never endanger his
life for your cause," Leiah said.

"His life is endangered already. I don't think you realize how many people
would kill him to prevent the Ark's discovery. He may spend the rest of his
life running from assassins."

"You're overstating this ridiculous situation," Leiah said. But for the
first time she considered the possibility that she had just heard a strain of
truth. "This whole thing's absurd!"

"I'm only asking you to help us learn just how absurd it is. If the Ark isn't here, we'll leave you in peace—you have my word. If the Ark is here, better we discover it than the Arabs, trust me."

"Trust you? And how do you expect me to help you?"

Rebecca turned, crossed her arms, and paced, tilting her head to look at the domed ceiling.

"You're his mother. Surely in all these years he's mentioned the key." She faced Leiah again. "Not a physical key, but a clue to its location. If you were to tell me, we could leave Caleb out of this altogether."

"Yes, we could, but he didn't. I don't think your key exists. You're right, he would have mentioned it, but he didn't. So have your look around and leave us."

"I'm afraid we can't do that. We're here because of an authentic letter—a piece to a puzzle that archaeologists have been scratching their heads over for centuries. The letter was given to us by a man who knew Father Matthew— an old blind Falasha priest named Raphael Hadane. I don't believe he was lying."

Leiah blinked. The name rang in her mind like a gong. Hadane. Alone it might not have meant anything, but a Hadane who was a Falasha priest? She had heard that name. Caleb had told her that name.

"What is it?" Rebecca asked.

"Nothing."

"I'm not an idiot. I just said something that made your eyes light up like stars. You've heard about the priest?"

"No. I don't know." And what if she told Rebecca? Would it be in their favor or work against them?

"I don't know?" Rebecca said. "I don't know means yes."

"Maybe, but either way it's got nothing to do with a key. The name Hadane might be familiar—so what? There are probably a hundred priests with the last name of Hadane. It's a common Falasha name."

"But do you know anything at all about this particular priest named Hadane? Did Caleb know him?" Rebecca sounded more like an officer interrogating a prisoner than a God-fearing zealot now.

"I don't know. Honestly, I don't. Hadane might have been a man in the desert—a friend of Father Matthew. But I swear that doesn't mean a thing. Like I said, there are probably a thousand Hadanes."

Rebecca glared at her. "You don't believe me when I say your son is in danger?"

"Listen to me! You go ahead and look for your precious relic, but if you touch one hair on my son's head, I swear I will—"

"You'll what, scream at me? Spit in my face? Maybe even scratch my eyes out! I'm not sure you realize what you're dealing with."

"And I'm not sure you realize who you're talking to."

They stared at each other for a few seconds, silent.

"You love your child, that's good," Rebecca said. "My mother loved her child too. The child was five years old and knew how to count to one hundred and I loved her as much as my mother did. And then one day a bus bomb killed them both. It happens. The Messiah will change that. The Ark will bring the Messiah."

Rebecca walked away and Leiah wasn't sure whether she wanted to run after her and issue an apology or throw a shoe at her.

———

Caleb slowed to a walk and slogged forward on numb legs. The questions drummed their way into a monotony that took the edge off his panic. Darkness had settled in a stillness broken only by the repeated calls of jackals in the night.

He stumbled on the spring near midnight and gorged himself with its cold water. In his best moments, he was grateful for the cool. If he was very lucky, he would make the desert before the sun rose. In his worst moments, he felt sure that when he did reach the desert it would bake him and leave him in a pile of bleached bones for the next traveler to step over.

The jackals faded in the wee hours and Caleb knew it was because not even jackals traveled this close to the salt flats. The only life in this desert, other than the occasional rat, would be found under a microscope. And yet he plodded on. A hopelessly blind fool, trudging to his own death.

A dozen times he thought about turning back; a dozen times he reluctantly discarded the notion. His bones told him to walk on. Never mind that those same bones would end in a heap, eaten clean by the rats; never mind that each step took him further from the only life he'd ever known. He had committed himself to head east, and he would head east.

When dawn began to gray the landscape, he saw that he was very near the white sands of the desert. He'd come a long way, but he still hadn't reached the true desert. He plodded on.

Then the sun cleared the eastern horizon, a huge orange ball of flame. It had been twenty-four hours since his last rest, and his muscles were rebelling.

Caleb stopped and looked around. He'd come to a shelf of rock scattered with pockets of sand. The rock faded into the blazing white salt flats two hundred meters ahead.

He turned slowly and looked at the hills he'd crossed during the night. They rose slowly to a pale blue sky. From where he stood he couldn't see a single shrub or tree. A few browned plants pocked the hills, but if rain had fallen here in the last year, there was no sign of it.

When he turned back to the desert, vertigo nearly took his legs from under him. He had to rest. But he couldn't stop here without shade. It would be like lying down in an oven. He would fall asleep and dry up. No, he had to keep moving.

He moved one foot forward, and then the next. His sandals settled on their first patch of rock-hard salt. He took three more steps and then stopped again.

It was as if he'd crossed a barrier, the one that separated life from death, maybe. Walking out onto the endless flats, exhausted and parched, without the slightest inkling of where he was headed struck him as a terrible thing to do. Maybe even evil.

His legs suddenly folded and he sat hard on his rump.

He couldn't do it.

"Promise me one thing, Caleb."

"Have you ever crossed the desert, Dada?"

"No."

"Then please stop your talking and pass me that cool water you just drew from the well. I am very thirsty."

The thoughts drifted through his mind as if on stray clouds.

"Christ, have mercy on me, a sinner," he said, but he didn't hear his own words. Maybe he hadn't said them at all.

Yea, though I walk through the valley of death . . .

Caleb slumped to his back and lay spread eagle, facing the burning sky.

I will fear no evil.

Just keep the sun off my back and I'll be okay.

Blue faded to gray and then to black.

9

D AVID BEN SOLOMON SNATCHED UP THE white satellite phone on its third ring, his fingers trembling with anticipation. "Hello, Rebecca?"

"Hello, Father."

The connection was filled with static. It was her second call—the first was from the ship halfway down the Red Sea.

"So?"

"So we are here."

"At the monastery? You've taken it?"

"We've taken it. But Caleb escaped—"

"What?" Solomon sat heavily. "How could he escape? You allowed a monk to escape?"

"He's not a monk. And he escaped through a tunnel out the back. Don't worry, we'll have him soon."

"And the Ark?"

She hesitated. "We don't know. But the name Hadane is familiar—"

"I knew it! It's there, Rebecca! I can feel it in my bones."

"We have a visitor. A Palestinian, I think. He shot Peter."

Solomon stood, knocking his chair to the floor. "That's impossible! How could they know?"

"I don't know, but we suspected it at the roadblock, and now we have a sniper. The old priest may not be as tight-lipped as we assumed. I'm afraid the sniper has gone after Caleb. I've decided to go after him myself."

"No. You can't leave the Ark. Listen to me, Rebecca. You have the future of our people in your hands. Under no circumstances can you abandon—"

"We don't have the Ark, Father. It may be here, but without Caleb it might as well be hiding three kilometers under the sand. Without Caleb there *is* no Ark. We don't have time for one of the others to fail—I have to go myself."

She did have a point. He began to pace. "If the Arabs are on to us, how do you know they won't take the monastery? If they were to get their hands on the Ark—"

"I'll stay in contact and I'm only taking one man. The place is built like a fort; the rest can hold it for a week if they have to. There's no way the Arabs would dare try a full assault. We're in Ethiopia, remember? Besides, I'm pretty sure the gunman's alone."

"Then neutralize him before he has any idea that you've found the Ark. It will be impossible to return to Jerusalem if they know."

"Consider him dead." She paused. "And we haven't found the Ark. You seem so sure, Father."

"I am. The lights have come on, Rebecca. The Ark is in that monastery. I cannot tell you how monumental this is. We are writing history, you and I. There was the day Joshua fought the battle of Jericho and there was the day Solomon built the Temple, and now there is the day that the Ark of the Covenant was found again. It's no less significant."

"I hope your peers in the Knesset are as sanguine. If you're right, all of Hades will break loose."

"The Knesset will have a fit, but no true Jew can ignore the call of the Ark. Not even Hades can stand against the power of God."

"Shalom, Father. I will contact you when I have Caleb."

"Shalom, Rebecca. Godspeed."

Solomon set the phone down. Sweat drenched his shirt. He stood still for a few seconds and then recovered his chair and sat. Perhaps he was too optimistic. His daughter was right, they hadn't found the Ark yet. But the old priest's story had wailed in his mind for three days now, eroding his doubts.

It made absolute sense. He had pored over history texts that spoke of Manasseh's reign and the Jewish temple on the island of Elephantine, where Hadane had insisted the priests had taken the Ark. And he had read the accounts of the Templars who had come to Jerusalem to find the Ark only to abandon the city and take up residence in Ethiopia. He had even taken a small corner of the knight's letter to the university and had the antiquities department analyze it. The tests had shown that it was eight hundred years old if it was a day. They'd tried to confiscate it.

Under the lights of the priest's story, the puzzle began to look like no puzzle at all but a clear map of history. The kind that can only make sense in retrospect. That map led directly to the Debra Damarro in northeastern Ethiopia.

And then there was destiny. The will of God. He felt God's will like he felt his clothes.

Perhaps he was being too optimistic, but he didn't think so.

"Godspeed, Rebecca. Godspeed."

The camels were nasty old beasts who hadn't been ridden in over a year, according to one of the monks. Neither Rebecca nor Michael were strangers to mean old beasts, so she forced the creatures to the front gates and cinched the reins tight enough to make a statement.

She figured they had two hours before sunrise. She had decided to head south, away from the desert, and circle around to pick up Caleb's trail before daybreak. The fact that she was nearly certain of his destination afforded her that luxury. And his tracks would be impossible to hide in the sand.

As for Avraham's insistence that the sniper had fled, she simply dismissed it. He hadn't put a bullet through Avraham's head because he wasn't after Avraham. Either way it was unlikely that he would be on the south side, where two of her men waited in their hilltop post. That's where she would go, over the hill in the dark without detection and then back north in a search for Caleb's tracks.

"We have enough water for three days," Michael said.

"We won't be gone three days. He's on foot. With any luck we'll be back by afternoon. I hate camels, and this one seems to hate me. More than a day and one of us just might kill the other."

He chuckled.

They led the camels up the road, keeping the animals between themselves and the eastern hills in case the sniper drew a bead and decided to take a potshot. Only after they'd crested the hill and passed the post did they mount the beasts and begin their swing back to the east.

Rebecca's camel evidently assumed that its yearlong respite from duty earned it the right to nip at her legs. One good kick to the teeth and the matter was settled. The camel spit in the dark as if in disgust, but plodded forward willingly enough.

She found Caleb's trail at dawn, five kilometers east of the monastery. The tracks were stretched, those of a staggering man. She pulled out her binoculars and studied the diminishing hills. Beyond lay the great white expanse of desert known as the Danakil Depression.

"You will die if you go to the desert," one of the older priests with a scratchy gray beard had told her. "The desert has no mercy."

"If I die, then so will Caleb. Do you think he's dead already?"

The man had only turned his head.

She lowered the glasses and checked her gear. A bedroll, a small knapsack with enough bread for a few days. Some kind of jerked meat. Her bowie knife, rifle, and enough ammunition to fight off a band of Afar tribesmen if they decided she looked like the edible kind.

In this country a gunshot would announce your presence for kilometers. The knife would be the better bet. She could take the head from a viper at ten paces with it. A Palestinian—that was a different story. Bigger target—easier kill. She'd only used a knife once. The man had been in her hands, and his blood had flowed over her fingers.

Rebecca swallowed, sickened by the memory. A year ago, she'd sworn to herself never to kill another man as long as she lived. Her mother and her little sister had been brutally murdered, but she in turn had brutally murdered. At times she wasn't sure if the Mossad was any better in God's sight than the Hamas. Either way, it was all in the past. She wasn't a killer. She was simply a woman who had killed out of necessity. No more.

Yet here she was.

She remembered the first time her father had read her the story of Samson, single-handedly killing a thousand Philistines in a day.

"What happened to all the blood?" she'd asked.

"When he was finished, he was red," her father said. "Does that scare you?"

She thought about it. "No. As long as it wasn't Samson's blood."

He'd chuckled. "God isn't in the business of killing Jews, Rebecca. Remember that."

"What about the Holocaust?" she'd asked.

She would never forget the look that darkened his face. "That was Hitler, not God. First it was Philistines, then it was Hitler, and now it's Palestinians. Never forget that either." He slammed the book closed.

It was the end of the lesson.

"Let's go," she said softly.

Michael nodded beside her.

She nudged the camel and they headed into the hot sun.

First the Philistines, then Hitler, then the Palestinians, and now Caleb, she thought. When will it end?

10

ISMAEL ADJUSTED HIS RIFLE BETWEEN the large boulders he'd spent the night behind and brought his eye to the scope. From his hole he had a clear view through a side window into what appeared to be the kitchen. The soldiers inside had walked by a dozen times, and right now one had stopped so that his head was framed perfectly in the window. He could see the man's face as if he were within arm's length. A bright red scar sliced down his right cheek, and Ismael imagined putting it there himself. He could have taken the man's head off at anytime, but doing so would be tipping his hand. The woman had to come out of the monastery at some point, and Ismael had no intention of delaying the moment unless he absolutely had to. Rebecca's first step out into the sun would be her last.

During the night he had carefully considered his options. He had a full bottle of water, retrieved from the well behind the monastery before the sun rose. He'd brought enough food to survive for a few days—mostly honey bars and seeds. If, by some impossible feat, they did slip out of the monastery and make it to the lorries parked behind, he would simply take out their tires. And if they made a run for it on foot, he would take a horse from the corral he'd seen in the small village five kilometers down the road and hunt them at his leisure. He still had the Land Rover, of course, stashed a mile or so down the road, but off the road it would be useless. He would use it only when the killing was done. Now it was simply a waiting game, like waiting for a fox to emerge from its den.

A hiss cut the still air and Ismael froze. A snake . . .

"Perimeter's clear. He's gone."

A radio! An Israeli was just below him! The realization sent a chill through Ismael's skull. He hadn't seen a thing. The soldier was good.

A reply came, but Ismael couldn't make it out.

"He may have followed Rebecca to the desert . . ."

Rebecca was gone?

More words were spoken, but Ismael couldn't hear them over the thumping of his heart. She had gone to the desert? It was impossible! It occurred to him that he was in a very precarious position, maybe twenty meters from a soldier, and yet his mind had been snapped away by the Jew-witch already.

He'd seen tracks in the sand last evening, but they had been made by sandals, not by boots. He spun his glasses to the corral behind the monastery where three camels had slinked about the day before.

Two of the camels were gone.

It came to him then, crouched behind the rock in his perfect killing perch. The one the boy had called Caleb—the one the Jews needed to find their relic—had escaped, and somehow Rebecca had gone after him without his knowing. They had gone to the desert. A tremble swept over his limbs.

The air was suddenly very quiet. Swearing steadily under his breath, Ismael pulled himself back and ran behind the hill. He would have to follow, of course. He would have to get the horse and follow. Going on foot would be impossible. It was still morning. How long had she been gone?

He broke into a run, working his way into a small ravine that led away from the monastery towards the west. It would take him at least an hour to reach the village where he'd seen the horse. Then he'd have to take the animal—he doubted they would just give it to him. By the time he picked up Rebecca's tracks she would have as much as eight hours' lead on him.

Eight hours! Ismael bit his tongue hard enough to draw blood. The Jews were like snakes—the moment you had them within your grasp they slithered out of reach. In Palestine it was Jerusalem; here it was Jew-witch. You had to exterminate them like you would exterminate a nest of vipers.

And now this viper was headed east on a camel while he ran west on foot.

Ismael spit blood and leaned into his run.

———

Abu Ismael stood and looked out of his fifth-story office window at the sprawling city of Damascus. It was a paradoxical blend of the old and the new. An ancient city in the heart of Syria, struggling to burst into the twenty-first century. Like a mother in childbirth—a breech birth.

Clay walls baked brown by the beating sun stood within spitting distance from shiny glass walls sealed to keep their conditioned air from spreading to the desert. A Mercedes beeped at a donkey that forced it to a crawl.

Damascus.

A knock rapped on the door and Abu turned. He was in one of the glass buildings, of course, and his office was decorated with plush corded curtains and thick burgundy rugs from the Turks. The huge marble map on his wall could easily buy one of the mud flats in the city.

"Come."

The door flew open and his wife and daughter streamed in like kites with their long colored skirts.

"Morning, Papa!" His daughter held his grandson in her arms.

"Good morning." Abu smiled and stretched his arms out. "Good morning. How are my delightful ladies?" He kissed each one on the cheek and quickly turned his attention to baby Abu, whom he pried out of his daughter's hands. "And how is the little general doing?"

"The little general is still pooping his pants every hour," Mishana said, tossing her bag on a guest chair.

His wife chided her halfheartedly. "Remember where you are, Mishana."

"How could I not? My father is the most important man in all of Syria, and I am in his filthy rich office"—she plopped in a stuffed velvet seat—"sitting in a chair made for kings."

"Ha! If the king heard you say that, you might find yourself in a cement cell," his wife replied. "I would watch my tongue if I were you."

They were modern Arabs, no less devout than more traditional Arabs, but, as Abu had once said, lifted by the grace of Allah above most.

He handed his grandson back to Mishana. "I'm sorry you can't stay, but I'm expecting company." He glanced at the clock. "They are due now."

"Of course," his wife said. "Mishana insisted you needed Abu to brighten your morning. We're shopping."

"Ah, my ever concerned daughter. Is it bringing Abu or shopping that really interests you?"

"Neither. It's seeing you," his daughter said.

Abu smiled and took her face in his hands. "As smart as your father," he said and kissed her forehead.

They laughed and gathered their bags. His wife turned at the door. "Any word?"

"No."

She dipped her head and closed the door.

She referred to Ismael, of course. Abu had made the mistake of telling her that their son had gone into northern Africa on a mission. Ismael's leaving the family to support the Hamas cause had never met her resistance, but Abu knew it broke her heart. Ismael had always been a fanatical zealot, and fanatical zealots who threw themselves into the line of fire rarely lived long. Never mind that the people would sing your praise in the streets for a day; your mother would weep for a year.

Abu paced to the window and stared at the southern horizon. Ismael had made contact two hours ago, by satellite phone. They had made a mess of the first attempt at the roadblock, an event that Abu had already suspected as his son's handiwork based on the news stories.

Now Abu had learned that his son had gone after them alone. It wasn't necessarily flawed thinking—he might have done the same. Less chance of detection. Taking an army into Ethiopia would be impossible.

But the fact that Ismael hadn't yet succeeded was a cause for concern. There was no evidence that the Ark actually existed down there, but the monastery did, exactly as the boy had said. From the first, Abu had known that, for Ismael, the mission was more about killing Rebecca Solomon than the relic. Now Ismael was down there in the desert, and the Jews were in a monastery digging around. The thought of what they might actually find made Abu's stomach feel light.

The buzzer sounded. "General Nasser is here, sir."

"Send him in."

Abu's concern had prompted this meeting.

If the army was the most powerful branch of the Syrian forces, General Nasser's air force now played a close second. In fact, a full two-thirds of the country's military budget had gone into upgrading their air power since the

Gulf War. Iraq's overwhelming defeat had made a case for technology and, more pointedly, for airborne technology.

The general walked in without knocking, removed his hat, and greeted Abu warmly. For ten minutes they exchanged common news. First of their families and then of the city and then of the never-ending Palestinian cause. Although Syria wasn't in direct armed conflict, the PLO was. And the PLO was nothing less than an extension of their own military, even if it was still fragmented and hopelessly underarmed.

Nasser took a sip of tea and crossed his legs. "So tell me, what's on your mind, Abu? Surely you didn't invite me here to talk about Arafat's granddaughter."

They chuckled.

"Let me ask you a question," Abu said. "What would be the worst thing that could happen in the Palestinian struggle for freedom? In strictly hypothetical terms, of course."

The general frowned. "The worst? I can hardly think of anything that isn't worst. Anything short of the Jews vacating all of Palestine and going back to Europe is the worst."

"Of course, and we all share your sentiments. But indulge me. Realistically, the worst."

Nasser thought for a few moments. "The worst would be a strengthening of Israeli resolve to hold Jerusalem. Where Jerusalem goes, the whole land goes. We have gradually beaten Israeli resolve down. Their hearts are slowly being squeezed."

"An example in Jerusalem?"

"Turning Solomon's Stables into the Marwani Mosque under their noses was perhaps our greatest achievement this decade." A soft grin spread over the general's face. "Imagine, turning a Jewish holy place into a mosque without a single bullet fired."

"Solomon's Stables. The Temple Mount. *Haram al-Sharif.* And what could possibly happen to strengthen Israeli resolve in this regard?"

"The West could embrace old sentiments—increase military funding."

Abu waved a dismissing hand. "Israel doesn't need more weapons. It has nuclear weapons. What Israel needs is a renewed spirit."

He stood, put his hands in his pockets, and fingered his car keys. It was a delicate subject he was broaching—rumors could often do more damage than the truth, and in this case, he didn't even know the truth.

Abu picked up his porcelain cup and sipped at the tea he'd poured. "There's a passage in the Koran which I'm sure you know. It speaks of the *Children of Israel who will twice corrupt the land.* You know it?"

"Of course."

"It says they will enter the Al-Aqsa Mosque, as they entered it the first time, and utterly destroy that which they conquered."

"Yes, it's retelling the history of the mosque."

Abu smiled and nodded. "My son does not see it as the telling of history. He insists that it is prophecy, and as it turns out, he's not alone. The apocalyptic reading of this passage is gaining popularity, especially among the Palestinians."

"So they believe that the Jews will one day try to take the Temple Mount and destroy our mosque. Let them believe it—it fuels their fight."

"They actually believe that the Jews already have a master plan to retake the Temple Mount," Abu said. "It's not plausible, I know. The Israeli government is terrified of setting foot on the Mount, much less taking it from us."

Abu took a deep breath. "But their Temple, Solomon's Temple, which they claim was built on the Mount, was built for one reason. To hold the Ark of the Covenant. What would happen, Nasser, if the Ark of the Covenant were actually found and brought to Jerusalem?"

The general blinked and for a moment Abu thought the older man had not heard.

"That could never happen," Nasser said.

"No. But if it did happen?"

"No, I mean we could never let that happen." General Nasser sat forward. "What are you telling me, Abu? You ask me what would be the worst thing that could happen to Palestine and I can't tell you so now you're playing games with the Ark? You're speaking of a nightmare."

Abu sat in his chair. "So then, perhaps we should have a plan to deal with this possibility."

Now the general's humor left him altogether. "Stop playing games, Abu. What are you saying? Someone has found the Ark?"

"No. It's something my son is doing. He believes that the Ark may be found." Abu couldn't explain the details nor mention his involvement—not yet. There was a fine line to be walked here. "But it has made me think."

"If the Ark of the Covenant were found and brought to Jerusalem, every Islamic army from Sudan to Iraq would descend on Israel to protect our holy mosque. We would demolish the Jews."

"And they would allow this?"

"What could they do? Bomb themselves into oblivion? Perhaps it would be best."

"And you believe that Jordan and Egypt and the others would agree?"

"Without question."

Abu looked at the large wall map to his right. "As I said, it's my son. He believes this may actually happen." He turned and smiled.

Nasser wasn't smiling. "And if your son is right, then Allah help us all," he said.

"Yes. Allah help us all."

11

C ALEB . . ."
"Yes, Dada?"

"If you peel back the skin of this world, what will you find?"

"I will find an oven."

"No. You will find the kingdom of God. A kingdom where the meek inherit the earth and mountains are moved with words."

"No, Dada. I will find a white hot oven called the desert . . ."

The voice faded and Caleb faced a black world. He blinked and slowly opened his eyes. The sky was blue and a round ball of fire hung above his head. The sun.

He jerked up and pain spread through his skull. He slumped back to the hard earth and groaned. But in that moment he saw that he really *was* in the desert. The previous night's events crashed through his mind.

He was in the Danakil Desert. The monastery had been taken by bandits. He was looking for help. He had to find help!

Caleb pushed himself up to his elbow and fought to focus his vision. The white salt flats ran to the horizon, like a huge marble slab. A very thin film covered the ground. He lifted his hand and touched the tiny grains to his tongue. Salt.

He eased back down, rolled to his side, and began licking the white salt. *I'm licking the salt like an animal,* he thought. *I've become like an animal.* But he kept licking because nothing seemed as appropriate at the moment. He had to go—that much he knew—but first he had to lick because his body craved salt.

Then the taste grew bitter and he stopped.

It occurred to him that while he was here nuzzling the ground, his parents were held at gunpoint. He struggled to his feet. The heat felt like it had weight. Hot enough to dry the tongue if you happened to open your mouth. He ran his tongue along the rough edges of his lips without managing to wet them.

Caleb wavered on his feet for a few long seconds, unsure which direction to walk. He looked back towards the hills and considered trying to make his way to the monastery. The spring he'd stopped at last night was back there.

But Father Joseph Hadane was not.

He looked out to the featureless desert thinking that it was mad to wander aimlessly in this white oven. But he had to, didn't he? Still he couldn't. His muscles refused to walk. It was like standing on the edge of a cliff and knowing that you had to step off. Just because you knew you had to didn't make taking that first step easy. Every corner of his mind recoiled at the thought. He stood there weaving in the sun, unable to move.

Going back might not be such a crazy thing—*I'll drink and find my energy and then plan something logical. Father Hadane isn't the only man who can help; there've got to be others. The lepers—why didn't I just go to the lepers? I could have taken their horse . . .*

Why hadn't he thought of that last night? But now it was a full day back and then another day to help . . . at least.

On impulse he took a small step forward with his right foot. And then he brought his left foot up to join the right.

Without really knowing why doing so made any sense, he began to take small wobbly steps forward, like a penguin teetering across the ice.

Only this wasn't ice. It was blistering salt. And he wasn't a penguin. He was a madman. An ant wandering into a furnace. Already after only ten steps his sandals felt like they might be melting. At least he was wearing khaki slacks and a long-sleeved cotton shirt—they would keep his skin from melting. For a while.

Caleb swallowed hard against a lump gathering in his throat. Tears of frustration blurred his vision. He could hardly see, but it didn't matter—he didn't know where he was going anyway.

Professor Daniel Zakkai crouched alone in the monastery's root cellar, outlined by the torch's amber flames, and began tapping the floor with a small ball-peen hammer.

The first day of exhaustive search had ended in a few hours of sleep during which it had become clear to him that, absent Caleb, he could still carry on, albeit in a very limited fashion. Maybe even dig a little. And if he was to actually dig, there was no part of the site that begged to be further examined more than the root cellar. He'd awoken and asked them to move the racks of potatoes from one end of the six-by-six-meter room to the other.

He tapped lightly on the hard stonelike surface, listening to the tone of the echo. The urgency for discovery had evaporated after the night search. Clearly they were stuck without Caleb. But this fact did less to dampen his enthusiasm than to settle him into a more cautious pace. He often told his students that the greatest finds were exposed by the last hair on the brush in an inadvertent sweep. An exaggeration, obviously, but one filled with truth nonetheless.

Zakkai tapped slowly, judging the depth of the concrete with a discerning ear. Most of the floors he'd tested produced a deep, dull *thunk* consistent with earth or rock. The walls gave off a higher toned report, and in several places the root cellar's floor gave off a similar sound. But it was the hollow ring that his ears begged for. As of yet the sound had alluded him.

He worked on his knees, down to the east wall, and then he began a diagonal crossing pattern to the corner. The cool air smelled musty, like earth—an odor he'd grown to love over the years, like a soldier might love the smell of gunpowder.

If they found the Ark . . .

Zakkai stopped himself and looked blankly at the wall. *If they found the Ark* . . . The phrase had an absurd ring to it. His mind drifted back to the day David Ben Solomon had first stepped into the doorframe of his office. He knew Solomon from the news, of course. The rogue Knesset member who spoke boldly about the Temple's restoration. It had always surprised

Zakkai that the man continued to win his seat in the government. And then Solomon walked into his office and wooed him with words that made Zakkai wonder why he hadn't become prime minister yet.

"There was a time when God dwelled with Israel," Solomon had said. "Without God, Israel always has been and will once again become like the dust of the desert. And even knowing this we refuse to build his house?"

Somehow those words had led to the imperative that Zakkai take an extended sabbatical and join Solomon in a new plan of his. This plan to find the Ark of the Covenant. It was as if Moses had walked into his office and given new orders. *Watch thou* Raiders of the Lost Ark *and do thou like-wise.*

Of course, his methodical search was nothing like Indiana Jones's, not nearly so romantic or adventurous. Until now. Now he was tapping—Zakkai resumed his tapping on the floor—alone in a subterranean cellar thinking thoughts like *if I find the Ark.* Absurd.

And yet, one thought of the Templar's letter and the . . .

A hollow thud echoed in the room and Zakkai froze, his hammer cocked forty centimeters above the floor. He tapped the floor once and blinked.

He hit it again, harder this time.

It was like hitting a drum.

Zakkai's heart crashed into his chest. He slid his hand closer to the wall, noting that it held a tremble. He struck again.

The sound swallowed him—the sweet, sweet tune of emptiness.

Zakkai scrambled to his feet. "Rebecca!" Rebecca was gone. He spun for the door. "Samuel!"

The radio! The radio, you idiot. He snatched up the hand-held and pressed the toggle. "Samuel, I think I may have found a room."

There was a pause before Samuel's voice rasped over the box. "Come again."

"I need a couple men down here right now. I think I may have found something."

"You have found the Ark?" a stunned voice asked.

"No! A room."

"I can't spare any men, Professor. We have a perimeter to watch."

"And I have a relic to find!" He paused, his head spinning. "Send Jason down."

"Without a guard?"

"We are in the root cellar . . . put a man at the front tunnel if you want. But I need some help. And make sure he brings a pick."

Samuel didn't respond.

Zakkai dropped to his knees and began tapping quickly, marking the rough outlines of the soundings with white chalk. The chamber below crowded the cellar's wall, behind the racks which had held the potatoes. Now a square, roughly one meter by two meters, marked the black floor.

"Now you're going to start tearing things apart?" Jason demanded, ducking through the small wood door.

"Jason! It was behind the racks. I knew there had to be a cavity here somewhere." Zakkai had decided yesterday that he liked the man, despite the natural tension drawn by the circumstances.

Jason dropped a large pick to the ground and stared at the markings. "What does that prove? A hollow spot in the cement."

"But you wouldn't have built over an opening this large! Don't you see?" Zakkai grabbed the hammer and struck the floor. It echoed satisfactorily. "You built on a floor, but we're hearing a chamber *under* that floor."

"And?"

"And? Don't be daft, man!" He was perhaps too expressive in his exuberance. "We have found an entrance into Caleb's childhood chambers."

Jason stared at the chalk marks and finally nodded. "Maybe. I guess that's something."

"It's more than something, my fine friend." Zakkai grabbed the pick.

"So now you're going to ruin our root cellar?"

"Please, Jason. I personally will pay to have your precious cellar restored to its moldy old self. We are talking history here!"

"*If* you find the Ark."

"Worth it, don't you think?"

Jason eyed him. "You swear to fix it. Either way."

"Yes."

With a glint in his eye, Jason stepped forward and took the pick. "So what are you waiting for? Not sure how to handle a pick?"

He swung the tool with the ease of a man who'd dug too many holes without the advantage of a backhoe. The sharp point buried itself in the rock.

12

T HE SPRING WAS A BLESSING. The fact that Caleb's tracks led beyond the spring towards the desert was not.

They traveled in silence mostly, Rebecca to the front and Michael to her left and behind, half a camel. The beasts plodded on soft hoofs, rocking with each step. Their tan hides twitched with the occasional fly, and they blinked against ever-present gnats eager to feed at the moisture in their eyes. They smelled of hay and dung, but perched so high on the hump, Rebecca caught a full whiff only occasionally.

The terrain had flattened from its steady descent, and patches of white salt replaced the loamy sand of the hills. They came to an acacia tree—the last one before the desert by the looks of it—and Rebecca pulled up under its meager shade.

"I thought the Negev was hot."

"Wait till we get to the desert," Michael said.

"I don't think we'll be going into the desert. Only a proper idiot would walk in on foot."

"Maybe he *is* a proper idiot."

She humphed and nudged her camel forward. They moved on with the sun at their backs now. To anyone seeing them trudging along on camels dressed in tan khakis with desert hats and leather boots, they might look like two lost archaeologists. Not that there was anyone to see them this far out.

"Do you mind if I speak frankly, sir?" Michael asked after a while.

"Go ahead. I don't think we have curious ears out here."

"What do you make of this mission?"

She knew what he was asking but played along anyway. "What do you mean?"

"We're over fifteen hundred kilometers from Israel, laying siege to an empty monastery and now chasing a monk into the desert."

"He's not a monk and I don't think he went into the desert."

"A madman then. You can't seriously believe we'll find the Ark of the Covenant."

There it was. "You don't believe it exists?"

"Sure it exists. But I'm not sure it will ever be found. There are other ways to wage a war than to walk through deserts on camels looking for a gold box."

She eyed him sharply. "A gold box?"

"The Ark is—"

"I know what the Ark is. I don't know your faith—for all I know you don't believe in God. But for any Jew who still believes in God, the Ark is no gold box."

"Of course, I know—"

"No, I don't think you do, or you wouldn't have said it," she said. "The Ark of the Covenant is Israel. Do you understand this? We have never been a true nation without it, and we never will. It's the dwelling place of God on earth. The Temple was built to house it, and our religion has always centered around it. Without the Ark there is no need for a nation to protect it, is there?"

"We have a nation now."

"You call this tiny experiment which has sputtered along for fifty years a nation? No, Michael, we're trying to *become* a nation, but we are not really a nation, not yet. My father says that we're a sapling trying to become a tree. But every day the dirt is being washed from our roots and we watch it float downstream and argue over its color. There's your nation. And we refuse to turn to the gardener—to God—for help because we've forgotten why we were planted."

The desert was fast approaching, and Caleb's tracks did not stop.

"I've never heard it said like that," Michael said.

"I don't know if we will actually find the Ark—frankly I doubt it. But I can tell you that this evidence we have is enough to bring most archaeologists panting."

She turned to him and smiled. "It's pretty amazing, isn't it? In New York a thousand traders are yelling at the Big Board, desperate to make a few dollars; in Paris lovers are sitting beside a canal for a portrait; in Jerusalem two rabbis are sitting at the Western Wall, arguing about whether a woman should be allowed to hold a weapon. And here we are, in the most remote corner of the earth, on the heels of literally the greatest discovery of all time. Who knows what treasures are hiding under this sand, but believe me, soldier, we're not looking for a gold box. We're looking for the presence of God. The only hope for Israel. No bomb, no politician, no man—not a million men—can accomplish what the Ark can accomplish for Israel."

They rode on, and Michael remained silent. It was no wonder Israel was losing its soul, Rebecca thought. Not even her soldiers understood her destiny.

They came to the edge of the desert an hour later. It was then, for the first time, that Rebecca realized their prey was no ordinary man.

"His tracks go in," Michael said.

Sure enough. She could see where the light coating of dust had been disturbed. He'd walked in twenty meters or so, then laid down before standing and continuing into the heart of the salt flats.

"He's tired," Michael said, pointing to the weaving trail.

The footprints disappeared into a seemingly limitless horizon. He could be a kilometer out, he could be ten kilometers out, although unless he had some protection from the sun and a tank of water she guessed it would be closer to a kilometer. Either way they would find him soon.

She shook her head. "I would take on a battalion of Palestinians over this any day. What possesses a man to go in there on foot?"

"What possesses Palestinian children to throw rocks?" Michael responded.

"Brainwashing."

"So maybe his brain is washed. It's a hot day."

"Well, let's just hope he still remembers what will lead us to the Ark." She slapped her camel. "Come on, he can't be far. Let's get him and get out before nightfall."

The camel snorted, reluctant to step onto the salt.

Rebecca smacked the beast again, and it finally slumped forward. The last of the sand fell away, and they rode out onto the forbidden flats.

It had been a leper colony, not a village, and the fact had sent Ismael into a fit of sorts. He blamed it on the frustration the woman had brought him. The Jew-witch made him kill the three lepers—a man, a woman, and a child, who'd come out in their rags to ask him why he was taking their prized possession.

At least that's what he assumed they were asking him. It didn't matter. He was so startled by their sagging faces that he spun and shot the first through the head. Seeing the man topple backward filled him with a sense of purpose. The girl and the woman lepers became Jews in his mind, and he shot them too.

Unfortunately, the shot had frightened the horse and it took him half an hour to get his hands back on the animal.

Now it was midday and he had only just found the camel's tracks.

Ismael rode without a saddle, and the mare's sweat had soaked his pants. When this was done, he would shoot the horse. He lifted his rifle and sighted at the distant desert. Waves of heat shimmered across its surface. He had grown up in the desert; he doubted the Jew had. Her camel could outlast his horse, but she could not outlast him. Not in the desert. It was the one bright side to this unfortunate delay.

Ismael lowered the glasses and kicked the horse.

Zakkai stood back, panting. It had taken them nearly six hours to carve out the two holes that stared up at them like black eyes. The first had ended in a shallow chamber, no more than seventeen centimeters deep and maybe fifty centimeters wide. What purpose it served was beyond either of them. It had taken Zakkai twenty minutes to persuade Jason to continue.

Now it looked as if his argument had vindicated itself.

"So what do you make of it?" Jason asked.

"Hand me the torch," Zakkai said, reaching his hand out.

Jason plucked the fire stick from the wall and pushed it into Zakkai's hand. "How big is it?"

Zakkai dropped to one knee and lowered the flame into the hole. He bent over and waved the torch to his right. An underground wall glowed three meters further in. "Big. It's a full room."

"Empty?"

"No."

Zakkai dipped his head through the opening. The torch's flame suddenly seared his arm, and he instinctively jerked it back, dropping the fire.

"That was smart," Jason said.

Zakkai ignored him. The room below flickered in the torchlight, a treasure trove of artifacts. Not artifacts of antiquity, but those of a recent day— simple furniture, bookcases stuffed with dusty books, a couple of chairs. And on the far side, another opening, gaping black in the shadows.

Zakkai scrambled to his feet. "Help me in."

"You sure? Is it safe?"

"Please, just do as I say." He stretched out a hand. "Lower me in."

Jason grabbed his hand and lowered him into the hole. It felt like his shoulder might pull out of joint, but Zakkai hardly cared.

"Are you down?"

Zakkai looked down. The floor was a meter below him. "Let go," he called. His voice sounded dead in the hollow room. Jason released him and he landed easily among the pile of rubble they'd hacked from the ceiling. He picked up the torch and turned it slowly around the room.

The chamber was roughly three meters by five meters, hewn from solid rock and worn smooth over many years. A small table and a lone glass lamp sat to his left, both covered in a thick layer of dust. Behind the table, two old wood chairs. To his right, short bookcases lined the wall, housing dozens of books.

"Should I come down?"

"Come," Zakkai said. The word sounded too loud for the small room.

A rope dropped down beside Zakkai. Jason eased himself into the chamber. For a moment they stood, side by side, silent.

"I . . . I recognize this room," Jason said softly, as if afraid to disturb the stillness.

"You do?"

"It's where I first met Caleb. This is where Father Matthew brought me. I wonder why we never found it when we rebuilt . . ."

Zakkai turned and motioned towards the far wall. The entry to what appeared to be a collapsed tunnel faced them, choked with large slabs of rock.

"That's why," Jason said. "The tunnel has collapsed."

"But Caleb must have known that his room was here. Why didn't you just excavate?"

"We were building new lives," Jason said. "Not digging up old ones."

Zakkai turned back to face the opening beside the table. "And have you been in there?"

"No. Caleb came out from there."

Zakkai swallowed and bent down to read the spines of the books nearest him. The bookcases were low to the ground. He blew and dust puffed. *The Seven Storey Mountain*—Thomas Merton. Another dozen books by the same author. A collection of works in Hebrew, others in Amharic.

"Does Caleb know Hebrew?" he asked.

"Yes."

"This is incredible. He lived down here?"

"Yes."

"I've heard some things. But I couldn't have imagined this. It's not where you'd expect to find a ten-year-old boy."

"No."

Zakkai stood. He could nearly hear the voices of Caleb's old teacher echoing softly off the stone. The workmanship of the walls took Zakkai back to the blind priest's story. How long ago had the room been carved out of the rock? And by what kinds of instruments? If the old man's story was right, the Templars themselves had brought Celtic masonry and construction methods to Ethiopia. This monastery and, if so, this room could have been carved under the supervision of a lost order of the Templars.

Jason stood in silence, taken back in time by the images that now surrounded him. He looked stunned.

Zakkai walked up to the arched entry into the second room and Jason followed. He fed the torch into the room and knew immediately that they were looking at Caleb's bedroom. He stepped in. A wool blanket neatly covered the small wood-frame bed along one wall. Above the bed, a single painting of Christ on the cross. Beside the bed, a nightstand with a dusty oil lamp. And on the other wall, more books. As many as there were in the main room—ancient books written by monks and scribes—names unfamiliar to Zakkai except by the titles preceding them.

"What kind of boy lived here?" he asked in wonder.

Jason looked around. "He was abandoned at the gate as an infant. A war child. Father Matthew took him in and raised him as a son. Until the day the monastery was leveled, Caleb never once stepped outside these walls. He was ten then. We took him to the United States because we thought that would be best for him."

"We?"

"Leiah and I. She was a Red Cross nurse then." He paused. "His pure faith changed America in ways we could never have imagined. But America changed him too."

"The miracles," Zakkai said. He'd heard the incredible stories.

"Yes. But most people don't know the price he paid. Caleb has lived a tormented life, divided between two realities." Jason averted his eyes, but Zakkai could see the moisture glistening in the torchlight.

"I'm sorry," Zakkai said.

"I think Caleb is one of the few who knows why Christ sweat blood when he asked God to remove the cup. It wasn't the physical suffering; it was a greater suffering, the kind that tears at your soul. Caleb never has recovered."

Zakkai looked away, suddenly awkward in the heaviness of the moment.

Jason seemed to come to himself. "I'm sorry, I don't mean to go on about Christ to a Jew—"

"No, no. Not all Jews despise the man."

They stood in silence for several long seconds.

Zakkai took a deep breath. "Well, I think it's time we begin our search."

"The closest thing to an Ark you'll find here is a picture in one of these books," Jason said.

"Forgive me for pointing out the obvious, but we are in Caleb's room. The same Caleb who may very well hold the key to the Ark's location. Short of the man himself, we could have hoped for no better find."

"It's the room of a child."

"And according to Hadane, Caleb was a child when Father Matthew hid the Ark." Zakkai stepped into the main room and planted the torch into an old bracket on the wall.

"What are you planning on searching?" Jason asked, following.

"We need more light down here. Two more torches at least. And we could use some help. Do you think your wife would be willing?"

"I guess that depends. I'm pretty sure she won't be up to swinging a pick around. What are you planning to search?" he asked again.

"Everything," Zakkai said through a grin. "Every square inch. Every piece of paper, every page, every bit of furniture. Everything. There is something here; I can feel it in my bones. And believe me, my friend, I know bones."

———

The sun beat at his back and Caleb thought he was only a few meters from death. How he had managed to walk this long he could not remember because his mind had started to close down an hour ago.

If there had been a breeze, his sweat may have provided some relief, but the air refused to move. Or if it did move, the movement was straight up, rising with the force of heat, like a blast furnace reaching up into his pant legs and baking his knees. The only thing that was missing was the roar of the flames.

Each footfall sounded with a dull thud, and the thuds had slowed as of late. His mouth had dried completely, so that if he tried to open it—which he no longer did—his lips at least objected. They had glued shut. Water became a desperate dream. Waterfalls crashed through his mind, and he spent the hours tasting each drop of mist they threw in the air. He would've cut off a leg for a splash.

The horizon was flat except for the lump to his left. And even that lump wasn't a lump at all, but a node in his mind, rising to mock him.

In fact, maybe the desert wasn't a desert at all. Maybe he was walking through his own life. Plodding into his own heart. A landscape stripped of its water and left to die.

How had he come to this point? There was a time not too long ago when he could sing and fill the desert with rivers and a thousand trees. But even the memory of that time sat like an obscure lump in his mind.

A lump like that lump on the edge of the desert ahead of him.

His right leg suddenly gave way and he fell. His upper torso slammed onto the hard salt before he could move an arm to break the fall. His breath left him and he lay, arm pinned under his body, suffocating, thinking that the moment of death had finally, mercifully come.

But then his wind returned. He thought about licking the salt, but decided that prying his lips apart to get his tongue out would be too difficult.

It took him a long time to maneuver his body to stand because his right arm had stopped functioning. Pain throbbed through his side when he tried to use it. Maybe it was broken; maybe it was dislocated; maybe it was just gone.

Caleb looked around, disorientated. Which direction had he been walking? He turned slowly with his right shoulder dipped. The lump on the horizon filled his vision. Yes, he had been walking towards the lump. The node in his mind.

He shuffled forward.

And what was he doing in this desert? Looking for water. No, looking for a priest named Hadane who could give him water. No, looking for help from a priest named Hadane because his mother and father needed help. Although right now a cup of water seemed more like help than any of . . .

Caleb stopped. It was the lump that stopped him. That lump on the horizon which, now that he thought about it, had been there for a while. He straightened and squinted at it.

A wet squishing sound filled his ears. His heart had decided that this lump might be important. What if it wasn't a lump?

The image jumped into focus, as if his mind had been waiting for that question to connect itself to his eyeballs. It was a rock formation! Not a round lumpy rock formation, but a square one that jutted out of the white flats like a cluster of skyscrapers on the horizon.

Caleb couldn't contain the emotion that flooded his eyes. He let out a sob that parted his lips. He could feel the skin tear, but the pain hardly registered.

Hope, sweet hope, was swallowing him. He shuffled forward without removing his eyes from the rock. "Oh, God, thank you! Oh, God, thank you!"

The first blister appeared ten minutes later. One moment Caleb was unaware that his right foot was rubbing raw, and the next he was limping through a jagged pain.

And the rock formation had not come any closer. Which meant that it was very large, and that was good. And very far, which was not good.

The sun was in the western sky, halfway to the horizon. He had to reach the rock by nightfall.

13

REBECCA PULLED OUT HER BINOCULARS AND carefully scanned the horizon, then looked down. Caleb's footprints looked less distinct, like he was dragging his feet. He was slowing, but he still was nowhere in sight. Because of his head start, she was beginning to think they might not catch up to him by nightfall. And once darkness fell, they would not be able to follow.

She saw the rock formation then, through her lenses. "The rocks. He will head for the rocks."

Michael had his glasses up as well. "How can you be sure? His tracks are headed to the right now."

"His trail goes to the right because when he was here he couldn't see the rocks without binoculars. When he sees the rocks, he will change course towards them."

A distant wail carried thinly through the air.

She lowered the binoculars. "Did you hear that?"

"Sounded like an animal."

She nodded. "Okay, we'll cut him off. There's no way he can make it past the rocks by nightfall."

They veered from Caleb's tracks and headed directly for the distant formation.

————

Caleb limped on, through the pain. A second blister swelled on his left foot, where his sandal strap crossed over his foot. The sun had baked the skin from his toes, he saw. He stopped and tried to adjust his sandals, but the attempt failed. He took both sandals off, but immediately put them back on—he might not have heard the sizzle, but the heat had burned his soles already. The Danakil reached temperatures in excess of 140 degrees and the salt more than that.

But he was going to make it. He had made it this far. Caleb struggled forward in an awkward limp that sent searing pain through both feet.

And what if he couldn't make it?

A desperate desire swam through his mind. *I have to make it. I have to make it.* Suddenly nothing beyond this one thought mattered.

He walked for another ten minutes, and if he thought about it hard enough, the rock formation did look closer, didn't it? A slight shiver of anticipation rippled through his bones. There, just ahead, was shade and relief and maybe a city with water. A small blister on his foot was not going to slow him, much less stop him. The resolve filled his legs with new strength.

Caleb managed a full half-hour before the worst of it hit. The first hint of discouragement settled during one of the squinting sessions he'd taken to every few minutes. This time when he squinted the rock formation actually looked further away. Certainly not closer.

The notion stopped him in his tracks. He blinked rapidly. The distant shape stood clearly in the rising heat. A wedge of heat ripped up his spine. It was, wasn't it? It was as far away as it had been half an hour ago!

He thought he should run, so he did . . . five steps before a screaming pain shot up his shins and spread through his loins.

He uttered a cry and looked at his feet. At first he wasn't sure what he was looking at. They were puffy with blisters and bleeding where some of the blisters had broken. Like boiled tomatoes with split skin. Behind him a thin trail of blood spotted the white salt.

He looked up and stared at the rock formation, suddenly terrified. He looked back at his feet, and for a moment he thought he might throw up. *No, you can't throw up, Caleb—the vomit will draw desert rats. Desert rats will eat a disabled man to the bone. And the blood will draw more desert rats.*

You can do this!

Caleb looked ahead and took another step. Pain shot up his leg.

It was then that Caleb realized he would die in this desert. But it wasn't for another full minute of desperate, halting steps that the realization passed from his mind to his heart and squeezed tight, like a vise.

He gripped his hands to fists so that his arms trembled and forced his right foot forward. His sandal was wet and made a soft slurpy sound. He grunted and forced another stop. Fire spread up his ankles.

Caleb slogged forward, every muscle strung like a wire, trembling from head to foot now. Tears sprang to his eyes and something in his mind snapped. He took a long step, and then another. And another. Now the flesh in his feet began to tear in earnest.

But something had changed.

He suddenly threw out his arms, spread his fingers wide, and lifted his chin to the sky. The scream came from his belly and tore past his throat, a wail that sounded like death.

But instead of crumpling to the ground, he marched on. His feet were falling apart, he knew that, felt that. His flesh quivered and twitched like a horse's fighting off flies. He was in shock, and he walked on knowing it well. He no longer cared if he lived or died. Only that he walked.

So he walked. His scream gave way to sobs which eventually gave way to a clenched jaw. The only sound he could hear was his heavy breathing. That and the sound of his feet tearing.

The pain soon faded into a numbness that rose up his legs. He was walking to his death. He was dying, from the feet first. Soon it would reach his heart. But he didn't care anymore.

In his mind he had already died.

———

Zakkai paced in the subterranean room, stepping carefully around the piles of ancient texts they had worked through. Three torches crackled lightly in the silence. Jason and Leiah sat on the old chairs by the table, looking at him with sagging eyes, exhausted.

Leiah had refused to be part of the search at first. They had just discovered her son's childhood bedroom, and tearing it apart sounded like an abomination to her. But once she understood that with or without her help the room would be searched, she elected to help, which evidently translated to "oversee" in her mind. Now they had come to the end of the search and she had already suggested once that they put everything back exactly as they had found it.

"Please, Professor," Leiah said. "You haven't found anything."

He didn't answer.

"We've searched every page of every book," she said. "We've examined the table and the bed with a magnifying glass. We even searched the floor, for heaven's sake. There's nothing here. And if there is, we aren't going to find it in this light."

Zakkai barely heard her. His mind had taken a different track. "You are both certain that Caleb has never made any mention of the Ark."

"Never," Leiah said. Jason shook his head.

"And you honestly don't believe he knows anything?"

"I really don't see how he could," Jason said. "He's told us everything he remembers."

"Then perhaps we should assume for a moment that you are correct."

"That would be generous," Leiah said.

Zakkai ignored her. "Suppose Father Matthew didn't mean for Caleb to know about the Ark's location. Suppose he planted the key to its location without Caleb's knowledge."

"That doesn't make any sense," Jason said. "What's the use of a key if no one knows it exists?"

"Someone does know about it. Just not Caleb. The old blind priest, Hadane, knew about it. And he knew about it because Father Matthew told Hadane's brother, a Falasha Jew who has supposedly converted to Christianity. Joseph Hadane. The point is, under this scenario, Father Matthew obviously wanted to protect Caleb by keeping the knowledge from him."

"So you're saying Caleb isn't the key after all?"

"No." Zakkai wagged his finger. "I'm saying that maybe he doesn't *know* he's the key. Knowing it would place an undue burden on him. But if the Ark came into danger of being discovered, then something would tip Caleb off. Show him the key."

"What? That doesn't make any sense," Jason said. "Why would Caleb need to know—"

"So that he could protect it, of course." Zakkai looked around, suddenly excited.

"We haven't found anything that looks like a clue meant to tip Caleb off," Leiah said.

"Exactly. But perhaps because Father Matthew didn't want Caleb to find it unless there was a significant threat." He paused and turned around, thinking. "The question is, what would Father Matthew consider a threat? If someone were to find Caleb's room and search these books for clues to the Ark, would that pose a threat? No! We're going about this wrong."

"What do you suggest?" Leiah asked. "That we tear into the walls?"

Zakkai spun to her, wide-eyed. It made perfect sense.

"You can't be serious," she said.

"Why not? If the Ark is hidden, then an excavation would pose a threat to its uncovering. Something would have to be exposed to tip Caleb off as to the Ark's true location." Zakkai strode to the wall and felt it with his palm. "Something only Caleb could understand."

"But why here? It could be anywhere?"

"Because this is where any archaeologist would begin. This, Leiah, is the heart of the monastery, as far as I'm concerned. Caleb holds the key; these are Caleb's quarters." Zakkai felt a faint chill snake down his spine. He hurried to the table, snatched up his hammer, and approached the wall.

"Please, Professor. Let's at least talk this through before you begin to beat on the walls."

He tapped the stone lightly. They hadn't even tested the walls. Jason suddenly grabbed one of the torches and disappeared into the bedroom.

"Jason?" Leiah called after him. "Are we just going to let him smash these walls?"

Jason didn't reply.

"I have no intention of smashing your walls," Zakkai said. "I'm not even scratching them. But if you are right about Caleb not knowing, and I am right about why Father Matthew wouldn't want him to know, then we have no choice but to at least look."

"You're not looking at the wall. You're hitting it with a hammer."

The stone was thick along the wall Zakkai tested. He moved to his right a meter or so and tapped again, from the top of the wall down to the floor. He could be wrong, of course. The whole line of reasoning he'd followed had been based on the vague presumption that Father Matthew wanted to protect Caleb from . . .

"Professor!" Jason's voice echoed through the chamber.

Zakkai turned to the call.

"Uhh, you might want to see this."

Zakkai brushed past Leiah and spun into the room.

Jason stood on the bed with the picture of Christ in his hands. But Jason wasn't looking at the frame in his hands, he was staring at the wall behind it.

A thin crack angled across the surface. Jason knocked on it with his knuckles. Hollow.

Leiah pushed past Zakkai and immediately saw what they saw. The archaeologist in Zakkai was speaking now. Telling him that they should slow down because they had made a discovery and all discoveries should be handled with the utmost care. He stood there, unmoving. Yes, it was time they slowed down and applied the meticulous standards he'd committed his life to. Never mind that this was an illegal military mission with guns and soldiers. They had just found something that screamed of value and they could not just . . .

Leiah suddenly took the hammer from his hands and jumped onto the bed. She tapped the stone before Zakkai could stop her.

But it wasn't stone. It was plaster and it crumbled to the wool bedspread.

"Easy! Easy. Don't damage anything!" Zakkai took the hammer, brushed past her, and examined the plaster. Jason and Leiah stood back and allowed him to work carefully around the hole, tapping with just enough force to dislodge the material in small amounts.

He worked in silence for five full minutes. No one spoke.

A slab of white plaster suddenly broke free and Leiah gasped. A nook gaped at them—a dark hole behind the wall, roughly a third of a meter in diameter.

"It's empty," Leiah said.

It did look empty. But Zakkai already saw the single sheet of paper which hugged the bottom. He reached in and slowly extracted it.

The paper was in good shape, clearly of modern manufacture despite its textured stock, nothing like the ancient letter the blind priest had given them.

"A letter?" Jason asked.

Zakkai carried the sheet into the main room and laid it on the table. Together they crowded around and studied the words under the flickering flames.

> *Caleb,*
>
> *You alone know the secrets of this majestic rock we shared for a home. It was a gift from God. My dear sweet one, you will know. Where the brine mixes with the oil, there you will find God. Only you will know.*
>
> *I am flying now, Caleb. We will fly together again. I cherish you more than life.*
>
> *Matthew*

Heat rose through Zakkai's neck. He reread the letter three times, feeling his heart tighten with each reading. He lifted his chin and took a deep breath. Leiah sat down in one of the chairs and lowered her face into her hands.

"So then maybe you're right," Jason said quietly.

"We are right," Zakkai said. His voice wavered with emotion. They might have just as well uncovered a placard with the words *Within these walls lies the Ark of the Covenant.*

14

THE TRIBE CONSISTED OF THIRTY-THREE SOULS. Twelve women, seven children—eight if you counted the one with child—and fourteen monks. Only seven of the monks had taken the vow of celibacy, but they had all made simple vows unique to the tribe that no less committed them than any vow taken anywhere by any monk. In fifty years they had never been less than fifteen and never more than thirty-four. The harsh reality of the desert played more than a small role in their numbers.

Like most people who depended on the desert for survival, they were a nomadic tribe, rarely staying more than two weeks in any camp. But the Oasis of the Towers was one such camp, and they had stayed a long three weeks before the Father had suggested it was time to move on.

The oasis wasn't much more than a brown puddle to the east of the towers. The rock formation shielded the hole and the camp from the afternoon sun. There were only three commonly known springs in the Danakil, eight if you really knew, and twelve if you knew how to wring water from a rock. Fortunately the tribe had a few "rock-wringers." But only the spring at the Tower Oasis remained wet year around. Not wet enough to support more than two spiny trees and not wet enough to wash down your camels, but wet. Enough to filter the soupy, brown water for drinking, at least.

The tents were already loaded and the water jars filled. They would leave at sunset as always. Within the half-hour.

Three of the children ran circles around Mustaf, the oldest and, without argument, the most ornery of their fifteen camels. Mustaf objected loudly and bared his lips, turning clumsily and spitting at the children, which only perpetuated the game. As was to be expected, Daniel led the charge, skipping like a jackal, edging the old camel close to its limits.

Two of the women were sweeping the salt, clearing marks of their stay as a courtesy more to themselves than to any other visitor. In all likelihood the next visitor would in fact be the tribe, three months from now. Excepting Mustaf, the last of the camels were already strung together in a long train for the journey.

It was then, just after Brother Elijah had told Daniel to leave the camel alone, that Miriam's cry cut through the air and stopped them all in their tracks.

"Brother Elijah! Brother Elijah, come quickly!"

After a momentary pause, a dozen of the tribe ran towards her. She waved to them urgently. "Hurry!"

"What is it?" Elijah demanded. Little Daniel was on his heels with the other children, and behind them Brother Isaac and two of the women.

Without answering, Miriam spun and walked around the tower.

Brother Elijah drew abreast. "What is it?"

"A man."

"A man? You haven't seen a man before?"

"Please, Elijah. This isn't the time to play around." The rest had caught up and trailed her, some snickering at the exchange. The tribe wasn't easily excitable, but they were easily amused.

"When you see, you won't be laughing," Miriam said. She turned and ran through a group of boulders to the west side of the tower.

The man lay on his face, unmoved from where Miriam had stumbled upon him. She slowed and walked around the body. A hush enveloped the others. They formed a rough circle around the body.

"Who is he?" Daniel asked.

No one answered. The man was dressed in western clothes—khaki slacks and a white shirt, the latter stained by sweat, the former by blood. His sandals were embedded in blistered feet. Flies buzzed around the glistening flesh, feeding on the blood. None of this was so uncommon in the desert.

The color of the man's skin was. It was tan, not black. This man wasn't from the desert.

"He's a white man," Daniel said, undeterred by the silence.

"Hush, Daniel," his older sister, Ruth, said.

"I was doing a sweep for garbage and found him here," Miriam said. The man's back rose and fell in gentle undulations. Dark hair concealed his face, which was planted in the sand.

They stood looking down at the strange sight together. It seemed to have frozen them into inaction. And then suddenly they were all moving. Brother Isaac knelt by the feet and began to pull up the man's pant legs.

"Give me water," Elijah said, taking a bottle from one of the women. Miriam dropped to her knees and pulled matted hair from the man's face. "We have to turn him over onto his back."

The children crowded for a better look, and Ruth shooed them back. "Give them room. This isn't a painting to gawk at. This is a man who is dying."

"It's okay, Ruth," Isaac said gently, placing his hands under the man's legs. "Let them look. It won't harm them."

Together, Isaac, Elijah, and Miriam eased the body over onto its back. If the man felt any pain, he didn't show it. He was unconscious.

Miriam placed her hand under the man's shirt. "His body temperature's too high." She ripped the shirt open, and Elijah poured his water on the chest. They worked as a team familiar with the task set before them. They had to reduce the body temperature as quickly as possible.

"Water," Miriam said, blindly reaching her hand to the others like a surgeon asking for a scalpel. A bottle filled it. She uncorked it with her teeth and spilled a thin trail onto the man's cracked lips. Then onto his forehead and cheeks. She emptied it over his neck and hair. Beneath the blisters the skin was smooth; he was a handsome man with a finely shaped face.

Miriam took another bottle of water, gently pried his lips apart, and dribbled the cool liquid into his mouth. The water seeped past white teeth.

Isaac had removed the man's sandals. "It's not as bad as it looks, but we have to get some salve on these blisters."

"We can't move him until he responds," Miriam said.

"Yes. Daniel, fetch the stretcher, please. Ruth, please tell the Father that we have a guest. He will know what to do."

They ran off, Ruth chiding her younger brother for always having to be the man of the hour.

The stranger first responded ten minutes later—a gentle swallow—and a satisfied murmur swept through the onlookers. Within minutes the man was moaning, and his temperature had fallen to reasonable levels. Brother Isaac had covered his feet in a thick layer of salve, then wrapped them in white linens.

The Father had instructed Ruth to take binoculars and climb the highest rock to look out to the west. She was clambering up the boulders now, proudly announcing her mission to the rest.

"We are taking him with us? Or are we staying?" Miriam asked Brother Isaac. It was not their way to leave a man in need.

"I should think we will stay," he said. "But that will be up to the Father. Either way this man isn't going to walk around on his own tonight. Help me put him—"

"There's more!" Ruth suddenly yelled down from her perch. "There are more coming!"

Miriam jumped up and gazed out at the red sunset. "More? You mean more travelers?" She could see nothing but flat salt.

"Yes, more! Two on camels, I think. No wait . . . three! Another further behind!" She spun down towards them. "Three!"

"What did the Father say?" Isaac demanded.

"That if there were more coming we should leave immediately!" Ruth was already scrambling down from the rocks.

Isaac grabbed the stretcher and rolled it out next to the man. "Well, now we know. Let's go."

Isaac and Elijah lifted the limp man onto the stretcher, grabbed the poles on either end, and hurried for the caravan. If the Father had insisted they leave, it could only mean that the approaching travelers posed a threat. Obviously the Father knew something they did not.

Miriam insisted that she be the one to stay by the man until he recovered. Brother Isaac raised a brow, but no one objected. The process of attaching the makeshift bed to her camel took no more than five minutes. The stretcher angled to the earth and would slide like a sled. If the ground wasn't so even, the ride might be rough, but the desert was as flat as marble here.

With a final sweep of the camp the caravan left the Tower Oasis, dragging their newest member behind. They left a trail, of course—two lines in the sand left by the stretcher, leading due north.

Ismael first caught sight of the two camels one hour before sunset, and the sight had him off the horse immediately. He brought the glasses up and peered at the distant animals edging away. They were headed for the tall rocks on the horizon.

Ordinarily he might have used the speed of his mount to flank them and take a position in the rocks before them. A horse could outrun a camel any day.

Unless the horse was an old dehydrated mare, wheezing with each step. Ismael wasn't sure the horse would make the rocks at a walk, much less at a gallop. A camel was the wiser mount in this cursed heat.

And there was another small fact that held Ismael back. The simple reality that if he could see them with his glasses, they could also see him with theirs.

They might not expect that they were followed, but he couldn't take that chance. He remounted, eased his horse off their trail, and angled south. It was less likely that they would check their flanks than their rear. Unfortunately the maneuver would add a couple of hours to his ride, but the sun would soon be down. Even if the horse gave out, he could walk to the rocks in the night.

Like him, the Jew was following tracks—without a moon she would have to stop for the night or risk losing them.

Ismael smiled for the first time that day. The distant camels had neither increased their pace nor altered their course. Soon it would be dark and he would come up on them unexpected, not from their rear, but from their flank, on his belly. Even if they had spotted him, they wouldn't see him in the dark.

He would pick them off like two rats in a cage. And if he was lucky, the monk they pursued would be with them.

Three rats in a cage.

Rebecca had scanned their rear with a scope every half-hour, but saw nothing. She had no reason to believe the sniper would follow them in the first place, but if by chance he had, he still wasn't in sight.

Caleb's trail was unquestionable. He'd left drops of blood in the sand that a blind man with a bag over his head could follow.

The largest rock had looked like a shaft of red light in the setting sunset. Now it loomed over them, an ominous monolith in the dark.

They pulled up their mounts a hundred meters from the rocks and listened. Nothing. Rebecca slid off her camel and Michael followed suit. They walked for the tower, staying on the protected side of the animals, pausing and listening every dozen paces.

Still nothing.

It took them another twenty minutes to reach the rocks. Nothing but silence met them. They had no reason to believe Caleb would be violent, so their search went quickly. He was gone.

"So . . ." Rebecca said, staring at the twin lines in the sand. She knelt and traced one of them with her index finger.

"So, indeed. We won't be able to follow these easily without a moon."

"No. What do you make of them?"

"Something was obviously here. Travelers. Maybe a caravan."

She stood and brushed off her hand. "They took him with them. I don't see any more blood. He has help now. It's hard to believe he got this far on foot."

Whoever this Caleb was, he wasn't proving to be the easy pickup she'd imagined. They were already a full day from the monastery, and he was taking them further.

"What now?" Michael asked.

"We get a few hours rest and head north. The going will be slow, but we can't afford for him to gain another eight hours." She looked at the mudhole. "At least we have water."

"You call that water?"

"We can strain it."

"Where's the air force when you need them?" Michael asked wryly.

"The air force is picking off stone-throwers. We're saving Israel."

"And here I thought we were riding camels through hell." He smiled.
"Funny."

"Have you considered the possibility that these travelers he's hitched a
ride with might be armed?"

"It's a possibility," she said. "A single soldier held off a battalion of tanks
in the Sinai in '73. There's two of us. What are a few camel jockeys?"

"And I'm the funny one? I might prefer ten tanks over fighters who
have the backbone to live in this godforsaken desert."

"You have a point. Get some rest and dream of Jerusalem. It will clear
your head."

Rebecca set up the satellite phone thirty minutes later and made contact
with the monastery. According to Samuel, Avraham was positive he'd heard
the sniper on his morning round at about eight. But a further search had
proven fruitless. Otherwise, all was quiet—at least as far as security went.

Zakkai had found a chamber under the root cellar. The professor got
on the line, excited. He told her about finding Caleb's old room and their
methodical search. And then he told her about the letter, and Rebecca had
to sit down.

"It actually says that?"

"Yes, it says that. Where the brine meets with the oil—that is where we
will find the Ark."

"So we definitely need Caleb then. Unfortunately he's still one step ahead
of us."

"When will you have him?"

"Soon. Have you made contact with my father?"

"We're scheduled to call in the morning."

Rebecca cut the connection. Zakkai could smell the Ark. Imagine! The
thought sent a thrill up her spine. Everything her father had worked for;
everything she had lived for; everything her mother and her baby sister had
died for—it just might finally be in their reach.

Rebecca laid out her bedroll at the base of the huge rock and told Michael
she'd wake him in three hours.

She stared at the stars and begged God for his redemption, as she did every night. That redemption would be found in the Messiah's coming went without saying. Any true Jew knew that, even if most Israelis did not. The Messiah's coming meant rebuilding the Temple.

And if the Temple was rebuilt? Then she would find a handsome young man who didn't mind being married to a woman with her past and make lots of children. A whole flock of little Israelites.

She turned in her blankets and began to picture that man. But she fell asleep before his face was fully formed.

And then suddenly she was awake. Her eyes peeled wide and her heart slamming in her chest. She had heard something that didn't belong.

She held her breath, listening intently. Her handgun was at her head— the Glock. Safety on or off? Off.

There it was again, a scraping, like a branch on a rock. Except for the few trees by the mudhole, there *were* no branches here! And even if there were, there was no breeze to move them.

The sound came again and fire spread through Rebecca's veins. She moved on instinct. She palmed the gun, rolled from her bed, and came to her knees at the base of the towering boulder. Without a break in her movement she slid silently around the boulder and flattened her back to its cool surface. She took her first long slow breath and willed her heart to slow its pounding.

For a few moments the night was silent again. She guessed they'd been resting at least two hours by the crescent moon which now sat on the horizon. It cast just enough light to turn the salt flats a dull gray.

Whap!

Rebecca blinked. The sound registered—the sound of a bullet spitting into the ground. Or a body. A silenced rifle!

Michael!

She spun around the rock.

Whap! Whap!

The rocks forty meters across the clearing momentarily brightened with two silenced muzzle flashes. Rebecca stared in unbelief at the bedroll three meters from her own. A low groan rose through the air; the bedroll moved. Michael was still alive.

Rebecca dropped to a crouch, prepared to run out to him.

The sniper was intentionally luring her, she knew. He'd seen her escape too quickly for a shot and now had wounded one in the hopes of bringing out the other.

Michael began to push himself up.

"Down!" Rebecca whispered urgently.

Whap!

Michael dropped to his chest like a sack of rocks.

Rebecca yanked herself back, fighting off panic. She closed her eyes and breathed steadily. *Easy, Rebecca, this is Golan. This is the West Bank. This is what you were trained to do.* How could the sniper have followed them? And why?

It didn't matter. She had to kill this man now before he did any more damage. And how do you kill a deadly sniper hidden in a position of advantage?

You don't.

You save the camels before he kills them, if he hasn't already. Without a camel her mission would be over and she would be dead.

There was a saying the Mossad commander who'd trained her IDF special forces team had drilled home: *Extreme, excessive force creates confusion; confusion creates mistakes; mistakes determine battles.* The politicians might favor gradualism, but the military did not.

It took Rebecca only a few seconds to settle on her course of action. Her decision was a matter of instinct, not reasoning. Five years in the field had taught her to trust her instincts, like a man trusts his pulse.

She rechecked her safety, rolled her head as a matter of habit, and bolted from her cover. The nine-millimeter Glock held eight rounds and she methodically fired six of them at the sniper's flash point while in a full sprint. Only an idiot wouldn't seek refuge from the barrage. The sniper might be deranged but he was clearly no idiot.

The camels were already scrambling to their feet in the echoes of the unsilenced gunfire when Rebecca reached them. She turned the gun on the camel closest to the sniper and put a round in its head.

Boom!

The camel toppled to the ground, dead. The other screeched and bolted past her, out of the enclave. She had one round left.

Rebecca dropped behind the fallen camel and the sniper's bullets came, *smack, smack, smack, smack,* plowing into the carcass.

"You're dead now, Jew!" a voice screamed in Arabic.

Michael's pack sat on the animal's hip, in better position than she could've hoped for. She reached up, slipped her hand into the pack, felt the familiar ball of cold steel, and pulled out a grenade.

This Jew has a little gift for you, my dear neighbor.

Rebecca crouched behind the beast, pumped her last round at the rocks hiding the sniper, hurled the grenade, and sprinted after the fleeing camel without waiting.

She'd taken five long strides when the night shattered with a bellowing explosion that rocked the ground. Four more steps and she was around a boulder, tearing after her own camel.

You see what it means to mess with an Israeli soldier in the night?

Rebecca ran for five hundred meters, weaving on the flat to spoil any aim the sniper might have in the moonlight. A single unsilenced pistol shot rang out over the desert—the Arab was telling her that he was still alive.

The sniper was alive and Michael was dead. She didn't allow the thought to linger. The Mossad had a saying: *There was a time to mourn, a time to kill and there was a time to survive.* Now it was the time to survive.

It took her twenty minutes to close the gap to her camel, another ten to coax it into her hands and mount it. A predicament that should have presented itself to her earlier now filled her with a small horror.

The satellite phone was in Michael's pack, back at the oasis. Not that she could have taken it out with the sniper bearing down—but she could have killed her camel and not his. It was a mistake.

Mistakes determine battles.

She'd had no choice but to shoot one of the camels—she couldn't chase down both, and she couldn't take a chance that the sniper might take one. He had his own mount, of course, but handing him another one broke with basic military doctrine. Putting the sniper on foot in this desert would be as good as killing him.

Forty minutes later her reasoning proved itself. She stumbled upon a dying horse one kilometer to the northwest of the rocks as she circled in a wide berth. It was still twitching. The pig had ridden his animal to death.

Rebecca reluctantly dismounted and cut its throat. Now the sniper *was* on foot. And she was without a communications link to the others.

They would hold the monastery for a week before retreating, as they had agreed, should communications be cut. The thought of heading further into the desert alone sent a shiver through Rebecca's bones. But she had no choice. She couldn't just hop over to the monastery for reinforcements, and they couldn't send a search team into this abyss of salt.

She wouldn't need a week, of course. She'd have Caleb in a day.

An hour later she picked up the twin trails of the caravan headed north. A tremor still lingered in her bones as she turned her camel onto the trail. *Now* it is time to mourn, she thought. But she didn't feel like mourning. She felt like going back and killing. Or being killed.

But that wasn't her mission. Roughly four hours ahead in the night there was a man named Caleb who held the key to Israel's future.

He was her mission.

15

ISMAEL SAT ON TOP OF A BOULDER thirty meters above the salt flats, eyes closed, slowly rubbing his temples. It had taken him less than five minutes to understand his predicament. He was stranded in the desert without a mount.

It had taken him another hour to make the first call to his father on the sat phone, only to reach an answering machine. He had waited three more hours without a callback. All the while Rebecca Solomon extended her lead.

He'd replayed the attack a hundred times in his mind's eye, each time telling himself that his failure wasn't due to his own mistake, but her good fortune. She had somehow managed to wake. She had moved with surprising speed, caught him off guard with her mindless attack, and then escaped. A brilliant maneuver, he couldn't deny. But just the same, it was her fortune that had awoken her.

He'd found the horse dead. She had slit its throat and headed north.

The sat phone burped beside him and he snatched up the receiver.

"Yes."

"Good evening, Ismael. So you're alive. That's a good start."

"She's better than I thought. I need a Jeep flown in to me," he said. "She's headed north on a camel."

"A Jeep?" Abu's voice tightened. "Where *are* you?"

"In the desert. You can triangulate my position from the call—"

"I know I can triangulate your position from the call. That's not the point. The point is you've allowed yourself to become stranded in the middle of the Ethiopian desert. She should have been dead days ago!"

"She's better than that!"

"What happened?" Abu demanded.

Ismael told him in broad terms.

Abu took a deep breath on the other end. "Okay, Ismael, now you will listen to me. No more games. You will do exactly as I say. I don't know any better fighter than you, but now we are past fighting to soldiering, and there is no better soldier than me. Do you hear me?"

"You are threatening me?"

"I am trying to help you, you fool! And in case you don't see it clearly, you need my help."

Ismael blinked in the dark. Abu could be a man of terrifying fury if pushed too far. He knew because he'd pushed too far on more than one occasion and still had the scars to prove it.

"Well, I'm stranded in the hottest desert this side of hell. Yes, I suppose that I do need your help. Either way I will kill her."

"Yes, I'm sure you will. But this isn't simply about one woman."

"Do you already forget your other son?"

Abu remained silent and Ismael knew he had crossed the line with the stupid accusation. He was thinking about apologizing when his father spoke again.

"How much food do you have?"

"I have a whole camel—enough meat for a week if it doesn't spoil. I'm at a spring."

"It's been two days and the Israelis are still at the monastery," Abu said. "Why? Have they found something? In the end, Rebecca Solomon may be the least of our problems. Do you understand this, Ismael?"

"Yes, of course."

"We will do this my way now. I will call you tomorrow at noon."

Abu cut the connection and Ismael lay back on the rock. *We will see, Father. We will do this your way only if it means killing Rebecca Solomon.*

———

David Ben Solomon stood on the Temple Mount early in the morning. He stared down at several hundred Jews already wandering in the courtyard below—stray souls draped in black and white, nodding at a foundation that was at best erected by Herod, not King Solomon as many supposed. No, the original Temple had been behind him, under the Dome of the Rock. But the Jews seemed satisfied to touch a few remaining stones at the base while the Muslims paraded around on top, as if they owned the whole Mount. For all practical purposes they did.

Ahead of Solomon lay the Old City of Jerusalem, surrounded by the old wall, roughly a thousand meters squared. They had divided the city into four quarters: the Muslim to his right, the Christian adjacent that, the Armenian next to the Christian, and the Jewish below him—four pieces to a square puzzle. Of all these, only the Jewish truly belonged. Until Israel realized that, the puzzle would remain unsolved. Peace would elude them all.

"Come, Messiah. Come quickly." Solomon turned his back to the Old City and looked across the Mount. Since that day in the war of 1967, when he himself had marched through the golden gate with the very first Jews and stood on the Mount, the de facto policy had been that, although Jews could visit the Mount, they could not turn it into a place of prayer. And the rabbis had agreed because of their belief that the Mount was too sacred for the unpurified Jew. What would happen if a man stepped over the Holy of Holies and prayed without purifying himself first, they asked.

There is no Holy of Holies! Solomon argued. *Which is why we must build it.*

Unfortunately, common sense had fled the leaders. Rather than redeem a holy place now defiled, they preferred to turn it over to Muslims to further desecrate! It was the fear of guns and bloodshed speaking, not the fear of God.

Three weeks ago a young woman of twenty had been arrested for closing her eyes on the Mount. The Muslim *Waqf* accused her of praying. She was thrown in prison for a day by the Israeli police, themselves afraid to confront the Muslim guards. So now the police had joined the rabbis and the Knesset in playing this silly game. Absurd.

Meanwhile, the Muslims flocked to the Temple Mount, their *Haram al-Sharif* as they called it, thousands at a time, treading over a Holy of Holies that did not exist. Israel might technically possess sovereignty of the Mount, but the Muslims possessed its soul.

Solomon glanced at the huge gold dome. He would never forgive himself for not blowing it up then, when he had the chance in 1967.

His phone vibrated in his robe pocket. He always wore traditional clothing on his visits—it helped take him back to the ancient days. But he didn't mind bringing a little technology with him either—it helped connect him with the future.

He walked briskly for the gate. Several Muslim *Waqf* guards watched him carefully as they always did; they wouldn't stand for his use of a cell phone. As far as they were concerned, atom bombs could be concealed in cell phones, and he was the kind of person who would use an atom bomb.

Solomon flipped the phone open as soon as he passed the gate. "Hello."

"David!" It was Zakkai and his voice was strained. "We've found something, David."

Solomon looked around and ducked into an enclave which would offer him some semblance of privacy. "What do you mean something?" The air suddenly felt too heavy to breathe. "You found . . . it?"

"No. But we found Caleb's old room under the root cellar. It hasn't been touched in fifteen years, since the monastery was originally destroyed. And in the wall above his bed we found a letter, hidden by Father Matthew." Zakkai paused, as if the moment deserved some recognition.

"Yes, go on. What kind of letter?"

The archaeologist explained in detail. He read the letter twice.

"So it means that the Ark is there!" Solomon said.

"I think so, David. I do."

"When did this happen?"

"Last night. The Ark is hidden in this monastery—we can hardly doubt that now."

"And where is Rebecca? She hasn't found Caleb?"

"Not that we know. She made contact last night. They believe Caleb was picked up by some travelers headed north. But they're closing in. She seemed confident that they would have him very soon."

"So. The letter is saying that the Ark is somewhere where the oil and the brine mix. There's no way to make sense of that without Caleb?"

"It sounds like a riddle. We're open to any thoughts, but it makes no sense to anyone here. Don't worry, Father Matthew would never have been so cryptic unless he was sure Caleb would understand."

Solomon took a deep breath. He felt as though a small bomb had been dropped in his skull. They were actually going to find it and honestly he could hardly stand the thought.

"You know what this means, David?" Zakkai said. "This means you'd better start making preparations. You know we've had a visitor—if the Arabs even think we're onto something, we may have difficulty transporting whatever we find over the sea. Have you talked to our friend?"

"Not yet. I will now. Don't worry, my dear archaeologist, you find our lost treasure and I will make sure it gets to Jerusalem. If we're lucky, Rebecca has already eliminated our visitor. Dear God, I pray she has. In the meantime we must maintain absolute security. I don't have to tell you how important this is."

"No, you don't." Zakkai paused. "It's nearly impossible to believe, David."

"Yes, it is. But you haven't found it yet. You've found a piece of paper which will do nothing for our people."

Zakkai cleared his throat. "You're right. We'll call the moment we hear from Rebecca."

"Please do."

Solomon closed the phone. He walked out onto the path and struck for the street, busy now with pedestrians. They looked dreamlike now, hustling through another day, pretending to be Jewish in a country which had already sold its soul.

Your soul lies hidden in a monastery, fifteen hundred kilometers away. And my daughter is closing in.

It was time to begin softening the political ground. Solomon shook his head, hoping against hope that they were not being led down a path to an empty hole. Either way they had crossed the threshold now. The Knesset had to be warned. He would begin at the top.

It was time to call Gurion. Simon Ben Gurion, prime minister of Israel.

16

THE DESERT SKY ARCHED BRIGHT BLUE far overhead, like an inverted ocean. Caleb could still hear the distant sounds of singing and tambourines, blended with other instruments into a mystical kind of music that had lured him to join in. But he could no more join in than he could dive into that blue ocean suspended over him.

He was dead.

Caleb blinked rapidly several times, adjusting to the brilliant white light that swam on either side. Somewhere angelic voices talked quietly. He was maybe on a cloud, floating into . . .

He jerked his head up. He was in the desert. On the salt flats. Alive.

Caleb blinked again, struggling to remain propped on an elbow. A strange sound groaned from his mouth.

"Shhhhh. Easy now." A cool hand rested on his shoulder, and he turned to look at a dark-haired woman kneeling beside him. Behind her a white tent stood on the sand. And beside that tent, a dozen more, forming a large arc. Two camels lay on the sand three meters from his head.

"What . . . Where am I?" he asked through slurred speech. It occurred to him that his shirt had been stripped off.

"You are with our tribe. We found you near the tower and tended to you," the young woman said, smiling. "You are very lucky—we had almost left."

Caleb looked around, noting now that a handful of children in loincloths and tan wraps were staring at him, all kneeling in a row, several paces to his left. Their browned faces smiled wide, but they remained perfectly silent. One of them had a thin trail of mucus leaking from his nose.

"Are you Afar people?" Caleb asked dumbly.

The girl laughed and spoke to the children. "He wants to know if we are Afar." At this they all giggled, the one with the dirty nose, hysterically.

"I think that if we were Afar you would be dead, City Boy," the woman said. "My name is Miriam. We are not Afar."

"Are *you* Afar?" one of the boys asked, grinning.

"Don't be silly, Daniel," Miriam chided. "That's not even funny."

The other children cackled in long strings that suddenly struck Caleb as infectious. He chuckled once. Miriam looked at the boy with the mucus. "And, Peter, it's impolite to walk around with a leaking nose. We have a guest."

Peter, the smallest of them, ran his forearm along his upper lip shyly. The others smiled but didn't seem at all put off.

"What is your name?" Miriam asked.

"Caleb."

"Caleb." She smiled. "You must be very hungry, Caleb. I saw you stirring and sent Ruth for some hot cereal."

Caleb looked at her, unsure what to say. Like him, her skin was tanned dark, but not black—not what he would have expected for desert people. She was pretty, and when she smiled, her teeth flashed as white as the salt. Her tunic was tan, like the others'.

"Where am I?" he asked again.

"I've told you. You are with our tribe."

"No. I mean where are we? I walked into the desert . . ."

"You're still in the desert." She motioned to the surrounding salt flats. "We have traveled one night north of the Tower Oasis. Do you know the Tower Oasis?"

"No."

"Then you are even more fortunate than I had guessed. Perhaps God has brought you."

"How far are we from the hills?"

"Two nights' travel. And two nights the other way to the sea. But I don't think you will be ready to go anywhere for a few days." She nodded at his feet. He saw for the first time that they were bandaged with gauze strips. "The tops of your feet were badly blistered, but they will heal quickly. Thank the Father your soles were not hurt. Would you like to try walking?"

"Who is the Father?"

She looked at him with her dark brown eyes and blinked. "God."

"God." He nodded. "I came into the desert to find a Father Hadane. Do you know him?"

"Yes."

"You do?" Caleb shoved himself up to a sitting position. "He's here?"

"You'll have to talk to Elijah about that. Please, there's no rush. First you must eat."

The one she had called Ruth suddenly ran around the nearest tent holding a bowl. She pulled up when she saw him awake. The girl looked to be in her teens.

"It's all right, Ruth," Miriam said. "You've never seen a grown man before? I can see you're not one to take the vow." Ruth flashed Miriam with a look of warning and then approached Caleb, smiling.

"Miriam said that you would be hungry. I have put salt in it for you." She set a steaming bowl of porridge before him.

"Thank you." Caleb picked up the spoon and took a bite. It tasted like grits. He shoveled the food into his mouth.

The children giggled, amused by whatever he did, it seemed. Caleb smiled with them and ate anyway. The meal was delicious after two days without food.

"You like our food?" the boy called Daniel asked.

"Yes. It's very good."

He grinned wide. "Then you should join our tribe. My sister is looking for a man to join us."

Ruth picked up a handful of sand and flung it at Daniel. She took after him like a sprinter out of the blocks, and the two raced away, chased by hilarious cackles from the others. To Caleb's surprise, even Miriam laughed.

She saw his look. "You will forgive us, Caleb. Daniel is an unforgivable pest and Ruth is too testy for her own good. A good man is hard to find in this desert, as I'm sure you can imagine. It's not something we can afford to be too subtle about."

She brushed her hands of sand and stood. "Now I'm sure you're eager to meet the men. Time to see if those feet of yours still work." She offered a hand

and Caleb took it. Ruth and Daniel had come back already, Ruth leaning on her brother's shoulder as if he hadn't said a thing to embarrass her.

Caleb pulled himself up with Miriam tugging. His feet were tender, but not so that he couldn't walk. He hobbled in a small circle, testing.

"The tops hurt a little."

"Yes, they will for a couple days. But you seem healthy enough."

He nodded and walked with a few even strides. "Good as new," he said. "I'm a fast healer."

"Good." Miriam handed him a large white tunic, which was little more than a thin blanket with a hole cut for his head. "This will keep the sun off you."

He pulled it on and then followed her when she took his arm.

"Run along now, children. He's not going anywhere soon. I'm sure he'll be here for your amusement later." They ran off, all except Ruth who watched from a distance, pretending not to be interested.

"It's time to meet Elijah," Miriam said.

———

All of the men wore the same long white or tan robes, which swished above the sand as they walked. Some wore hemp ropes to secure the light gowns at their waist, others flowed by like curtains over the ground, and Father Elijah was of this later stripe.

The short Friar Tuck–looking monk was as jovial as he appeared, but he spun a heady philosophy that made Caleb blink. "I've been given the task of introducing you to the tribe," he said with a twinkle in his blue eyes. "And I'm enjoying it already, like a bee who's found a particularly sweet flower. You're the flower, my dear lost traveler. You don't mind if I feed for a few hours, do you?" He'd smiled and Caleb couldn't help smiling back.

The man was an enigma if ever Caleb had met one. Actually the entire *tribe*, as they referred to themselves, was an enigma, but Elijah personified the heart of what made them so mysterious.

"Feed all you like. But you might find that my petals have wilted in this desert," Caleb had said.

"Wilted? It's a good start, my friend. Soon they will be dead." He winked and turned for the flap. "Come now, let me show you the way the salt lies around this tribe."

Elijah had led him from his sprawling tent and run through a litany of basic facts, as if he were the schoolmaster and this was Caleb's first day of school.

There were fourteen tents in the tribe now, each staked to form a rough arc beside a large group of boulders. Several fires lay dormant on the eastern side of the camp, out of the wind's worst, in case it took a notion to blow up. They built fires only twice a day and then only small ones because wood did not come easily—they either hauled it in from the hills or traded for it.

Traded?

Yes, the tribe cut blocks of salt from the flats, the size of any household brick, and traded them at several outposts on the edge of the desert. It was enough to sustain them, and not enough to ruin them.

They ate mostly meal and dried meat, with the occasional pudding. He rubbed his stomach and informed Caleb that, despite what some of the men might say, not all puddings were created equal. Miriam's tapioca pudding, for example, was created with more equality than the others. He winked and strolled on.

They had lived on the desert for about eighty years, he said. Four generations for some. A mixture of old Falasha Jews and travelers of every stripe. Half of them had wandered in and stayed, and the rest had been born in. They lived simple lives in a harsh land, moving from camp to camp every few days or weeks, depending on food and water.

"Our quest is spiritual, away from the murderous din of materialism," Elijah said. He took Caleb's arm and tipped his head, as if intending to make a joke. "You won't find a Mercedes or Corvette under our flaps, my friend." He chuckled and walked on. "To us poverty is a blessing which bares the soul."

Caleb was familiar with most monastic traditions from his studies, but the tribe fit none that he knew of. "You are monks," Caleb observed. "What tradition do you come from?"

"No tradition, friend. Our own tradition. We follow One, and his name is Christ. Each man and each woman follows the same Lord, although not necessarily on the same path."

"So you are Christian, converted. But you don't all follow the same rules?"

"We are not Christian—not in name. We are apprentices of Christ alone and his teachings through the Gospels and the apostles. And yes, of course we follow the same rules. But not all of us subject ourselves to every rule of man."

He motioned to a woman bending over a loom of some kind. "You see that woman there weaving? Her name is Elizabeth. She is forty-five years old and loves to dance. She has taken a vow of celibacy and is childless. But there, next to her, is Mary who is fifty-four. She is happily married to one of the monks, Brother Isaac, and has three children, one of whom is Miriam, your nurse, who has incidentally taken a vow of celibacy herself." Elijah shrugged and chuckled.

"Married to a monk? How is that possible?" Caleb asked. "I've never heard of a monk that's married. What makes him a monk then?"

"Well, my friend, I don't know what men call a monk in your far-off land, but here, we call a person who has taken the vow to pursue God a monk. Whether man or woman, they must be old enough to hold a vow, but if they dedicate their lives to chasing after their Creator, we call them a monk."

Caleb stopped at the explanation. "You're serious? Then what are you giving up?"

Elijah turned back to him. "Giving up? You mean in your world monks are expected to give *things* up? We don't toss up a few coins or a Mercedes in exchange for the kingdom. We give up our *lives*. And we gain him. We give up the unreality of meaningless pursuits and we find God." He lifted a finger, as if to make a point. "There is no greater disaster in a spiritual life than to be immersed in a false reality. We abandon the false reality for the sake of a greater reality. Knowing God."

The words swam through Caleb's mind like a tide from the past. They could have been his own at one time, but they were spoken by this man in a robe who called himself a monk. This witty Friar Tuck who cared for no rule but the rule of God in his life.

Like Dada.

A small current of electricity buzzed down Caleb's spine, and he shivered on the hot desert floor. For the first time in many years Caleb felt the once-familiar stab of desire swim through his chest. He wanted to be like this man. Like Dada.

"There is no greater disaster than to think that what we see with these eyes is the real life," Caleb said.

"That would be another way to put it, yes."

"I used to say that."

"Used to? But no longer?"

"When I was a child," Caleb said, avoiding the question.

"Then perhaps you are here to become a child once again."

They walked again, in silence for a few minutes.

"You were saying that anyone may become a monk here, by chasing after the Creator. And how do you do this? How do you chase?"

"The pearl of great price," the monk said immediately, as if everyone should know it intimately. As a matter of fact, Caleb did. He finished Elijah's thought for him.

"Sell everything to buy the pearl. To do so you must first desire the pearl," Caleb said.

"Yes. Then you also know that desire doesn't come from the mind, but from the heart. The hope that burns under the ashes of our poverty."

"Yes." Caleb breathed deep. He became acutely aware of his steps over the hard salt. Suddenly he wanted to cry, and he wasn't sure why. These pearls from Father Elijah—he had owned them once. What had happened to him?

He swallowed and walked on. "Do you take other vows?" he asked.

"Yes, yes, of course. All kinds of vows. Vows of poverty—we have all taken vows of poverty. It wouldn't do to have a Mercedes drive through camp, now would it?" Elijah winked and grinned.

"You seem to think that a Mercedes is the definition of wealth," Caleb said.

"A traveler once showed me some pictures of many cars. I fell in love with the big white Mercedes. At the time I thought about shooting my camel and leaving the desert with the man."

They laughed.

Elijah thought for a moment. "But really, poverty is not about living without. Living without can be a fruitless death full of misery. Poverty is about needing. It is clearing space in your heart so that God can fill it, as the Father would say."

"The Father. You mean God?"

"No, now I mean Father Hadane. Our teacher."

Caleb spun to Elijah. "Father Hadane!" He had misplaced the urgency of his coming here. "I have to speak to him—"

"Yes, I know you do, Caleb. You are here because there is trouble at the monastery Father Matthew served in. Joseph told us."

"You know? Father Hadane supposedly knew my father, I know, but how did he know there was trouble?"

Elijah shrugged. "Who's to know? The Father could have told him, but now we have too many 'fathers' and you'll forgive me, but my mind is spinning with them. I am a father, and Father Hadane is my Father, but my Father is really God. You have a father and I know it wasn't Father Matthew because Father Matthew took a vow of celibacy. So perhaps we should just use names."

"You knew Father Matthew?" Caleb asked.

"Yes. He was twenty when he left the tribe to go to the monastery."

"Which was where I was abandoned as a child," Caleb said. "He raised me as his own son. I'm now adopted by American parents who rescued me from the monastery when it was destroyed. Jason and Leiah."

Caleb paced and bit at a fingernail. "Please, I have to speak to Joseph Hadane. Father Matthew told me to find him if there was any trouble at the monastery, and now there is. It's been overrun by Jews, I think. They're holding my parents captive."

Elijah absently stroked his jaw with his hand, but made no move to lead him.

"Actually, I don't know why I've come here," Caleb said with sudden frustration. "I don't know what a band of wandering desert monks can possibly do. What I really need is a way back to the monastery with some help."

"A Mercedes."

"No. Please, this is serious."

"Yes, of course it is. And you are being pursued; that also is serious."

"I am? We have to do something immediately!" He looked out to the desert and saw nothing.

"But we *are* doing something. I'm indoctrinating you. I may not be able to give you a Mercedes or guns, but I can point you to the way."

"What's that?"

"That's more than you'll ever need to set a few Jews straight."

"Please, stop talking in riddles and take me to Hadane. I nearly died finding you; the least you can do is let me talk to him."

"As I recall, we found you. I'm sorry, my friend, I can't take you to Father Hadane. Not yet. You're not ready. But I can tell you this. It's the *Tabotat* the Jews want, not your parents. They will be safe. And without you, no one will find this *Tabotat.*"

"*Tabotat?* You mean an Ethiopian Orthodox replica of the Ark?"

"Yes."

"Why would they want one of those? They're in every Orthodox church in the country."

"Exactly." Elijah shrugged. "Evidently they want this one. Father Hadane has instructed me to tell you that if God dragged you across this desert, it was for your sake, not theirs. You may find solace in those words."

"Solace! I'm stranded in the desert while my parents are at gunpoint, and you want me to find solace in the words of an old priest who won't even talk to me?"

"So you have faced some adversity," Elijah said, still stroking his chin. "That also is good. Adversity introduces a man to himself. And we must know ourselves before we can know what needs to die."

"Stop the riddles. I was handing out riddles when I was ten. You don't have to feed them to me now."

Elijah looked at him, silent. Caleb immediately regretted his tone. He scratched his head and turned away.

"It's okay, my friend," Elijah said. "You're a delight to watch. It's not often that God leads a man to us with bandits on his heels—my goodness, you are all the talk. But you should really rest in Father Hadane's words. He's sure that Jason and Leiah are safe."

"Then ask Hadane to speak to me himself."

"He will speak to you, my friend."

Caleb turned to face the monk. "When?"

"He will speak to you when you are ready to listen."

A WAS CALLED BLESSED   131

17

REBECCA CROUCHED IN THE ROCK formation and peered down at the monks' camp through her binoculars.

The sun had already dipped into the western sky when she first saw their camp. She'd circled around the large field of boulders, secured her camel at the base of a small rock mountain, and climbed up to her position an hour ago. Judging by the shadows, it would be dark in about three hours. She had already decided to wait for nightfall to make her move. But she hadn't decided what that move would be.

The tents were little more than squared canvas drapes, simple and effective in this environment. They were white, like most everything in the camp. The only exceptions were a few large blankets that they gathered on at the tents' entrances.

Rebecca slowly scanned the camp for the hundredth time. A light breeze moved the tent walls like sails. Children romped at the base of the rocks, sixty meters from where she hid in her perch. Most of the people had retreated to the shade of their tents. But the two she was interested in sat by the southernmost tent, cross-legged, talking.

She knew that the man was Caleb—his tunic was different from the others' and his feet were bandaged. What he could possibly have to say to the pretty young woman, Rebecca had no clue. She'd have thought he would be making a fuss about the monastery, not loitering in the afternoon heat, talking with a woman.

The woman was in her twenties, Rebecca guessed, with long dark hair, not unlike her own. Her skin was darker, a deep tan, and her eyes were brown, like her skin. She laughed and engaged Caleb without a care, it seemed.

She'd never seen Caleb before now, and what she saw was nothing like she had expected. Somehow this man sitting on the desert did not meet her image of someone who'd hidden from the world in an Ethiopian monastery, serving lepers. For starters, he wasn't Ethiopian. In fact, his skin was lighter than the woman's. His hair was dark and hung nearly to his shoulders, which were square and strong.

But it was his eyes that had arrested her attention. Even from where she sat, eighty meters away, their green hue shone in her magnified lenses like twin emeralds.

Know thine enemy. It was the first rule of engagement. And what exactly was the purpose of her engagement here? It was to gather information from this man named Caleb. He knew the location of the Ark, and it was her objective to get that information from him.

Rebecca thought about that as she studied him, listening intently to the woman. *The woman's a desert wanderer, Caleb. What does she have that interests you so?*

There would be two ways to take information from the man. The first was by force. The second was to try to coax it from him. The two alternatives seesawed in her mind, and the longer she looked at him the less clarity she felt about which course would be best.

Forcing information from a man who was not eager to give it could be an unpleasant task. She could only assume that he wasn't ready to spill his guts, or he wouldn't have crossed this inferno to escape her. And any man who had the fortitude to walk as Caleb had walked, bleeding from his feet, was a man of unusual character. Even if she was willing to threaten him for the information, she doubted he would respond to threats. For that matter, she wasn't sure she could effectively threaten any man, much less this one with green eyes. Perhaps her heart was growing soft.

From the start, she and Michael had agreed that once they caught up to Caleb, they would simply force him back to the monastery and deal with him there. But now the game had changed. She could take Caleb by gunpoint, but without a radio or a GPS, heading into the desert might be the end of both of them. She needed assistance, and she doubted the monks would be eager to help in a kidnapping.

She watched Caleb stand and walk in a circle, as if deep in thought. His lips moved and he brought a hand to his chin. What was he saying?

Rebecca watched the woman for a few moments—she was using her hands to explain something as she talked. Caleb was asking questions. But not the animated questions she would have expected. He seemed more introspective. If he'd come for help, he had a strange way of asking. If he'd come to escape, he had come to the wrong place. This desert was a hell, not the local sheriff's office.

A bead of sweat trickled past Rebecca's ear and down her cheek. The sun was taking its time, crawling down the sky. Regardless of what she did, she would do it in the dark.

The second alternative, coaxing the information from Caleb, had its challenges as well. It might take time. She didn't have time.

She looked at his face in the setting sun. *Are you the kind of man who can be coaxed, Caleb? Or is your skin too thick?*

He suddenly spread his arms wide and turned in a circle, with his chin lifted to the sky, as if crying out. Rebecca blinked at the sight. She could hear the soft murmur of his voice on the breeze, and it wasn't a cry.

Caleb sank to his knees and gripped his hands to fists. His face wrinkled in a kind of remorse. For several long seconds he remained in the posture, hands flung wide. And then he bowed to the earth, slumped to one side, and rolled onto his back.

It occurred to Rebecca that she had stopped breathing. She could feel the man's desperation through her glasses. What a strange thing to do.

The woman touched his forehead, as if taking his temperature. She stood and walked away nonchalantly, leaving Caleb spread on his back. He lay unmoving, eyes closed. They were a roving band of lunatics down there.

After a few minutes, Caleb pushed himself to his seat and sat, staring out at the endless white flats in a stupor. She could still see his eyes, green and unblinking, lost in deep thought.

What secrets are you hiding, dear Caleb? Hmm? Would you open your heart to me?

The notion of engaging this man suddenly struck her as appealing. He was a man; she was a woman. A gun wasn't the only weapon in her arsenal.

She would see what this strange man was made of. In the end, if she failed to lure the key from him, she could always resort to some form of force.

Rebecca turned away and leaned back against the rock. As soon as the sun went down she would wander into the camp, a lost soul in desperate need of water. They would take her in because they were monks, and then she would find Caleb.

"You may call me Delilah," Rebecca whispered.

18

THEY SAT IN A SITTING ROOM off Prime Minister Simon Ben Gurion's office, three men from the Israeli government. The good, the bad, and the ugly. He, Solomon, was the good for obvious reasons—he stood for God and God was good. Stephen Goldstein was clearly the bad—not only did he head up the Labor Party, which was for the most part bad in Solomon's book, but he wasn't even sure there *was* a God. And Ben Gurion was the ugly because, in spite of his belief in God, he lacked the political backbone to build God a house.

Ben Gurion reminded Solomon of Benjamin Netanyahu with his short cropped head of gray and sharp nose. The consummate politician who hardly knew how not to smile. Goldstein, on the other hand, made it to the top of his party without a pretty face. He wore a scraggly goatee, a mustache, and narrow glasses that rendered his eyes as slits. He looked like a goat.

"Don't be absurd, Solomon," Goldstein said. "We live in the twenty-first century, not in the pages of the Bible. Our nationality drives us, not some antiquated religion. We have children to educate and cities to build and two thousand years of lost time to make up. And 70 percent of Israelis agree with me."

"Of course," Solomon returned. "With thousands of atheists who call themselves Jews flooding in from the Orient, you should have no problem getting your percentages. But that doesn't make you right. There's a call to righteousness hidden in every Jewish heart, even yours, my friend. That call holds us together."

"Our nationality holds us together."

"Our nationality? Walk the streets of Tel Aviv and tell me what brought these people together. You have a black man from Ethiopia, a yellow man from China, and a white woman from Poland, and you cannot say that they came to this narrow strip of land to eat dinner together. They don't even eat the same food. No, they came because they are Jews, and Jews are Jews because of Judaism. That is what unites us."

Goldstein nodded but not in agreement. "We're all entitled to our own beliefs, Solomon. And to your good fortune there are just barely enough Israelis who agree with you to give you a seat in the Knesset. But it's only *one* seat. You should remember that."

"And there is only *one* God," Solomon said. "That doesn't make him wrong either."

The prime minister sipped at a glass of red wine and let them go.

"Please, don't throw God in my face," Goldstein said. "Not even his spokesmen, the rabbis, share your conviction of rebuilding the Temple."

"The rabbis?" Solomon demanded with a forced chuckle. "The same rabbis who urged millions of Polish Jews to stay in Poland rather than cause a disturbance by leaving? How many Jews died because of what the rabbis said then? The subtext of history is agony, my friend." He paused to still his heart rate. "My mother was one of those Jews. She too died. Now our well-intentioned rabbis urge us not to build God's house because of the disturbance it will cause among our neighbors. It's God's prophets we should follow, not the rabbis. And God's prophets tell us to build the Temple."

The outburst effectively shut the old goat up. Unfortunately, he probably hadn't heard a word—his ears had been plugged with the quest for power before he'd learned to talk.

Ben Gurion cleared his throat. "I sympathize with you, David—"

"I don't want your sympathy, Simon," Solomon interrupted.

"What is your point?" the prime minister asked sternly. They were all accustomed to this heated banter, but even politicians had their limit.

Solomon stood and walked to the picture window overlooking Jerusalem. He'd considered a dozen approaches and none of them felt like they would land softly. His point was to make these two face the music, but he couldn't start full blast—he had to ease the volume up slowly. His exchange with Goldstein had been a little too loud.

"My point, gentlemen, is that one day our hand, your hand, may be forced." He turned and faced them. "Not by political winds, but by much more powerful ones."

Goldstein silently eyed Solomon over his thin spectacles.

"Speak plain English, David," the prime minister said. "We know that you're talking about religious zeal, so just say that."

"Not religious zeal. The zeal of God. There is a difference in magnitude."

"I've heard this a hundred times," Goldstein said, sighing. "If you two gentlemen don't mind, I have a meeting I have to get to." He started to stand.

"If a million Jews were to surround Jerusalem, demanding that we rebuild Solomon's Temple, what do you suppose would happen?" Solomon asked.

The Labor Party leader hesitated. "Then I suppose we would have to rebuild the Temple. And five hundred thousand of those million might die." He shrugged.

The prime minister was not so dismissive. "You're saying something, David. But I don't think we're hearing you."

"Is there any scenario that comes to mind that would motivate a million or ten million Jews to demand the Temple's rebuilding?" Solomon asked.

Goldstein sat back, evidently interested enough to linger for a while. "You're planning another Temple building rally and you expect Jerusalem to turn out with more than the usual contingent of Red Heifer nuts to deal a decisive blow—"

"Surely this isn't about the Ark of the Covenant," Ben Gurion said with an incredulous smile. Solomon suspected he said it as much to cut Goldstein off as to ask a meaningful question.

Silence settled over them.

The prime minister eyed Solomon carefully. "You're not planning to make a claim that you can't back up."

Solomon did not answer.

"What do you mean?" Goldstein asked.

"It's been suggested before," the prime minister said without removing his eyes from Solomon's. "Think of it, a respected leader claims to have discovered the Ark of the Covenant. The Jews begin to demand a Temple, the Arabs go ballistic, and battle lines are drawn before anyone can discover that the gold box is really a fake."

Goldstein glared at Solomon.

"At least you know your people," Solomon said. "Something we can't say about our friend here."

"Now you're talking about a fable," Goldstein said. "Not Judaism. I never said that a fable could not destroy a nation."

"Destroy? Or unite?"

"Please don't play with words, David," Ben Gurion said. "What is your point?"

"My point is that you'd better fuel your F-14s, gentlemen. The Ark is not a fable."

"Please, we have been down this road a dozen times. Over 90 percent of the country believes the Temple Mount is more than just another piece of real estate—they aren't saying it's a fable—"

"You're not hearing me. The *Ark* is not a fable."

"What, you've found it, Solomon?" Goldstein said with a small smile.

"I didn't say that. But let's assume for the moment that I have. Would you support the rebuilding of the Temple?"

Any good graces that Ben Gurion had harbored up to this point seemed to fade from his face. He knew that this kind of rhetoric could do more damage than good—he'd made the point clear on several occasions.

"Okay, David. I understand your passion, but you're—"

"You asked me to make my point. Please answer my question."

The prime minister and Goldstein exchanged glances. "Would I support the rebuilding of the Temple if you really did have the original Ark of the Covenant?" Ben Gurion asked.

"Yes."

"I would take the Ark away and drop it in the sea."

"And defile God? The people would crucify you."

Ben Gurion closed his eyes and stretched his neck. "I've answered your question; make your point."

"So I take it you wouldn't—"

"Frankly, I don't know what I would do. It's a hypothetical question I've never given a lot of thought to. Make your point."

Solomon looked at Goldstein. "And you?"

"The discovery of the Ark would destroy Israel, surely you know that. Deep down where romantic notions don't have the air to breathe. We're surrounded by enemies, and at the moment the Temple Mount flies *their* flag, not ours. Burning it would bring World War III. Don't be absurd."

"So I take it that if I were to unveil the Ark on national television for all of Israel to see, you would approach the dwelling place of God with a flamethrower and reduce it to a lump of gold? Then I won't count on the support of the Labor Party. The Likud Party will see this differently."

"I didn't say I would burn it."

"Oh? Then what would you do?"

The fact was, they couldn't possibly know what they would do. It was akin to being asked what you would do if you knew an atomic bomb would fall on your house in ten minutes. The options were silly.

The prime minister spoke quietly. "Why are you asking this, David?"

He dropped his own bomb then. "Because I may have found it."

They stared at him in stunned silence.

Ben Gurion raised an eyebrow. "May have?"

"Yes. And I need you to begin thinking about how to handle this to Israel's ultimate advantage. I will demand that the Temple be rebuilt, and I know without the slightest doubt that the people will enthusiastically agree. The rest is up to you."

Goldstein came out of his shock. "That's absurd! You'll kill us all!"

"We're already dead! I am bringing us back to life!" Solomon thundered. "You may live as a Jew or die in your defiance to God!"

"What do you mean, may have?" Ben Gurion demanded, ignoring the eruption. "Where?"

"I mean that I have evidence that is staggering and I have some people on the ground. They have found some things."

"Where?"

He paused. "In Egypt." It was a justified lie, considering the circumstances. "But you will never find us. If you don't cooperate, I swear the first you'll see of the Ark will be on national television."

Goldstein was red. "I will see my own family slaughtered before I cooperate with you. If you bring the Ark to Jerusalem, Israel will be forced into war, regardless of who cooperates with you. You know that!"

Solomon had hoped for a more reasonable audience, one he could begin to plot with. But he knew now that reason wasn't on the agenda. He would need to let them stew.

"Then, as I said, I suggest you begin to fuel your F-14s, gentlemen."

Solomon turned abruptly and walked for the door. "And sending the *Shin Bet* after me would be a very bad idea." He left them staring.

———

Ismael hunched under the towering rock and keyed in the numbers over the satellite phone, for the fifth time that day.

Noon had come and gone and Abu had not been available. The heat was like an oven despite the shade of the rocks, and flies buzzed around the camel's carcass, six meters off. He had cut strips of flesh from the beast and laid them on the rocks to roast. The raw meat was too warm and wet for his tastes, and it was already starting to rot.

The line hissed in response. "Abu."

Ismael sat to his haunches, relieved. "I've been calling all day. What happened?"

"Some things take time. If you would have handled this right from the start, we wouldn't be here. But that's immaterial. I've made the arrangements."

"Good. I'm in a hellhole down here. If you hadn't answered, I might have decided to walk out on my own."

"Well, you'd better get used to your hellhole because you're going to be there another two days."

Ismael jerked up. "Two days! That's crazy! What about Rebecca? I can't just sit here in this stinking pit for two days!"

"You can and you will. Unless you want to go after her on foot."

Ismael closed his eyes and swallowed.

"I've arranged for a team of elite forces to be transported to Yemen, fully armed and provisioned. They will be joined by a guide who knows the desert, and then flown in a Hercules to your location. We're assuming they can land on the salt flats. Is this right?"

"Yes. How many men?"

"Ten men, a dozen horses, and two Jeeps. I will put them in your command, Ismael, but only on one condition."

"Of course."

"You will have twenty-four hours to track down the woman. If you find her, you will kill both her and this Caleb. But either way you must return to the monastery and kill whoever you find there. The monastery is the prime objective. Do you understand? They wouldn't still be there if they hadn't found something to keep them there."

"How will you know my location?"

"We already have it from the satellite phone. You cannot afford to fail, Ismael. And you can't afford to be exposed. The men will be dressed as civilians, but we don't have the time to remove markings from all the gear. The Ethiopian government will take exception to Syrian troops shooting up their country."

"Don't worry—the only people out here are natives."

"No, Ismael, you are wrong. The Ethiopians actually believe they had the Ark. They will defend it to the death. The Jews are not your only concern."

He hadn't thought about that. Either way, with fresh horses and ten men, completing his mission would be a simple matter of execution. Failure would be nearly impossible.

"Just get the Hercules here. I won't fail you," he said.

"Forty-eight hours," Abu said. "Go with God, my son."

"Go with God," Ismael said. But he didn't really feel like going with God. God had deserted him.

19

DEEP IN THE WHITE DESERT CALEB slowly began to lose himself to the heat. Or perhaps he was finding himself.

He'd spent several hours with Elijah wandering the camp, learning of the tribe's strange ways which really were not so strange at all. They held a kind of inexplicable appeal that put a lump in Caleb's throat. Something that screamed of his youth—a simplicity of devotion. A look of delight in their eyes that drew him. The monks, married or single, male or female, all shared the same obsession: Christ. Not the Christ known by the world, necessarily, but the Christ of the New Testament. The one who'd said you cannot enter the kingdom of heaven unless you become like a child.

Elijah was Hadane's right-hand man, it turned out, and despite his jovial attitude towards nearly everything they encountered, he struck Caleb as a treasure chest stuffed with truth. Hardly surprising, actually, considering he'd lived in the desert for forty years.

What was slightly more surprising was Miriam's wisdom. She was twenty-five, he learned, and not only had she taken the vow of celibacy, she seemed thrilled with the notion of spending her days staring into God's face, alone. But of course, it was never alone, because God always lured and touched seekers who stumbled into camp.

"You're so isolated out here," Caleb said.

"And this from a man who lives in a monastery?"

"We serve whole communities. Lepers."

Miriam smiled. "Most people seem to be under the false notion that small doses of religion on a weekly basis somehow sustain the spiritual man. We don't see it that way, Caleb. If you're dirty, you become clean by taking a bath. Imagine trying to clean yourself with a few droplets of water each day—no matter how good your intentions, the droplets will never amount to enough water to wash your body. Isn't it better to be doused with buckets of water?"

"And who is the water?"

"God is. He drenches us. And when someone like you wanders into our camp, they inevitably walk away dripping wet." She smiled. "You'll see. What is better, to sprinkle hundreds of people each year with tiny droplets of truth, or to immerse those few God brings us in the springs of life? It was the way of John the Baptist."

He'd never thought of it that way.

Neither Elijah nor Miriam seemed capable of appreciating the danger he'd fled, not because they were dimwitted, but because they seemed convinced that all was safe at the monastery. When he asked for an explanation, both of them smiled and told him that the greatest battles were always fought in the heart. And Father Hadane had told them that this battle was indeed for the hearts of man, not a gold *Tabotat* hidden in a stone building. By midday his worries of the monastery had faded. In an odd way, Caleb felt like he had come home.

By midafternoon he began to cave in on himself.

He sat by Miriam, listening to her soft voice talk in ways he hadn't heard since Dada had died, and his chest ached to taste Dada's passion once again. But it was God's passion, Miriam told him, and maybe he'd misplaced it.

She hadn't known Father Matthew—Dada had left the tribe before she was born. But her mother had known Dada, and she'd told Miriam that she'd never met a man with such devotion.

A buzz had come to Caleb's head while she talked, and he could not dislodge it. It was as if an airborne intoxicant hovered over the whole camp, and he'd breathed enough of it now to send him around some invisible bend. A bend of sorrow and desperation, a kind of smothering panic.

"I heard about you, Caleb," Miriam said quietly. "When you were a child, you were a pure vessel. I can't understand why you have turned your back on the Father."

Caleb had settled back on the sand at the words, swallowed by his own agony. Miriam let him lie there, in anguish, for a long time before touching his forehead.

"I have never seen such a sensitive spirit," she whispered. "God loves you dearly, child." And then she had left him.

When Caleb stood two hours later, it was growing dark. He took a few steps on numb legs and then turned to face the camp. Something was happening to him because he was standing here in the desert, swaying on his feet, staring at these monks' tents thinking that he should become a monk. But that was crazy, because Jason and Leiah were being held back at the monastery!

"Caleb."

He turned and faced a man standing in the breeze, his white robe whirling around his ankles, like Moses. It was Elijah.

"He will see you now, Caleb."

———

Elijah took Caleb to the last tent, winked, and pulled aside the flap. Caleb ducked in and the canvas closed behind him.

Two amber lamps flickered on a small desk in the middle of the room. Behind the desk, a single cot lay in the shadows and beside the cot, one bookcase filled with books. There was no other furniture—only the same rainbow-colored rugs and pillows Caleb had seen in the other tents.

He stood still, not sure what to expect. Hadane was not in the room as far as he could . . .

"Hello, Caleb," a deep, soft voice said.

He spun to his right. A man sat cross-legged by the wall, hidden in the shadows of several large pillows.

"Forgive me, I didn't mean to startle you." The man stood and walked out to Caleb. He was a frail man, shorter than Caleb by a foot, and bald on top.

He came right up to Caleb, looked up with light blue eyes, and smiled. Caleb saw the fading pigment immediately—on the Father's nose and his cheeks. It wasn't advanced yet, and it might not be easily recognized if you didn't know, but Caleb knew.

Hadane was a leper.

The man reached up and touched Caleb's cheek lightly. "So, you've come after all."

After all?

"And do you still believe?"

"Believe? Yes . . . I think so."

Hadane turned away and walked toward a large red-and-yellow rug at the tent's center. "Well, if you don't mind sitting with a leper, then sit, my son." He clutched his white robe, pivoted, and sat cross-legged to his haunches with practiced ease.

Caleb sat in front of him, matching his posture.

An awkward silence settled over them. Aware of Hadane's gaze on him, Caleb looked around the tent, feigning interest in the pillows and desk. At any moment the old man would speak and set the meeting at ease.

But Hadane didn't speak. He only smiled and watched. What could the man possibly be thinking?

"Is there something I can help you with, my son?" Hadane asked.

The gentle voice drew Caleb, and he looked into the man's soft baby-blue eyes. They seemed to swim in pools of mystery.

Caleb dropped his eyes, suddenly afraid he might not be able to control the emotion that suddenly rose through his chest.

Outside he could hear Ruth shriek as she chased after Daniel, but the noise didn't take his mind away from the tent. Out there, a woman was laughing and the fire was crackling, but in here Hadane was just smiling, perfectly silent, and it made Caleb's heart pound.

"I knew your father," Hadane said. "I have spent my life trying to love God as he loved God."

Caleb swallowed at an ache gathering in his throat. It made no sense, really. Nothing had happened to make him so emotional.

"Matthew used to visit us often. He was very proud of you. He told me once that you had a belief so pure that it put him to shame. That you took Christ at his words, without question." He paused. "I think that you have lost your first love. You have misplaced your belief."

It was the last straw, although only one of the very first straws. Caleb lowered his head and fought to keep from crying. His head swam and he began to panic. What was happening to him? He was beside himself for no reason. The questions that had spun through his mind all day felt silly sitting next to this man whom they called Hadane.

Then Caleb couldn't contain himself. He sat there on the rug and began to weep long tears of sorrow that took his mind from the tent. He was in the monastery with Dada; he was in the old American theater singing with the wind full in his face; he was at the foot of his bed, begging God not to turn his face.

"Do you know what children like to do, Caleb?" Father Hadane asked. "They like to dance."

Yes, they like to dance.

"Do you know what King David did around the Ark of the Covenant, Caleb? He danced."

Caleb glanced up at the Father.

"Do you know why David danced around the Ark? Because he was in the presence of God. And in the presence of God you sometimes become like a child. We are keepers of the secret of the Ark, Caleb, and we like to dance."

The old man suddenly grinned mischievously. He scrambled to his feet and began to dance a strange jig of some kind, across the rug and then back. A large smile lit his face.

Caleb stared in shock.

Hadane looked at him and winked. He seemed to double his efforts in a loud clear song. He waved to Caleb to stand.

"Dance with me! Dance with me!"

Unsure of what else to do, Caleb stood on shaky legs.

"Dance, Caleb! Dance like David."

The sight struck him as so odd that he let out a short laugh, which only seemed to encourage the old man more. He stopped suddenly and faced Caleb. The tent fell silent. A child yelped outside.

Father Hadane let his arms fall to his side. He began to bob up and down, vertically. Then his bob became a bounce, straight up and down. Caleb felt his heart tighten.

"Do you remember this, Caleb?"

"Yes."

"Father Matthew used to dance like this. Do you remember?"

"Yes." Tears were flooding Caleb's eyes now, and Hadane was bouncing higher.

"You used to dance like this when you were a child. Do you remember, Caleb?"

"Yes. Yes." When he was a child, he had danced like this. Like a child in the kingdom. Like the old man was dancing now. Across the stage for the whole world to see through their cameras.

"You must learn to dance again, Caleb. Dance with me!"

Caleb's knees refused to move. He bobbed a little with fists clenched, furious and humiliated and wanting to jump as he had never jumped. But he could not dance. It seemed ludicrous to him. He was not that little boy any longer. He was a grown man, and for whatever reason, the idea of jumping like a fool horrified him. He was crying in earnest now.

Hadane threw his chin up and yelled at the ceiling, uncaring of Caleb's humiliation. "Come on, Caleb! Dance, dance, dance! Become a child with me. We are in the presence of God! We are in the presence of the Ark. Become like David!"

Caleb gritted his teeth and hopped once. Then twice. Then he groaned loudly and began to bounce.

The weight fell from his chest like a sack of grain cut loose.

He began to leap as high as he could, sobbing still, but now with desperation.

"Dance, dance, dance!" cried the old man on each hop.

Caleb wasn't sure exactly when it happened, but somewhere in there he connected with his childhood for the first time in a decade. He was hopping up and down as he had in the fields with Jason and Leiah once, but he could just as easily have been flying like Peter Pan.

And then they weren't just hopping. They were skipping and dancing. Caleb was the first to roll, and then Father Hadane rolled on his heels, a somersault that would make any young boy envious. He came out of the roll laughing and leaping. They were making a ruckus, but those outside either couldn't hear or didn't care.

It took Hadane and Caleb fifteen minutes to settle down. They sat, panting between laughs. No words, just laughs and heavy breathing. Nothing else had been said.

Father Hadane finally took a deep breath. "Now, that's better, don't you think? You came for help. What is it?"

"My father, Father Matthew, told me once that if I ever didn't know what to do, I should find you."

Hadane nodded. "They are after the Ark of the Covenant, the resting place of God. But the resting place is not there."

"And if it was, surely Father Matthew would've told me."

"I didn't say the *Tabotat* wasn't there; I said the resting place of God isn't there." He smiled and tapped his chest. "It is here. As for the *Tabotat*, only you will know."

"So . . . when you said that we were in the presence of the Ark, you meant here?" Caleb tapped his heart.

"Yes."

"Then why did my father insist I come here?"

"Because the resting place is in danger."

"I thought you said . . ." Suddenly Caleb understood.

Hadane nodded. "Yes. The child who once focused the eyes of the world on Christ has lost his own sight. Misplaced his love. His faith. That is why you are here."

"But I *do* still believe!"

Hadane hesitated and looked deep into him. "Do you? You believe what?"

"I believe in the power of Christ. I may not be living up to those beliefs, but I do believe."

Hadane smiled sympathetically. "I am going to tell you a few things, Caleb. If you are willing, they will change your life, but you must open your heart."

"My heart is open."

"We will see. But your beliefs are wrong and so your love is gone."

"No. I don't think my beliefs are wrong. But tell me—"

"I have just told you. Your beliefs are wrong. You say that you may not be living up to your beliefs, but by definition, this is impossible. We always live up or down to our beliefs. Beliefs are the rails which govern our lives. Our trains roll on them whether we like it or not. If your train is not rolling on the set of rails which you claim are yours, it's because you have diverted your train to another set of rails—these are your true beliefs now, not the rails you left. Unless you first understand this, you can never find what you seek."

The words floated through the air, like notes of a magical melody. Even before Caleb had the time to piece Hadane's reasoning together, he knew it was true.

"If I *say* I believe, but do not follow, then I do not believe at all," Caleb said, more to himself than to Hadane. The brother of Jesus had said that. James.

Hadane nodded once. "It is the greatest misconception in Christianity today. That what you once believed, you will always believe. That to profess is the same as to believe. That a profession made twenty years ago somehow trumps what you really believe today."

Hadane stared directly into Caleb's eyes. "In reality, most people who call themselves Christians do not believe in Christ at all. Their train is not on his rails. They do not live what they say they believe, because in reality they don't believe it. Not really."

Father Matthew had said the same a hundred times, and it came back to Caleb like a long lost tune. Caleb spoke, mimicking his own father. "To believe in Christ is to follow him. To be his apprentice with full intention of living as he lived."

"In his footsteps," Hadane continued. "Casting all aside for the sake of the treasure." They were quoting the same teaching of Father Matthew's, and it was like oxygen to Caleb's soul.

"Tell me more," he said.

"There *is* nothing more until you face the truth about yourself. You cannot surrender what you do not possess. You cannot truly surrender yourself unless you possess yourself. The first thing you must possess is the truth about yourself—that you have allowed your beliefs to drift. This truth must reach beyond your ears and your memory and sink into your spirit or nothing else will matter."

At one time, Caleb might have said these very words himself. Now the notion that he might not really believe as he once did struck him as a vile thing.

He blinked and shifted his eyes from Hadane. *Is this possible, Father? I would never forsake you!* A lump rose to his throat again.

"Blessed are the meek," Father Hadane said. "Blessed are those who are persecuted; blessed are they that mourn; blessed are the poor in spirit. Very few really believe these, Caleb. Very few even really *intend* to follow this path. It is the narrow path."

"You're saying that if I really believed, I would show the kind of power I did as a child?"

"No, no." Hadane lifted a finger and wagged it. "The kingdom of God is not about what we see with these eyes. It's not about eating or drinking or walking or throwing away the crutches. Those can be good gifts, like wealth and prosperity. But they touch only the surface and they are quite incidental. His kingdom is about peace and joy and love and a kind of power that will turn your heart into a herd of thundering horses if you let it."

It could just as easily have been Dada sitting here, teaching him. None of this was new—it was simply new to his grown mind. What he had once taken for granted as a child now sounded profound.

"What has happened to me, Father Hadane?"

"You must remember that the spiritual life is first of all *life*. It is something to be lived. But like all other life it, too, can grow sick and die when uprooted from its proper element. Perhaps you have been uprooted."

"I've been in a spiritual element . . ." He stopped, knowing again what his father would say. Hadane said it.

"Living in a monastery or a church or a desert hardly counts as walking in the kingdom."

Caleb hung his head, closed his eyes, and took a deep breath.

"You have come here to rediscover your place in the kingdom, Caleb. It's a struggle for most men to even believe in the kingdom, and when they do, they spend their years hobbling along, confused about what they really believe. Like a man who looks in the mirror and walks away forgetting what he looks like. But you . . ."

Hadane took a settling breath. "You are destined to run, my friend."

He chuckled, and then suddenly caught himself, as if he'd bitten his tongue. "Oh my, my! Oh, dear God!"

Caleb looked up. Hadane stared at him with wide eyes, mouth open. He clutched his chest. "Oh my, my, my!" The old man closed his eyes. "You are going to run, my boy." He looked at Caleb again, stunned. "Oh my, my." He jumped to his feet and paced a few times before turning back to Caleb.

"You *must* find your faith, my dear boy! Normally I would tell you to spend a year on your knees, walk a thousand kilometers of desert. But you don't need a thousand kilometers. You need to walk the fifty centimeters between your mind and your heart. You *must* recover the faith of a child."

It occurred to Caleb that he'd stopped breathing.

Hadane rushed up and knelt before him. He gripped Caleb by both shoulders. "You will run, boy! Do you hear what I'm saying? Like Elijah, down from the mountain. You will *run* through the kingdom, if you yield. So you must! He must be allowed to sweep you off your feet! Do you understand?"

Caleb nodded.

Hadane shook him once. "No, I'm not sure you do understand." He spoke urgently now and Caleb started to cry. "This is beyond you. You must enthrall your mind with God. You have no idea of the breathtaking power that awaits you there."

Hadane stood and backed off. He spread his arms wide. "You want to know how to rediscover the kind of belief you once had, as a child? Enthrall your mind with a ravishing vision of God. Find the pearl, Caleb. *Waste* your life for the treasure—this extravagant love for Christ. Swim in his ocean and breathe his water." Hadane chuckled and twirled around once. "And then . . . then, my sweet child, you will run." He spun again. "Run like the wind through his kingdom." He chuckled and bent to make a point. "*You,* my dear boy, will be fortunate to survive the herd of horses that stampedes through your heart." Then he spun away, laughing.

Time seemed to fall still. Caleb had no idea what the old man meant, other than the simple demand that he surrender to this whirlwind even now sucking at his heart. It was an old axiom, spun with new colors. Desire and surrender and believe, as Dada used to say. The words were breathtaking and terrifying, and he knew then that he would either run in the kingdom or die in this desert.

"I will," he said. It came out very soft.

He lifted his chin, tears streaming down his cheeks. "I will waste my life for Christ."

He opened his eyes. "I will run. I will swim in his ocean, I swear it!" he said through gritted teeth.

But the tent was empty. Father Hadane had left him.

20

REBECCA HID HER GUNS IN THE ROCKS, changed into a tunic she'd brought from the monastery, and led her camel into camp.

It was almost dark when she approached the first tent, the one Caleb had sat beside, talking to the young woman. They had led Caleb into one of the other tents over an hour ago, and he hadn't emerged as far as she'd seen. He was her main objective, of course, but the young woman would be her first.

The children were the first to see her, and they ran through the camp, thrilled at her approach. *Okay, Rebecca, you are the distraught traveler, remember. You are eager for nothing but water and a place to lay your head. You are now a woman first and a soldier second. Or not a soldier at all, not until you have Caleb alone. Then you are Delilah.*

Miriam came out of her tent and saw her. The children ran up and led her, skipping and arguing over who should hold the camel's bridle. They approached Miriam.

Rebecca offered a beleaguered smile. "Dear God, thank you! You have no idea how good it is to see another human being. Do you have water?"

Miriam nodded cautiously. "As much as you need. Where have you come from?"

"I was separated from my party yesterday. We're surveying the Danakil on contract. Do you have a radio?" She knew they wouldn't, of course. But any sane person would want to be rejoined with their party immediately, and the radio was the only form of communication out here. They certainly wouldn't have a satellite phone.

"I'm sorry, but a radio's useless to us. Where's your party now?"

"If I knew, I'd be with them. Back there somewhere. I think I understand why Nesbitt called his book about this desert *Hellhole of Creation.* This heat is obscene," Rebecca said, shaking her head.

Miriam looked at her with a raised brow. "I haven't read the book. But not everyone who walks this desert finds hell."

She turned to one of the children. "Take the camel to the water, Daniel." She reached a hand out to Rebecca. "My name is Miriam, and I welcome you to our tribe. We may not be able to reunite you with your party, but we gladly offer food and shelter to all who come our way." She smiled, but it wasn't an entirely genuine smile, Rebecca thought. Miriam was not an idiot, and she might be wondering how a light-skinned woman had wandered this far into the desert, in spite of the survey story.

"Thank you. And God bless you." Rebecca dipped her head. "My name is Rebecca. I'm a Jewish archaeologist on loan to the University of Michigan."

"Hmm. I've never been there." They came to what Rebecca presumed was Miriam's tent. "You may stay with me tonight. Father Hadane will know what we should do in the morning."

"Father Hadane?" The name took Rebecca off guard. The old blind rabbi, Raphael Hadane, had spoken of his brother, a Joseph Hadane, who lived in the desert. Surely . . .

"Yes. Our leader."

"What's his name?"

Miriam looked at her. "I've just told you. Father Hadane."

"But the rest of his name."

"Father Joseph Hadane. You have heard of him?"

"Maybe. I knew a rabbi once. His name was Raphael Hadane and he was also from Ethiopia." She shrugged, covering her interest. "Probably a coincidence."

"Raphael is Father Hadane's brother! He will be thrilled to hear of this!"

"Really! Your Father is a Falasha Jew?"

"He was. But we follow the way of the Messiah now."

"You are Jews who wait for the Messiah? Out here in this godforsaken desert?"

"No, we are Jews who swim in the Messiah's love. This is our ocean. Come."

Christians.

Miriam turned and led Rebecca towards the main camp. "We will find you some water and food. The others will be glad to meet you. And if you like, you may join us in our evening dance. It will begin after dark."

———

After several introductions to other members of the tribe, Rebecca washed two days of dust from her body and combed her hair in Miriam's tent. Her host might suspect that there was more to her story, but it didn't interfere with her hospitality. She even offered Rebecca some perfume, a gift which came from a Hungarian traveler two years ago. Miriam evidently wore it very rarely.

She learned of the tribe's strange customs. Miriam was actually considered a monk here—she'd taken simple vows including celibacy. She seemed delighted by the prospect.

"I will leave you now," Miriam said. "My tent is yours. Do as you please." She smiled kindly and was gone.

Rebecca smoothed the clean tunic Miriam had given her to wear. The smell of lilacs lingered in the air. For the first time since leaving Jerusalem, nearly a week ago now, she felt like a woman.

Far away her father was pacing, no doubt. They would be worried because she'd missed her morning, noon, and evening contacts. Short of sending helicopters, they could hardly search for her. They would be forced to wait the three days previously agreed to.

Zakkai would probably be digging by now, she thought. It wasn't like him to sit idly. He would find some corner to chip away at, to keep his mind occupied if nothing else.

Meanwhile she had stumbled into Rabbi Hadane's brother, of all people! One more confirmation of the blind man's story. All the more reason to proceed very carefully. Caleb had fled the monastery and struggled across a blistering desert to find these monks. These robed Jews who thought that they swam in the Messiah's love. This tribe led by Hadane, the very one who had first told his brother, Raphael, that the Ark was in the Debra Damarro. There was more here than met the eye.

Rebecca set the brush down and took a deep breath. "I do believe we are onto something, Father. Maybe we will find the Ark after all." It was time to do what she'd come to do. *Dear God, give me strength.*

She skirted the long row of tents in the dark, looking for Caleb. Three small fires burned in the night and most of the tribe had gathered to eat around them. But not Caleb.

Her heart beat steadily. *Ease up, Rebecca. You're going to seduce a man, not face a mob of Palestinians. You're acting like a child.*

Seduce? I am not going to seduce a man. I'm simply going to talk to a man. I'm going to trick him into telling me what he knows.

And that's not seducing? You will seduce him.

She peered around a tent, three down from the one he'd been led into. Surely he wasn't still in . . .

"Good evening."

She spun. It was one of the older monks. Elijah.

"Rebecca, is it?"

"Yes."

He held his hands behind his back and wore a wide smile. "I didn't mean to frighten you. Miriam tells me that you're interested in the Messiah."

"Yes."

"Good. Very good, my dear!" He dipped his head and turned to leave. "I will pray that you find him."

She stood, watching him walk towards the fire. Another misguided Jew.

Rebecca hurried around the tent and made her way down the line, but she still saw no sign of Caleb. She rounded the last tent and was about to head back when she heard the mumbling to her right, from the dark.

She pulled back. Caleb suddenly walked by, in full color, not two meters away. How she'd missed him, she had no clue, but he was here now, walking with purpose in his long robe, arms spread at his sides, mumbling at the sky.

She had watched him for hours through the binoculars, but now, seeing him so close, she was surprised by both the strength in his arms and the beauty in his face. A handsome man who was pacing like a fool, talking to the sky.

Rebecca's heart hammered in her chest. She couldn't step out now—he'd think she'd been spying on him.

Caleb walked past, then suddenly reversed direction and paced back behind the tent, out of sight. She could step out now and . . .

He was back again! Marching in the sand as if to make a point. And then suddenly he turned and walked straight between the tents, towards her. She had no choice now.

Rebecca looked towards the fire, away from Caleb, and stepped out casually, as if unaware of him. He nearly ran into her.

"Oh!" She stepped back, feigning surprise. "I'm sorry."

Caleb stopped. He stared at her with wide green eyes and she wasn't sure if he even saw her.

"Hello," he said. He suddenly glanced around, as if unsure of where he was. He started to turn.

"I didn't expect anyone back here," she said. "I don't recognize you." She held out her hand. "I'm Rebecca."

Caleb turned back and took her hand. "Hello, Rebecca."

She held his fingers, surprised at their warmth. "And your name?"

"My name? My name is Caleb." They stood holding hands.

She had to keep him talking. "Caleb. Are you new to the tribe?"

"No. I'm old to the tribe. But I've been lost."

"Lost? Yes, me as well. I was separated from my group yesterday and somehow I ended up here." She smiled. "It's good to meet someone who isn't a monk." She chuckled deliberately.

Rebecca wasn't even sure if Caleb had heard her. He was looking at her, but his gaze seemed distant. They were still holding hands and she suddenly felt foolish for it.

She dropped his hand and cleared her throat. "You're old to the tribe? What does that mean?"

"It means that I used to believe like they believe," he said. "It means that I used to swim deep in this ocean of love as well, but I became accustomed to the dry land, and now I have this crazy notion that breathing underwater is impossible."

For a moment they locked eyes and she thought she might have been chasing a madman. He spun and strode away, robe trailing at his heels.

"Wait!" She hurried after him and slowed by his side. "Do you mind if I walk with you? I feel strange with them."

"Sure," he said. "Sure."

"Where are you going?"

"I don't know." He looked at her sideways. "Do you want to breathe underwater?"

The discussion wasn't remotely like any she had imagined. "I . . . I'm not sure I understand what you're talking about. I walked through the desert and it nearly cooked me. A good swim might be nice."

He stopped and put his hand on her arm. "I'm not talking about splashing around a pond. I'm talking about free-falling into an ocean of love and sucking it in. That's the kind of water I'm talking about. When that kind of water is in your lungs you can't help believing, can you?" He paused. "Do *you* believe in that kind of love?"

She blinked, aware of his hand on her arm. *Think, Rebecca. Remember why you are here. Take control of the conversation. Be Delilah.*

"Yes, I believe in love. I'm a woman; all women believe in love. Have you ever loved a woman?"

Caleb hesitated, searching her eyes, then released her and walked on. "I don't need the love of a woman. I'm after a true lover. And to find him I think I might have to die."

Caleb halted, tilted his head up and flung his hands out to the starry sky. "Take me, Father!" he cried to the stars.

Rebecca started. He was indeed losing his mind out here in the heat.

Caleb spun to her, his eyes brilliant with the distant fire's reflection. "You should seek his love, Rebecca. We all should. We'll never find a treasure like God. I should know. Do you know why I should know?"

"No."

"Because there was a time when I could walk in his presence as if it was another world, right here around us. And it is! There's another world right here, waiting to be opened. An ocean tempting us to dive in. The kingdom of God is here, Rebecca!" He pounded his chest three times. "It's here."

She wasn't quite sure what to do with his show. Was he deluded?

"Are you always so dramatic, or has the heat gotten to you?" she asked with a smile.

"Dramatic? You haven't seen dramatic, if you think a man on a quest looks like anything more than an ant walking across the ground."

"See? You're talking in terms that make no sense. What does an ant walking across the ground have to do with how crazy you're acting?"

"That's the point, it's not dramatic at all. You want to see dramatic? I've seen dramatic, believe me I've seen dramatic, although not for a long time. In fact, that might be my problem."

"Maybe. But it's not every day you find a man walking around in a robe, spreading his arms to the sky, begging God to kill him. At least not in my circles." She knew that she had to earn his trust, but she had no sense of how to affect such a man.

"Then maybe you walk in the wrong circles," Caleb said.

"I'm Jewish. The notion of God isn't foreign to us."

"I'm not talking about a notion. I'm talking about the real thing. The parting of the Red Sea. The sun standing still. The fire in the bush. When was the last time you saw the fire?"

"I haven't ever seen the fire. But then I'm not Moses, and I don't think you are either."

He just stared at her, at a loss for words.

"I'm sorry," she said. "Look, maybe we should just start over. I really didn't mean to disagree or anything—you just took me by surprise." She laughed and wondered if it sounded manufactured. She should just drag him out into the desert and get what she needed from him. But studying Caleb as she was now, she knew that would be impossible.

"You don't look like the kind of person who would associate with these monks," she said. "I'd expect to see you in a uniform, ordering armies around."

He continued looking at her as if he hadn't heard.

"Okay, well maybe not . . . How long have you been here?"

"Two days."

"Two days?" She hesitated. "You just wandered in? Are you ready to leave?"

He didn't answer.

"Surely you didn't just stumble into camp without a past. Someone, some-where, must be waiting for you."

Still no response. She decided to throw him some bait, now while his mind was preoccupied with this ocean of his. He might respond to a question linked to the Ark.

"There must be a key to the presence of God, don't you think?" she asked. "Where the oil and brine mix."

Caleb just stared at her for an inordinate amount of time, and she thought she might have been too obvious. "Enthrall your mind and your spirit with a ravishing vision of God," he said. "Swim to the bottom of his ocean, and there you will find a pearl of great price behind a piece of white coral. Waste your life for this pearl and you will be in the door without a key."

The words hardly made sense. She couldn't think of what to say in response. The sound of a drum broke the night air. It was quickly joined by ouds and a flute.

Caleb grabbed his flowing tunic and pulled it around himself like a prophet. He strode past her towards the campfires, evidently drawn by the music. *Oh no, you don't. Not yet.* She wasn't ready to let him go.

"Caleb, wait. Please, I need to—"

Caleb whirled back to her, grinning wide. "Are you willing to abandon yourself, Rebecca?" He gripped his tunic in both hands and jumped up in the air.

Rebecca started. What in God's name was he doing, jumping like this?

"Yes?" He laughed, delighted with himself. "Dance with me, Rebecca. Dance!"

He jumped again, straight up nearly a meter, and then again, like he was a pogo stick. "Abandon yourself! Dance, Rebecca! Dance! We are in the presence of the Ark! That's the meaning of the dance."

The absurdity of the moment froze her to the sand. *The Ark?* It occurred to her that her mouth was open.

"Find God with me!"

Caleb landed a last time, spun back to the camp, and ran for the fires.

21

I DON'T THINK YOU APPRECIATE THE DELICACY of the situation, David," Ben Gurion said. They sat alone late that night, in David's own apartment, sipping wine. It was the least Solomon could offer his old friend. "You have Goldstein tied in a knot."

"Has he talked?" Solomon asked.

"No. But he threatened to call the Egyptians in an effort to close the borders." He paused. "I made a call to Lerner, down at the university. He tells me that the Ark cannot be in Egypt. It's impossible."

"Lerner? This is the same man who agreed with the Muslim *Waqf* that bulldozing the entrance to Solomon's Stables was not threatening to antiquities? I'm surprised you would *call* him much less listen."

"He's also Israel's leading authority on archaeology—"

"No, Zakkai is Israel's leading authority on archaeology. And Zakkai is finding it hard to sleep these days, trust me."

"So, you do have Zakkai in on this. Lerner guessed as much." Ben Gurion shook his head. "If what you say is true, David, I'm not sure I disagree with Goldstein's suggestion to close the border."

"It would be paramount to turning the Ark over to the Muslims. First we give up our Temple Mount and now you would give up the Ark? What's next—Judaism? You're determined to make a name for yourself in the history books. The man who put Judaism in the grave once and for all."

"Don't be ridiculous." Ben Gurion eyed him carefully. "And the alternative would be leading our country into war; you know that. Goldstein may be godless, but he's no idiot." The prime minister stood and walked to the same window David had gazed through while the old blind priest had spun his tale nearly a week ago now.

"How long have we known each other, David?"

"Since the war in '67."

"Over thirty years. We have come a long way in thirty years."

"We've come nowhere," Solomon said. "We were closer to our objective then than we are now."

The prime minister turned to face him. "Yes, it all depends on the objective, doesn't it? I don't expect you to ever agree with me ideologically—I will concern myself with building a nation and you may concern yourself with building a people prepared for the Messiah. But we both must be very careful not to wipe out ten million Jews in the process."

Solomon didn't respond. It was old ground, covered a dozen times over the years. More talk seemed pointless.

"I must know how likely it is that you will actually find the relic, David."

"You mean the Ark—it's not just a relic. Assume it done."

"You have it?"

"No. But assume I will in a matter of days. And if I don't, consider this a dry run, because one day I will."

"There are no dry runs with the Ark. Our neighbors will explode if they even *think* we have it."

Solomon ignored the point. "You have two choices: you'll either give the Ark to our enemies and destroy Judaism's foundation, or you'll allow me to unveil it and risk war."

Ben Gurion sighed. "Yes."

"Let me help remove the confusion which might surround these two options. What Goldstein and his group of bandits don't realize is that we are surrounded by enemies because of *who* we are, not because of our policies. Nothing will ever change the fact that we are Jews. Unless we all become Muslims and change the name of our country, we will be Israel, and as Israel we will always be the enemy. Neither the Temple nor the Ark will bring war—it is who we *are* that will bring war! All the Ark would do is reaffirm who we are, and this will bring war."

"I'm not sure I see how this makes the matter any less confusing."

"Don't you see, Simon . . . Israel and her neighbors are destined for war either way. I'm saying you're not faced with a decision of war or no war—

that's out of your control. The only question is whether you want to enter the next war *with* the Ark or *against* the Ark."

Ben Gurion raised an eyebrow.

"You don't believe in the power of the Ark? It handled Jericho quite nicely."

"It doesn't matter whether I believe in the power of the Ark, does it? There are enough Jews who do, and they won't like the idea of taking tanks into battle against the Ark. Is that it?"

Solomon nodded. "Close enough."

"So you're saying that war is inevitable either way, and it would be a mistake to allow the Ark to fall into enemy hands. I agree. How about giving it to a third party?"

"Put it in an American museum? Absurd. It's our heritage! War would still come. No, you must have it in your hands. There is no other way."

"But you're wrong. There is another way. Leave the Ark. Simply don't find it. As long as it's hidden, it poses no problem."

"And if we wouldn't have resurrected the nation of Israel, we wouldn't have the problem of protecting it, would we? You can't hide the truth just because you don't want to face it. You don't just sweep God under the rug because he gives you a headache."

"Then you're basically insisting on war."

"I didn't commission the building of the Ark, my friend. God did. If his instrument brings war, so be it. I insist on nothing but to do his will. Perhaps you should take this up with him. He is accepting prayers at the Western Wall, below the Al-Aqsa Mosque, from what I hear."

"Please don't patronize me. I'm not your enemy—you have plenty of those as it is."

Solomon turned from him and sighed. "You're right, forgive me." He stood and joined the prime minister by the window. They looked out to the Temple Mount together.

"I see you keep your goal clearly in view," Ben Gurion said.

Solomon nodded. "I need your help, Simon. If I find the Ark, I want you to help me bring it in safely."

"I would rather you didn't find it."

"Yes, but that's beyond my control now." He thought briefly about Rebecca's missing status and a barb pulled at his chest. He could only pray that she was safe. He would like to say that Rebecca had been in much worse situations and could handle herself easily, but he didn't know the situation in the desert. Zakkai and the others were giving birth to cows, waiting for her call. They'd come to a standstill. Without Caleb, the prime minister would get his wish.

"I could put you under arrest," Ben Gurion said.

"You could, but that would stop nothing. It's simply a matter of managing the inevitable now."

"The Knesset—"

"I will deal with the Knesset," Solomon interrupted.

The prime minister arched an eyebrow. "Oh?"

"It's getting the Ark into the country that concerns me."

Ben Gurion stared at him.

"I may need a submarine," Solomon said.

"Through Eilat?"

"If there is any trouble, it would be safer than through the Sinai."

Ben Gurion set his glass down and turned for the door. "I'll give it some thought. I'm not sure whether or not you're doing a terrible thing, David. But I think that when the dust settles, most of the world will conclude it is a terrible thing."

"Half the world already thinks that our God is a terrible thing."

22

REBECCA SLEPT THROUGH THE NIGHT only because her body refused to stay awake after three days with little rest. Caleb's last words about the Ark haunted her dreams. Caleb haunted her dreams. When she awoke at dawn, she felt as though a truck had run over her.

She quickly splashed water on her face from a basin in the tent and wandered into the camp wearing the tunic Miriam had given her. She had to find Caleb immediately.

But Caleb was nowhere to be found. The boy, Daniel, on the other hand was, and he took it upon himself to educate her about the camp. Her mission loomed large in her mind; she didn't have the time to discuss desert life with a child. Then again, Caleb was nowhere in sight.

Two other small children, a boy and a girl, tagged along, but Daniel was twice their age, and he kept them towing a line of respect with surprising ease. Visitors found their way into the camp perhaps once a month, he informed her, usually traders and scientists—the Danakil Desert was too harsh for even most seasoned adventurers. Was he going to be a monk? Yes, of course, the boy responded. In this desert? He'd looked at her as if she were dull in the head. Yes, of course. If you want to swim, you must find water. The desert was a good place to swim.

It was Caleb-speak. Or had Caleb been speaking Tribe-speak last night? They were all preoccupied with this business of swimming in God's ocean. They evidently thought he'd moved it to the desert.

It took her an hour, wandering about with Daniel to find what she was looking for. Caleb was sitting in the sand a stone's throw from the camp, by the rocks, staring out to the desert.

Rebecca excused herself and walked to him. In light of last night's failure, she'd decided that engaging him on an intellectual level would be inadvisable until he showed some sense. That had been her problem—she had tried to engage him as a reasonable person rather than as a woman. He was too busy looking for an ocean to swim in to use reason.

Rebecca approached him from the side and caught his glance while she was ten meters off. He closed his eyes and pretended not to see her. She suppressed a smile. Was he embarrassed? That was okay, because honestly she was a little embarrassed herself.

She eased herself down beside him and folded her legs to one side. He seemed determined to ignore her, and she was tempted to reach over and blow into his ear. Clear out the cobwebs. Instead, she looked out to the desert.

"Stunning, isn't it? It's hard to believe that something so white and beautiful can so easily kill. I led my camel . . ."

"Excuse me," Caleb said. He pushed himself to his feet and walked away from her.

Rebecca stared, dumbfounded. How could he do that? What kind of man could just stand and leave a woman without the slightest hesitation?

She stood, furious. So then, perhaps force was her only recourse. If he refused to even engage her, she had little choice.

But you don't want to force him, do you, Rebecca?

No. She wanted him to respect her, at least. Not as a soldier with a gun, but as a woman. It struck her that his disregard for her was as frustrating as her failure to move the mission forward. And the fact that she would allow her feelings to influence her decisions frustrated her even more.

Maybe he is taken with you and can't stand to be distracted.

"Hello, Rebecca."

She spun to the rocks. Father Hadane had materialized from behind and watched Caleb go. He turned his head to her.

"He won't be easy, you know."

"I'm sorry? Easy to what?"

"Easy to deceive. You are here to deceive him, aren't you?"

Rebecca still hadn't completely recovered from his sudden appearance. Caleb must have been talking to the old man behind the rocks earlier. About her?

"Is that what he told you about me?"

"No. He hasn't mentioned you."

The old man was dressed in a simple tunic; he looked like what she imagined an old Hebrew prophet might look, walking out of the desert.

"I'm sorry, I don't believe we've met," she said. "I don't know what you've heard, but you've obviously been misinformed. I walked into camp—"

"Yes, I know, Rebecca." He smiled. "I know where you've come from and why you are here. You're here because you believe Caleb holds the key to the Ark's location, and you intend to take the information from him."

He knew? How? "Really?"

Hadane just held his smile.

"And how do you know this?"

He waved a hand in the air. "I know, I know, I know. That doesn't matter. You won't deceive him, and the truth can't be forced from him. So I'm afraid that you've walked a long way for nothing, my dear."

Clearly the old man knew her intent. Hiding it now would be a waste of time, and she had wasted enough already. This strange leper seemed to be larger than life despite his small frame. He'd gotten his fingers into Caleb's mind.

"Is it in the monastery?" she asked.

"Your Ark? Only Caleb can tell you that."

"Do you know where the oil and the brine meet?" she asked, thinking of the letter Zakkai had read to her.

"It sounds like a question for Caleb."

"You like him, don't you?"

"He's a tortured young man. So very near to God and yet so far. Yes, I like him very much."

"And you really don't think I can deceive him?"

"No, my dear, you cannot deceive him."

"How can I deceive him if he won't let me near him? Let me test him and we'll see what happens."

He eyed her quizzically. "But you *are* testing him. And you have failed twice now."

"Yes. But what kind of test is this? He's preoccupied. If you believe the truth you've given him can withstand a real test, then put him in the cage with me and we'll see what he does."

"Oh? A cage?"

"A cage," she said, mind racing. "Charge him to watch over me. What good is the light if he can't shed it on the path of a wayward soul who's wandered into camp? Assign him to me so that he can't simply walk away every time I talk to him; that's all I ask."

The old man hadn't moved an inch since first appearing. "And you will try to trick him into telling you what you want to know?"

"Not necessarily. I will test this truth you've filled him with. I will try to persuade him to reject it. That would be the true test of his faith, wouldn't it?"

Hadane stared at her, smiling, silent for a few moments.

"And if you succeed?"

"If Caleb stumbles from your truth in any way, then you'll ask Caleb to tell me what I want to know. He'll listen to you. If I fail, I will leave you."

A glint filled Hadane's eyes. He suddenly broke to his right, fingers on his lips, pacing. And then he paced back again. "Yes. Yes, yes." He looked up. "You have your wish. Although I doubt you understand why." He waved a hand. "It doesn't matter. I will tell him to watch over you."

Hadane turned and strode for the camp. He spun back after five paces, grinning wide. "You are transparent, my dear, but I like your spirit. You do realize that this is for *your* sake, not his? No, of course you don't. But in the end you will. In the end the whole world will see."

He swiveled about and marched for his tent.

———

Rebecca was seated behind Miriam's tent an hour later when Caleb walked up, expressionless. He stopped beside her and folded his arms, looking to the horizon. Then he sat with crossed legs. Rebecca did her best not to grin. It was good to be in power again.

For a full minute they said nothing. She had no intention of rushing. Although it was true that Zakkai was probably climbing the walls back at the monastery, their entire mission depended on her ability to manipulate this man beside her. And she saw that manipulating Caleb might take the full two days she was now allotted. Climbing into his mind and pulling out what she needed was now her only concern, and to be honest, she relished the idea.

She would use wit, and if wit failed, seduction, and if seduction failed, then reason. And if all of these failed, she would finally resort to force.

"The Father has asked me to stay with you," Caleb said. "It is his way to show kindness to strangers and illuminate their paths. We feel you may need some illumination."

Rebecca smiled at Hadane's clever use of her own imagery. "Well I'm lost, that's for sure. I was beginning to get the impression that you weren't interested in me."

He cast her a side glance. "Yes. I'm sorry, but I was preoccupied." He looked back to the west, in the direction of the monastery, now two days' ride away. "I came here confused and lost. But I've started seeing things clearly again. Believe me, when you see things of the kingdom clearly, they tend to preoccupy."

Yes, of course they do, my dear innocent boy.

Rebecca pushed herself from the sand and pulled him up by his arm. "I want to hear all about it, but first let's walk. I'm tired of sitting around this camp. Aren't you?"

He staggered to his feet, off balance. "No, actually, I'm not really. We could talk to Miriam if you—"

"No, let's explore the rocks." She pulled him and he stumbled after her. "Come on, a change of scenery will do us wonders." She laughed, partly because the moment called for laughter, and partly because of the astonishment that lit his face.

Rebecca eased back next to him, but she didn't release his hand. Instead, she swung it in her own.

She smiled and looked into his eyes. They were deep pools of green, and for a brief moment she imagined they were the ocean he had talked about.

"I'm not sure it would be wise for us to go far," he said, clearly uncomfortable.

"What's the matter, Caleb? You're afraid to shine your light on my path? Don't be silly. I want to hear your story. Tell me, where do you live?"

He paused and they strolled towards the boulders. "I live in a monastery."

"Where is your monastery?"

"Two days that way." He pointed west.

"And who lives there with you?"

"My mother, Leiah, and my father, Jason."

"They know where you are?"

"No. No, they don't. I had to leave suddenly when bandits overtook it."

"Bandits! You're not serious! You just left? What about your parents?"

"Oh, they're safe. The bandits were after me and will leave as soon as they realize I'm not coming back."

"How do you know that?" Rebecca asked, surprised.

"Father Hadane told me." He shrugged. "I believe him."

"And would you jump off a *cliff* if Father Hadane told you it was okay?" she asked in a biting tone.

He smiled. "I might. If the ocean was down there."

Yes, of course, how could she not know. The ocean. They walked through a narrow canyon formed by two large boulders. The shade felt good, and Rebecca deliberately slowed the pace. He pulled his hand from hers and she let it go naturally.

"And how long have you been in this monastery of yours?" she asked.

"I grew up there. That's the problem, I think."

"Living in a monastery?"

"No. Growing up. Growing up isn't a bad thing, of course, physically or spiritually. But to grow up spiritually means to mature in spiritual ways, not to bring human maturity to spirituality."

"Hmm."

He scratched his head with one hand. "I've grown up in my own wisdom, and now I know why Christ said that unless you *become*—not are, not want to be, but *become*—like a child you cannot enter the kingdom! I am becoming again."

Caleb seemed to have forgotten his shyness. "That's what this is about!" he said, turning excitedly to her as if the realization had just dawned on him. "It's a renaissance; it's a rebirth! I'm beginning to walk where I once walked."

"Is that right? A renaissance? And what can a child know that a man can't? I've seen your renaissance, and frankly, it makes me wonder."

He stooped, picked up a fistful of sand, and flung it into the air. "Wonder! Exactly! Wonder, that's what a child sees better." They'd come to a small pile of rocks and he jumped up on one, spinning to her. "And do you know what follows wonder?"

She smiled. "Tell me."

"Belief! Ha!" He leapt from the rock. "Belief!"

"Belief. Yes, but belief in what, that's the question. I'm sure you expect me to believe that you've cornered the market on truth. No offense, but while you and your leader are jumping up and down like jack rabbits, the real world is finding a slow, painful death. Only the Messiah will change that." She didn't mean to inject her own beliefs, and she immediately chided herself for doing so.

"The Messiah? The Messiah is here." Caleb thumped his chest. "He is the ocean. That is the light Father Hadane has asked me to shed on your path, dear Rebecca."

He was taking the whole thing about light too seriously, and she decided it had to stop. She would do the influencing, not Caleb.

Rebecca walked up to him, smiling. "Enough of the ocean. It's making me thirsty." She reached up and gently pushed the hair from his forehead, allowing her finger to linger, but only barely. "I want to know about *you*. About your life. Tell me how you came to be who you are today. Tell me about the monastery."

Caleb instinctively looked away, uncomfortable.

Not too fast, Rebecca. Goodness, listen to her! *Not too fast,* as if she, who had never even dated a man, somehow held the secrets to seduction. She was more accustomed to *killing* men.

I am a woman. Seduction was born into my blood!

She turned from him and walked a few steps with her arms behind her back, swaying just barely.

"Tell me about yourself, Caleb," she repeated. Was he even watching her?

Was he seeing how she moved with such grace and stepped as only a woman can step? She turned slowly.

No. He was staring off, thinking of how to answer her question.

"I was left at the monastery as an infant," he said. He began to tell her his story, exactly as she had asked.

At first she just looked at him, still plagued by questions about how to best lure him. But as he continued, she found herself drawn into an incredible tale she would never have guessed possible. There was no rush—he was letting her into his world, and that alone would disarm him, she thought. So she encouraged him with a few questions, asking for details.

Caleb sat on the rock and gave her details. They came out of him like water from a broken dam. It was as much self-reflection as telling her, she thought, but she was so taken by his story that she no longer cared.

They talked for a long time, into the afternoon. Several times they walked, and each time Rebecca led them deeper into the boulders, away from the camp. Caleb had shed any sign of apprehension at her company. He relived his life with her, using animated gestures and laughing, and on two occasions, even crying. His tears did not concern her as much as the fact that she felt a few of her own gathering in her eyes.

It struck her, after he told how he'd spent the last five years struggling with deep loneliness, that she liked this man. She at least cared for him. The notion of seducing him suddenly felt absurd.

Stop it! It is absurd that you are allowing emotion to compromise your mission. That is what's absurd!

He asked her about her past, and she fabricated a story about archaeological studies in New York, where she met and married an American who later died in Jerusalem, the victim of an assassin's bullet. She thought it would be good for him to feel what she felt about her own loss, so she wove it into a tale of true love. Now *her* talking was as much self-reflection as telling.

They had worked their way deep into a canyon by midafternoon. Soft sand, not rock salt, covered the ground here. They had spent the last hour talking about small things, the kind of things old friends talk about. This was good. He had let her in. They had even laughed together in a way that

Rebecca found genuinely pleasing. She was most definitely in character, she thought. It was time to teach Caleb that she was a woman.

He was sitting in the sand, cross-legged, looking at the sky in reflection. Rebecca walked up and eased to the ground beside him with her legs folded to one side so that she leaned on her right arm.

"It is amazing how people are drawn together," she said, looking to the sky with him. She smiled. "Here we are in the desert, far away from our homes, two strangers, yet seeking the same thing."

"Hmm."

The desert air was hot, despite the shade. Rebecca was suddenly terrified to say more. But she did anyway.

"I've been lonely too, Caleb."

For a long while she didn't know what his response would be because she was afraid to look at him. They just sat there, close, but still innocent. It wasn't too late to pull back and suggest they return.

"I think the worst kind of loneliness comes from not belonging," Caleb said.

Rebecca's heart spiked. He wasn't discouraging her.

"You're right," she said softly. "I'm not sure I've ever belonged, really— not to a people, not to a country, not to a man."

"Then you understand my problem as well," he said. "I feel like I'm stranded between worlds."

"I would give anything to belong."

He sighed. "Yes."

It is now or never, Rebecca thought. She slipped her left hand towards his shoulder. He didn't move and she glanced up to see that he wasn't looking. She touched him.

Caleb might have flinched; she wasn't sure. Natural enough.

Rebecca let her finger run down his biceps. She turned toward him, so that her face was at his shoulder. She could smell his musky skin. He still didn't move.

She eased over so that her mouth was near his neck.

"You are a very handsome man, Caleb." Her voice sounded sultry yet innocent. "We are connected, you and I."

She was breathing steadily now, from her own uneasiness rather than desire, but he wouldn't know the difference. He still did not budge. She couldn't see his face, but she assumed his stillness was a good sign.

"You have what I want, and I have what you want," she breathed softly in his ear and leaned closer. She closed her eyes and let her lips touch his hot cheek. "You want what . . ."

He suddenly jerked away and leapt to his feet. Rebecca nearly fell forward.

"What are you doing?" he asked.

She righted herself. One look at his round eyes, and she knew she had misjudged him. Blood flooded her face.

"What do you mean, what am I doing?"

"You . . . You were kissing me!"

"Yes, I was kissing you. I was kissing you because you said you were lonely, and I said I was lonely, and when I put my hand on you, you encouraged me to kiss you."

He blinked, still stunned. "I didn't *encourage* you."

"You didn't move."

"I was frozen. I couldn't move!"

Rebecca scrambled to her feet, furious now. She had bared her soul to this man, and he was appalled by it?

"What is wrong with you?" she yelled at him. "Don't you have warm blood anywhere under that skin of yours? Haven't you ever been kissed by a woman?"

They stared at each other—he in shock, she in anger. She'd never kissed a man, but that hardly mattered. He was being unreasonable to resist her so easily.

"No," he said.

"Exactly! That's your problem! It's time you grew up. This may come as a shock to you, but you're not a child anymore! You're a man. Men fall in love with women and kiss them and they have children and grow old together. They don't hide away in the desert looking for oceans to dive into!" She had said too much.

"And have you kissed a man?" he asked.

His question took her off guard. "Of course! I was married, remember?"

"You really were? I thought you were just making that all up."

He knew?

Rebecca felt as awkward and embarrassed as she could ever remember feeling. He was impossible. She did the only thing she could think to do. She walked up to him and slapped him on the cheek.

"You're impossible!"

She stormed off, horrified. What in God's name had she just done? Other than make an utter fool of herself?

That's it, Rebecca. No more games!

23

THE SUN WAS ALREADY SETTING WHEN the Hercules circled once over the Tower Oasis and fanned out for a landing on the salt flats. After two days of perfect silence, the turbine's whine sent a disturbing chill through Ismael's skull.

A large man who walked with a Republican Guard gait (more like a rooster than a man) was the first off the plane. He strode towards Ismael. The others waited by the rear door, which was now lowering.

The man stopped and saluted. "Captain Asid reporting, sir. Can I tell them to off-load?"

"Yes."

The captain signaled to the men who immediately began leading horses out of the tail. His father had kept his promise to keep him in charge; that was good. For the first time in days, Ismael felt the familiar surge of power run through his veins.

"What men and provisions do you have?" he demanded.

"Ten men, all Republican Guard cavalry. Twelve horses and two Jeeps, sir. We have automatic weapons and enough explosive munitions to wake up the dead if you want us to, sir."

"What have you been told about our mission?"

"Only that we're in Ethiopia without authorization, engaging Israeli soldiers who are also here without authorization."

Ismael nodded. "Good." Two Jeeps mounded with provisions rolled off the large prop plane behind the captain. "Where is the tracker?"

"Hasam." He spun and whistled over the engines.

A thin man dressed in tan cotton pants, which were ragged at the heels, ran towards them. He made an awkward attempt to salute. "I am Hasam."

"You know this desert?" Ismael demanded.

"Yes."

"Two days ago a caravan left these springs and headed north." He pointed in the direction the tracks had led. "Unfortunately, the wind has erased their tracks. Do you know where they were headed?"

"If they headed due north, then they would either stop at the Manessa, an outcropping of boulders one and a half day's journey, or beyond at the Tagasal Springs, three days' journey. Or they may have gone west, headed for—"

"They didn't go west. I said north. If you were going north, where would you stop?"

The Hercules revved up, screaming over the man's response. Ismael waited patiently while the transport taxied through a U-turn and then lumbered over the sand and into the air.

Ismael looked at the tracker and raised his brows.

"I would always look for a watering hole," he said. "But if I were in a caravan leaving from here, I would probably have water—"

"Please, the answer to my question will do. They left from here and they were a caravan. I told you that. Where would they go?"

Hasam glanced at the captain who stared ahead. "To the boulders for a few days, until my water was low, then on to the spring."

The men led groups of horses towards the boulders. Both Jeeps blazed along the flats, spewing salt behind. "Have your men water the horses. We'll eat and leave by midnight, while it is cool," Ismael said. "I want to be in their camp before the sun sets tomorrow."

———

Sleep had come hard for Rebecca. Her failure with Caleb loomed in her mind like a laughing monster. She'd first considered going back out to collect him and then drag him back to the monastery with her, but doing so would be impossible without the tribe's help. And there was the small problem of Caleb himself. She knew that he would never respond to force. He would probably choose death over anything she demanded of him. Especially now, in light of her seduction.

She finally decided that there was only one way to resolve the problem. The most difficult part would be approaching him again after making such an idiot of herself.

No one knew where he was the next morning. She searched the rocks and found him on a sandy shelf above the camp. He stood with his arms spread and his chin tilted up, dressed in the same tunic he'd worn last night. If she wasn't mistaken, he'd spent the night out here.

She approached him from behind. "Good morning."

He didn't move. This was not a good sign.

She leaned back on a rock, crossed her arms, and watched Caleb's face. His eyes were closed. "You are supposed to watch over me, or did you forget?"

"Good morning, Rebecca. Did you sleep well?"

"Yes. And you?"

"Yes, I slept wonderfully." He smiled, opened his eyes, and lowered his arms.

"You slept out here?" His eyes seemed greener than she remembered. His dark, wavy hair hung to his neck, slightly disheveled.

"Yes."

"You look refreshed."

"I'm seeing clearer, I think."

Rebecca raised an eyebrow. "Does sleeping on the sand always make someone see clearer?" He didn't seem at all affected by the episode yesterday. It was all slightly unnerving.

"No. But being with God does."

She nodded. "I have to ask your forgiveness—"

"Done," he said. "Never happened."

She looked at him and decided he was right. They should pretend it never happened.

"So what have you been doing all night? Really."

"Staring into the eyes of God," Caleb said.

What an odd thing to say. "And what was he doing?"

"Staring back into my eyes." He turned and faced the desert, hands limp at his sides.

He was both intoxicating and frustrating at once. Intoxicating because the way that he looked at her made Rebecca want to stare into God's eyes with him; frustrating because she knew that the notion was absurd. Surely there had to be a thread of reason left in him.

"And what does God tell you when you stare into his eyes? What are you accomplishing out here, Caleb?"

"God tells me nothing, Rebecca. We enjoy each other's company. I think it's why he made me." He twisted his head to her and his eyes flashed mischievously. "What could be better than to enthrall the mind with the eyes that blinked you into existence?"

She swallowed and forced herself to continue down her line of reasoning before she gave it up altogether. "Yes, but to what end, Caleb? While you're here enjoying God's company, the world is coming apart at the seams somewhere. My people are being killed. Is that what the Nazarene ordered?"

He was beyond reasoning. It was time to bring Caleb into the real world.

She looked out to the desert. "I want to tell you something, Caleb. A part of my story that I omitted yesterday."

Caleb looked at her, amused perhaps.

"This is why I am really here." She took a deep breath. "My father, David Ben Solomon, was conceived in Auschwitz in 1942. His mother, Zelda, managed to escape with a German's help, three weeks before giving birth to my father. But she was so traumatized by the ordeal that she died in childbirth—the Nazis had killed her after all."

"I'm very sorry," Caleb said.

"Hold your sorrow—I'm not finished. My father was six when the nation of Israel was born in 1948. He was twenty-five and newly married to Hannah, my mother, when Israel was attacked at the onset of the Six-Day War in 1967. On the fifth of June Israel bombed Egypt's air bases in a massive preemptive strike. The battle in Jerusalem lasted three days. Against international pressure Menachem Begin ordered Colonel Mordechai Gur and a brigade of young paratroopers to take the Old City, held by Jordan. My father was one of the paratroopers."

Rebecca paused, remembering the story told to her by her father a hundred times.

"They entered through the Lion's Gate, on the northeast, with Colonel

Gur leading a column of half-tracks that rattled through smoke and fire from Jordanian legionaries camped on the walls. They pushed past a burning bus that blocked the gate, firing in every direction. They screamed down the street, turned through another gate onto a path lined with trees, and into a plaza. An octagonal building with a golden dome stood before them. And the men were off the vehicles and running to it, guns in hand. Gur lifted his radio and spoke words which ring through Jerusalem to this day: *The Temple Mount is in our hands."*

Caleb watched her, eyes wide.

"The Temple Mount was in our hands. My father was in the last Jeep. He jumped off and ran for the Temple Mount, carrying a Torah scroll under one arm and a ram's horn in his other hand. Soaked with sweat he ran, uncaring of the bullets from Jordanian gunfire. David Ben Solomon was roaring out in song. He was the herald of the Lord, and he arrived on Gur's heels, blasting the shofar. He dropped to his knees and bowed to the Holy of Holies, where the Dome of the Rock stands now. Then he stood and blasted the shofar again, this time on the radio so that all of Israel could hear."

Rebecca tossed a rock into the desert below. "The general had arrived, and soldiers were wandering around in a daze. For the first time in a very long time the site of Solomon's Temple, to which the Messiah himself would one day return, was in Jewish hands. My father ran up to the general. 'Uzi,' he said. 'Now is the time to put one hundred kilos of dynamite in the mosque and be done with it, once and for all.' The general laughed and my father insisted. They hauled him from the Temple Mount in handcuffs."

Rebecca briefly wondered whether Caleb was even believing all of this. She had lied to him once, and he'd found her out. But this was different. He would hear the sincerity in her voice.

"The war ended on June 10. Three days later, on Shavuoth, 200,000 Jews gathered at the Mount in a festival of victory. Four days after that, the military of Israel decreed the new status quo. Under Israeli rule, the Temple Mount would remain a Muslim religious site, to be guarded by Muslims. Jews could enter the Mount but they could not pray there—that would be relegated to the new square that the engineers had cleared at the Western Wall. That was over thirty years ago and nothing has changed. In the middle of

Judaism's most holy city lies Judaism's most holy site, originally built to house the presence of God. Only there is no Temple for our God—there is a Muslim mosque. Isaac's inheritance has been stolen by Ismael."

She faced him. "My father says that if he had blown up the *Haram al-Sharif* when he was on the Mount, the Messiah would have come in 1967."

"I'm so very sorry—"

"No, I'm not finished. My father made a vow to God the day he was taken from the Temple Mount. He would not rest until Solomon's Temple was rebuilt. It has become his calling. To many in Israel, David Ben Solomon is a prophet, a voice crying in the wilderness, 'Prepare the way of the Lord.'" She stared into his eyes.

"Now I've come into the desert, and I see that we have the wrong prophet calling out."

Caleb just looked at her, unsure.

"*You* are the one who will prepare his way, Caleb."

If her meaning sank in, he didn't show it.

"You have in your power the key to Israel's restoration, as foretold by the prophets. If the Temple is not rebuilt, Israel will fade like this desert—it's a foregone conclusion. But with the Temple, Israel will return to God and thrive. You, Caleb, have in your hands the power to allow Israel's destruction or bring about her restoration. And I will ask you again, do you really love the Jew?"

He stared at her with a blank face. "I'm afraid I don't understand you."

"The Ark of the Covenant, Caleb. The Temple was built to house the Ark. If the Ark is returned to Jerusalem, then Israel will be obligated to rebuild that Temple. You alone can lead us to the Ark."

There she had said it.

He blinked once. Then again.

"Where do the oil and the brine mix, Caleb?" Rebecca asked.

"You are with the Jews who overtook the monastery!" he said.

"Yes."

"You . . . Then my mother and father are safe?"

"Yes. In fact, they have helped Zakkai dig into your old sleeping place below the monastery. They found a letter from Father Matthew that talks about the place where the oil and the brine mix. We believe the Ark is hidden there."

For a long time, Caleb looked into her eyes.

"I'm sorry, Caleb. I know I misled you, but considering the circumstances, I'm sure you can understand." She told him Raphael Hadane's story, and that Father Matthew had told his good friend, Father Joseph Hadane, about the Ark. "Israel is on the verge of finding her salvation, and you now hold Israel captive."

Caleb finally spoke. "The presence of God is not in an Ark any longer, Rebecca. It's here in the desert. It's in the ocean. In his eyes. In the heart."

"Yes, well I haven't seen you knock down the walls of Jericho or defeat armies. The Ark belongs to Israel."

Caleb closed his eyes. "I would like to be left alone," he said.

"You're supposed to be my guide," she said. He didn't respond. "Okay. Talk to your God and see if he doesn't urge you to help me. If he's the God of Abraham and David, I think he will. I will pray that you listen."

She left him like that, standing with eyes closed, perhaps staring into the eyes of God. It would be the last time she left him, she thought. She had now committed herself, for better or worse. If he didn't agree to help her, she would at least make an attempt at force.

24

THE REPUBLICAN GUARD TEAM MADE excellent time through the cool hours of the night, covering more than half the distance to the boulders before the sun began to warm the desert.

Ismael rode in one of the Jeeps, leading the horses at a steady fifteen-kilometer-an-hour clip. The animals wouldn't be able to maintain the pace in the heat, but with an hour's rest and a good watering at dawn, they would have the strength to continue through the day. It all came down to water, and they carried two hundred liters of it between the Jeeps and all the horses.

Now the sun was halfway up the sky, and the captain was sweating profusely. "This heat is as bad as I was told," he said. "The faster we move the worse it feels. It's like a blast furnace. God has given Ethiopia a corner of hell."

Ismael ignored the comment. They rode for another few minutes in silence.

"We will come into their camp at dusk, on horses only," Ismael said. "The vehicles are too loud. Tell the tracker to halt us two kilometers before the camp."

"Reasonable," the captain agreed.

They rode on.

"Tell him," Ismael said.

"Yes, I will."

"Now."

"Now? He's behind us, with the horses."

"You don't know how to walk? Get out."

Captain Asid hesitated for a moment and then stepped out onto the sand. The Jeep rolled on, a steady five kilometers per hour now. Ismael closed his eyes and let his mind wander to the killing ahead. They had the firepower to wipe out a small army. Whatever lay before would soon be dead. If they were lucky, they would find both Caleb and Rebecca. And if not, they would level the monastery anyway. The thought made the heat bearable.

Caleb missed the midday meal, and Rebecca began to worry. She might not have so much experience handling a man without a knife or gun in hand, but she could've sworn that she had moved him this time.

Elijah had informed her that the camp would leave for a watering hole in the morning. One way or another she would take Caleb with her tonight—she couldn't afford to travel further from the monastery.

She waited another hour, expecting him to walk into camp at any moment. But the desert lay still and hot. No sign of life, much less Caleb. If he had come to his senses, he would have done it by now.

Rebecca grunted and walked for the boulders. Maybe he had fallen and hurt himself, or lost himself in the square kilometer or so of rock, though the latter seemed unlikely. Then again, with Caleb, nothing was really that unlikely. She decided to return to the spot where she'd discovered him this morning. From there she would follow his tracks—with some luck he hadn't run a marathon out here.

Rebecca entered the small sandy enclave overlooking the camp and pulled up, startled. Caleb stood with his back to her, on the rock's edge, in nearly the same position she'd left him. He even had his arms spread, as if he were trying to calm this desert he called an ocean.

She pressed into the rock on her right and watched him. A light breeze pushed his cotton robe around his ankles. His wavy hair curled at his shoulders; from behind he reminded Rebecca of a picture she'd once seen of the prophet Elijah being fed by ravens.

She saw that he held a stone in his right hand.

"Have you ever ridden a bicycle, Rebecca?"

His voice seemed lower than she remembered.

"How did you know I was here?" she asked, stepping out.

"Do you remember the first time you rode a bicycle?" he asked, still facing away.

She had no intention of following him on one of his crazy lines of thinking. "What are you doing out here, Caleb? I've been waiting. The camp is moving in the morning."

He turned around. He looked different, again. Not as though he had actually changed, but different, in the subtle lines around his smile and in the color of his skin. And in his eyes. Everything seemed brighter—his cheeks redder and his eyes greener.

But it was more than the color. Caleb was staring at her and she was feeling her heart pound without understanding exactly why.

"I am learning to ride my bike," he said.

"I . . . I'm not sure I understand."

"It's something Father Hadane told me, and I'm beginning to comprehend. When you learn to ride a bike, you don't just learn that you *ought* to ride it; you actually *attempt* to ride it and then you *do* ride it. Belief works the same way. I am learning to believe; I am riding my bike."

He said it with a delightful awe—you'd think he had just mastered the secret to atomic power. And the way he was looking at her, with such compassion, eyes swimming in an innocence she could not grasp, Rebecca wasn't sure he hadn't.

It was her turn to speak, she knew that, but the words weren't bubbling out. She spoke anyway, and it sounded stupid.

"What is the stone for?"

"My bicycle," he said. "I was attempting to float it."

She swallowed.

Caleb shrugged and dropped the stone to the sand. "Not really. I don't think this bicycle has wheels." He grinned. "Even if it did have wheels, there's no place for it to go. I think a bicycle has to have a place to go, don't you?"

"Makes sense." Actually it didn't. She broke eye contact and walked towards the edge. "Did you talk to Hadane today?"

"No. I'm sorry. I haven't had the time yet."

No, you're too busy staring into the eyes of God and floating rocks to con-cern yourself with saving Israel. She wondered if that constituted a fall from grace. She had tested him and he had failed. Hadane would never buy it.

"Have you thought about our conversation?"

"The Ark. Yes."

"And?"

"And I would like to go with you, back to the monastery."

She spun to him. "You would?"

"Yes, but I don't think I'm finished here. And I really don't think I can help you find the Ark. If it is in the Debra Damarro, Father Matthew would have told me."

"He did! In the letter."

"No. My father often referred to the human heart as the Ark of God, Rebecca. The Spirit of God dwells in the *heart,* not in a golden Ark. That is the answer to your riddle. The oil and the brine mix in the heart. The oil is the presence of God and the brine is sin. I'm very sorry, but you're mis-taken about the Ark."

Rebecca felt her face drain as his words sunk in. The *heart!* What if he was right? But no, there was other evidence. Too much corroborating evi-dence. "What about Raphael Hadane's story? He said that Father Matthew told of the Ark."

Caleb smiled politely. "Again, the heart. In Father Matthew's mind, I was the Ark. He was the Ark. But I can understand him using the term in speak-ing about me. I was very special to him, and I was hidden in the monastery, wasn't I? In the letter you found, he's reminding me. Father Matthew was very creative."

Rebecca felt her heart sink, but she refused to dismiss Zakkai's evaluation outright. There had to be more to the blind priest's story than imaginary hearts.

"I could be mistaken, of course." Caleb must have seen her disappoint-ment. He crossed his arms and stared out to the west. "Either way, the Ark isn't what you think it is. If you will wait another week with me, I will take you back to the monastery."

"A week? Your parents are back there!"

"And they are safe. You may want the Ark, but you're not a killer, Rebecca. I was meant to be here and I don't think I'm ready to leave yet."

"You have no *idea* what I am! Not a killer? If you knew, you might not be sitting around with rocks in your hands."

He looked at her without a shred of concern, still smiling softly. "How could someone who tried to kiss me yesterday try to kill me today?"

Rebecca suddenly wanted to slap him. "Uhh!" She gritted her teeth. "You're clueless!"

He arched a brow. "Am I?"

"I don't know what kind of woman you think I am, but I'm not her," she said. "I'm fighting for my *life!* For my country's life—not some relic you think of as a simple golden box. Just because our beliefs differ doesn't mean you don't have an obligation to respect mine. How dare you claim to possess the presence of God's power while dismissing the true resting place of his power!"

"I only believe—"

"I don't care what you believe!" she interrupted. "I don't see any stones floating, and I sure don't see any bicycles wheeling around. You're living in a fantasy world, and it's time you joined the real one. Whether you like it or not, the Ark is in that monastery, and you're going to help us find it."

She spun and walked away.

It was time to retrieve her guns.

25

ISMAEL GAZED THROUGH HIS BINOCULARS at the large outcropping of boulders the tracker called Manessa. They had made good time through the day's heat, thanks to the water they carried. Now the sun sat on the horizon behind him like a large orange, spreading fingers of red across the western sky in a brilliant sunset.

The white tents at the base of the rocks were unmistakable.

"They're here!" he said. His heart pounded steadily and a tremor took to his hands. "The camp is here." He lowered his glasses and snatched up his AK-47.

"Nothing lives. Do you hear me? We kill every animal and every man and every child—everything! And every tent burns. We go in hard and smother them before they know what's hit them."

"Yes, sir." The captain was already checking his weapon.

"Horses only. Leave the tracker with the Jeeps. Weapons on automatic."

Ismael stepped into the stirrup, mounted his horse, and yanked the bit tight in its mouth. It was a fresh mount, and he didn't have time for the black stallion to question his authority. The horse's eyes spread wide and it backed up, snorting. The others mounted. They were two kilometers from the camp.

Eleven horses now stood abreast—the ten Republican Guard and Ismael. He nudged his horse and they trotted forward, maintaining their file. Whatever else these men were, they were excellent horsemen. Ismael had no doubt they would shoot as well as they rode. His father had sent the best.

The plan to take Caleb by force wasn't really a plan at all. The tribe didn't have a defensive bone in their bodies. She would just take him and head due west, with or without the tribe's help. Eventually they would run into territory that Caleb recognized. Rebecca was only waiting for the sun to remove its heat.

She made her way around the rocks and climbed to the perch where she'd hidden her weapons and gear. She pulled out a leather saddle pack and flipped the flap up. Thirty seconds later she was dressed in the khakis, the Glock loaded and holstered. She gripped the rifle, hoisted the bag over her shoulder, and turned to leave. An orange sun glowed on the horizon. In twenty minutes it would be dark, and she would be riding her camel west with Caleb in tow.

She glanced at the camp below. The monks loitered about, at peace with the ending of yet one more day. A nuclear bomb could go off in London or New York or Tel Aviv and these people might never even hear about it. In some ways she coveted the simple lives they led. In other ways she pitied . . .

Something caught the corner of her eye and she turned slowly to the desert. What she saw stopped her heart. A line was moving towards them, black against the shimmering heat rising through the sunset, like a row of ants.

Rebecca instinctively jerked down, into cover.

Eleven dark horses marched towards them out of the red sky, in even step. She knew immediately that it was the Arab. The assassin had found them and was coming in force! Dear God, she had to save Caleb!

A cry suddenly sounded from the tribe, and Rebecca spun for it. Half a dozen monks ran for the edge of the camp, robes flowing behind. They were going to reveal themselves!

Rebecca jumped up and shouted at the monks. "Get back!" Didn't they see the horses? "Get back!"

But they didn't seem to hear, much less get back.

Hadane was among them—*leading* them, actually. They came out of the tents like pack rats now, the whole tribe running for the front edge of the camp, as if to welcome the Messiah himself. But this was not a savior. This was death, and it was marching with guns loaded.

Rebecca jumped over the rock. Below her Hadane yelled instructions at his tribe, motioning them to line up beside him. All of them, monks and women and children. A man with dark hair pushed in eagerly next to Hadane and she saw that it was Caleb. They had lost their minds en masse.

Rebecca ran across the boulders, heart slamming in her chest, desperate to take up a firing position close enough to stem the attack. *Dear God, help me.*

It occurred to her with that prayer that she didn't have a chance against eleven armed men. If she fired, she would give her position away. She could not save the tribe alone. She should be hiding, not scrambling to attempt an impossible rescue.

But Caleb was with them, wasn't he? And without Caleb, her mission would fail.

Rebecca ducked her head and leapt over the rocks.

———

The tents looked red in the setting sun's light, like a field of uniform boulders with pointed tops. Ismael swallowed against a dry throat and took a deep breath. He checked his safety one last time and glanced down the line of trotting horses.

The men stared ahead, soldiers proud at the edge of battle. Never mind that this battle was a foregone conclusion—they had been trained to sniff out a slaughter, and they could smell the blood now.

Ismael felt a bead of sweat break over his left eye and he let it run. His only prayer was that the Jew was still there.

"Ready to charge," he said. His voice sounded high with excitement. He kicked the stallion, and it broke into a gallop. The others followed immediately, lagging momentarily and then catching up.

They charged abreast, bearing down on the sleeping tents like an eagle rushing in for an unsuspecting mouse.

———

Rebecca bounded down the rock pile, yelling at the tribe.

"Get back! They're Arabs, you fools!"

A muted thunder rolled across the flats and she glanced up to see that the horses were in a charge.

"Get into the rocks!" she screamed.

But no one seemed to pay her any mind. They strung out in a long line, with wide spaces between each person. Hadane stood with his feet spread and planted, staring directly ahead with head tilted down, like a gunslinger in the desert, facing off with Pecos Pete.

Rebecca landed on a boulder ten meters from Hadane, then crouched behind another to give her cover. Caleb stood between her and the leader, copying the monk's stance. The Arabs' horses pounded towards them, less than a hundred meters off now.

Hadane threw his arms wide, as if he were on a cross. He twisted his head to face Caleb, and Rebecca saw his bright eyes clearly.

"Do you believe, Caleb?" the man yelled over the approaching roar. His eyes flashed and a maniacal grin split his face. He yelled again.

"Do you believe? Do you remember the day the sun stood still? The day the sea parted? Believe, Caleb! Believe!"

Caleb kept his eyes on the monk. He lifted his arms. The whole tribe stood with arms lifted now, like scarecrows in flowing robes, facing the horses. Several of the younger children chased about their legs, jumping, oblivious to the predicament that faced them. The others ignored them.

"Look into the eyes of God, Caleb! Look and believe!"

Hadane stretched his arms over his head, fists clenched, to form a *V*. He lifted his chin and cried out, "Belieeeeeve!" It sounded like a scream.

Rebecca watched, stunned. Caleb threw his head back and wailed at the sky. "I belieeeeeve!"

Rebecca spun to face the horses. The riders were in view, led by a black stallion, its rider's kaffiyeh streaming back in the wind. They galloped with rifles in one hand and reins in the other, leaning into their charge. Firing into the rogues would accomplish nothing until they slowed. When they did, she would kill as many as possible. But the tribe stood defenseless. They would be slaughtered, and in the end she would die with them. But still, she could not simply watch as the Arabs butchered such sweet, innocent . . .

Rebecca swore at her sentimentality and lined her sights on the leader. He would be the first.

Down below her, Hadane and Caleb were still screaming at the sky;

from the desert, the horses still thundered in. They showed no sign of slow-ing. Now they were thirty meters off, at a full gallop.

Rebecca's finger snugged the trigger to fire.

It struck her then that something was happening—something that felt disjointed in her mind's eye. The Arabs were not bringing their rifles down to fire. They were not bracing for any kind of impact. They were simply rush-ing forward, full tilt.

Rebecca saw this through her sight, and she pulled back slightly for a broader view.

Sound suddenly began to fade. Her ears felt stuffed with cotton. Caleb stood with his head cocked back and his mouth spread in a silent scream, wail-ing at the sky, but the sound did not register. Two horses were now barrel-ing down on him, no more than twenty paces off. She could see the flare of their nostrils, the sagging of their lips with each stride, their huge eyes peeled in horror.

But their riders . . . they weren't even *looking* at the tribe!

The lead rider suddenly reared back, three meters from Hadane. His black stallion clawed at the air. The other riders pulled up hard on taut reins. Their horses braked to a halt, protesting vigorously. The tribe stood still, arms stretched up and faces tilted to the heavens with Hadane, screaming in silence.

It occurred to Rebecca that she wasn't breathing. The horses stamped and the riders looked at the tents beyond the tribe. For a moment silence settled on the eerie scene and Rebecca stared in total disbelief. A buzz filled her mind.

A child laughed.

Rebecca heard the laugh and immediately saw the young girl from the corner of her eye, hiding behind her mother's tunic, peeking and smiling at the soldiers.

But the soldiers didn't hear her. Or see her.

"Where are they?" the leader demanded in Arabic. "Where are the tents?"

The buzz in Rebecca's head faded to a high-pitched pinging sound. What she saw was an absurdity that refused to connect with her mind. The Arabs did not see the tribe. Nor the tents.

"On the other side of these boulders," one of them replied.

"Shut up, you idiot! They were right here."

"The sun plays tricks in the desert," another said.

The leader walked his horse right up to Hadane, and then right past him, as if he didn't exist at all.

But Hadane did exist. And he was still screaming silently at the darkening sky.

A tremor shook Rebecca's limbs.

The leader stopped his horse behind Hadane, centimeters from his head. The other horses stamped forward on stiff legs, their flesh quivering, stepping through the tribe. The leader spun his horse around twice, his eyes darting around, scowling.

He kicked the stallion. "Hiyaa!"

The horse bolted. The rogues followed, galloping into the camp, past the tents, and through the other side. The sound of their hoofs faded into uncanny silence.

Rebecca crouched, every muscle strung tight.

A scream started, very soft, as though far away, and then swelled to full volume. Hadane's scream. Caleb's scream. All of them screaming the last syllable of *believe.* " . . . ieeeeeeve!"

It rushed to full volume and then ceased, as if someone had pulled the plug. They lowered their arms and looked around with wide eyes.

Some began to laugh.

Hadane grinned from ear to ear, and Rebecca slumped to her seat behind the boulder.

They were jumping around and dancing and laughing for ten minutes before Rebecca made her way out of the boulders to face them. The horde of Arabs had gone, in search of the tribe.

Caleb stood limp, staring out to the desert with his back to her, but Rebecca made for Hadane who was holding a small child and spinning in circles. He set the child down as she approached.

An odd resentment had settled on her in the Arabs' wake. In an inexplicable way, Caleb had proven himself to her with the demonstration of power, but she couldn't accept his proof. For one thing, her mind was still having difficulty believing what she had seen. The tribe had found a way to blind the Arabs to their presence, and even thinking about it made Rebecca feel stupid. Either way, she could not agree with Caleb's beliefs, regardless of his proof. He was a Christian. She was a Jew. Their beliefs clashed.

"I will take Caleb now," she said. "I have to go."

"Did you like it?"

He was talking about the Arabs. "Interesting. Madness."

"We were simply riding our bicycles," he said. "One day you should try to ride."

"Please. I've heard enough about bicycles and oceans and the eyes of God to keep me entertained for a month. I don't know what kind of sorcery you work, but I can see why you keep it in the desert. You dance and hop and carry on like children and you practice this magic. Frankly, it feels laced with madness. Now I have no choice but to take Caleb."

"If you take Caleb, you will take the madness," he said with a gentle smile.

A voice spoke behind Rebecca. "I will go."

She turned. Caleb stood looking at her with those impossibly green eyes. She felt oddly disarmed and averted her stare.

Caleb turned to Father Hadane. "I owe you my life, Father."

"You owe me nothing, my son. You only owe it to God to run when he asks you to run."

Caleb stepped forward and knelt in the sand, taking Hadane's hand. "I owe you my life." He kissed the elder's hand and stood. They looked at each other for a few long seconds.

"We have a long journey tonight," Rebecca said.

"You understand that you aren't *taking* me," Caleb said. "I am going. And I'm going because I'm meant to go."

"Yes, of course. Then let's go."

Hadane reached up and ran a thumb over Caleb's cheek. "Visit again, my boy. Remember what I told you. Be bold. Cowardice keeps man double minded, hesitating between two worlds. True faith abandons one option for the other. Hesitation is the death of faith."

"Yes," Caleb replied. "What's the use of asking, if we don't dare ask for anything we can't satisfy in our own power? I will remember, Father."

"Good."

They hugged. Miriam led two camels out to them—Rebecca's and another for Caleb. Had they prepared for this already?

Five minutes later, after Miriam had told them which stars to follow and which mountains to keep in sight, Rebecca led Caleb out of the camp, leaving a throng of well-wishers waving in the last light.

It was going to be a long journey, and in all honesty, Rebecca wasn't even sure where they were going.

26

DARKNESS HAD BLACKENED THE DESERT for a full hour before Ismael pulled up on the far side of the boulders. He stared forward into the night, blinking. A slight tremble shook his hands. She had escaped again.

The caravan's tracks had been everywhere, but they hadn't led anywhere. The troop had marched the perimeter once already, with the tracker, Hasam, searching in the failing light for the signs of a caravan's exit into the desert. Nothing. Their horses were nearly dead; they had no choice but to stop for at least a few hours.

Ismael slid from his stallion. "We will camp here and leave at midnight. Water and bed the horses."

"Should I send the Jeep back around the backside?" Captain Asid asked. "The tracks are everywhere on that side. They still could be hiding."

"No. They couldn't have hidden so quickly. They're gone. We can't afford to spend the fuel."

The captain looked back into the night. "I could have sworn I saw—"

"You saw boulders, Captain. The desert plays tricks. The Jew is gone. Our objective now is the monastery. Get the horses watered."

The captain turned his sweaty face away and barked the order to set camp.

Ismael slung his saddle from his horse and dumped it on a rock. If the Jew had left for the monastery with Caleb, he might miss them both. There was now the possibility that she could reach the monastery and be gone before he arrived. If the godforsaken horses had any more strength, he would make a run for it now.

The men dismounted and struck a quick camp. They had used nearly half of their water supply. Two more days and they would be out. They would have to swing by the springs he'd passed through nearly a week ago now.

Ismael spit into the darkness and closed his eyes. The anger had lodged in his gut like a bitter pill, refusing to budge. During his five years with the intifada he had been in a dozen situations that would make an ordinary man cry with frustration. But none had produced the heat that flowed through his veins now. He wasn't sure how to deal with the devastation he felt. He only knew that he couldn't allow the men behind him to see. They would never understand. To be Arab and Muslim was one thing. The Egyptians did a fine job of being Arab and Muslim. But to be Arab and Muslim and Palestinian and to see your own brother butchered like a cow by a Jew was another thing altogether. The Syrian Republican Guard had some of the Middle East's best trained and best armed soldiers, but not even they had the fuel of hate driving them like the Palestinian forces did. Nothing could motivate like the death of a brother or the loss of a home.

Ismael took a deep settling breath. The Jew was killing him with this cancer of hate that ate at his gut. He would track Rebecca down until his own death if he had to.

He reached for his pack and pulled out the satellite phone. It was time to tell Abu the news.

———

Professor Zakkai paced in the monastery's kitchen, their makeshift op-center. It had been four days since Rebecca's last contact. Even Samuel, a trained soldier, had lost his steadfast patience judging by the sweat on his face. Avraham was the only one who didn't seem too worried, and then only because the prospect of losing Rebecca obviously didn't bother him.

Zakkai, on the other hand, was literally begging God for her return—she was not only a dear friend, but she might hold the key to the Ark. He felt like his stomach had been cinched into a small knot.

"We should send a search party after her," he said to Samuel. "She's obviously in trouble."

"Or dead," Avraham said.

"We can't afford to send any men," Samuel said. "Not only do we have no clue where to send them, but we can't afford to weaken our defenses here."

"Defenses for what?" Zakkai demanded. "There *is* no threat! We're sitting here on our hands, while she's out there, bleaching in the desert. How can we *not* send a team out?"

"To where? The desert is huge. She left nothing but tracks, Doctor. Tracks that are blown away by the wind. Don't worry, if anybody knows how to survive, it's Rebecca and Michael. I've served with a thousand men, and not a single one of them holds a candle to either of them. Rebecca's alive, and the only reason she's not here is because her mission requires her to be somewhere out there."

"Ha." Avraham wore a smile. "You hope to marry her someday, eh, Samuel? She's gotten into your head with her pretty face. She's a *woman!* If you hold her over any man in the army, you're a fool!"

"Don't be an idiot! She has a record that puts yours to shame. And she handled you nicely enough, didn't she?"

Avraham scowled. "She did not *handle* me. I gave in to her authority for the sake of the mission—there's a difference. One day you'll see that. It's been four days; our agreement called for only three days. We should have killed the hostages and left yesterday."

"We'll leave when I say," Samuel said. "We wait."

"We can't kill the hostages," Zakkai said.

Avraham looked at him with a raised brow. "On the contrary, Professor, we *must* kill the hostages. How long will it take for them to spread the word of our little exercise here? An hour? Two? We might never make it back to the Red Sea, much less Israel."

"There'll be no killing of hostages," Samuel said. "We take our chances without the blood of innocents on our hands."

"You can't be serious. This is a military operation."

"We're here for the Ark, not for killing."

They stared each other down for a few long seconds, and Zakkai wondered if Avraham would snap one of these times. The man wore a pistol—maybe they should remove it.

Avraham suddenly turned to Zakkai. "This mission is turning bad,

Professor. The longer we wait, the higher the chance of our discovery. As long as we're waiting, we should use the dynamite and begin excavations immediately."

"Dynamite could harm the Ark," Zakkai said.

"Not if it's used carefully. In the service, we placed charges on bridges so that they would collapse only when used with a heavy load. We could blow only those walls and floors that wouldn't compromise the structure of the building, and only with enough dynamite to make pickax work easy. No harm."

Zakkai weighed the suggestion. In truth, he had already considered using dynamite, in spite of Rebecca's order not to.

"And if we do happen to find the Ark," Samuel said, "do we have the evacuation plan?"

Zakkai shook his head. "No, but Solomon has it. He told me this morning that he's confident the prime minister will lend a submarine."

The others looked at him, surprised.

"Yes, Ben Gurion is more of a friend than you might think. Goldstein, on the other hand, is not. He has evidently already started to form a coalition against the Ark being brought to Jerusalem, if it is found."

"They know?" Avraham asked.

"They know we're looking."

"God help us if this gets out," Samuel said.

"Either way, we should begin laying the explosives," Avraham said.

Samuel hesitated. "No. We'll give them another twenty-four hours. Then we'll talk about alternatives." He turned and walked out.

27

THE NIGHT HAD PRODUCED A WEARY plodding that had left Rebecca numbed. She led, to the front and to the left of Caleb's camel, staring at the rising moon, feeling awkward in their silence. She had no idea what he was thinking back there, and she hardly had the courage to ask. As it was, they had talked enough in the previous two days to leave her with a headache. At least that's what she told herself.

But there was more, wasn't there? It wasn't just her head that was hurting. It was further down, in her chest, where her heart belonged. Where a hole now struggled to push blood through her veins. In all honesty that's how it felt, like a vacant black space, and she wasn't thrilled to feel it.

He made no overtures. The moon rose and began to sink again and he said absolutely nothing. They had just come from a dream world where anomalies and impossibilities took center stage, and Caleb had settled into an austere silence that seemed to rub salt in her wounds. She didn't have any wounds, of course. She was simply exhausted beyond reckoning. That's what she told herself. But still it hurt like she had been wounded. A hole had been drilled through her chest.

Rebecca had looked back once and caught him looking at her, wearing a small smile. She had grunted and faced forward. She almost spoke to him a dozen—two dozen—times. But always the words refused to surface past her throat. And as the time stretched on, the prospect of speaking to him dwindled. She wasn't sure what she might have lost back there at the camp, but she still had her pride.

She looked back at him again, much later, and saw that he had slumped over on the camel, asleep. She slowed her own camel until they walked abreast. Only then, when he made no move, did she nonchalantly study him. His head barely bounced with the camel's slow gait. His black hair fell over his cheek and his lower lip stuck out further than normal, relaxed in sleep. His hands still held the reins gently—large hands accustomed to work. If not for his peculiarities, Caleb might be the kind of man she would consider spending time with. He was gentle and very kind and he would make a good father. Perhaps a good lover—

She blinked and looked back at the moon. It was absurd, of course. He was also a fool. And a Christian.

Her heart thumped unnecessarily hard. She nudged her camel forward and swore she'd never think such mad thoughts again.

If you take Caleb, you will take the madness, Hadane had said.

She answered him in a whisper. "The madness is in Israel, you old bat. I've been surrounded by it all my life. This is child's play."

She dozed in the early morning hours, waking every half-hour to verify their course. They entered the foothills as the horizon grayed with the first morning light. She recognized the terrain now—they were back on the same path she'd followed Caleb on. The spring should be another two hours ahead. She glanced back and saw that Caleb still slept.

The next time she looked back, nearly an hour later, he was awake.

"Good morning," he said, smiling.

"Morning." She faced forward, glad for the break in endless silence.

His camel strode up next to hers. "We're back on the same path I came," he said. "There's a spring ahead."

She looked over and offered a forced smile. "You doubted me? I learned to navigate by the stars before I was ten."

"Not bad. If you can navigate your life as well as you navigate camels, you'll do well."

"Meaning what?"

"Meaning what I said."

His cryptic talk had started already, and Rebecca wasn't sure if she hated it or loved it. But his voice carried a strange thread of comfort, and maybe for this alone she continued.

"You are preoccupied with finding the path of life, aren't you?"

He looked to the hills ahead and his smile faded. "I'm preoccupied with

Christ now. He is the path, and I've found it again. It's easy to miss, you know. Because it's quite narrow. I walked it as a child, but somehow I wandered to the side. I never abandoned it, you understand, but what was once so clear and evident became foggy, and I lost sight of the path. Then I think I lost interest." He shrugged. "It's hard to be passionate about something you can't see. Hadane helped me see again. The way of Christ has become obvious to me again."

"Just like that, huh? Like flipping a light switch."

"Yes. Just like that. And Christ is the light."

"The Nazarene." She shook her head and turned away. "The Jews crucified your man two thousand years ago, and Christians have been after us ever since. You almost wiped us out in World War II."

"That was not us, but I am so very sorry."

"It was Christians. You're not a Christian?"

"Not if that's a Christian. I'm an apprentice of Jesus. I am his bride, his lover, his slave. His way is to love, to turn the cheek, to die for another."

"So then you would die for me?" The question came without thought and she immediately regretted it.

He looked at her with those green pools for eyes and it made her feel funny. "Yes."

"Well, no offense, but I don't think I would die for you. I would die for Israel."

"That's a start. So did the Nazarene."

They traveled in silence for a while.

"You believe the Ark is really at the monastery?" he asked.

"I think there's a good chance."

"God's presence does not dwell in the Ark. You do realize that, don't you?"

"No, I don't realize that," she said. "You don't believe the book of Exodus?"

"Exodus is only the beginning of the story. You don't believe Isaiah?"

"Of course I do."

"Then you know about the Messiah."

She paused. "I am here because of the Messiah," she said.

"So am I."

She knew what he meant, of course. They fell silent. The sun was hot behind them now.

"When we get to the monastery, will you help me search for the Ark?" Rebecca asked.

He didn't answer right away. She was aware that she had said *me*, instead of *us*, and it made her feel good. In a strange way she wanted Caleb to help her.

"I don't know yet," he said.

"I would appreciate it if you made up your mind."

"If I don't, will you try to force me?"

She looked at him and saw that he was smiling. She couldn't help returning the smile. The notion of her forcing him seemed absurd. "I will tie you down and tickle you until you confess," she said.

He raised a brow. "Then I would have to tickle you back, until you swear never to tickle me again." He lifted a hand and wiggled his fingers. "These are very good ticklers, you know."

It was a ridiculous moment and they stared at each other, caught by the exchange. He suddenly snorted in a short laugh. The sound was so strange that Rebecca chuckled.

"Oh, that was an appealing sound," she said.

"Yes, I'm trying very hard to appeal to you."

They began to laugh aloud, as much to break the awkwardness as for the humor of the exchange. Their laughter fed more laughter. The reprieve came to Rebecca like a desperately needed rain on a blistering hot day.

They came to the spring twenty minutes later, still chuckling now and then with offhanded comments. If Caleb was as mad as she had thought, his madness was infectious.

Umbrella-shaped mimosa trees formed a ring around two small brown pools, each roughly three meters across. A small cliff broken by several inlets formed a barrier on the south side, so that the spring remained shaded for most of the day—its only salvation, Rebecca assumed. Through the morning hours, they had left the white salts of the desert and entered the sandy soil of the hills. Vegetation grew in small pockets, scattered haphazardly over the hills. She had passed this way six days earlier, thinking that she was headed into the land of the dead. Now it all looked fresh and full of life.

Caleb reached the spring first. He dropped to the ground and immediately came around to her camel. He lifted a hand up to help her. Rebecca's first inclination was to wave him off—she hardly needed help dismounting from a camel, especially from a man. She'd served in a man's war and bested most of them; if anything, she should be the one helping him. She couldn't recall ever allowing a man to help her like this.

But the thought was immediately supplanted by another—that she should take his hand because he *was* a man. Because this was not about helping, but about Caleb being a man and she being a woman. Both notions flashed through her mind in under a second, and she reached her hand out to his.

His grip was strong and warm. Their eyes met for a moment and she thought that maybe she really was losing her mind. It was the fact that she was hesitating, sitting on her camel with her hand in his, staring into his eyes. She should be dismounting!

She slid off the hump and landed lightly on the sand. "Thank you," she said, unable to hide her smile.

"You are welcome."

They let their camels drink in silence. A very light breeze blew through the canopy over their heads. In a way she stood at the crossroads of absurdities, she thought. She a Jew, he a Christian, both watching their camels slurp at muddy water in the middle of nowhere, while the end of the world loomed somewhere nearby. In Jerusalem.

Then suddenly something else was thrown into the crossroads. A small sound that didn't belong. She lifted her head.

It came again, a light pounding.

Hoofs!

Adrenaline flooded her veins. Caleb jerked his head up—he'd heard it now as well.

Rebecca scanned the spring and assessed their situation quickly. They couldn't outrun horses. They could make for the breaks in the cliff, thirty meters off, but their tracks . . .

"Quick! Take the camels into the cliffs." She grabbed a blanket off her camel and swept it across the sand.

"Where—"

"Go!" she snapped. "To the cliffs."

Caleb yanked on the reins and dragged the two reluctant camels around the pools. Rebecca followed, erasing the tracks behind her as well as she could. The horses came into view just as they entered the break in the rock. It was the Arab troop!

Rebecca cast one last glance over the covered tracks. She had no idea where the canyon behind her led. If the Arabs followed them, it would come down to a firefight. Her only hope was that the Arabs were heading directly for the monastery.

Then again, that would be a problem as well, wouldn't it? They had horses and would easily reach the monastery first.

Rebecca pulled back into the rocks, breathing hard now. She grabbed her camel from Caleb. "Hurry! We have to take up a position that'll give us an advantage under fire!" she whispered.

"Who are they?"

"The Arabs from the desert. I'm obviously not the only one who considers the Ark important."

The small canyon cut fifty meters into the cliffs before angling to the left. Large boulders crowded the sandy bottom, and the walls on either side rose jagged. They turned a second corner and pulled up. A narrow path led from the canyon up to the plateau, two stories above them. Rebecca dropped her reins, ran up the path, saw that it ended in the plain, which offered no cover, and ran back down.

"We can't risk getting caught in the open with camels," she said breathlessly. "We'll hide here and take our chances. Leave the camels in those rocks." She pointed to a pile of boulders mid-canyon.

"What about you?"

"Don't worry about me. You just get out of sight and stay out of sight until I call for you. Hopefully they'll pass. We'll figure things out from there. Hurry!"

She already had the rifle in her hands, and she spun for the opposite side.

She couldn't do anything about the camels. If one of the Arabs walked into this part of the canyon, they would find a mouthful of lead. The unsilenced shot would bring on a full firefight, but she would have to take that chance. Better here than in the open.

28

THE REPUBLICAN GUARD RODE THEIR horses hard, beyond the point of exhaustion, only because Ismael knew about the spring they now approached. Their water was gone. They had abandoned the two Jeeps in the foothills, loaded the munitions on the horses, watered them well, and struck directly for the spring. The tracker had estimated that the camel tracks they followed were less than several hours old by the signs. So then, the Jew could not be far ahead—camels were slow beasts. With any luck they would catch them before the monastery.

Ismael reined his horse up at the edge of the spring and dropped into the sand. The others crashed in around him. They let the horses stamp up to the waters, sweaty and snorting.

"Another run like that and we'll kill them," Asid said.

"But they aren't dead, are they? If we fail with our mission, on the other hand, you might be." Ismael was studying the banks as he spoke. The camels had skirted the twin ponds, dragging something. His pulse quickened.

"How far till—"

"Water the horses," Ismael snapped. "I'll be back."

He slid his rifle from the scabbard, checked the load, and walked around the pools. The tracks led from the oasis to the cliffs, then into a canyon. He edged around the corner and saw that whatever they had been dragging had been lifted. A weak attempt to cover tracks. An attempt that a soldier as experienced as the Jew would make only in a hurry.

Ismael gripped the rifle in both hands and studied the sandy ground. The tracks disappeared around a bend. With a parting glance back at the oasis, he slipped into the canyon and hurried for a rock outcropping this side of the bend. Except for his steady breathing and the gentle murmur of voices from the watering hole behind him, the air lay still. He made his way up the canyon, running from rock to rock, keeping to the south wall.

At the next bend, he saw the large island of boulders in the middle of the canyon. And beyond the boulders, a path that snaked up a dead end. He thought immediately that he'd been too late. It must be a back way that Caleb knew, which would make sense if he'd lived in these hills all his life. But still, there was the fact that they had tried to cover their tracks, which meant that they might be only a few kilometers ahead. He should get back to the horses. The Jew would be a sitting duck in the open. Not to mention that camels—

A tan head suddenly eased out from behind the large boulders, thirty meters ahead.

A camel!

Ismael jerked back, his heart suddenly slamming in his chest. They were still in the canyon! They had tried to fool him, but now one shot to the head of their camels and they would be on foot.

Another thought crashed through Ismael's mind: if he had been seen, which he would not put past the Jew, she would know that he had seen the camel. She may have been holding off a shot, thinking that he might see the path and leave. But now she had seen him jerk back—the next time he wouldn't be so lucky. Speed. He had to act fast, before she expected him to.

Ismael ducked and ran into the canyon. He slid down at the base of the boulders, expecting a shot to ring out.

But none did. He inched around, keeping low at the base. The camels stood dumbly in the sun, not twenty meters off. Two quick shots and the Jew would be as good as dead. He pushed himself to one knee and lifted his rifle.

It was the first time Rebecca had seen the Arab's full face. He was Ismael. Son of Abu Ismael, brother of Hamil. She knew that because she had studied Hamil before killing him. Ismael, Hamil's mourning brother, had shouted obscenities at a camera crew once, naming Rebecca as a witch who was poisoning the land. His hate for her ran deep, and she hardly blamed him. She knew how losing a brother or a sister felt.

If it had been any other face peering around that cliff wall, she might have pulled the trigger. But to see Ismael here, deep in the desert so far from Palestine—her head spun with questions.

And then he jerked back. One glance and she saw that the camel had walked out. He knew! She swallowed. So it would come down to a firefight after all. *Dear God, favor Isaac.*

Ismael acted quickly, diving to the rocks before she could regain a target. And then he rose to one knee, filling her sights. He was going after the camels! She eased the slack on the trigger. *I'm sorry for your brother, Ismael. Now it's your turn to die as well.*

And maybe you as well, Rebecca. When the gunshot reaches the oasis, the soldiers will come. She had no choice.

Movement to her right caught her attention half an ounce from the hammer fall. It was the shape of a man, walking into play, and she knew in one unutterable moment of horror that it was Caleb.

She shifted her eye without losing Ismael and stared in shock. Caleb was walking towards the Arab! Dressed in a white tunic and strolling as if they had planned to meet all along.

Ismael rose to his feet, his rifle trained unwavering on Caleb's chest. Caleb stopped three meters from the Arab.

Why Rebecca didn't pull the trigger then, she would never understand. She told herself that it was because by coming out, Caleb was telling her not to. Ismael was standing there, his barrel pointed at Caleb, ready to send a slug through his heart with a twitch of his finger, and Rebecca remained frozen, like a block of ice.

"You are the Arab?" Caleb's voice sounded softly down the canyon, a decibel above a whisper. In its wake absolute stillness. Rebecca had stopped breathing.

"Why are you trying to kill me?" Caleb asked.

Rebecca slowly lifted her head from the rifle and looked at Caleb, twenty meters from her position. He stood with his arms limp at his sides— like a child.

Ismael took a step back, transfixed by the sight. His eyes were wide, trained over the barrel, but he didn't shoot.

"My Master once taught that the peacemakers would be blessed," Caleb said.

"Shut up!" Ismael's voice echoed in high pitch. His eyes jerked around the canyon. Why didn't he shoot? Because he knew that he was being watched. If Caleb had walked out to him, someone else surely saw him as well. If he shot, he, too, would be shot. He knew that, Rebecca thought.

Caleb lowered his head and looked at the man past arching brows. He took a step forward, then stopped.

"You know, when I was a child I sang once and a thousand people fell over. I closed my eyes and sang a simple song in Ge'ez, and when I opened my eyes, they were all on the ground." Caleb's voice held a slight tremor. "Do you know why, my friend? It was because the Spirit of God breathed over them. Man sometimes has a hard time dealing with the breath of God."

"Don't be a fool! Don't take another step! Where's the witch?"

So he knew it was she, Rebecca thought.

"You mean Rebecca? She's no more a witch than I am a magician. We're simply people. She's one that God's pursuing, and I'm one that God has caught. And that means I have a little power." He paused and lifted a hand slowly. "Now don't shoot. I'm only lifting my hand. But you know yesterday we lifted our hands above our heads like this"—he lifted both hands—"and you rode your horses right through our camp."

Ismael blinked rapidly several times. "You're lying! We saw no camp."

"Yes. That's the point. You were blinded, I think. Either that or we were made invisible, but I think blinded is more accurate because that happened before, in the Bible, you know. That's what Hadane knows; that's what I had forgotten. We still live in the time of the Bible, between Christ and the Apocalypse."

"What are you talking about? You're talking nonsense!"

"No, I'm not. Really, I'm not." Caleb lowered his hands slowly. "Do you want to see the power?"

Ismael didn't respond. He was still frozen.

"You know, this is amazing," Caleb said, looking down at his hands. "I'm really not sure if I even have the power to show you. To be totally honest I'm standing here terrified." He looked up. "Really, I am. It feels like I'm stepping

off a cliff here. One foot is over and the other is still anchored and I'm trying
to decide whether or not to jump. What do you think, should I jump?"

Ismael just stared at him, his face now ashen.

"*Courage, my son.* That's what Father Hadane said," Caleb said. "Courage,
my son. Cowardice keeps man double minded, hesitating between two
worlds. True faith abandons one option for the other. You ever wonder what
true faith is? I may be talking as if I was full of faith, but really, I'm trembling
under this robe. Look at it." He looked down at the hem, and Rebecca saw
that he was right. She could see the quiver in the gown from where she
crouched! The man was mad.

"So you see, I think I've just stepped off the cliff and I'm free-falling now,"
Caleb said, looking up at the Arab. "Now the question is whether or not I will
land hard and die."

Ismael just stared at him, completely off guard by the strange speech.
They stood like that for some time, long enough for a bead of sweat to leak
down Rebecca's cheek and drip on her thumb. Her palms were wet and her
breathing shallow, and she just stared at the two men facing off, immobilized.

"Are you going to shoot me?" Caleb asked.

It was an impossible moment. The Arab gripped his weapon, knuckles
white and shaking. But he did not fire.

"Then if you aren't going to shoot me, I think you should sit down,"
Caleb said. "I'm falling off a cliff; the least you can do is sit."

For a moment Ismael stood unmoving. He suddenly began to shake. His
face twisted in a sort of anguish, and he staggered back one step. His mouth
fell open in a silent cry of agony. For a terrible moment Rebecca pitied him.

He suddenly fell to his rump, with a dull thump. He still held the rifle,
and his hands pressed against its stock, white with pressure. He was trying
to pull the trigger, she thought. He was actually trying to shoot!

Caleb stared, his eyes wide with wonder.

The Arab was trembling all over now. He looked like he had acciden-
tally fallen on a high-voltage power line. Tears broke from his eyes and ran
down both cheeks. He craned his head back in agony, his mouth gaping and
his eyes clenched in a silent cry. The gun fell from his hands, and he slowly
drew his knees into his chest, like a fetus.

Rebecca swallowed, struck by a deep empathy. Ismael was being consumed with sorrow, she thought. He was crying for his brother—for his land, for his life—and suddenly Rebecca was fighting a balloon of sorrow that was trying to rise through her own throat. Tears blurred her vision and she wiped at them quickly.

Dear Ismael, I am so sorry.

The Arab toppled over to his right side and lay still.

The canyon hung in silence for a few long moments. Caleb looked down at Ismael, wide-eyed; the Arab looked unconscious; Rebecca hardly dared to breathe.

But an opportunity had presented itself.

She vaulted the rock and landed on the sand, facing them. "Let's go!" she whispered. "The others will come looking. We have to hurry!"

She grabbed the reins of both camels and tugged them towards the path which rose to the plateau above. Her mind buzzed like a tuning fork, stunned by the events. But they had to flee, didn't they? Yes, of course. *Dear Ismael, I am sorry?* She had thought that? How could she think that? Rebecca grunted and shook her head.

It occurred to her that she was alone on the path. She spun back. Caleb stood, planted where she'd left him, facing the Arab.

"Caleb! Hurry! We have to get out of here!"

He hesitated one moment longer and then followed in an uneasy gait. Pulling off a disappearing act with the tribe, at the side of Father Hadane, was one thing, Rebecca thought. Now he had done this on his own, and she wasn't sure he knew how he'd done it.

She sure didn't know.

The path dumped out into rolling hills, and she mounted her camel. Whatever had happened, his God was turning out to be not so bashful. Even so, they would be lucky to reach the monastery ahead of the Arabs. And either way there would be a firefight.

29

"SHEIK AYYUB SPEAKS FOR PALESTINE when he interprets the Koran's prophecy to say that Israel's second corruption of the land will be their attempt to retake the Temple," Muhammed Du'ad said.

The commander of all Palestinian Authority forces faced Abu Ismael and spoke past a frown. He'd come to Damascus in the night at Abu's urgent call. General Nasser sat on the sofa to Abu's right, watching with legs crossed. For the first time, they had shared the scenario of the Ark's possible discovery, and it was playing exactly as Nasser had predicted.

"If you don't believe that, you don't appreciate Islam the way that the Palestinian does," Du'ad said. "The Jews will try to retake the *Haram al-Sharif*—that much any half-witted Muslim knows. The only question is when. Now you tell me that they have the Ark, and you think we should wait? Their Ark will require a temple, you know that as well as I!"

"I didn't say they have the Ark," Abu said. "I said they seem to think they have something. It *could* be the Ark. And if you follow Ayyub's interpretation of prophetic events, then you also believe that the prophet Jesus will come again and lead the Muslims against the Jews."

"Yes, of course."

"So then perhaps we should wait to see if this Messiah of ours will come." It sounded absurd, referring to the Christian Jesus as Islam's savior, but the Koran was quite plain on at least that much. All three major religions had a savior—a Messiah so to speak. It was a fact not lost on most scholars that for Islam and Christianity that savior was the same prophet, Jesus. The same man that the third religion, Judaism, had crucified. In a strange way it united Christianity and Islam, though only in theory. In practice, the Christians were uniting with Jews. He could never understand why the West seemed so eager to embrace the very people who had killed their God.

Either way all three religions claimed their savior, and in all three cases that savior would come to the Temple Mount. For the Jews, a Messiah to deliver them from Islam; for Islam, a savior to destroy the Jews; for Christians, the savior to come a second time to destroy both Jews and Islam. How had the world come to this?

Du'ad stared at Abu with dark eyes. "The prophet Jesus will emerge in his time. Until then we will make our own future. Ayyub also teaches that God has brought the Jews to Palestine so that they can be destroyed with one swipe of the sword. Does this mean we are to let them walk over us until the day we rise up and destroy them? No. If we discover that the Jews have even a *thought* of retaking the Temple Mount, we have no alternative but to defend it to the death. No Muslim leader in all of history has ever willingly abandoned sovereignty of a holy place. It would make them a pariah to the Arab world."

Abu nodded. He was right, of course. And he believed that the other Arab states would agree without argument.

"Well, Colonel, we did not bring you here to debate. We have no intention of allowing Jerusalem to fall into Jewish hands. And whatever you think, we aren't fools. We know the importance of the *Haram al-Sharif.*"

Abu stood and walked to the large rotating globe to the left of his desk. He spun it and watched the marble inlaid countries turn. "You know my son, Ismael, perhaps better than I do. He's not a man given to failure. The Jews have eluded him so far, but he's a capable man who is now well armed. It's unlikely these Jews will ever return from Ethiopia. It's even more unlikely they will return with the Ark. But in that unlikely event . . ." He let the sentence trail off.

Du'ad's jaw clenched.

"How many in your force now?" Abu asked. They were getting down to the meat of the matter, and Abu preferred it over philosophy.

"A hundred thousand."

"How many are properly armed?"

"Forty-five thousand in organized militia. Armed with machine guns, light antitank missiles, grenades . . . some land mines and explosives. We also have over five hundred Strela and Stinger surface-to-air missiles."

It was far more than most of the West assumed by watching television, but nothing compared to the armed weight of their enemy.

"And how quickly could you mobilize?"

"Twenty-four hours. Our best units are always on alert—Force Seventeen. But we are powerless without the Arab states."

"Perhaps. But if the Ark of the Covenant is brought to Jerusalem, you will not be alone. I am sure of that."

Abu glanced at Nasser who nodded. They had come up with a plan a year ago over coffee, and the air force commander had surreptitiously dubbed it *Dirty Harry,* a reference to his favorite American movie, in which a cop played by Clint Eastwood shot first and asked questions later. They hadn't thought at the time that they would be discussing it as a viable plan this soon.

General Nasser unfolded his legs, stood, and walked to a flask of hot tea, which he poured. He took a deep breath. "Your small force may be the key to the defeat of Israel, Colonel." He turned and faced Du'ad. "Not through the slow pestering of an intifada, but in a full-scale attack. In fact, without you, I'm not sure we *could* prevail. Israel may be small, but it contains as much firepower as all of our states together. Not to mention a tactical nuclear arsenal that we know they would use if forced."

"We tie them in knots with a few stones," Du'ad objected. "You don't think you can crush them with your collective armies? Our problem is that Arabs are unwilling to unite."

"No. I don't think we could defeat them." Nasser hesitated. "Not without you. Israel has three Achilles heels, despite their power. Their geography, their dependence on reserves, and their dependence on air power. Their geography because the Arab world now has a country *within* Israel's borders: Palestine, which has slowly accumulated, as you say, forty-five thousand armed troops, at the heart of Israel."

Nasser turned and paced with his arms behind his back. "Secondly, their dependence on reserves because it takes them twenty-four hours to activate them. For the first twenty-four hours of any crisis, Israel is scurrying about, activating its soldiers and bringing its pilots from their synagogues to their airfields. Once they have their air force fully active, they present a huge obstacle to our forces. But only if they get their fighters into the sky. That is their third weakness—their dependence on their air force."

Du'ad nodded slowly, understanding.

"In the war of '73 they discovered our plans before we could strike. They demolished us from the air. The way to win a war with Israel, my friend, is to cripple their airfields from the inside. One massive attack that begins on the fourth front—at the heart of Israel—through the deployment of Palestinian soldiers to destroy their airfields before they can activate their reserves. Only then do we come in from the other three fronts—Egypt on the south, Jordan and Saudi on the east, and Syria on the north." He smiled. "I call it *Dirty Harry*. We run and shoot, and ask questions later."

Du'ad blinked. "Give me two days and I will have a thousand four-man teams, armed with missiles, within striking distance of their airfields. Most of their air bases are within forty kilometers of Palestinian territory. A day and a night by foot. An hour by car."

"Exactly. But the mobilization would have to be very quiet. They are very—"

"You don't need to tell me how the Jews fight, General. I live in Palestine, remember? I have men who can work their way deep into Israel. And I have another forty thousand who can take to the streets with more than stones. But without a full-scale armed attack on our heels, I would be throwing their lives away. We would last a day, destroy a few airfields, and then be slaughtered."

"The Israelis don't believe that your scattered forces could deliver a coordinated attack from multiple locations," Nasser said.

"Three years ago they were right," Du'ad said. "Today they are wrong, and to our good fortune, they don't know it yet."

"How long can you keep your men in place near the airfields without detection?"

Du'ad shrugged. "A day on some airfields. Three days on the ones with cover nearby. A week if we are very lucky. We run patrols regularly and in some cases have arms cached behind lines."

"That would suffice. We are interested in their airfields and the roads to the bases, Colonel. You understand? If we delay their reservists from making it to their bases and their fighters from taking off, our chances are very good. But if you fail, our own armies could very well be destroyed at the border. We depend on you as much as you depend on us."

Muhammed Du'ad stared at Nasser for a very long time, expressionless. "You are serious about this? What do you want me to tell the council?"

Abu spoke up. "For the moment we are only talking. Exploring our options. But any plan to engage Israel would depend on you. We have brought you to ask if you are prepared and willing."

"I am not only prepared and willing, I demand it," Du'ad said.

Abu nodded. "We have drawn up the plan in detail." He took a folder off the desk and handed it to Du'ad. "There's a specific list of targets and a coordinated outline of attack for your benefit. Subject to your approval, of course. In addition to air bases, the plan recommends the seizure of the electric power plant at Hedera, the oil refineries of Haifa, the chemical tanks of Gelilot, and the telephone company in Bezek. In one single coordinated attack. Confusion must cripple their mobilization. This plan may not leave this room."

Du'ad took the folder and glanced inside.

"The plan is sound, Colonel," Abu said. "Our only question is whether we are willing to trust the fate of our collective armed forces to a small band of Palestinian soldiers."

"My soldiers aren't vagabond *Ashbals*, trained in the desert without enemies, General. We have cut our teeth on daily conflict. Palestine is our homeland, and we know it better than we know our wives. We will die for Palestine."

"Yes, but dying is not the objective. Destroying Israel is."

"No, General. If the Ark is coming to Jerusalem, then protecting the holy site is our objective. We are first of all Muslims. Whether we die or destroy Israel in the process is secondary."

Abu stared at him, struck by the simple logic. War had a way of distilling the issues to a few basic realities. Colonel Muhammed Du'ad had lived through his share of war, and his realities were crystal clear. For that Abu envied him. In a strange way he hoped the Jews did bring the Ark to Jerusalem. Ismael and Du'ad would then have their war as they wanted it: to the death. Islam would finally have its day. One way or another, someone's prophecy would be fulfilled.

"You are right. And I would fight by your side, my friend."

Du'ad dipped his head after a moment. "What shall I tell the council?" he asked again.

"Tell it to be prepared. Tell it that I am consulting with our neighbors today, beginning with Jordan—if Jordan agrees, I believe the rest will as well. If we have a consensus, then I will send word. Prepare your men, but do not deploy them until you hear from me. And then they must only take their positions. You understand that this all depends on the highly speculative event that these Jews find the Ark and bring it to Jerusalem? We aren't starting a war, Colonel. We're merely preparing for the possibility of war. In the event war is justified, our efforts must be perfectly timed. If you attack prematurely, many good Muslims will die without purpose."

"No death is without purpose, but I understand your point."

Abu eyed him. "We have to keep this strictly silent. We don't need another Yom Kippur War." The Israelis had sniffed a rat then and launched a preemptive strike that had crushed Egypt's air force.

General Nasser cleared his throat. "We know that some of your leaders would find it difficult to resist stirring things up with rumors. But doing so would also stir up the Jews and neutralize our plan. We depend on absolute silence about the Ark. It's not an issue of avoidance—it's integral to our strategy."

Du'ad didn't respond to the insinuation.

"Allah will be glorified," he said.

30

HOW THEY'D MANAGED TO BEAT the Arabs to the monastery, Rebecca couldn't know. Maybe the other soldiers hadn't discovered Ismael as quickly as she'd assumed they would. She had led Caleb in through the back, and her soldiers couldn't have appeared more relieved.

Zakkai had hovered over her like a father, beside himself to see her with Caleb in tow. His key had arrived, and he could obviously hardly wait to give him a try. He couldn't seem to look away from the man. He ordered them to eat and drink—there was much work ahead.

Rebecca immediately dispatched guards to the perimeter and a sniper to the tower. The Arabs would be coming at any time.

They sat in the kitchen with Samuel, and she quickly ran down the events of Michael's death and her subsequent tracking of the caravan. She left out details then, of course. There was no way to describe what she'd seen without sounding half mad. She had taken Caleb; that's what mattered. He was here. They had their key.

Rebecca avoided eye contact with Caleb for the simple reason that she was afraid that looking into those green eyes of his might be regarded by one of the others as more than it was. Of course, there would be no *more-than-it-was* to her looking, because there *was* no more than it was. On the other hand, he seemed to have cast a spell over her and the last thing she needed was to show it in front of her men.

Actually the whole thing was a bit confusing. Rebecca concentrated on the task at hand. They had a mission to finish, and at any minute they would find themselves in an engagement with the Arabs.

"May I see my parents?" Caleb asked.

She looked at him. Now his eyes did sink into hers and she took a drink of water. "Where are his parents, Samuel?"

"In the study."

"And where is Avraham?"

"Below."

"Below doing what?"

Samuel glanced at Zakkai. "Laying dynamite."

Rebecca looked at each of them. "I thought I ordered you not to use dynamite."

"You have to understand, we thought—"

"Regardless of what you thought, we did not come to Ethiopia to blow up monasteries. This was Avraham's doing? Is he using timed charges?"

"It was Avraham's idea. But we agreed. I don't know what kind of charges."

If not for Avraham, Zakkai would never have agreed, she thought. "And if Avraham suggested killing the hostages, would you do that as well?"

"Actually, he did. And no, I did not agree."

For a moment no one spoke. Rebecca set her mug down heavily. "Bring Avraham to the study. And hurry, we don't have much time."

———

Caleb's mother ran to him, took his face in her hands, and kissed each cheek. "I was so worried."

"It's okay, Mother. I was in good hands."

Leiah glared at Rebecca.

Jason put an arm around Caleb's shoulders. "Boy, you had us worried. Where have you been?"

"In the desert."

Jason lifted an eyebrow.

"A caravan of monks found him," Rebecca said.

"No thanks to you," Leiah said.

"I brought your son back in one piece," Rebecca returned. "You should remember that."

"You laid siege to his home and chased him into the desert. You should remember *that!*" Leiah said. "If it served your purpose, you'd probably slit his throat."

Rebecca wondered at the anger behind those words. The boy's mother was obviously a strong woman, but she hadn't expected such a biting resentment. *Why are you so angry, Leiah? Your son is a good man, and I've grown to care for him.*

The door suddenly slammed open and Avraham walked in. He stood by Samuel and stared at the gathering. "All together like a happy family, are we?" He eyed Caleb. "I'm surprised you made it back alive."

"Surprised?" Rebecca asked. "Or disappointed? I want you to remove the charges you've laid immediately."

Avraham's jaw flexed. "Has he told you what you need to know?" he demanded, glancing at Caleb.

"No."

Avraham grinned. "You couldn't . . . coax it out of him?"

Heat flared up Rebecca's neck. "We were in the desert, you idiot."

"Yes, exactly. All alone, together, in the desert. Plenty of time to be . . . persuasive," he said, drawing out the last word. "If you don't have the key yet, then either *you're* the idiot or he doesn't know it."

The room suddenly felt very stuffy. Rebecca could feel Leiah's glare on the side of her face. "Keep your fantasies to yourself, Avraham. I don't have the time to argue with you. We were followed by a band of Arabs who may be coming over the hill as we speak. You'll remove the charges or I'll have Samuel put you under arrest."

A shadow crossed his face, but it didn't mask a thin smile. "Give him to me for five minutes and I promise you, he'll tell us what he knows."

"If you lay a single finger on him, I'll kill you," she said. She meant it to be matter of fact, but it came out like the hiss of a snake. Avraham's eyes squinted very briefly. He saw it, she thought.

"You have a soft spot for him, do you, Rebecca? The mighty soldier has discovered that she is a woman after all?"

"I've discovered what we came to find. Caleb. Without him we are lost. Samuel, please take Avraham and see that he removes the charges. If the Arabs arrive, then leave the charges and take your positions. But if I find that you've laid any charges set to go off after we leave, I will charge you with insubordination. Insubordination in the field is punishable by death. I promise you that I'll kill you myself. Now leave."

Avraham left wearing a scowl that sent a butterfly through Rebecca's gut. She glanced at Caleb, saw that he was staring, and immediately removed her eyes. They met Leiah's, who had a brow arched. *Dear God, help me.*

Zakkai saved her.

"Rebecca, we must hurry. We must take Caleb down."

"Of course. The radios work down there?"

"Yes."

"Then show us what you've found, Professor."

———

Two torches blazed on the wall of the ancient subterranean room in which Caleb had lived as a child. An old table, its chairs, and a long bookcase loaded with over a hundred books were the only furniture. Rebecca took it in, lost in the wonder of how a boy could have lived here, so removed from the world.

Caleb was the last to enter. The ladder creaked, and Rebecca turned to see him descend, feet first. Jason and Leiah stood on her right. Zakkai waited in the shadows by the entry to another room, like a science fair winner, waiting to show off his exhibit.

Caleb set his feet on the dusty clay floor and stopped, his hands still on the ladder. He turned slowly and looked at the walls as if lost in a dream. The torchlight glinted off his eyes. He was going back to the past, Rebecca thought. For a moment she let herself go with him, a child in a musty room full of books. A lonely child.

Caleb's eyes watered. A faint smile crossed his face.

No, not a lonely child. A sacred child.

"You remember your room, Caleb?" Zakkai asked softly.

"Yes." He looked at Rebecca. "This is where I grew up."

She smiled, unsure of how to respond. Caleb was addressing her instead of his mother. Leiah was looking at her again; Rebecca could feel her eyes.

"I spent many days here with Father Matthew," Caleb said. "I can't believe the room survived intact." He reached out and touched the bookcase with his fingertips. He suddenly turned back to Rebecca, smiling wide now.

"I read all of these books, you know! Every one of them."

"That's a lot of books for a child," she said.

"Yes, it is." He walked towards the arched entry by Zakkai, excited now. "And that was my bedroom! I can't believe my bedroom survived!" He stooped and entered. "My bed's still here!" They followed him in.

"And the painting above your bed was still here, Caleb," Zakkai said. "We removed it and found that space."

The plaster was broken, revealing a small cubbyhole.

"Father Matthew left you something. Go ahead; it's still there."

Caleb glanced at Zakkai and then reached in and withdrew a rolled letter. He pulled it open and read it. The note was short—the same Rebecca had been read over the satellite phone.

Caleb,

You alone know the secrets of this majestic rock we shared for a home. It was a gift from God. My dear sweet one, you will know. Where the brine mixes with the oil, there you will find God. Only you will know.

I am flying now, Caleb. We will fly together again. I cherish you more than life.

Matthew

"Where do the oil and the brine mix, Caleb?" Zakkai asked.

He looked up, wide-eyed. "In the heart."

Zakkai nodded. "And where is the heart of the monastery?"

"The heart of the monastery?" He looked puzzled. "The foundation below the study," he said from memory. Of course! The heart was a place! The thought hadn't even crossed her mind.

Zakkai exchanged a quick glance with Rebecca. The torchlight glistened off his sweaty brow. "You are sure?"

"That's what Father Matthew used to call it. You think . . ." Caleb blinked.

"Show us, Caleb."

———

Caleb led them to the corner behind the last bookshelf, a dimly lit section of the room that housed rows and rows of dark brown leather books. He pointed to the floor. "Somewhere under here," Caleb said.

"Somewhere?"

"When we rebuilt, we covered over it, but there used to be a small hole in the floor where Father Matthew kept papers and a few very old books. He called it the heart of the monastery. It was here"—he moved his hand in a small circular motion—"in this area somewhere."

"A hole. What size?"

"Small. Like a shoebox."

Zakkai looked at Rebecca.

"Not exactly the size we were looking for," she said.

"Okay, please stand back everybody." They did. He paced the bare floor, roughly six by eight. From his belt he withdrew his ball-peen hammer and lowered himself to his knees. He began to tap on the concrete.

"Any idea what kind of papers he kept in this safe, Caleb?"

"No. But they were very important to him." He looked up at Rebecca. "Maybe something from the desert."

"What was in the desert?" Zakkai asked.

Rebecca answered. "The tribe of monks Father Matthew used to live with, before coming to the monastery. They have their own codes."

"Hmmm." Zakkai tapped several times every eighteen centimeters along a line and then started back up another line. They watched him silently now—only the dull clack of steel striking thick concrete sounded. At any moment her radio would crackle with news that the Arabs had come. Rebecca felt her palms tingle with the thought. They were on the verge of failure here and time was nearly out. They could hold off the Arabs for a day or two if Ismael didn't have explosives, but she knew that he must. Grenades at least—she had seen those on several horses back at the camp. If they had grenades, they probably had dynamite. She had nine men including Avraham. The Arabs had ten and Ismael. If Avraham—

A distinctly hollow sound interrupted her thoughts. She jerked her eyes to where Zakkai knelt, frozen over the cement.

He glanced at them and then struck again.

Deep below their feet the blow echoed, as if he'd hit a cement drum. Zakkai swallowed and spun to her. For a moment they locked stares. And then the professor was on his feet.

"Give me the pick!"

Jason gave him the pickax.

"Stand back!"

"Easy, Professor," Rebecca said. "You're using a pickax."

"Of course I am! We don't have all day, do we?"

"No."

"Then please stand back. The fragments can sting." He swung once, with all his weight, and the tip chipped an inch deep. He swung again and sparks flew. Ten swings later he stood back, panting. He'd managed to do little more than dent the floor.

"Give it a go?" he said to Jason.

Jason took his turn. For five minutes the two beat at the floor, switching off every minute or so. A six-inch slab suddenly dislodged itself and Jason picked it up.

"This is the new floor we poured over the old." He pointed at the rough gray floor now exposed in a rough six-inch circle. "That's the old."

Zakkai took the pickax and swung at the spot. They worked without talking, chipping up the floor in tiny bites. Rebecca became aware that Caleb was standing next to her, and she looked at him. He watched the work, unsure. They were demolishing what was probably once a sacred part of his life. Or perhaps he was worried about what they would find. The Ark wouldn't bring peace, and Caleb didn't know anything but peace. Why would he want the Ark discovered? He wouldn't. He had led them to this spot almost incidentally, without really thinking they would find anything.

In truth, she herself couldn't imagine finding anything. It was a last-ditch effort in a long line of last-ditch efforts. They would find nothing but an old black hole and then they would fight their way home.

And if they did find a golden Ark? The notion wasn't unlike the notion of finding Atlantis.

Rebecca wasn't even sure she *wanted* to find the Ark any longer. Hadane had said that the Ark wasn't the vessel of God. He was. Man was. If Hadane and company had turned out to be a band of witless fools, she might feel differently. But they had proven their wit with power, and they believed that the Ark would bring nothing but war. For a fleeting moment, the idea grew in her chest, and she found herself hoping the Arabs would arrive.

But that was crazy. She had dedicated her life to rebuilding the Temple! Finding the Ark would mean rebuilding the Temple, regardless of what Hadane, or Caleb for that matter, said. She wiped her palms on her dungarees and watched the dismantlement. She was losing her moorings, she thought.

Her radio suddenly squawked. "We have men and horses on the eastern perimeter. They're here!"

As one they froze. Zakkai had just swung and he looked up, wide-eyed and panting. Sweat drenched his shirt, rendering it translucent against his hunched back. His hair was a disheveled tangle.

"They'll pin us down, Professor," Rebecca said. "If we lay down covering fire from the tower, we could get out now to the west before they know we've gone. We have the lorries."

"And leave this mystery unanswered? If we leave, they'll kill the monks. And Caleb."

Rebecca didn't answer. He was right, the Arabs might very well let them escape and take over the monastery. She turned on her heels and keyed the radio.

"Where are you, Samuel?"

"The bell tower."

She strode for the door. Behind her Zakkai began to swing again. "Open fire. Let them know we're here and don't want to be bothered. Hit them hard."

"Daniel, how many do you see from the road?" Samuel's voice was calm. High above them the sound of his M-14 boomed.

"Ten. Eleven," came the reply.

Behind Rebecca, Zakkai suddenly gasped. She stopped at the door and keyed her mic. "That's all of them. Keep them in sight, and don't let them get close enough to use grenades. If you lose them, I want Daniel back inside."

Above her the M-14 boomed again, joined by short bursts of automatic weapons fire to her flanks. Zakkai was staring down at the floor. He jerked his head up. "There's a room!"

Rebecca spun around. "A room?"

Zakkai dropped to his knees and peered at a small hole in the concrete. "I think I've broken into a room." His voice echoed softly. "It's dark and quite large."

They had to deal with the Arabs, or it wouldn't matter what Zakkai had found. "How long will it take you to clear a hole big enough to enter?"

"Fifteen minutes." Zakkai sprang to his feet and attacked the hole like an animal.

"I'll be back," Rebecca said. "The rest of you stay here." She ran from the room. A loud explosion suddenly rocked the ground near the west end. The Arabs weren't messing around.

31

ISMAEL SAT ON HIS HORSE BEHIND an outcropping of boulders and studied the monastery through his binoculars. His men had dismounted at the first engagement and returned fire from cover along the hill overlooking the valley. The Jews had opened up with a full assault even before they were in range, which could only mean that Rebecca and Caleb had arrived and expected them. They were sending a message. One of the men had managed to launch a grenade, but had been forced to retreat under heavy fire.

"Sir, we should flank them," the captain said beside him. "They might try to escape out the back."

Ismael lowered the glasses and pointed to the hills across the valley. "Put two men on that ridge and two men on the north ridge. Make sure they let the Jews know they are there."

"Immediately."

Captain Asid left and barked orders down the line. Four men scrambled back, mounted their horses, and galloped off under the cover of the hill.

The episode back in the canyon still haunted Ismael like a bad nightmare. The one they called Caleb had stripped him of his dignity with a few words, and Ismael still could not comprehend what had followed. He'd been overcome by sorrow. The world had become transparent for those few moments and the thought of pulling his trigger to send this robed man to his grave had felt obscene. Then he'd actually tried to kill him anyway, and his finger had refused to cooperate. The sorrow had taken over his mind then. It had become unbearable and he'd fallen. When the captain found him, he'd sworn the man to secrecy. He'd become ill, he insisted, and the men had no business knowing.

Ismael had heard of sorcery before, mystics who had their own way with evil. There was no sense of evil in the monk's eyes, but Ismael knew he had to be such a mystic. In some ways he now wanted to kill Caleb as badly as he did the woman.

"We have them trapped," he said to the returning captain. "There's no escape. Tell the men to cease fire."

Asid twisted his head. "Cease fire!"

"We have the high ground. They don't have a chance."

"We have the high ground, but they have the fortress," Asid observed, looking down.

"And we have explosives."

"The structure's strong."

"How much dynamite do we have?"

"A hundred sticks."

Ismael smiled. "Then it's not strong enough, is it? As long as we keep them penned in, we will have them. As soon as it's dark, I want your best men to begin laying explosives around the backside. We will attack before dawn. A full frontal assault while they deal with the dynamite behind."

"Use it all at once?" the captain asked, more of himself than Ismael. "And if we fail?"

"We won't. But if we do, then the Syrian air force will provide an air strike." He faced Asid. "One way or another we'll stop these Jews. No one leaves alive."

"The monks?"

"They've seen too much."

———

Rebecca sprinted down the hall towards the study, her heart pounding like a sledge. The Arabs had encircled the monastery, fired off one last salvo, and then pulled back. They were waiting for darkness; she was sure of it. Clearly, Ismael's high ground did him no good against a fortress built like the monastery, especially with Samuel's M-14 parting their hair. But darkness would shift the advantage. They had four hours till nightfall.

Four hours to make a break for it before the Arabs closed in with whatever explosives they had. It would be safer to run and shoot now, when Ismael least expected it. She would take Caleb and his parents with her.

Unless, of course, there was something in Zakkai's room.

She spun into the study's doorway. "Well?"

Zakkai knelt over a three-foot hole they'd hacked into the floor. Leiah and Caleb peered over his shoulders. They looked up as one.

"We have a room," Zakkai said.

Feet pounded down the hall, and Rebecca turned to see Jason running for the study, a flaming torch in one hand and a rope ladder in the other. He stepped past her into the room.

Rebecca walked over to the circle and peered into Zakkai's room. Light fell into the subterranean darkness, graying a floor two-and-a-half meters below them. Beside her, Caleb stared down, stunned. This room had obviously existed without his knowing, even as a child. None of them was speaking. Rebecca's pulse quickened.

"What's inside?" she asked.

"We can't see the whole room without getting light into the hole," Zakkai said.

Rebecca knelt and lowered her head carefully through the opening. A musty odor laced with the smell of vanilla wax filled her nostrils. She blinked and let her eyes adjust to the darkness.

The room looked about two-and-a-half meters wide, carved from gray stone. It ran to her right, but she couldn't see how far because the light faded to black. A drop of sweat fell from her forehead and made a dark splotch on a thick layer of dust that carpeted the floor. As far as she could see, the room was empty, but the light faded before it reached the back wall. If they had a flashlight, she would be able to see more, but she couldn't hold a flame below her without getting burned.

Rebecca pulled up. "It looks empty."

"Go in, Rebecca," Zakkai said.

"Me?"

"Yes."

She looked at the others who all stared at her. She nodded. Jason handed the torch to Zakkai and tossed one end of the rope ladder into the hole. It unrolled and landed with a dull slap.

Rebecca stepped down the ladder rungs, swaying with the rope. Her head was already into the opening before she reached up to Zakkai for the torch. With a last look into his bright eyes, she dropped to the floor.

Yellow light splashed on ancient stone walls. The musty smell was very strong now; dust filtered up from her landing. She held her breath and peered forward, towards the far end.

"Anything?" It was Zakkai above. He was already lowering himself into the room.

The far wall glared back at her and it took a moment for Rebecca to understand what she was seeing. She was looking at another stone wall.

"It's empty."

A peculiar warmth washed over her skull—a curious blend of comfort and disappointment. Perhaps in these last few minutes she had actually allowed herself to believe that they would find the Ark, buried in this lost cavern beneath the remote monastery hidden in the Ethiopian Abyssinia.

But the room was empty. The Arabs were digging in outside, David Ben Solomon was pacing back in Jerusalem, and the room was empty.

Zakkai took the torch from her hand. She turned to see Caleb lowering himself on the rope ladder behind her. So now she was left with only one responsibility: to save these people whose lives she and Zakkai had endangered in this search of theirs. She'd come to find the Ark and she had found Caleb—a madman who claimed that *he* was God's Ark.

Caleb looked around. The others were coming down behind him. "It's empty," he said.

Rebecca turned back to Zakkai. The professor had moved over to one of the walls and was drawing his index finger through a thin layer of dust.

"The detonations that destroyed the monastery must have flooded this room with a film of dirt," he said. "This room must be eight hundred years old, from when the monastery was built in the thirteenth century."

"It's empty, Professor," Rebecca said gently. "Now we have to go."

He ignored her and ran his hand over the stone, dislodging a thick layer of dust that rained down to his feet.

"So," Leiah said by Rebecca's side. "There never was an Ark in the monastery."

Zakkai was rapping his knuckles on the stone. It sounded as thick as the earth.

"I'm sorry," Rebecca said, turning to Leiah. "We are only Jews, you understand—trying to recover a spiritual identity that was lost a thousand years ago. Please, Professor, we're running out of time." She turned to climb the ladder.

"There's a Templar cross here," Zakkai said.

Rebecca spun back. The Templars?

Zakkai quickly cleared the stone with his palm revealing a faded cross etched into the wall. It ran about thirty centimeters high, and it was indeed the unique cross with flared ends used by the Knights Templar.

Zakkai shoved the torch out to Rebecca. "Hold this!"

She took it. He began to wipe the dust from the wall in wide swaths, using both hands. It fell to the ground in heaps and rose in a haze, choking them. But Zakkai didn't stop. He wiped in a frenzy with his forearms until the dust was so thick none of them could breathe.

Coughing echoed through the room, and finally Zakkai stopped. Slowly, the dust settled. The Templar cross stood alone on a gray wall. The professor tapped it, but the stone behind was solid.

"The Templars put their mark on everything they built," Zakkai said. "This must have been the foundation of the monastery, built by Templars in the thirteenth century. It would confirm theories that the Ethiopians had help carving the stone churches in this area."

They looked at the cross silently.

"But it has no bearing on the Ark," Rebecca said, wiping her mouth of dust. "Right?"

Zakkai seemed not to have heard. He leapt over to the far wall and attacked it as he had the other. Immediately Rebecca saw the marks, and her heart froze in her chest.

The Hebrew letters were unmistakable.

Zakkai went rigid. And then he cleared the wall, using his forearms like giant windshield wipers. The dust flew, once again smothering them. He stepped back from the cloud he'd created and faced the wall, panting, legs spread and planted. The torch crackled and the dust began to settle. There on the wall a Hebrew inscription materialized from the haze.

Zakkai's high-pitched voice spoke, barely above a whisper. "The kingdom of God is within you."

A chill ran up Rebecca's spine. Caleb had said that to her in the desert! "That's the heart of the monastery," she said softly, as much to herself as to the others. "The presence of God is in the heart, not in the Ark. It's what Father Matthew believed."

"Jason, get me the pickax!" Zakkai snapped.

"What can you do—"

"Just get it. Hurry!"

Jason clambered up the ladder and dropped the pickax into the room. It landed with a metallic clang. Zakkai bounded over to it, snatched it up, and faced the wall again.

"Professor, there is no Ark. The *heart* is Father Matthew's Ark; that's what Hadane meant—"

"If this is stone, it won't be hurt, Rebecca. The kingdom of God is here. Within *you*." He pointed at the wall. "Within this *wall*, not in man! Stand back!"

He lifted the pickax and swung at a spot a foot below the inscription.

A soft boom startled her, and Rebecca's first thought was that someone had dropped a grenade into the room. She crouched. But it hadn't been an explosion. Thick roils of billowing dust engulfed Professor Zakkai.

Then silence.

"Zakkai?"

"I'm all right!" His voice echoed around her. The sound of his voice had changed.

"What happened?"

He didn't respond. The dust began to settle. On her left, Jason and Leiah had covered their noses with their shirt sleeves. On her right, Caleb stood with his mouth slightly agape. She thought that he was still reeling from the whole discovery of this room. In front of her, Zakkai's form emerged from the settling dust.

Rebecca stepped forward, holding the wavering torch into the haze for a better view. A tiny glint caught her eye through the shadows and her legs seized, midstride.

Rubble littered the floor. The whole wall had fallen down with Zakkai's blow! There was a cavern beyond. And this cavern was not empty—she knew that as if the knowledge had come to her riding a bolt of lightning.

Two small statues of angels, with wings swept towards each other, suddenly emerged from the settling dust. No, not statues; they were attached to a gold plate.

Could it be?

A large gold object began to emerge. A box that looked like it was rising out of a fog.

It had to be!

The Ark of the Covenant. It was.

I am.

Rebecca's heart slammed in her chest, threatening to tear itself free. For a long moment they gaped at the golden chest, stunned into silence. And then beside her, Zakkai let out a single, loud sob. He dropped to his knees.

"Oh my dear God." It was Leiah, behind Rebecca, muttering a prayer. "Oh my God."

Dust roiled at their feet. The torch's light flickered over a brilliant chest covered with a pure gold that looked as if it had been poured yesterday. Two golden angels—cherubim—knelt on the top, facing each other with wings extended over the Ark's cover. The Mercy Seat. The gold carrying poles still ran through their hoops at the base of the Ark. A simple wooden table supported the chest.

She had seen a hundred renderings of the Ark, but now looking at it she was struck by its brilliance. Like a perfect block carved out of God's throne and lowered here to earth.

Rebecca took a step forward on numb legs.

She knew the exact dimensions by heart—114.3 centimeters long, 68.58 centimeters wide, and 68.58 centimeters deep. Interlocking circles had been etched along the length of the lid—she'd never seen a rendering with them. Three inlaid panels ran the length, but the gold was not broken. The panels were made of the acacia wood beneath, then covered with molten gold.

Rebecca glanced at Zakkai. The archaeologist knelt, trembling, muttering prayers. Long wet streaks ran through the dust on his cheeks. His eyes looked like pools of sorrow. "Don't touch it," he rasped. "Nobody touch it."

Caleb stood in the shadows behind Zakkai, arms limp at his sides. She couldn't read his expression.

The room beyond the Ark was black in shadows. "This . . . this is it, isn't it?" she said. It was a statement.

"We have found it. We have found the resting place of God," Zakkai said. "Israel will be restored once again."

The rectangular panels were capped with a decorative ridge that ran the perimeter of the cover. "There's no dust on it," Rebecca said.

Zakkai stood and walked haltingly into the room, to the right of the Ark. He reached a hand out to one of the carrying poles, but then withdrew it. Rebecca eased to the left. The walls were covered in a waxlike substance. Vanilla wax—it was the source of the odor. She carefully stepped through the narrow space between the poles and the wall. They were both breathing deliberately, like accompanying bellows in the small chamber.

Only when she had passed the chest did she see that the shadows at the rear of the room were not shadows at all, but an opening. A tunnel ran into the wall, disappearing to black.

"Professor . . . ," she whispered.

"Of course! An escape route to take the Ark out! The Falasha Jews were no fools."

"Is it possible . . ." She trailed off.

"That it comes out beyond the Arabs? It must. God is with us! We must take the Ark out immediately." Zakkai's face glistened in the torchlight, wet with sweat.

Rebecca looked at the Ark again. Her mind seemed to be crawling through molasses. She had come to find this relic, but she hadn't actually expected to—that much she knew by the tremor in her bones.

"The Arabs will attack tonight—they're waiting for dark," she said.

Preparing the Ark for transportation would take some time. But if this tunnel led where she thought it did, they might have a chance. The equation had changed now. The Ark had to be saved at all costs.

Rebecca stepped into the tunnel. It ran straight back into pitch-darkness.

"Wait here for a minute."

She ducked and hurried down the passage, keeping the torch above her head so that it left a trail of soot along the arched rock ceiling. Her breathing chased her into a jog.

A hundred meters later she pulled up, panting. There was still no end in sight. She spun around and ran back. When she broke into the chamber, they were exactly where she'd left them, in the dark, wide-eyed and immobilized, like three children visiting prep school for the first time. Three, because the fourth, Caleb, still hung back in the shadows behind Jason and Leiah, and Rebecca still couldn't read his expression in the shadows.

"How far?" Zakkai asked.

"I don't know. Far enough, I think." She faced Jason, catching her breath. "Do you have wood and nails for a crate?"

"Some. Yes, I think so."

"Crate it, Professor. No one opens it. No one touches it." She eased around the Ark. Her skin tingled as she passed, and she wasn't sure if it was her own reaction or not.

"As soon as it's dark, I'll send two men out to scout and move one of the trucks to the leper colony. It'll be risky, but I don't think they'll chase a single truck on horseback if they know the rest of us are still here. Those remaining will leave through this tunnel on foot and meet the others at the village."

She reached the ladder and turned back. The world was about to change, she thought. The gold box sitting there would see to that.

"Be ready to leave as soon as I give the word."

32

IT TOOK DAVID BEN SOLOMON TWENTY-FIVE minutes to track down the exact location of the prime minister, primarily due to an overprotective administrative assistant who obviously had little regard for Solomon. It took another twenty minutes to drive to the Hyatt, where the prime minister was speaking to a large gathering of Arab Israelis, of all things. Solomon couldn't remember feeling as elated as he did walking through the revolving door. Not only was his daughter alive, but she and Zakkai had accomplished their mission. It was news that made him weak in the knees.

The cameras were out in force, and Ben Gurion was speaking with a volume to match. Solomon pushed his way past the security and strode down the center aisle, past five hundred important Arab businessmen who'd gathered to hear how all Israeli citizens, including Arab Israelis, made Israel, Israel—an oxymoron in Solomon's eyes.

He knew that he was out of place, marching down the aisle dressed in a flowing tunic, frowning like a prophet, but he shoved the thought from his mind. Israel's future was at stake. Zakkai's call had sent a quiver through his nerves, and it had not abated. This meeting in the Hyatt was a joke next to the information he now possessed.

Solomon walked right to the front, past the cameras, and only then thought it might be better to step to one side, out of the camera's view. But he discarded the notion and walked straight up the steps that led to the platform.

Several black-suited security men stepped forward, but he reached the podium first. Ben Gurion's speech stalled.

"Simon, we need to talk," Solomon said.

His approach had frozen the politicians behind the prime minister. A security man reached Solomon and placed a hand on his arm. The prime minister just stared, completely off guard.

"We have it!" Solomon whispered.

Ben Gurion blinked.

The security detail leaned forward. "I'm sorry, sir. You'll have to leave the platform—"

"Leave him," Ben Gurion said.

The guard stepped back.

Ben Gurion faced the crowd. "You'll forgive me . . . I am evidently . . . needed. I have said what I came to say anyway. As long as I am the prime minister of Israel, we will regard every Israeli citizen as the same." He had lost his flare.

Solomon stood with his back to the crowd and caught the defense minister, Benjamin Yishai's, glare. *Your life is about to be turned on its head by your enemies, Benjamin Yishai. And I am not your enemy. Stop glaring like an idiot.* Solomon nearly said it aloud.

"Thank you." The prime minister dipped his head and turned from the podium. The crowd hesitated, then offered a smattering of applause.

"This better be good, David," Ben Gurion snapped. "You either have the courage of a madman or the sense of a fool."

"But it is good. And it's terrible, depending on who you are."

"I'm the prime minister. And so far it feels terrible." He glanced at the others and walked past them, waving off another security man. His face was ashen. They walked towards a suite in the back. Ben Gurion's chief of staff hurried to catch them.

"Sir? You can't—"

"Not now, Moshen. Give me five minutes," he snapped.

They entered an empty suite decked out Hyatt style with high-back chairs and burgundy drapes. Solomon shut the door and faced the prime minister.

Ben Gurion looked at him, unblinking. "What, Solomon? What precisely have you found?"

"The Ark."

Their eyes locked for an inordinate time, while the words spun through Ben Gurion's mind. "What do you mean . . . the Ark? You actually have the original Ark of the Covenant?"

"Yes. We actually have the original Ark of the Covenant."

Ben Gurion turned to the table where he lifted a flask of amber-colored liqueur and poured a drink. "And how do you know this . . . that this is the Ark? You found something that looks like the Ark?"

"No, Simon. We have the Ark. And I know it's the Ark because Zakkai is there and he told me himself that there isn't the slightest doubt."

"Where?"

"In northern Ethiopia—"

"I thought you said Egypt."

"Yes. But it's in northern Ethiopia, in the bowels of an ancient monastery. Exactly where we thought we would find it. Do you realize what this means?" He could not contain the grin that spread over his face.

Ben Gurion frowned and tossed back his drink. "Actually, I *don't* know what it means. I do know that it's hardly something to grin about."

"We have the Ark, for God's sake!"

"No, we have nothing but a report that the Ark's been found. Meanwhile, Islam does indeed occupy the Temple Mount which is where the Ark would belong if it actually were to show up! It is a bad mixture."

"Yes, Islam holds the Temple Mount. That's the point, isn't it? But we have another problem."

"This whole *thing* has been a problem from the beginning. Dear God, if I had actually thought you might find the thing, I might have sent the army in to stop you!"

"Then you wouldn't have been the only one."

Ben Gurion twisted to face him. "What do you mean?"

"The Arabs. My people were followed. There's a unit of Syrian Republican Guard around the monastery as we speak."

"What!" Spittle flew with the word.

"Don't worry, they have no idea we have the Ark."

"Don't worry? Why didn't you tell me that the Syrians were involved?"

"They weren't involved! The Palestinians were involved, and they managed to pull the Syrians in for support. At least that's the best we can make of it. And as I said, they have no idea that we have the Ark."

"So you're telling me that a band of Jews have actually discovered the Ark of the Covenant in Ethiopia and are surrounded by Syrian commandos. And you have the audacity to suggest I not worry?"

"I can't imagine a better situation! We have the Ark, for God's sake!"

"So you've told me." He took a breath. "So you have the Ark. What now?"

"We can't let them have the Ark; that's what now. Under no circumstances can we allow the Arabs—"

"I *know* we can't let them have the Ark!" Ben Gurion turned back to the table, poured another drink, and stormed over to the window that overlooked the Old City to the south. "Dear God, I can't believe I'm having this conversation."

Solomon felt almost giddy. For nearly half a century he had dreamed of this day. The power was intoxicating. They could say what they wanted— they could wiggle and they could scream, but they could not deny the Ark. Its very existence trumped any possible political device.

"It's in a monastery? We should drop a dozen thousand-pound bombs on that monastery," the prime minister said. "You know that, don't you, David?"

"So you've said. Or throw it into the sea. But you can't blow up God and expect to survive."

The prime minister turned from the window. "You're absolutely sure about this?"

"Yes. I am. We have the Ark. And now we have no choice but to bring it to Jerusalem. For that we need your submarine."

The prime minister shook his head in disbelief. "Now you're the most powerful man in Israel; is that it?"

"Something like that. It would seem that I have God on my side now. You could be King Ahab and send out the ministers and we could have a showdown on Mount Carmel, but we both know who would win, don't we?"

The prime minister just stared at him.

"Can I have one of the submarines?"

"You can't just bring the Ark into Jerusalem and parade it down the street."

"I didn't have that in mind."

"What *did* you have in mind?"

Solomon hesitated. "Call a meeting of the leaders and I will tell you all what I have in mind. In the meantime, for God's sake, give me a submarine. We have three in the Red Sea, doing nothing. I need it off Massawa tomorrow. We don't have time. My people must leave tonight if they hope to escape."

"*Can* your people escape?"

"We don't have a choice, do we?"

The prime minister leaned against the window sill and ran a hand through his short gray hair. The door suddenly opened and an aide stood in the opening. "Sir—"

"Out! Get out!" Ben Gurion boomed.

The aide beat a hasty retreat.

Ben Gurion took a deep breath and faced the window.

"I need to know, Simon," Solomon said.

"I don't like to be cornered." He turned back. "Okay, you have your submarine. I'll call Admiral Bird myself. This could lead to war; you do realize that?"

"It will only lead where God intends it to lead. We've been at war for two thousand years, if not with guns then with our souls. In 1948 we found a piece of real estate we could call home. Now we are about to find God again, and the cost is God's to decide, not mine."

"I will have to tell Goldstein and the others."

Solomon didn't respond.

"We will meet at my offices at nine in the morning," Ben Gurion said.

"That will be fine."

"You realize that once on the submarine, the Ark will be in my possession?"

"I'll have to trust you with that, Simon. And you must know that my people have independent documentation that no one will be able to silence. If you destroy the Ark, the world will know." It was the weakest link in Solomon's plan, but he had his own contingencies in order.

Ben Gurion walked to the phone and dialed a number. He spoke quickly to the admiral and then hung up.

"He's expecting a call from you." The prime minister handed Solomon a slip of paper with a private phone number on it. "Work out the details with him."

"Thank you, Simon."

"Wait a few days before thanking me. You just make sure the wrong people don't get their hands on . . . that thing. God help us all if the Arabs find out that we have it."

"They won't."

Solomon left and hurried for his car. He pulled out a notebook, found a phone number, and quickly dialed it. A voice answered in Hebrew.

"We have the submarine," Solomon said.

The voice hesitated. "So, it's happening."

"Yes. We need your help, Admiral. One of the other admirals, Bird, is in charge. But the Ark must not be handed over to the government. Not yet. It has to stay in our hands."

"Don't worry, David. I don't need persuading. We will have our Ark. Dear God, I can't believe this is actually happening."

"Believe it, Moshen. It's happening. Just make sure Admiral Bird doesn't get in the way."

"He won't."

33

AVRAHAM WATCHED ZAKKAI AND TWO of the monks work around the Ark, like moles scurrying about a prize find. He had never actually believed they would find the Ark of the Covenant, but looking at its gold glimmering under the light from several torches, he was finally accepting the fact that they actually had it.

And that changed everything.

One of the trucks had made it out of the valley nearly an hour ago, although barely, judging by the fusillade of tracers that chased it over the hill. But with any luck it now waited at the leper colony as planned. The Arabs had blown the other one ten minutes later. He'd ordered his men to lay down heavy fire to persuade the enemy that the lone truck had escaped without more than a soldier or two. The plan seemed to have worked. They would not all fit in one truck, of course, but that suited Avraham just fine.

Zakkai had overseen the construction of the half-finished crate around the Ark, a process made slow by the hand tools available. To make matters worse, the wood wasn't exactly what you'd call dimensional lumber. Everything had to be cut at least once. The challenge had been to package the Ark in such a way that it wouldn't be recognized as the Ark. It wouldn't do to haul a box labeled "Ark of the Covenant" through Ethiopia. Neither the Arabs nor the Ethiopians would take the evacuation of the holy relic lying down.

"How long, Professor?" Avraham asked.

Zakkai stood, panting. "A couple hours. At least. We can leave by midnight."

"We don't have until midnight."

"I can only do what is possible. Maybe by eleven." He bent back down and resumed hammering a nail.

Actually, the delay played to Avraham's favor. He had the time to do what he needed to do. The soldiers had been placed strategically around the monastery, positioned at windows that overlooked all of the surrounding hills. The Arabs could sneak up close, but they couldn't engage the entrances without presenting themselves to an open field of fire. The only real challenge would be explosives. The Arabs were undoubtedly planting remote detonation charges around the perimeter, but this, too, played to his favor.

Avraham glanced at his watch and climbed out of the hole. It was time to deal with Rebecca.

He found her in the sanctuary, with several of the priests and the woman, Leiah. Avraham took a deep breath and approached her.

"The Ark will be ready to move in two hours," he said.

She turned to face him and he swallowed a wedge of revulsion. Her pretty face had become a symbol of all that he hated about the Israeli army, he thought. Everything so prim and proper and pretty. Everything always by the rules, while the enemy slowly nibbled at the borders. He had been disgraced by that army. The world thought Israel's army was too aggressive—in reality it was too soft.

"We have to make a decision," he said.

"What decision?" Rebecca asked.

Samuel walked in and she looked at him. "All quiet?"

"Sporadic gunfire, but no change," Samuel returned.

She returned to Avraham. "What decision?"

"What do you suppose the Ethiopian government will do when they learn that a small band of Jews has just hauled off their precious Ark? They do have an air force, you know?"

"Yes, I do know. And I think we accepted the risk of being discovered by the Ethiopian authorities before we left Jerusalem. With any luck we'll be out before they discover we were here."

"With any luck? So you'll put the fate of the Ark in the hands of luck?"

"We don't have a choice."

"Of course we have a choice." He eyed the monks. "We can eliminate the information at its source. Anything less would be stupid. You're not stupid, are you, Rebecca?"

She studied him carefully. "We're here on a mission for God's people. Killing innocents along the way doesn't strike you as ironic?"

"They're no more innocent than the innocents who died at Jericho. Perhaps less—after all, they do have knowledge that could keep the Ark from ever reaching Jerusalem."

"Not if they don't use that information."

"So they've given you their word, have they? You plan on risking our country's future on the word of a man you hauled out of the desert and his mother? I'm sorry, but it sounds stupid to me. Does it sound stupid to you, Samuel?"

The soldier didn't answer.

"I don't care how it sounds to you, Avraham; they will not be harmed," Rebecca said.

Avraham walked up within arm's reach of her and smiled deliberately. "You've given yourself to him, haven't you? And now you're willing to trade Israel for a few moments of pleasure with a man who's your enemy. You're playing the whore now?"

Her hand flashed out and struck his cheek hard. *Crack!* Biting pain shot down his neck.

"I won't tolerate insubordination," she said. Her voice held a tremor and he knew that he'd hit a nerve.

"So. You *do* have a soft spot for this Caleb? All the more reason to kill him. Don't be a fool; we can't let them live. Whatever you think of them, they're Christians and they're our enemies. They'll call the authorities the minute we leave. We have no choice but to kill them."

"A pig can justify lying in his slop too. It doesn't mean we should all do it. I won't stoop that low. And yes, they *have* given me their word. I trust them. The Ark will be safe until morning, and by then we will be past the border."

Avraham sneered. *No, you won't, Rebecca. No, you won't.*

He'd done what he had set out to accomplish by approaching her. He clenched his teeth, gave Samuel a long stare, spun on his heel, and strode from the room.

———

"That's impossible! Put my daughter on the phone immediately."

"I told you, she refuses to talk to you," Avraham said. He stood alone in the kitchen; it had taken him a full ten minutes to get David Ben Solomon on the line.

"Sir, you must realize that things aren't what you might think down here. The monks are witches, and it seems that Caleb has bewitched Rebecca. There's a state of confusion in the men, and I'm telling you that if we don't do something, this whole situation could go very badly."

"That's absurd!" Solomon stormed. "What are you talking about? Zakkai said nothing about this when I spoke to him."

"Zakkai? Zakkai's only concern is finding and packaging the Ark. Mine is getting the Ark back to Jerusalem. Your daughter spent nearly a week in the desert, sir. Most of it alone with this man. Her judgment has been compromised." He paused a beat. "I believe that they have plans to take the Ark themselves."

"Based on what? This is *nonsense*, Avraham!" Solomon was livid.

"If she would agree to it, you could talk to her yourself. But she has changed. I don't doubt that you would be able to hear it in her voice. Protecting this man, Caleb, who she's been sleeping—"

"Enough! Be careful, you're talking about my daughter!"

"Your daughter has given herself to this man," Avraham stated emphatically. "You may not like to hear it, but we now have the future of Israel to consider. We must take the appropriate action."

"What does Zakkai say of this?"

"I told you, Zakkai is in the cavern, boxing the Ark. He's hardly spoken five words to Rebecca since her return. We don't have all day. The Arabs are firing on us as we speak. I'll be lucky to get the Ark out as it is. The last thing we need is a conflict of power over confused loyalties."

"You're suggesting that *you* take over the mission?"

"Of course I'm suggesting that I take over the mission! Your daughter isn't thinking clearly. How else do you want me to put it?"

The line was silent except for Solomon's breathing.

"Sir, I only want to get the Ark out safely. We can sort out the details later. I realize how this must sound, but—"

"You have no *idea* how this sounds!" Solomon's voice trembled.

"And I'm sorry. But we're sitting on top of a crisis now. I'm only suggesting that you turn the mission over to me until we're out of Ethiopia. For the sake of Israel, David, I beg you."

Solomon paused and Avraham knew he had him. "The Ark is safe now?"

"Yes. For now. But I'm worried about—"

"Okay, you've made your point. For God's sake, get the Ark out of Ethiopia. But if I learn that you've touched one hair on my daughter's head, I will personally show you the wrath of God."

"Don't be ridiculous! I'm speaking about protecting her and bringing her home, not hurting her! Please remember who you are speaking to, sir."

"I do know who I am speaking to, and I also know that you have a heavy hand. Bring her home to me—and without a scratch, I'm warning you."

Avraham ignored the rebuke. "What are the coordinates and radio codes for the submarine pickup?"

Solomon gave them to him.

"Good. Now I have to insist that you confirm my authority to Samuel. Your daughter is strong willed, at the least. We don't have time for a power struggle—"

"Put him on."

"Stand by."

Avraham climbed quickly to the bell tower where he knew Samuel stood guard. He handed the phone to the soldier. "Solomon is giving me command of the mission. He wants to confirm it with you."

Samuel flashed him a look of astonishment and took the phone. "Yes?" He listened, and Avraham kept his eye on the man.

"Yes, sir, I understand . . . Well, yes I think she does seem . . . respecting of him . . . Yes, sir."

He handed the phone over. Avraham took it and spoke quickly. "Thank you, sir. We won't let you down."

"I'm counting on it," Solomon said. "*Israel* is counting on it. And, Avraham, perhaps it would be wise to encourage Caleb to stay away from my daughter. She's a Jew. He's a Christian, for God's sake."

Avraham smiled. "My sentiments exactly."

He hung up.

"You are now under my command, Samuel. Do you have any doubts about this?"

Regardless of his personal sentiments, the man was a trained soldier. "No, sir."

"Good. Then I want you to follow me."

"I'm covering the bell tower."

"Am I blind? When I ask you to follow me, you will do so."

"Yes, sir." Samuel keyed his handset and called up another man to cover the tower. He was a smart soldier; Avraham would give him that much. Someone to watch later.

Avraham followed Samuel down the stairs.

"Where to?"

"To arrest Rebecca."

Samuel stopped and turned back. Now his eyes were round like an owl's.

"Don't be a fool," Avraham said. "We don't have time to squabble over leadership now. You know that as well as I do. We have two hours before the Ark is ready. I have no intention of spending it arguing with a woman who has lost her sense of loyalty. And if you have any questions about my authority, I suggest you air them now. I will not be so cordial in front of others."

Samuel stared at him, and Avraham would have made his point with more force if it wasn't for the fact that he needed the man. Solomon had made his orders clear to Samuel. He needed his loyalty, at least for a few more hours.

"Do you question my judgment?"

"No, sir."

"Of course you don't. We are running out of time, soldier. I suggest we go."

———

The sun had been down an hour, and the Arabs had placed over a dozen explosives on the north side of the monastery. They had done so by engaging the Jews with small arms fire on the south side, just enough to hold their attention. Under the cover of night, the tracker, Hasam, and one of the soldiers had taken two trips each to the northern foundation and laid enough dynamite to knock a hole the size of Beirut in the heavy wall. But Ismael wasn't ready to detonate yet. This time he would be sure. As long as they had the time, he would lay every stick of dynamite.

A figure vaulted the rock to Ismael's right. It was the tracker, and he was covered with sweat. "Sir!" he blurted. He paused to catch his breath. "I have something to report, sir!"

Captain Asid spun from the wall of rocks overlooking the monastery. "Keep your voice down, you fool. They can hear you across the valley!"

The tracker collected himself.

"Well, what is it?" Ismael asked. The man looked like he'd seen a ghost downrange.

"I overheard the soldiers in the temple, sir. I believe they have . . ." He paused, searching for words. "They have the Ark of the Covenant."

Ismael had told them about the Jews' foolhardy mission, of course, and now Hasam had overheard the Jews discussing it himself.

"We know what they think—"

"No, sir." Hasam was shaking his head vehemently. "They have found the Ark in a cavern under the monastery and they are crating it up now for transportation."

Ismael stared at the tracker, unbelieving. Was it possible? "They have the Ark? That's impossible! You're sure?"

"I didn't see it, but I can tell you that they are sure. Nothing else could account for what I heard."

Ismael turned back towards the monastery. He had wondered why they hadn't fled the moment the Jew had arrived with Caleb. This would explain it. Because they had the Ark! They couldn't leave the Ark. And if they had the Ark, it would mean . . .

A small ball of heat mushroomed in Ismael's skull. He spun around and ran for his horse. The beast stamped in fear, and he quickly calmed it enough to pull the satellite phone free from his saddle pack. He switched it on and swore silently while it searched for a signal.

This changed everything. *Everything!* His discussion with Abu on the Temple Mount flashed through his mind. Their worst fears—the one scenario that hadn't really been a fear at all because it seemed so unlikely—had actually materialized! He had come to Ethiopia to kill one of Islam's worst enemies and instead he'd discovered one far worse.

The signal bar swelled and he punched in his father's number, hit an eight instead of a five on the last digit, cleared the screen cursing bitterly, and entered it again. This time he completed the whole sequence and lifted the phone to his ear. His whole body was wet with sweat. What if Abu wasn't . . .

"Hello."

"Abu!" The connection wasn't good. He covered his other ear with his free hand and turned away from the wind. "Abu?"

"Ism . . ." Static filled his ear for a moment. " . . . bad connection."

"Father, can you hear me?"

"Yes. Go ahead. I have you now."

"Abu. They have the Ark."

The phone filled with static again. He swore and turned again. "Abu? Abu, can you . . ."

"Yes, I can hear you. Settle down! What do you mean, they have the Ark?"

"They've found the Ark in the monastery. One of my men overheard them by the north wall—"

"How do you know—"

"I'm telling you, they have the Ark!" Ismael's voice sounded high in the night air. "Believe me, they have it."

This time there was only a stunned silence.

"Father?"

"You are absolutely positive about this, Ismael?"

"I believe so. Yes."

"They are in the monastery?"

"Yes."

"Can they escape?"

Ismael hesitated. "No. No, I can't see how they can. We have them surrounded."

"And yet they already have once."

Ismael blinked rapidly several times. Yes, they had, hadn't they?

"Listen to me, Ismael. I can't tell you how much damage will be done if they escape to Jerusalem with the Ark. It will bring a war. Do you understand? Not just a skirmish, but a full-scale war with full armies committed." A pause. "Do you hear me? You *must* destroy the monastery!"

His father paused. "And if they do escape, they must not be allowed to reach Jerusalem. You may want a war, Ismael, but I do not. Stop them, and all of Islam will be in your debt."

Ismael took a deep breath and settled himself. "Actually, you're right, it is war that I want."

"You will have your war. But not like this."

"If you don't trust me, then send in an air strike."

"Do I have time for that?"

"You see, you don't trust me. And no, you don't have time."

"Then I not only trust you, I depend on you. Islam depends on you. Allah depends on you."

Ismael glanced up and saw that Asid had walked up. "I will call you soon. Allah be praised." He cut the connection. His father was begging. When was the last time his father had begged anything of him?

"What shall I tell the men?" Asid asked.

"Tell them nothing. We will blow the monastery as planned. And if there is an Ark, we will take it ourselves."

———

Rebecca stared down the barrel of Avraham's nine-millimeter Browning. Behind her Leiah and Jason and the monks stood in stunned silence. To

Avraham's right, Samuel looked on, but he made no move to stop the man. That was the real problem here.

"Don't be stupid, Avraham," she said. "You'll never get away with this." She looked at Samuel. "Take his gun, Samuel."

"I'm sorry, sir. I can't."

"What do you mean you can't? You've forgotten whom you follow?"

"No, sir. I follow David Ben Solomon. He's put Avraham in charge of the evacuation. I'm sorry but—"

"Don't be a fool! My father's in Jerusalem! This is a mutiny; can't you see that?" If she moved quickly enough—while Samuel chewed on her words— she might be able to sidestep Avraham's shot. But who was behind her? A week ago she might not have cared. She lowered her hand near her revolver.

"Keep your hands up!" Avraham shouted, spittle flying from his mouth.

"You have to listen to me, Samuel," Rebecca said. She looked deep into his eyes. "We have the Ark of the Covenant, and we are taking it to Jerusalem. Have I ever not pulled you through? Avraham has other plans. Don't you, Avraham?"

He tilted his pistol and shot over her head. Several monks cried out, startled. Rebecca didn't flinch. If not for the monks, she would have made her move then. But they were in the line of fire.

"The next bullet will be in your head! Take her gun, Samuel."

They faced off, still for several beats. Then Samuel walked forward and Rebecca felt a tremor rip through her bones. This couldn't be happening! Her mind flew through several options. She considered grabbing Samuel and spinning him around as a shield, but she knew that Avraham would shoot him without a thought. Her draw was fast—she would have the time to kill Avraham, but not without sacrificing Samuel. How had he managed to pull this off?

Samuel reached her and lifted her side arm from its holster. Rebecca stood, hardly believing that she was allowing him to take it. But her mind was still frozen with the realization that if she made a move, innocent people would die. Caleb's people would die.

Where was Caleb? Down in his room the last she had seen him, pacing and meditating while the world fell apart above his head.

"I'm sorry, Rebecca," Samuel said. A shallow grin spread over Avraham's lips and he waved his gun for her to walk. She stood, paralyzed, her mind scrambling for orientation.

He's going to kill you, Rebecca. Look into his eyes—he has no intention of leaving you alive. She felt Samuel's nudge, and she walked out of the sanctuary on numb legs.

The sound of sporadic gunfire thundered from the tower. They had been exchanging rounds for several hours, each for their own purpose. The Arabs were laying explosives; she had guessed that much. But the Jews had no intention of being in the monastery when the charges blew. It would take the Arabs hours to discover that they had blown up nothing. At least that had been her plan.

Avraham dismissed Samuel and forced her down a long hall towards the monks' quarters. How long ago he'd planned this, she didn't know, but he was carrying through deliberately.

He chuckled behind her. "You should know better than to cross a man when you don't have your father to hide behind, Rebecca."

She ground her molars.

"I'm holding the gun and believe me, I haven't decided whether or not to use it," he said. "Don't tempt me."

They walked further and his breathing sounded loudly in the stone hall. "You know that I'm going to kill him."

Her pulse surged. He was talking about Caleb! She felt panic crowd her chest, and she almost threw herself back at him then, consequences aside. But she forced herself to walk on without showing emotion.

"The Arabs will kill the rest of you," Avraham said. "But Caleb is different. He has violated David Ben Solomon's daughter and I can't let that go, can I?"

"If you touch him, I swear that I will hunt you down and rip your throat out," she said.

"You terrify me. In there!"

She stopped and looked at the room to her right and then stepped in. It was pitch dark—only the lamplight from the hall showed her the cot. A bedroom. A lock had been hastily, but firmly, latched to the outer side of the door. Avraham had been busy in her absence.

"The state of Israel thanks you for your services, Rebecca. We never expected you to actually find the Ark, but now that you have, you're no longer needed. It is time to meet God."

"We?"

"Yes, we. You don't think I'm working alone, do you?" He chuckled again. "I've been assigned to your father from the start. You think I work with the old goat out of a passion to see the Messiah come? You're as stupid as he is. Your days were numbered long ago, Rebecca. It's only a convenience that they will end in Ethiopia, fifteen hundred kilometers from anyone who cares, under a mountain of rubble." He motioned at the wall behind her. "This room is on the north wall. If I'm not mistaken, our Arab friends are busily lining that wall behind you with explosives, a pleasant surprise really. At least your death will be a quick one."

He had been their enemy all along! The revelation sent a chill to her heels. "Why?"

"Why? You poor little innocent girl. Not everyone wants the Temple rebuilt. Good-bye, Rebecca. Say hello to God for me."

He slammed the door and she heard the latch clank shut. Tiny pinpoints of light burst in her eyes, but they faded quickly, leaving only a thick blackness. A knot rose in her throat as the full reality of what she'd just heard settled into her mind.

For a long time she could do nothing but stand there and stare into the dark.

34

IT TOOK THEM LESS THAN HALF AN hour to complete the crate under Avraham's supervision. In the end, it wasn't nearly as stable as Zakkai kept insisting it should be, but Avraham overrode the man with a few forceful words. There was no telling how soon the Arabs would begin their attack, and he had no intention of being around when they did.

The seven Israeli soldiers dropped through the hole into the Ark chamber one by one.

"What about the prisoners?" Samuel asked.

"It's their monastery, not ours," Avraham said. "We leave them to the Arabs."

"And where is Rebecca?" Samuel asked as the last soldier lowered himself by the rope ladder. Zakkai looked up from his position by the Ark. He didn't know about Rebecca yet.

"I'll bring her last, after you have the Ark safely out," Avraham said. "Let's move it!"

"Where's Rebecca?" Zakkai asked.

"She's in custody, as ordered by her father."

Zakkai blinked. Several of the others turned, surprised.

"Tell them, Samuel. Your dear Rebecca has had her ear twisted by Caleb. She's no longer sure about taking the Ark. We had no choice."

Zakkai looked at Samuel, eyes round in the torch's flames. "Samuel? Is this true?"

"Yes. I spoke to David myself. He put Avraham in charge."

Avraham breathed an internal sigh of relief. He had stretched the facts, but now Samuel had played his part as a good soldier and affirmed them. "Now, I suggest we move while we still can," he said.

They stood still, looking at him as if frozen in this chamber like mummies.

"Move!"

They moved.

Zakkai had wrapped the poles in canvas and fixed them on the crate's corners. At his instruction, four men hoisted the box and followed him and his torch into the tunnel.

Avraham watched them go, like pack rats into the dark, hauling their oversized coffin. That's what they would say in the unlikely event anyone asked—they carried the body of a deceased monk and his possessions for burial.

Avraham had already checked the tunnel's exit himself. It came out behind a rock beyond the hill, nearly five hundred meters from the monastery, well beyond the Arabs' perimeter. The leper colony and the truck waited a half-hour march to the west.

Avraham waited five minutes, long enough for the others to near the tunnel's end. Then he followed, alone. He'd had no intention of bringing Rebecca, of course. Her fate was sealed with the monks'.

The thumping of his boots followed him down the tunnel. Water dripped somewhere.

He'd thought about killing Caleb as he'd promised Rebecca, but it would have been a risky indulgence. The men's loyalty for the next few hours was more important than his personal revenge. Both Caleb and Rebecca would die anyway—Caleb in his own dungeon where he'd sequestered himself and Rebecca in her prison. If Caleb had come up, he would've shot him. But the man had remained in the bowels of the monastery, lost to the world.

Avraham eased around a large boulder and stepped into the night ten minutes later. The others were already gone. Gunfire sounded to the east—unreturned this time. It was only a matter of time before the Arabs noted the lack of gunfire from the tower, and then they would attack.

He lifted his hand to his cheek, took a breath, and raked his nails down hard enough to draw blood—a necessary wound. Pain throbbed through his jaw. He gritted his teeth and struck out for the leper colony.

A tingle of pleasure spread over his skull, like a warm, thick milk. For all practical purposes, the Ark was his.

———

The bedroom was furnished with a cot, a nightstand, and a single oil lamp, that much Rebecca discovered by feeling her way in the darkness. She had spent the next ten minutes in a meticulous search for matches, and then abandoned the search with a deep ragged breath. The room was her tomb, and she was suffocating already.

The blackness was thick enough to smell, she thought. The musty odor probably came from the grate in the corner, a gray-water drain. Rebecca worked her way around the room a third time, doing her best to ignore the tremble in her fingers as they searched for anything that might lead to an escape. She breathed through her nostrils in steady pulls. Sweat snaked down her neck, and slowly a desperate sense of doom crowded her mind. The door's latch refused to budge under repeated assaults. She sat on the cot, shaking from head to foot, fighting off panic.

There was no way out.

Dear God . . .

She stopped, unsure of what to pray. When had God heard her prayers and responded? An image stuttered through her mind: the monks, standing in the desert with their hands and chins raised, screaming silently at the sky while the Arabs walked around them. How could she deny such a power? She couldn't. But the fact that the monks were Christian was a problem, wasn't it? It was like watching a Muslim heal the sick.

Rebecca shook in the darkness, suddenly furious. She grunted aloud. The sound echoed hollow, surprisingly comforting. She screamed impulsively. A long piercing shriek that bounced off the walls and flooded her with rage.

She was going to die in this room. Avraham's guess that the Arabs had placed dynamite along this north wall was probably right. It's what she would do. There was no way a soldier could cover the whole length from the monastery without exposing himself.

The explosion would be sudden, a blinding wall of white fire, projecting chunks of concrete into the room at eight hundred kilometers an hour, like missiles from a gunship. One of those blocks would take her head off. She blinked in the direction of the wall. At any moment. It was how her mother had died.

Rebecca swallowed and reached back to lie down. Her hand hit the lamp and it toppled to the floor with a crash. Glass. She lay down on the cot, uncaring.

A thought ripped through her mind, and suddenly she cared very much. Glass. What were the walls made of? Stone? No, only the outer walls and tunnels were built of stone. The rest were poured concrete. But it was a rough concrete. She bolted upright.

And what about the grate?

Her heart now pounding in her chest, Rebecca dropped to her knees and felt for the glass. A sharp edge sliced into her finger, but the pain hardly registered. She grabbed the pillow from the bed behind her, pulled off the pillowcase, and wrapped it around her hand. The glass would probably do nothing to the concrete walls, but the grate might be a different matter.

She got her padded hand around the largest piece of glass and scrambled over to the corner, knocking the nightstand over on the way. With her left hand, she felt for the edge of the grate, and with her right she brought the sharp glass to its rough surface. She scraped.

The surface yielded!

She dug at the edge, scratching a hard claylike substance off the surface. The steel grate was roughly twenty by thirty centimeters—too small to crawl through, of course, but large enough to use as a tool. The thought of the wall exploding behind her suddenly brought a new terror. Accepting fate was one thing any good soldier learned to do in battle. But Rebecca was no longer accepting that fate.

Star bursts spotted her vision, and she forced herself to slow down. All she needed now was to pass out. She worked the grate quickly, uncovering first one edge and then two others. She jammed her fingers through the slots and yanked.

It came out with a soft popping sound. For a moment she knelt, paralyzed, stunned by her success.

She jumped to her feet and rushed for the door. She slapped hard concrete for a few seconds before realizing she was on the wrong wall. She walked parallel along the wall and around two corners before her fingers found the wood door.

Rebecca attacked the wood like an animal, swinging the heavy steel grate like a pick, grunting with each swing. The boards were less than an inch thick; she had seen that when she'd first entered.

It took twenty good whacks and one bloodied hand for the first plank to split. When it did, the hall's lamplight looked to her like the light of heaven, and she began to sob with her swings.

Two minutes later she crashed through the splintered planks, the pillowcase red around the grate. She gasped at the cool air, and waves of heat crashed down her spine. She dropped the grate with a jarring clank, pivoted to her left, and sprinted up the hall.

Rebecca slid to a stop at the outer hall and flattened herself against the wall, still breathing hard. The air was strangely silent. Gunfire sounded in the distance, but not from the monastery. Her people weren't returning fire.

Could they have left?

Dear God, they had left!

She sprinted for the study, spun through the door, and ran for the hole in the floor. The room below was dark and vacant. The rope still hung, limp in the shadows. She thought about dropping into the cavern and racing after them, but an image of Caleb filled her mind. Avraham would have left him. And the others. If she could get the monks out through the tunnel before the attack . . .

Rebecca whirled and ran for the hall that led down to the root cellar. As far as she could tell the monastery was empty.

"Caleb!" She called out before she reached the hole Zakkai had knocked through the floor. "Caleb!"

Amber light glowed from the hole in the root cellar's corner, like at the top of a jack-o'-lantern. She dropped to her knees and bent over it. "Caleb!"

"Yes?" He stepped into the light from his old room, smiling.

The sight was absurd, this man dressed in his tunic, at peace with the world, while Arabs prepared to storm the monastery. He must have seen something in her face because he dropped the grin and blinked.

"What is it?"

"Thank God, you're okay," she said. "What are you doing down here?"

He hesitated. "Talking to God."

"Of course, how silly of me. We have to get *out!* You can talk to God later."

He climbed up the ladder and followed when she ran. "Did God happen to tell you what happened to the Ark?" she asked.

He answered as if she were serious. "No. But I think I understand now."

"That's good, because I don't. Avraham has taken the Ark. While you were talking to God, he managed to lock me in a room and take over the mission. The throne of God is in the hands of a madman. I could've used your help." She said it all, surprised that she actually felt some anger at him for missing the entire episode and talking so placidly about it. In his own way he was impossible.

"He locked you in a room? I thought he was one of your soldiers."

"He was! Never mind. Right now we've got to get the others out of here before this whole place goes up." She rounded a corner and headed for the front of the monastery.

"So the Ark is gone then?"

"Yes."

They ran into the sanctuary and pulled up. Jason stood with an arm around his wife, Leiah. Eleven others waited where they had waited for many hours now, on the floor in the center of the room. Six monks and five servants. They were all here.

Jason dropped his arm and strode towards them. "Caleb! What's going on here?"

"When did the others leave?" Rebecca asked.

"I didn't know they *had* left. We haven't seen anyone for half an hour. What's happening?"

"Avraham has hijacked the Ark," Rebecca said. "That's what's happening. And if I'm right, this place is about to blow. We have to get you to safety. Hurry, follow me!" She headed for the door.

"They're going to blow up the monastery?" Leiah asked. "We can't let them—"

"If you want to live, I suggest you follow me. We don't have time!"

They broke for the door as one.

She led them, clopping down the hall like a pack of mules. From the hills outside, a voice called out in Arabic. They were getting suspicious. Shots rang out again.

Rebecca herded them into the study and handed Jason a torch from the wall. "Take them through the tunnel. Find a place to hide until morning. Then take them to the leper colony."

"What about you?" Jason asked.

She looked into his eyes. "The Arabs may find this room. If they do, they'll assume the Ark is on its way to Jerusalem and follow Avraham. I can't allow the Ark to fall into Arab hands—it would be the only thing worse than what's already happened."

"That's crazy! What can you do? You don't even have a gun!"

"Don't worry about me. I've been fighting these Palestinians since I turned twelve. I know how they think better than they do." She forced a grin. "You just stay alive."

"I'll go with you."

They turned to Caleb who had stepped forward.

"Don't be ridiculous," Rebecca said.

He lifted his right eyebrow.

"You can't come with me," she objected. "Not only would you be in the way, but you would end up dead. This isn't like the desert." Even as she said it, she knew it was sounding stupid to him, but the thought of putting him in harm's way again made her stomach turn.

"I don't think you understand, Rebecca," he said with a slight smile. "I have to go."

"Why, because you lost the Ark? The Ark is inconsequential to you, remember?"

"You're right. And that's why I have to go. Because the Ark is inconsequential. Powerless."

He was talking in riddles again.

A full burst of weapons fire suddenly filled the air. Distant yells sounded in Arabic—they were attacking!

"Go! Take them, Jason." She spun to Caleb. "I'm going alone!"

"Rebecca . . ." He spoke her name softly, as if tasting it on his tongue. A strange warmth spread over her head. She stopped, suddenly at a loss.

Caleb turned to his mother. "Don't worry, Mother. I know what I'm doing."

Leiah glanced at Rebecca and then walked up to her son. She lifted a hand and stroked his cheek. "Please be careful."

Rebecca could hardly believe that they were carrying on as if her instructions meant nothing. The Arabs were attacking and here they were, in the study, saying good-byes.

"Go with God." Leiah embraced him and then turned to Rebecca. "You will be careful with my son. And learn to listen to him; he knows more than you might think." She shot Rebecca a wink and a smile. Then she entered the hole and the others followed in single file.

Rebecca stared after them at a loss for words. An explosion shook the monastery. Caleb just looked at her.

"Stay close," she said and ran for the kitchen. They didn't have much time.

She and Caleb.

———

Avraham caught the team halfway to the leper colony.

"Who goes there?" Samuel's voice called out.

"It's me, you idiot. Get that gun off me!"

Avraham pulled up, panting. That they had gotten this far so quickly while lugging the heavy Ark was surprising. The rumbling started behind them—the Arabs were blowing up the monastery.

"Where's Rebecca?" Samuel demanded.

Avraham looked back in the direction of the monastery. "They're going to level it," he said. "Let's go."

"Where is Rebecca?" This time Samuel's tone was belligerent.

"Dead, I presume. The Arabs stormed the monastery before I could get to her. I barely escaped myself. If we don't move, none of us will escape. Now let's go!"

"No! We can't assume that she's dead!" Samuel said, stepping up. His eyes were wide and his face red. "I'm going back for her." He started back.

"And risk capture? I can't let you do that. They would force you to talk."

Samuel spun back. "We can't leave her, Avraham! You may be in charge, but she is our commander. We have to go back!" He turned and walked.

Avraham palmed his pistol.

"Samuel!"

The soldier turned.

Boom! The gun bucked.

For a full second, the soldier stared wide-eyed, a round hole punched through his forehead. He fell to the ground like a sack of beans.

Avraham turned from him and faced the others. "We have the Ark of the Covenant, gentlemen. Our objective is to return it to Jerusalem. I am in command of that mission. If you stand in my way, I will kill you. Do you understand?"

He lowered his gun arm. Jude, the senior among them now, just stared at him blankly. No one spoke. "Good. Strip him. Let's go!"

Jude stripped Samuel of his weapons, and the troop left, single file except for the Ark, which required four of them to carry. If they'd been in a fog about Avraham's authority, he had cleared the air for them.

35

THE NORTH SIDE OF THE MONASTERY was crumbling under heavy explosives—fortunately the kitchen was on the west side, but even then it was being shaken to bits when Rebecca and Caleb sprinted through.

Rebecca's mind raced through their options. She knew what she had to do, and it was looking as if there was only one way to do it. Avraham had stripped her weapons and radio. She had nothing but her hands and her mind, and she wasn't sure how well those were working. They were telling her that she had to get past the falling cupboards and flying mortar, and that was a start, but she knew that beyond the outer door she would meet flying bullets, hardly a proposition to favor.

She snatched a kitchen knife from the counter and seized the wooden door handle. "Keep your head down and make a beeline for the stable. No hesitation!"

"That's on the north side!" he said. "There are explosions—"

"That's right. The smoke will give us some cover. Just follow me!"

She pulled the door open and slid out into the night. She glanced back and saw that Caleb was on her heels, crouched low. Muzzle flashes spotted the hills—the Arabs were in a full firing mode, waiting for the air to clear. Another explosion thundered to their right, and she instinctively dropped to her belly. Caleb tripped over her feet and sprawled facedown on her back. They both grunted and Caleb rolled to the right.

Rebecca sprang to her feet and tugged on his arm. "Come on! Now! Run!"

She vaulted the corral fence and ran for the shack they called a stable. The air was clouded with dust and smoke—this was good. The monastery's north wall stood directly to their right—this was not good.

She slammed into the side of the stable and ducked inside just in time to avoid Caleb who crashed in from behind. They pulled up on the straw floor, panting. All three camels stood quivering in the far corner. Behind them, another explosion rocked the monastery, and the beasts honked in terror.

Caleb ran to them, speaking softly in his mother tongue, Ge'ez.

Rebecca scanned the shack and found what she was looking for. Along one wall stood a feeding bin—a rectangular box roughly two meters by one meter. She pulled it over, spilling the hay it held.

"You have any blankets here?"

"The camels haven't been stripped down yet."

Of course! They had been too preoccupied to take the bedrolls and saddles from the beasts since she and Caleb had ridden in earlier today. God gave his favors still.

"Help me put this on one of them," she said.

"The feeding trough?"

"Strapped to the back of a camel and covered with a blanket it becomes the Ark. Grab the end!"

She lifted one end and they hoisted it to the back of the nearest camel. It took them less than a minute to secure and cover it.

"You want them to think we have the Ark?"

"That's the idea. Draw them off." She saw his apprehensive stare. "It wasn't my idea that you come, just remember that. We have only one objective now. We run and we make sure the Arabs see us run."

"I would think that actually escaping would also be a reasonable objective," he said.

She cast him a sidelong glance. "Obviously. They catch us and they find out we don't have the Ark—that's a problem." She cinched the strap holding the blanket and grabbed the camel's reins and led it to the door.

"We wait for the next explosion . . ."

As if to answer her, a detonation split the air, sending a cloud of debris skyward.

"Now!" She yanked her camel into the open and forced it to the back gate. It protested loudly. She had wanted the Arabs to know—well now they knew.

She fumbled with the gate. Too slow! They would be sitting ducks!

Caleb suddenly pushed her aside, flipped a latch, and threw the gate open. He made a kissing sound and quickly guided the camels through. "Follow me!" he said, leaping to the camel's back. He pulled the second camel by its lead rope and kicked his animal into a startled run.

Rebecca clambered onto her camel and nearly fell off when it took after its cousins. Bullets whined about her and she ducked, kicking the camel into an awkward gallop. How they managed to reach the first draw without collecting a few slugs, she didn't know, but they made it and then galloped up the rocky incline.

Caleb kept looking back. Maybe it was good that he'd come.

They crested the first hill, and Rebecca knew that the Arabs would have to be blind not to see the large box silhouetted on the back of the second camel. But she had to make sure. At the last minute, she pulled back on her reins. The camel stamped to an impatient standstill.

She screamed at the top of her lungs. "Run, Caleb! Run with the Ark and with God!"

She kicked the animal under her, and it bolted over the hill into the next draw. Caleb had stopped and she raced up to him.

"Keep going! That was for the Arabs' benefit, not yours. Get us out of here! I guarantee they're coming. They have horses."

He nodded and took off down the hill. Far off, voices began to shout in Arabic. *That's it, follow us,* Rebecca willed. *Come on, Ismael.* Caleb made a sharp turn to the east at the bottom of the draw and she followed.

Come on and kill me.

———

Captain Asid ran up to Ismael, frantic and breathing hard.

"They're gone! All of them! They've taken the Ark!"

"Slow down! How can you be certain?"

"I sent a man in as soon as the team on the north reported the camels. The monastery's empty. And my men are sure that one of the camels was loaded with the Ark. They saw it—there's no mistake."

"And how could over a dozen men and women walk past your men?"

The idea that the monastery could have emptied without their knowing was impossible. There was the report of the camels, of course, but that had been only three.

"They had to have taken an escape route somewhere," the captain said. "But the Ark is headed north on the back of a camel. We saw it."

Ismael stared down at the monastery. Half of its north wall was gone and the bell tower had fallen over. They hadn't heard a single gunshot from the windows in ten minutes. The Jews had escaped. The main party had eluded them completely, but if Asid was right, the Ark had not. It was the only explanation. And Rebecca and Caleb were the two leading the Ark north. The thought made him sick. He could not make the same mistake twice.

"Set off the rest of the charges and order the men to the north hill," he said. "We're going after the Ark."

There was the possibility that he had it wrong—that the other Jews had the Ark and the two on the north hill were a decoy. He doubted that Rebecca would leave the Ark in another soldier's charge, but it was possible.

He snatched up his satellite phone and keyed in his father's number. The Arab world was about to receive a little shock, and at least half of him wasn't disappointed. Abu would pull out the stops now.

It was time for Islam to crawl out of hibernation.

36

ABU ISMAEL WALKED ALONG THE HEDGE of roses beside the Egyptian presi-dent, hands folded behind his back, head lifted to the palace gardens. Yusaf al-Zeid strode tall, wearing his patented slight smile, listening carefully without much sign of emotion. Not much, but some. Abu had met with him on three other occasions in years past and found him to be a man thoroughly in command of himself. But the information Al-Zeid had just ingested was challenging the man's impeccable facade, Abu thought.

"I have full authority from the king to commit all Syrian forces on the one condition that you agree to join us," Abu said.

"And the others?" President Al-Zeid asked.

"Jordan is dependent on both Syria and Egypt. Their military is a fraction of ours. But they clearly understand the threat we face. Not to defend the *Haram al-Sharif* will cost us Islamic unity. I'm sure you see that."

"Yes, I see that. I may be getting older, but I haven't lost my sight. Islam will never lose the *Haram al-Sharif*—you have my full support on that objective."

"Then we should have your support on the military operation. If the Ark arrives in Jerusalem and we don't move in the appropriate time, while surprise is still on our side, we will face an escalation which will only bring in the West. And we aren't in a position to engage the United States."

Al-Zeid nodded. "My predecessor tried the surprise route with your country once before. Do you like airplanes, General?"

"Airplanes. Yes, I suppose so."

"We lost almost all of our airplanes while they were still on the ground in that surprise attack. As it turned out, the Israelis surprised *us*."

"We didn't have 40,000 armed Palestinians in Israel's borders in '73 either.

They are preparing to mobilize already. Of Israel's 87,000 air force person-nel, 55,000 are on reserve. That's two-thirds. We believe that the Palestinians can ground half of their air force with their raids. Israel has 475 fighters and roughly 130 attack helicopters. If half of these are rendered inactive, your air force alone will have even odds. In 1973 your air force was dominated by MiGs. Now you have over 200 F-16 or Mirage fighters, not to mention over 80 modern attack helicopters. In '73 you had none. On the ground, we have an overwhelming advantage—9,000 tanks to their 4,300. We have nearly three times as many infantrymen, and they're far better trained than they were in '73. We outnumber them in nearly every category of armaments, and most importantly we will be engaging them on four fronts." Abu sighed. "It all boils down to their air force. If we can limit their air power, we could take them in three days."

President Al-Zeid chuckled. "We may be twice as large, but half of our equipment is obsolete."

"But we still hold the advantage. I could go on—nearly two-thirds of your tank force has now been upgraded to M-60s or M-1As. We both have advanced guided missiles that could cause havoc in their cities. Together we have five times as many antiaircraft guns and three times as much artillery. We have—"

"Yes, yes, General. I know what we have." He turned to face Abu and raised an eyebrow. "It seems that your country has boosted its intelligence budget."

Abu ignored the innuendo.

Al-Zeid nodded. "All right, I agree that we now have the tactical strength to overwhelm Israel with a four-front assault, as you've described. Frankly, I've thought so for a few years now." He lifted a finger. "You're forgetting Lebanon—they will be a thorn in Israel's north. I believe you still have over 30,000 men stationed there. But there's one small detail you are missing, aren't you?"

"Their nuclear arsenal. Yes, but they won't use nuclear weapons close in, on their own country. If we can get into Israel quickly enough, we elimi-nate their nuclear option. We're proposing a three-phase attack we don't think they will anticipate."

Abu took a breath.

"Yes, go on."

"The Palestinians attack Israeli airfields with every man they have. This before either Syria, Egypt, or Jordan has openly mobilized. But we already have limited mobilization. As you say, we have 30,000 men in Lebanon and 40,000 men in the Golan area, including the 14th Special Forces Division which recently moved from the Beirut area. Supported by a massive artillery attack from the rear, we could invade the Golan without warning. Our 5th and 7th Mechanized divisions are in the region and we have five more armored divisions between the Golan and Damascus. If Israel's air force is hampered by the Palestinians, we could easily push through the Golan with a massive assault in ten hours. Egypt would engage in a similar move to the south and Jordan to the east. We have geography on our side—Israel is a very small country. Syria will commit 300 MiGs to flood the northern skies. Obsolete or not, they will provide a significant complication for the Israelis, leaving the south open for your air force. How long would it take to reach Tel Aviv with 200 of your F-16s and Mirage fighters?"

"Not long. It would have to be very well coordinated."

"But not so well that it foretells itself. That's the key, sir. A sudden attack without warning. You're currently running a joint armored division exercise with the Saudis outside of Dhaba?"

"Yes," Al-Zeid said.

"Move the tanks to Jordan's border," Abu said. "Keep your air force and your armored divisions in the Sinai on high alert, and move only if the Palestinian forces are successful in inflicting significant damage to Israel's air force."

"No, General. I will not commit to a limited engagement. If we go, we go full force. But I'm still concerned about their tactical nuclear weapons. We should be discussing this with my generals."

"And we will. But first I need your commitment in principle."

"And all of this is precipitated by the Jews' discovery of the Ark of the Covenant." The president shook his head. "You are absolutely sure about this?"

"Our sources are impeccable. Either way, we would not attack unless the Ark actually reached Jerusalem, and then only if we felt certain that the Knesset would act on it."

"By voting to rebuild their Temple."

"Yes. But we can't wait until they've mobilized and gathered support from the West. We will have lost the advantage."

"And just where is this Ark supposed to be at this time?"

They came to a table with a silver tea set, and Al-Zeid invited him to sit with a sweep of his hand. In truth, Abu had no clue where the Ark was now. He wasn't even positive it existed. If it didn't, none of this would matter. If it did, on the other hand, all of this would matter very much.

"The archaeological expedition has left the monastery I told you about and is headed for the sea. The Saudis have agreed to triple their patrol over the southern sea, and I will ask you to do the same over the northern sea. We also have a commando team on the ground in pursuit. All routes north are being blocked. But in the event they slip through, they could be in Jerusalem as soon as two days from now."

"Two days! So soon!"

Abu nodded.

"The others can move that fast?"

"Yes. Without a full mobilization, yes. It could work, sir. It really could work. In fact, this may be the *only* time it could work." Abu sipped at the green tea. "I'm sure that there are those who are praying for the Ark to arrive in Jerusalem so that we will be forced into war. In their mind it is a gift from Allah."

"Gift? A gift that would cost many lives."

"A small price for the sanctity of Islam, some would say. We can't allow the Jews to take away the *Haram al-Sharif.* In the end, many more would die. Muslim masses would stampede, from Teheran to Jakarta."

The Egyptian president lifted his cup. "The Ark of the Covenant. It's like something right out of the Koran. The end of an age."

"So you agree then? You will commit Egypt?"

"If the Ark arrives in Jerusalem?"

"Yes."

The president looked off towards the high rises of Cairo on the skyline.

A prayer call echoed in the far distance. "I'm not sure either of us has a choice, my friend. The people will have their own say, and we both know what that say will be. I will commit our full support."

Abu had known that he would, but hearing him say it sent a chill down his spine. He could not hide a small smile.

"I've taken the liberty of preparing preliminary battle plans which I would like to review with your generals," Abu said.

Al-Zeid lifted his hand and snapped his fingers at a man in tailored civilian clothes. The man jogged over. "Call an emergency meeting of the chiefs of staff in one hour. If any of the chiefs can't be there, make sure the next in command can."

The man hesitated. "Yes, sir." He left at a run.

"Can you trust the Palestinian forces, General?" Al-Zeid asked. "It would seem that your plan depends on them."

"Yes, it does. But their futures are at stake. It's their homeland we are talking about. They will fight to their deaths; that much I can depend on. I only hope our soldiers have as much heart as they do."

"They will. We're talking about the *Haram al-Sharif*, Islam's third most holy site. Believe me they will." Al-Zeid's mouth curved to form a slight smile. "Those who believe that this is a gift from Allah may end up being right," he said.

———

The night was both kind and impossible to Rebecca and Caleb. Kind because it kept the heat down and provided cover from the Arabs. Impossible because the same darkness made following Avraham's lorry almost hopeless, and their first priority was intercepting Avraham. They had no communications and no weapons—for all practical purposes they were at the mercy of whoever happened upon them. Worse, they had no way to warn Solomon that Avraham had hijacked the Ark. That was how Rebecca read the situation.

Caleb evidently saw their predicament differently. He had taken charge, leading into the night as if he knew precisely where he was going, and it wasn't up the rough road they both knew the truck had taken.

They had doubled back to the leper colony after putting some distance between themselves and the Arabs, who, despite riding horses, were in the difficult position of following *their* tracks in the dark. If the Arabs somehow managed to stay on their trail, it would be a testament to their tracker.

The road leading north from the leper colony was filled with enough potholes to force Avraham's truck to a crawl. But after an hour Caleb had veered off the road and headed into the hills.

Rebecca had stopped on the road. "Where are you going?"

"This way's better," he'd said.

"And where does *this way* lead?"

"It's the right way, trust me."

"I am trusting you. I've been following you in the dark for three hours. But I would also like to know why you're taking us off their trail."

"You want to go to Jerusalem, don't you? We're going to Jerusalem."

"On camels? We need to stay on the road and pray for a truck to pass this way. I have to get to a phone!"

"There *are* no trucks or phones on this road." Caleb turned and walked his camel forward, to the top of a small hill overlooking the road. Rebecca held her camel by the roadside, furious at his presumption.

"Wait a second! You can't just—"

"Yes, I can." He stopped his camel and turned back. "And you must come with me. We have to get to Jerusalem! It's what this is about, don't you see?"

"No, I don't see! This is about the Ark and stopping Avraham. It has nothing to do with you!"

He looked at the horizon in front of him and then turned back. "I know these hills, Rebecca. Trust me, this is the shortest way to the sea."

"And then what? We'll have lost them!"

He didn't answer. For a few long moments they just sat there, facing each other in the darkness.

"Please, Rebecca. We must go this way."

His voice was strong yet gentle, and it made her want to follow him. She turned her camel up the hill and nudged it forward, frustrated but out of options. Without him, she would be lost in this country.

Caleb led the way without any further explanation. An hour later Rebecca was fighting the unshakable certainty that she'd made a mistake by following him. And if she had, its effects could run through Israel like a black plague.

What did Avraham have in mind?

They plodded north through the night, talking only rarely, and then only to discuss practicalities, like the crossing of tricky washes or the best route up some steep hills. Otherwise, Caleb seemed content to stay to himself, and Rebecca's frustration slowly built. Either way, she was relegated to following this madman as he led her towards the sea. Never mind that neither of them knew what to do once they reached the sea; never mind that Avraham was probably melting the Ark down at that very moment: she had committed herself to stay behind Caleb.

She'd been a fool to bring him.

On the other hand, he carried himself with a confidence she had not seen before. Gone was the wide-eyed child of the desert, stumbling around mumbling his prayers, eager to become like Father Hadane. Now Caleb led the way purposefully. Either he had gone completely off the deep end, or he'd found himself. Avraham had hijacked the Ark, and now Caleb had hijacked her mission.

They made steady progress. The sun rose and climbed the sky slowly. The thoughts from the night had faded with her own weariness.

Rebecca slumped over her camel and dozed near noon. She woke on and off, each time to the same sight of endless hills and Caleb's back to her.

Once she saw him begin to nod off, and for some reason she found the sight amusing. In a way she could not explain, it felt good to be in his hands, she thought. A *Jewish* man like Caleb would be a good catch. Tall and strong with broad shoulders, yet as gentle as a summer breeze. Not timid, mind you—Caleb had enough courage for ten men. He was a bit strange, admittedly. She wasn't sure about him in that way, but she imagined he would make an interesting man to live with. And an interesting father . . .

She shook her head and adjusted herself.

Dear God, give me grace.

37

THE KNESSET BUILDING STOOD AT THE center of expansive mani-
cured grounds, seventeen kilometers north of the Temple Mount, a flat,
white rectangular slab from the sky. Its level roof overhung an outer walkway
lined with Roman columns that supported it on all four sides. In the immediate forecourt the eternal flame burned, its fire licking at an unconsumed
"burning bush." In the outer courts by the main gate, the menorah stood like
a pitchfork with seven fingers, each telling its tale of Israel. Thousands of visitors filed by the ornate structure every day. But very few ever found their way
into the secret places of the building, where this tiny country at the center of
human existence charted its path through history.

David Ben Solomon glanced at Prime Minister Simon Ben Gurion, who
had called these selected government and military leaders to the Government
Room today, a departure from his offices where they were more accustomed
to doing business. Thirty brown executive chairs snuggled against the large
circular table, which was open in the middle. Inset ceiling lights glowed over
each chair. It was the kind of place where dignitaries conducted important
business, and Solomon fully intended they do precisely that today.

Goldstein stared at Solomon with dark eyes as he drew out the Ethiopian
Ark theory. Apparently the prime minister hadn't told the Labor Party leader
everything yet. Most of the rest knew nothing and listened with vague interest—nothing more than an obscure history lesson that had an eventual rele-
vant point. Several of the Labor Party—the minister of education, Uzi Baram,
case in point—watched him sternly. Goldstein's inner circle. But none of
them knew what Solomon and the prime minister knew.

That the Ark had not only been found; it was now on its way to
Jerusalem.

Solomon took his time, walking around the group like a schoolteacher, enjoying his time on the floor for a change. He said nothing of Rebecca's expedition. He only led them carefully down a theoretical road which supported the Ark's existence in Ethiopia, and then bolstered his position that if the Ark were ever found, the Temple had to be rebuilt.

Only then did he tell them the rest.

"So, my friends. You may be wondering why the prime minister has invited me to bore you with archaeological theories about a lost holy relic." He took a deep breath for gravity. "It is because we have found the Ark. And we have found it precisely where this theory suggested it should be. In Ethiopia. Hidden under a monastery, unharmed and fully intact."

Some of them blinked; some of them just stared at him. Solomon doubted they completely understood what he had just said.

"The Ark of the Covenant is on its way to Jerusalem as we speak."

The air might have been sucked from the room for the silence that fell over everything.

Solomon glanced at the prime minister again and saw that he was watching them intently.

"The Ark is found?" someone said in a soft, unbelieving voice.

"Yes. Yes, it is." Solomon felt a sudden pressure of emotion behind his eyes. Saying it here, in front of Israel's leaders, had a certain weight he had not expected.

"You . . . you've actually found the Ark of the Covenant and are bringing it to Jerusalem?" Moshe Aron asked. The Speaker's cheeks seemed to sag with his eyes.

"Yes."

"No!" Goldstein's chair skidded back as he stood. "No, we can't allow that! It's suicide!"

"It is life!" Solomon thundered.

They glared at each other for several beats, and then the room erupted with ten voices, all demanding, all argumentative, all at full volume.

"Silence!" Ben Gurion yelled. "Be quiet, all of you! Sit! Sit, sit, sit." He'd stood and now walked around them. "Another outbreak like that and we will adjourn. I have invited you here out of courtesy—don't abuse it."

Those standing, sat—Goldstein lastly and most reluctantly.

"We will have a hearing on the issue of the Temple before the full Plenum if the Ark actually makes it to Jerusalem, but I can't stress enough the need for prudence in the days to come. Whether some of you like it or not, King David brought the Ark to this holy city. God's presence dwelt within that Ark, and King Solomon built the Temple for that Ark. Also, whether you like it or not, over 70 percent of this country's citizens favor the rebuilding of the Temple in the event of the Ark's discovery."

"Which is why we have no business uncovering the Ark!" Goldstein said.

"We're beyond that."

"Not necessarily. What's uncovered can be covered."

"Perhaps. But I refuse to be the man who covers up the discovery of the Ark. I may be a politician, but I am first a Jew."

The table broke out into heated discourse, and the prime minister held his hand up. "Please! Listen to me."

The room quieted.

"That doesn't mean I know what to do with the Ark. I would like to hear from some of you." He faced an older Orthodox gentleman, Shmuel Halpert of the United Judaism Party. "Rabbi, what do you think will be the position of the Orthodox?"

"It is forbidden to go on the Holy Mount before the Messiah comes. How can we take the Temple Mount without going up on it?"

"You're standing in the Messiah's way!" Solomon said.

"The Messiah's way? The Messiah's way is for man to overcome evil impulses. Not to hunt down lost treasures."

"We *are* overcoming evil! The evil that lives on our Temple Mount in the form of Islam! Satan himself has set up shop in God's Temple, and you have the gall to talk about impulses?"

"Please," Ben Gurion interrupted. "We've heard the arguments a hundred times. Are you saying, Rabbi, that the Orthodox community will not favor bringing the Ark into Jerusalem?"

The rabbi thought for a few seconds. "This is the original Ark; you're sure of that?"

"Yes," Solomon answered.

"Then how can we *not* bring it into the city?"

It was the typical double-mindedness that had frustrated Solomon for two decades.

"The Likud will favor bringing in the Ark as well," Ben Gurion said, "although I'm sure we can expect the usual squabbling. As will Meretz. That will give us a significant consensus, not only in the polls, but in the government. But I want you to understand that it's primarily out of my own convictions that I have guaranteed the safe passage of the Ark into Jerusalem, if it has indeed been found." He looked at Solomon. "It sounds like the Ark is coming, ladies and gentlemen. We should get used to that idea. The real issue facing us now is the Arab reaction once they learn that we have the Ark."

"We have no right deciding any matters without the full Plenum in session," the Knesset Speaker said. "Which committee would have jurisdiction over this?"

"No committee. I have jurisdiction," Ben Gurion returned. "We will get to the Plenum. I haven't stepped beyond my authority in bringing the Ark to Jerusalem."

The Speaker was accustomed to setting the agenda, and his frown made it clear he wasn't completely satisfied. "Perhaps not yet. But any decision regarding the Ark *must* be a matter for Israel and its elected leaders."

"What do you think this meeting is about?"

Several others jumped on the point, and Solomon walked calmly over to his chair and sat. They went back and forth, arguing a dozen angles for over twenty minutes with hardly a pause for breath. Thank goodness that Ben Gurion had decided to float the notion of the Ark's return with these before taking it to the Knesset. There were a few enemies in the room, but not like in the full Knesset. There it might come to fisticuffs.

Goldstein returned the discussion to his insistence that they halt the progress of the Ark immediately, but as the arguments were cast, it became apparent that he was in the minority. The prime minister fell quiet and let them argue—it was the way of their government.

"I would like to hear from the military," the prime minister finally insisted. "We won't stop the Ark's coming—your arguments notwithstanding, I've already made that quite clear. The real question is what we can expect from the Syrians. Or from the others." The place settled into silence. "Defense Minister Yishai?"

Defense Minister Benjamin Yishai nodded at another man in full military dress. "I will defer to General Gur for the moment."

The air force's top man cleared his throat and let them sit in silence for a few seconds. "If our enemies believe that we intend to take the Temple Mount, we will have trouble."

"Of course we will!" Goldstein said. "Only an idiot would think otherwise."

"Let the general talk," Moshe Aron snapped.

"Please, Stephen. You've had your say." The prime minister stood and paced to his right. "We will have trouble, yes. You'll remember the havoc of October 8, 1990. The Temple Mount Advocates put up posters announcing plans to lay a cornerstone for the third Temple." He cast a sideways glance at Solomon. It was Solomon's doing, and most of them knew it. "The Palestinians took the posters as a declaration of war. Thousands marched on the Mount, and within a few short hours a score of them lay dead. The Palestinians will riot; we can expect that much."

He turned to General Gur. "But what about our neighbors?"

"It depends," the general said. "If we take the Temple Mount, they will engage us. The whole world of Islam would engage us."

"And that is a matter for the full Knesset," the prime minister said. "But in bringing the Ark to Jerusalem, what risks do we face?"

The general turned to a dark-haired man on his right that Solomon did not know. "That's a matter for intelligence. Daniel?"

"That the Arabs would be forced to engage us over the Temple Mount isn't in question," the dark-haired man said. "The question really boils down to two issues. Their intelligence—how much they know—and timing. Obviously they can't act on what they don't know. If we were to bring the Ark into Jerusalem without their knowledge, we would be in a much better position than otherwise. But if they knew we had the Ark, and they believed that our possession of it would lead to an imminent assault on the

Temple Mount, they might attempt a preemptive strike of their own. This would be a potentially catastrophic scenario."

"They tried a preemptive strike in '73," Moshe Aron said. "It didn't work then."

General Gur answered, "It didn't work because we caught wind of it and struck first. But the landscape has changed. Then, we didn't have forty thousand Palestinian soldiers to think about. Now we do. A sudden coordinated attack on four fronts would be a significant challenge."

"Our military is far superior to any of theirs," Aron pushed. "We've faced challenges before."

"I'm not talking about anything like what we've faced before. Frankly, our superiority is in our air force, not in all of our armed forces. And the air force requires twenty-four hours to fully mobilize."

"Then mobilize now!"

Gur glanced at Daniel, the intelligence man, who spoke. "If we mobilize now, then *they* will mobilize. It's a quid pro quo we've operated under for some time. Mobilization alone could push us into war, and I would go one step further than the general. Our air force is *not* the dominant power it once was—the Egyptians have modernized considerably. Our real strength lies in unconventional weapons."

The table went silent. He was talking about nuclear weapons, of course.

"This is asinine!" Goldstein said. "I can't believe we're sitting here talking like this. We are *not* all powerful—we will always have our neighbors to live with. We can't risk war, and we certainly can't risk mobilizing! We're talking about an archaeological find, for God's sake. This Messianic fervor will be the end of us!"

"We are already at our end!" Solomon said. "Israel is nothing without God! Since our inception we have run from God because we fear our neighbors more than we fear him. Even the rabbis have supported the status quo with their excuses of not wanting to step on holy ground—for what? For fear of Islam! We live in blasphemy!"

"Stop!" Ben Gurion's voice rang out.

He glared at Solomon and faced the general again. "We have no reason to believe the Arabs know anything."

"Two-thirds of my men are reservists," General Gur said. "You had better be sure about your intelligence. And you'd better expect a fight like you've never had if the Knesset even suggests rebuilding the Temple."

"When will the Knesset meet?" the Speaker asked.

Goldstein stood and his chair toppled. "I strenuously object to bringing the Ark to Jerusalem! War will be unavoidable! Some of you might welcome death, but I am not ready to die."

"That is your problem," someone said.

Ben Gurion broke the following silence. "The full Knesset will meet the day the Ark arrives. Assuming the Speaker approves, of course."

Moshe Aron ignored the jab. "And when do you expect that?"

Ben Gurion glanced at Solomon. "Within seventy-two hours."

———

They traveled until the sun fell again. The Ark of the Covenant was on its way to Jerusalem. The fact that Rebecca had ended up here, in the desert, while Israel's finest hour approached saddled her with a dread she could hardly contain at times. A dozen scenarios regarding Avraham's intentions had spun through her mind. But in the end it all began to feel distant and impossible, and she found herself thinking more and more about the man seated on the camel, ten meters ahead.

She nudged her camel and closed the gap. His dark hair covered his head like a hood, to his shoulders, but the moon lit his face. She could no longer deny the simple fact that she was drawn to this man. She was a soldier who might fail in this mission to return the Ark to Jerusalem. But she was also a woman, and she was seeing Caleb not only as a man, but as one who claimed that he could rescue Israel somehow. It all seemed impossible, of course, trudging through this desert fifteen hundred kilometers from Jerusalem. He a Christian, she a Jew.

The scene of her failed attempt to seduce him played through her mind, and she stopped nudging her camel forward.

Caleb turned and smiled. "You slept? That's good."

"I wouldn't call it sleep. You did a little nodding yourself."

"The heat gets to you out here."

They walked on, towards the white moon.

"How far to the sea?" she asked.

"Twenty kilometers, I would say."

"And when we get there, what do we do?"

"I don't know yet."

She nodded. Whatever Caleb was, he wasn't a soldier. "You don't know? We're following your plan and you don't have one?"

"My plan is to prevent a war." He said it so matter-of-factly that she honestly thought he believed he could do such a thing.

"My, my, you just refuse to be normal, don't you? Is everything a game to you? We're powerless here, mounted on camels in Eritrea, and in Jerusalem the fate of Israel is probably being argued in the Knesset. They're deciding whether or not to nuke the Syrians, but that's okay because down in the desert Caleb has a plan. What is his plan? To prevent a war, of course. It doesn't sound just a bit strange to you?"

Caleb began to laugh. "You do have a sense of humor, Rebecca."

She grinned at the way he said it. Might as well. She was with him now, for better or for worse.

"Actually, I wasn't trying to be funny," she said.

He sighed and looked up at the starry sky. "Do you ever wonder why God placed so many stars in the sky?" he asked. "They say that if the sky were a beach, what we can see is like a single grain of sand on that beach."

She looked up. A million white pinpricks flickered against the black sky. "I've never heard it put like that. It's a good way to say it."

"I've found my love again, you know."

Rebecca's first impulse was to think that he was speaking about her. She cast him a sidelong glance, but he was still staring skyward and she knew he was back in Hadane's world.

"So you *lost* your love?"

"Yes. My first love. That crazy love I had as a child. Somehow I misplaced it."

The night suddenly felt very thick. "And you learned to love God by walking with him. In his kingdom, right?"

He looked at her, surprised that she remembered what he'd told her. "Yes. In his kingdom. Do you love God, Rebecca?"

"Yes. Yes, I think so."

"But you don't love Christ."

"I said that I loved God. The Nazarene was not God. I'm sure he was a good prophet—one that the Jews might have misjudged. But he wasn't God."

"Then how do you explain my love for him?"

She looked to the horizon. "Just because the Arabs love Mohammed doesn't mean that he was sent from God."

"True love is found by stepping off the cliff," Caleb said, ignoring her line of argument. "That's what Hadane taught me again. Faith and love are bound together inseparably. If you don't truly believe, you can't truly love. If you don't love, you cannot truly believe. Each is required for the other."

"So if you don't have belief, how are you expected to find love?"

He looked at her as if the answer were obvious. "By doing the one thing man can do. By stepping off the cliff." He chuckled and nodded. "Stepping off the cliff."

"Stepping off the cliff?" She smiled, caught off guard by his laugh.

"When you step off the cliff, you learn very quickly to love the one who catches you. Man's problem is that he has become too attached to the ground he's on. He might stick a foot over the edge, but everything in him rebels at the thought of stepping off."

"Maybe because when people fall off cliffs, they tend to end up splat. On the ground."

He grinned. "Splat?"

"Yes, splat."

"But anything less is not faith at all. Faith is believing in what you can't see. Like air. And faith is the kind of belief that makes you do things like jump—otherwise it's not faith at all. Christ's brother James knew that well, and I suppose it was because he spent so much time with Jesus. Most people who think they believe don't really believe at all—not the way Christ and his brother talked about. They only think they believe, but they never really step off the cliff."

Christ and his brother? She wondered what the Torah had to say about faith. Her own belief had always come at the end of a nine-millimeter Browning.

"And don't think that a cliff has to be very high," Caleb said. "I think for most people, standing in the market where they buy their food and telling the stranger next to them that they love Christ—I think this would be a cliff plenty high for starters. They would find themselves madly in love soon enough."

His words spun through her mind, like threads of gold on the wind. There was indeed something intoxicating about Caleb.

He tilted his head back and faced the stars. "Oh, my dear God . . ." He spread out both arms. "I have found true love, Rebecca, and it is for the Nazarene!" He spun and reached out to her, wide-eyed. "That's the point! You're not going to find God in a gold box called an Ark! You're going to find him in *man*. He is Christ, and he loves us madly."

He spoke it with such passion that the thought of disagreeing felt awkward. She just grinned stupidly.

Caleb cleared his throat and dropped his hand. After a minute, he pulled on the reins and his camel stopped. "We should rest for a few hours," he said.

"No, we should keep going. Plan or no plan, we have to at least get to the sea."

"No, we should stop." He slipped from his camel. "Please, you're committed to follow me, and I think we should stop."

Rebecca blinked in the darkness. He was growing more assured by the hour. Caleb led his own camel and the one in tow to a bush where he tied them up. He walked over to her and lifted a hand to help her down. She hesitated and then took it.

But she didn't dismount. She looked into his face. His eyes were green in the moonlight, and they looked directly into her own. She dropped her eyes and looked at her hand, small in his. His other arm was poised to catch her if she were to fall—as if she would ever fall. He was waiting for her to dismount, of course.

She looked back into his eyes. A wedge of heat rose up Rebecca's spine. For a moment Rebecca thought she wanted to fall into his arms and hold him tenderly. Her heart began to race, and suddenly her hand felt very hot in his.

But she'd tried that once and it had not gone well.

She jerked her eyes from his, dropped to the sand, and flashed him a courteous smile. "Thank you," she said.

"You are welcome." His voice sounded tender. Not merely soft or gentle, but tender.

They had stopped at the base of a small cliff that rose up to the full moon, and Rebecca walked towards it, at a complete loss. Behind her Caleb remained still, and she knew that he was watching her. Dear God, what was happening?

Then she heard him leading her camel to the bush and she breathed in relief. Her belly was still doing flip-flops. *Get ahold of yourself, Rebecca. Goodness, he is not some boyfriend, and this is not a high-school bar mitzvah!*

A loud crack sounded behind her. She spun around. Caleb walked quickly towards her, smiling, his arms full of dead branches. He dumped them on the ground and quickly arranged them for a fire. He stood up, hurried to his pack, and began digging through it.

"What are you doing? We can't build a fire."

"A small one," he said. "We're in a gully—and it's dark; they won't see the smoke." He returned with matches. "Just a small one, Rebecca."

She folded her arms and watched him bend over the wood, blowing, until a nice flame crackled.

"It would be wonderful to have some hot tea, don't you think?" he asked.

"You have tea?"

"The monks gave me tea in the desert. I'm sure it's still in the pack."

Fifteen minutes later they sat next to the fire, eating sweet bread and drinking an herbal tea that tasted like grass from black tin mugs. They hadn't eaten in twenty-four hours, and they devoured the food quickly.

A very soft but permanent smile molded Caleb's face, she thought, as if being in her presence suddenly made him nervous. Something had passed between them while she dismounted the camel. Something that she knew she would have to throw to the wind in the morning, when they entered the real world. But something that she couldn't dismiss right now. She felt as shy as he, and to be honest she liked the feeling.

Caleb suddenly stood and began to clap and sway, grinning from ear to ear. "Do you like to dance, Rebecca?"

She chuckled, surprised at his sudden courage. "I'm not sure I've ever danced like that." She looked around at the dark, instinctively.

"I used to dance as a child," he said. "God dances, you know."

"God dances?" She couldn't help smiling with him. "I've always pictured him as a little more reserved than that."

"No, humans are more reserved than that. Not God. He quiets us with his love, and then he dances and sings over us with delight. That's what the prophet Zephaniah wrote. You know Zephaniah?"

"Yes, of course. He wrote that? I'm surprised you didn't get it from Father Hadane."

Caleb stopped his swaying and settled to his seat. "Yes, Hadane told me about Zephaniah. He also talked about David, who danced around the Ark. Surely you know about David."

"Yes."

"That's why the tribe danced. An old tradition from the days they guarded the Ark."

Rebecca folded her legs to one side and leaned on her arm. She watched the fire lick at the black night. "Don't you think Father Hadane was just a bit . . ." She paused, searching for the right word. "Odd?"

"Father Hadane is like John the Baptist," Caleb said. "The Baptist lived in the desert like Hadane. The monks don't eat crickets and honey, but the flour cakes come close enough, don't you think? Or maybe you can identify more with Elijah—your own prophet. Hadane is like Elijah."

"And what does that make you?" she asked.

"That makes me Elisha."

"Elisha, huh? When was the last time the world saw an Elisha?" Caleb looked at her, smiling. They held their gaze for a moment before she broke off.

"What cliff are you stepping off, Rebecca?"

"Cliffs again. I try to avoid cliffs, actually. Not good for the legs." It occurred to her that she didn't just like Caleb; she liked Caleb very much. Not only his innocence and his warm smile, but the quirky way he talked about his cliffs and his love for God.

"Perhaps you should look for a cliff to jump off," he said. "It might change the way you believe. And then you would find a new love."

"Yes, because belief is love," she finished for him. She looked up across the fire. "What about me? Do you *believe* in me?"

The tone of her voice must have caught him off guard, because he blinked and sat immobilized. What was she thinking, asking such an obvious question?

"Yes," he said softly. "I think I'm starting to."

Except for the crackling fire and a slight breeze, the night was very quiet. She didn't know what to say.

Caleb suddenly stood. "We should get some rest. It's getting late and we should leave in a few hours." He pulled both bedrolls from the camels and returned, dropping hers at her feet.

"I will wake you," he said. And then he walked for a boulder, spread out his blanket, and lay down.

38

AVRAHAM DROVE THE TRUCK BACK UP the hill, to where he and Zakkai had left the others an hour ago—in the rocks overlooking the small harbor just south of Massawa, Eritrea. Zakkai sat next to him, bright-eyed for a change. And well he should be—they had just boarded the expedition ship and found it untouched.

They were going home to Jerusalem.

The trip north had been relatively inconsequential, all things considered. Other than the altercation with Samuel, of course. Avraham had commandeered the satellite phone and called Solomon once in private, assuring him that they were making excellent progress. Rebecca was with them and unharmed, yes, but she couldn't talk, not until they were safely on the ship. Solomon had assured him that the submarine would be waiting as promised.

Dr. Zakkai had hovered over the Ark like a concerned mother. He had expressed his outrage about Rebecca and Samuel on two separate occasions, but not with enough antagonism to warrant Avraham's wrath in front of the others. The archaeologist was a scientist, after all, not a soldier.

The Israeli commando team left Ethiopia with four fewer soldiers than it had brought. That left nine, including Zakkai. Three of them sat in the cab; the rest, in the back, with the crate. They had only been stopped once, at a small Ethiopian post before the border, and the story of the burial had worked well enough, although Avraham wouldn't have cared either way. They could have easily outgunned the three-man post.

Avraham steered up to the waiting soldiers and skidded to a stop, sending a cloud of dust into the morning air. "Get in. Keep the crate covered."

They piled in and Avraham took them back down the hill.

The city of Massawa lay to the north, a gray carpet of concrete on the brown hills. A few dozen fishing vessels slept in the muddied port waters below them. Thankfully, no one had paid the archaeological vessel any mind since the expedition had left it a week earlier.

It took them twenty minutes to load the crate in the hold. A single beggar wearing a big, toothless smile watched them silently on the dock, unaware of the significance unfolding before his eyes. Zakkai tossed him a coin and the grin widened.

They pushed off, turned the forty-foot rig around, and steamed out to sea. The harbor slowly disappeared from sight.

Zakkai stared at the diminishing coastline. "The Ark will be in Jerusalem tomorrow."

"We aren't home yet," Jude said, walking up. "If the Arabs had contact with their superiors, they've reported losing us by now. I'm surprised we made it this far."

"But they have no idea that we have the Ark," Zakkai said.

"Maybe, maybe not. But they had to have known we were after it. If they even suspect we have the Ark, they'll be all over the sea."

Avraham cut the power to a trickle and stepped from the pilothouse. "Which is why we're meeting the submarine," he said. "We should be approaching the rendezvous now, to the north. I want everyone here, watching. Call the others. Zakkai, take the front. The rest on the side."

Within the minute they were standing in a line, peering over the rail for a sign of the submarine's black hull on the surface. Avraham dried the sweat from his palms and slipped back into the pilothouse. He pulled the M-16 out from under the wheel and switched it to full automatic. Keeping the machine gun from view, he eased behind them. He'd rehearsed the move in his mind a hundred times; now his heart slammed in his chest with the realization that these men were soldiers who'd done nothing to deserve an execution.

"I don't see a thing," Jude said and began to turn.

Avraham lifted the barrel and pulled the trigger. A stream of lead crashed into Jude's chest, slamming the soldier back over the railing. The others spun around, and Avraham pivoted his fire down the row, then back up it. Daniel ran for cover and Avraham cut him down midstride by the bulkhead. Avraham jerked the gun back and sent a short burst into one of the others who was crawling over the side. He lifted the barrel, breathing heavy.

Zakkai's feet slapped on the wood deck as he ran from the bow. "What's happening?"

Avraham ignored him and methodically put one last bullet in each skull. The sight of the bloodied soldiers lying quietly suddenly struck him as obscene. These were Jews, not Arabs.

A splash sounded to Avraham's right. Zakkai!

Avraham spun and ran for the bow. The archaeologist was nowhere in sight. He'd wanted him alive, but now Zakkai had gone overboard!

"Ahoy, there!" A bullhorn sounded on the starboard side and Avraham spun to it. The submarine bobbed in the waves, two hundred meters off. He froze on the deck.

"Ahoy!"

"Ahoy!" he shouted back.

He would have to forget Zakkai. How far could the man swim anyway? But the bodies on the other side had to go. Had the sailor seen his gun? No, he didn't think so.

He ran for the bloodied bodies and heaved them overboard, praying that his inability to see the sub meant they could not see him. The bodies were heavy dead, but he managed. He ran for the pilothouse and saw that the sub was edging closer. He stripped his bloodied shirt. He shoved the throttles forward and steered the ship in a wide circle, back towards the sub. Zakkai was nowhere in sight. He had to keep the sub away from the bodies, in the event they bobbed back to the surface.

The sub parked off the starboard side five minutes later.

Avraham waved to the captain, who now stood on the submarine's deck. "Thank God, you came!"

"Where are the others?"

"Dead. I barely made it." He looked at the horizon, frantically. "We have to hurry! I think the Arabs know that I took the ship."

The captain hesitated. "They're *all* dead?"

"Yes. For the sake of God, hurry!"

"You have the . . . the Ark?"

"Yes. In the hold."

The captain ducked, spoke into the hatch at his feet, then rose. "Drop your anchor. We'll be right over."

Avraham had just enough time to push some canvas over the bloodied deck, rip the wires from the back of the radio, and drop his freshly fired gun over the far railing. He lowered a ladder for four sailors who boarded from a large inflatable they'd deployed.

It took them thirty minutes to off-load the Ark and set it into the submarine through the loading bay. He stayed aboard the ship, hurrying the crew and doing his best to keep them from exploring.

Captain Moses Stern, commander of the new Dolphin class diesel-electric submarine, one of only three in Israel's navy, wore a perpetually proud smile. Whether it was for his sub or the Ark, Avraham couldn't tell, but he disliked the man immediately. Yet he had made it, hadn't he? He took a calming breath and let the crew secure the Ark in the sub's hold.

"Is it advisable to leave a crew to take the ship home?" Captain Stern asked as they cinched the last tie-down.

"No. Impossible! They'd be forced to talk if they were captured. We can't risk it. You can retrieve the ship later."

"Then we leave immediately. And I wouldn't worry too much, my friend. We don't exactly have a lot of competition in these waters. Syria has four submarines, but three of them are in the Mediterranean. And even if they weren't, it wouldn't matter. Theirs are hardly more than floating tubs."

He grinned and turned. "Make ready to dive," he barked.

Rebecca and Caleb came to the dirt road midmorning, after several hours of sleep and six more hours of crossing uncharted territory, talking comfortably about small things. Their exchange from the previous night had lingered in her thoughts, a sweet aftertaste that drew her mind more to him and less to the mission. But now they had come out of the desert, and to Rebecca it felt like stepping out of a fog into reality once again.

"Do you know where it goes?" Rebecca asked, looking up and down the wide, dusty swath. A veritable freeway by Eritrean standards.

"It leads to Massawa," Caleb said.

"Massawa! How far?" She walked her camel onto the flat road, relieved and eager. They hadn't seen a single sign of civilization for over a day, and yet Caleb had managed to lead them to their precise destination.

"Five kilometers," he said.

"Good. We can be there in an hour."

"No, we can't take the road," Caleb said.

She turned back, stunned. "What? What do you mean we can't take the road? We're five kilometers from Massawa!"

"But we're not going to Massawa."

He turned his camel to the east and began to walk it. The camel with the trough tied to its back followed him on its tether.

"Please. Why do you have to be so impossible?"

He ignored her and continued up the hill.

In that moment she thought she could strangle him. "Caleb! Stop!"

He stopped. But he didn't look back.

"Let's at least talk this through. I have to get to Massawa—you know that as well as I do. Avraham's out there somewhere with the Ark of the Covenant and only God knows what he's planning."

Caleb turned in his saddle. "You're right, only God knows. You should follow me, Rebecca. You should definitely follow me."

"Then at least tell me why. We're practically on the edge of Massawa and you want to head back into the hills?"

"You no longer trust me?"

She was too frustrated to answer.

"The cliff I'm looking for is this way," he said. "Maybe yours is as well." He started the camel walking again.

Now Rebecca was facing an impossible decision. She could leave him and head into Massawa alone, or she could plunge back into the hills with him, trusting that he was onto something. That he would find his cliff.

She looked down the road, furious. It took her a full minute to make her decision, enough time for Caleb to reach the crest where he looked back and waited. To her, following him felt like falling off a cliff.

Dear God, you've abandoned me! This is no longer funny.

Rebecca grunted and kicked her camel for the hills. The startled animal broke into a gallop, nearly spilling her. Caleb started forward as she approached.

They walked side by side for several kilometers without speaking. If she wasn't mistaken, they were heading in the direction they had come from.

"Aren't we backtracking?" Rebecca finally asked.

"No. Not really."

He made some clicking sounds and nudged the camel into a near trot. Rebecca followed suit and pulled up beside him again.

"We have to hurry," he said.

"Why?" The terrain was changing she saw—more white sand, fewer rocks.

"We don't have a lot of time. They're very close."

"Who's very close?" Rebecca looked behind them. Nothing. "What are you talking about? Who's very close?"

His camel started to trot and she pushed hers to the same pace. They bounded up a long hill. "Caleb, what's going on? Tell me! What . . ."

They crested the hill and she pulled up. The sea sparkled blue two kilometers down the hill. But it wasn't the water that had Rebecca's heart lodged in her throat; it was the military compound on the shore. Barbed wire encircled eight or ten buildings and a single hangar. Two old Huey helicopters sat on cement pads; the blades on the further rotated slowly, as if it had just been fired up. She could see a dozen men, loitering about the grounds.

"An army base?"

"Yes," he said calmly.

"You knew about this?"

"It's been here for years."

"What makes you think they will be friendly? They're Eritrean!"

"They won't be friendly."

"Why didn't you tell me? You knew we were headed for an Eritrean army base all along and you didn't tell me?"

"I didn't think you would appreciate it."

"And you're right! This is crazy! We have to get back to the road!"

"That would be a mistake. The Arabs are behind us. Very near, I think."

She looked back. "How do you know? Never mind!" She spun her camel around. "I'm going back."

"Rebecca?" His voice sounded low.

Rebecca stopped and faced him.

"Do you believe, Rebecca?"

He was looking at her with his head tilted down, a faint smile curving his lips, tempting. His look reminded her of Hadane, speaking those same words as the Arabs galloped for their camp.

"Do you believe?" he repeated.

Before she could answer, Caleb kicked his camel and plunged down the hill towards the military compound, tunic flying like a cape. The trailing camel followed, honking in protest.

Panicked, Rebecca swore, jerked her camel around, and took off after him.

Ismael led the horses up the hill in a fast trot. The last camel dropping they'd passed was still steaming, and according to Hasam they were very near the sea. The tracker said he could practically smell the camels then, and for all practical purposes, so could Ismael. If not the camels, the Jew.

For nearly two days they had followed the tracks. Despite riding faster animals, they had been slowed by the darkness that first night, checking and rechecking the tracks. They would have caught the camels the following day if it hadn't been for the short detour they'd taken for water. Horses might be faster, but they needed hydration. By the time the second night had fallen they were too tired to continue, and Ismael had allowed them to rest for six hours before continuing. Looking at the tracks now, he cursed the decision.

They pounded up the long hill, urging the horses into a gallop. His phone call to Abu last night had been a bad one. His father had literally screamed at him. And Ismael had screamed back. Evidently the Arab leadership of the whole Red Sea region now knew about the Ark and were on high alert. Their eyes were all on Ismael.

Then why didn't they leave their palaces and fly their warplanes down here to take the Ark out, Ismael yelled. He could only do so much on these cursed horses. Abu had cut him off after swearing that he would put every square inch of the land and sea leading to Israel under guard. If Ismael couldn't kill a couple of Jews, then he would do it himself.

Ismael reached the crest and jerked back on his reins. The sea shimmered in the morning sun, less than two kilometers ahead, at the base of the hills. Barbed wire circled a camp by the sea. They had been led to an Eritrean military installation!

"What is this?" he demanded.

The horses stamped around him, snorting from their long run. No one answered.

"They came to the Eritrean army. Why?"

"There!" someone shouted. Ismael glanced to see one of his soldiers pointing down the hill towards the gates.

He saw them then, three camels galloping up to the main gate, a kilometer away. Rebecca, Caleb, and the Ark! Heat flared through his skull, and for a moment his sight shifted into doubles.

He snatched up his binoculars and trained them on the camels. So close and yet so far. He jerked the lenses to the gate. They were unguarded. Ismael dropped the binoculars and spurred his horse.

"After them!"

As one, the row of horses lunged down the hill towards the Eritrean base.

39

CAMELS REACH THEIR TOP SPEED AT roughly twenty kilometers per hour in a full gallop, and Rebecca's was doing every bit of that. She kept wanting to scream out for Caleb to stop, but she didn't. Maybe because she knew it would be futile; maybe because of Caleb's suggestion that the Arabs were behind them. Or maybe because his undaunted courage struck a chord deep in her gut, where she'd learned to draw judgment. But for whatever reason, she kept pace and hammered for the unmanned gates.

Several soldiers in the compound had noticed them and were staring past the gates, stunned by their charge. Or was it something else that had attracted them? She looked over her shoulder.

A thin line of horses broke the hill's crest in a full gallop, kicking dust up in their charge.

The Arabs!

"Hiyah!" Panicked, she slammed her heels into the camel's side. "Hiyah!"

Caleb rode on, his hair flying behind him in dark waves as he charged straight for the open gate. Then he was through and he veered to the right, towards the helicopters. A handful of soldiers stood unarmed, still transfixed by the sight. They were 150 kilometers north of a peaceful border—the Eritreans clearly weren't expecting trouble. Somewhere, one of them began to yell a high-pitched warning.

Rebecca followed Caleb, her heart now thumping like a piston. He galloped past the first helipad, reached the second, and stopped at its edge in a cloud of dust. Rebecca pulled her snorting beast to a stop beside him. Caleb stared at the helicopter, face beaded with sweat, eyes brilliant and eager. He dropped from his camel. A mechanic gawked at him, wrench in hand.

"Unlash the Ark, Rebecca," Caleb said without turning. His voice was low and soft. Unlash the Ark? He planned to use the helicopter.

She moved without taking the time to think further. Whatever they were going to do, they didn't have much time. The Arabs would be at the gate in two minutes.

Caleb strode up to the mechanic and stopped. For a moment he just stared at the man. And then he spoke softly in a local dialect Rebecca couldn't understand.

But the man did.

His eyes spread to their whites and watered, as if a dam of tears had waited behind those eyelids. The wrench fell from his fingers and clattered on the concrete.

Behind them men were yelling now—the alarm was spreading.

Caleb stared into the man's eyes and continued speaking in a soft voice that brought a chill to Rebecca's bones. There was something in his voice that seemed to ride the air and make for the spine, she thought. The man began muttering, as if overcome by a sudden anguish. He glanced beyond them to the Arabs and then scrambled into the cockpit, rattling in a high pitch now.

Caleb ran over to Rebecca and grabbed one end of the fake Ark from the camel's back. "He's the pilot. He will take us," he said.

"What did you tell him?" she asked, stunned.

"I told him that God wanted him to help us." He grinned and pulled one end of the feeding box from the camel. The sudden weight nearly knocked him over before Rebecca managed to steady her end.

"You just *told* him?"

"Yes! Ha! Believe, Rebecca. Believe."

Yes, of course. Believe. If you just clench your eyes and believe hard enough, you can move a mountain. How silly of her not to understand.

They hauled the box into the helicopter as it revved up to a deafening roar. Caleb leapt in and pulled her into the bay. She glanced over her shoulder—the first Arabs had reached the gate.

"Get it up!" Rebecca yelled. "Get it up!"

The helicopter roared and then lifted off the ground, sending both her and Caleb crashing back to the canvas bench. The Huey rose three meters, tilted forward, and picked up speed in the direction of the Arabs. For what felt like an eternity, the open side of the Huey faced the lead Arab who'd pulled his horse back so that its hoofs pawed at the air.

Rebecca stared into the whites of Ismael's eyes for the second time in three days. She blinked.

When the horse dropped to all fours, Ismael had his rifle at his shoulder, and a split second later the first slug crashed into the helicopter's metal frame, centimeters from Rebecca's head.

She ducked and threw herself back into Caleb. The bullets tore through the Huey's roof. The pilot banked the helicopter hard to the right and they soared over a tin roof, barely missing a loose sheeting of aluminum that flapped up like a jaw under the buffeting wind.

And then they were over the water, beyond the effective reach of an AK-47.

It occurred to Rebecca that she was lying back on Caleb's chest. He had thrown his arms around her stomach in a firm embrace. She glanced up. He stared directly ahead, out the front windshield, looking half lost and half transfixed by the distant clouds.

Rebecca pushed herself up, but his arms continued to hold her. She lay back down, encircled by his arms.

"Caleb."

He looked down, eyes distant. He suddenly came to himself and blinked.

"Oh, I'm sorry," he said. He quickly removed his arms and then helped her up. "I'm sorry. Are you okay?" She felt his hand on the back of her head, stroking, concerned. And then he jerked that back as well.

"Yes." She cleared her throat and looked at him. He was blushing and trying to look preoccupied.

She turned back towards the compound. The Arabs were surrounding the other helicopter, but Eritrean soldiers were pouring out of the buildings, with guns now.

"Where are we going?" she asked.

"To Saudi Arabia."

"Saudi!" She spun back. "That's like jumping into the fire! Do we even have the fuel? Saudi Arabia's over three hundred kilometers."

Caleb spoke to the pilot, who gripped the stick with white knuckles. The man looked back, unsure.

Caleb reached a hand out to his shoulder and spoke gently. The man nodded slowly and answered him.

"Yes," Caleb said to Rebecca. "We have the fuel."

"And . . ." She paused. Part of her hated to ask. This whole thing was now firmly in a world beyond her. "And what are we going to do in Saudi Arabia?"

He looked beyond her to the blue waters without answering.

"Caleb? Don't tell me you don't know."

"I *will* know."

She faced the open door to her left. Three times now she had seen things she had no business seeing. First with Father Hadane and the charging Arabs, then with Caleb and Ismael, and now with this helicopter pilot. Whatever else the implications might be, the most significant was that Father Hadane and Caleb knew something she didn't. Their source of power was greater than hers. Christianity.

No, not Christianity, but this strange notion of following in the Nazarene's footsteps, which wasn't necessarily Christianity, was it? Not according to Caleb. They actually seemed to think that following the crucified man gave them a power beyond this world. And to watch them, she could hardly dispute it.

Part of her wanted to jump out of the helicopter now. Go splat, as she'd put it earlier. If all that Caleb had said in the desert was true . . .

Goodness, the implications were too much. She stared out the doorway and let the beating blades dull her thinking.

———

Ismael shoved his pistol under the pilot's jaw. "Fly!" He motioned after the fleeing helicopter. "Get in! Get in!"

His men had taken cover by the hangar and exchanged fire with a band of Eritrean soldiers who'd come from nowhere, pouring lead into the horses. Three had fallen before they reached the helipads. The rest had scattered for cover like fools. Couldn't they make the simple deduction that the Eritreans wouldn't shoot their own helicopter unless it was their last resort?

Three fifty-five-gallon barrels of fuel lined the cement pad—if a stray bullet hit one of those . . .

"Get in!" he barked one last time, shoving his gun into the man's larynx. The pilot spun and jumped into the cockpit, muttering in a high pitch.

"Shut up and start it!"

Ismael ducked under the tail boom and trained his weapon on a soldier running across the compound for a better angle. He pulled the trigger and shifted his sights before the man fell. He'd always had the knack for quick target acquisition, and he used it now, pulling the trigger five times in under ten seconds. Each time a man fell; each time the balance of power shifted a little; each time catching the Jew became more possible.

The rotor wound up above him, like a jet. Some of the Eritreans saw that the deadly fire was coming from his position, and they began to shout out warnings. But the lull in their concentration only gave the Syrian Republican Guard the time they needed to pour steady unreturned fire into the soldiers' positions.

The first broke for cover and Ismael barked an order. "Let him go!"

The Republican Guard understood immediately—it was a common tactic used when you wanted to give the enemy an escape route. Disengagement was often preferable to a firefight. Within a few seconds two others saw that the man had retreated easily and they followed, leaving only a couple of stubborn soldiers to defend the position.

Ismael took one out with a bullet through the head and the other cursed and ducked behind a woodshed.

"In the helicopter!" Ismael yelled at his men. "Hurry!"

Six of the remaining eight Republican Guard fit easily. Two did not.

"Up!" Ismael pushed his pistol behind the pilot's ear. "Up!"

The helicopter whined and lifted off the ground. One of the soldiers grabbed for the skids, and Ismael shot him through the head. The other jumped back and then fled beyond Ismael's line of sight.

"Shoot him," he ordered.

Captain Asid stared at him as if he'd been ordered to jump. "He's my own man!"

"He also has information. Shoot him!" Ismael shifted his pistol to Asid.

The captain swung his rifle out the door and shot four times. Ismael saw the prone body when they made their turn.

The helicopter broke the shoreline and headed directly northeast after the other Huey. Ismael pulled a map from the console and studied it quickly. The Jew was headed for either Shuqaiq or Al Birk. Either way, they would have to go north for Jerusalem. He held the map up to the pilot, jabbed at it. "Where! Where are they going?"

The pilot spoke in his own language, but pointed to Al Birk.

Ismael pointed at Doqa, 150 kilometers north of Al Birk. "Take us there," he demanded.

The pilot shook his head vehemently, running off a string of unintelligible words. He pointed a trembling finger at the gas gauge.

"Doqa!" Ismael yelled. He drew a more direct line to the coastline south of Doqa, and then up the coast. They would get over land and then fly north towards Doqa. If they ran out of fuel, they could land in the desert. Either way they were going further north. Doqa was just a head start.

The pilot eyed the map and then the gas gauge. He nodded, but his face was white.

Ismael leaned back and took a deep breath. He caught Captain Asid's gaze. "We are finished chasing," Ismael said. "This time they come to us."

———

The first helicopter pounded its way over the sea for half an hour before either of them spoke again.

"Rebecca."

She turned to Caleb. He held out a large hand. She hesitated and then reached for it. He held her hand gently. "Thank you."

"Thank you? For what?"

"For . . . believing." His eyes searched hers.

"I'm not really sure I *am* believing anything," she said.

"You're believing me. Maybe you underestimate what that means."

"And maybe you underestimate the position you've put me in," she said.

"And you me."

"And me you what?"

"Maybe you underestimate the position you've put me in," he said.

"You're doing what you think you need to do, with or without me," she said.

"Two weeks ago I was dying in the desert. And then God sent you to me."

"I came to deceive you."

"And instead you brought me truth. Now I'm living with that."

"With what?"

"With you, Rebecca." He looked away, sheepishly. "And I have a confession. Back at the road, if you would have turned and gone on to Massawa, I would have followed you."

She tilted her head. "But you didn't, did you? You left me."

"I didn't leave; I led! And you followed! You believed in me. And I think I believe in you."

It struck her then that he was saying more than she was hearing. In his own way he was telling her that he cared for her. Maybe more. Heat flushed her neck and she turned away.

"As I said, I'm not sure what I believe," she said.

They were saying belief, but they were meaning love. Because love and belief were the same, at least that's what Caleb had said. Or maybe it was all in her mind.

She felt his stare on her and looked back. His eyes were green and soft, and she knew looking into them that it was not in her mind.

Not at all.

———

The phone was slippery with sweat in Abu's hand. How the situation had progressed to the point of making this call, he still could not completely fathom. Eleven of his best trained men, fully equipped, had entered the desert after one woman a week ago, but at every step the Jew had eluded them. Now Ismael was after her in a helicopter over the Red Sea. And she had the Ark.

The Ark of the Covenant was actually on its way to Jerusalem aboard a helicopter! The Saudis would stop them, of course—every unit along the coast had been put on full alert as a result of Ismael's information. Egypt was slowly easing the tanks it already had in the Sinai into a position that would enable rapid mobilization. The Saudis continued their military exercises with Egypt near Jordan's border, conveniently cutting off every road that led to Israel. If necessary they could have the equivalent of two full tank divisions on Israel's southern border within three hours. The Jew would have to pass through those divisions to reach Jerusalem. If the Ark was in Saudi Arabia, it had virtually no chance of reaching Jerusalem.

But Abu was taking no chances. Rebecca had proven surprisingly resourceful. *Dirty Harry* was about to go live. Forty thousand Palestinian soldiers were about to hear the words they had waited to hear for over fifty years.

Colonel Muhammed Du'ad's voice filled the phone. "Yes?"

"Colonel. You know who this is?" It was a secure line, but in the Middle East, nothing was really secure. They followed the protocol for all PLO transmissions.

"Yes."

"The time has come."

The phone was silent for a few moments.

"And our brothers?"

"Your brothers are all in agreement. All of them."

"I see. How long do we have?"

"Two days. Move into position, but do nothing before you hear from me personally. Nothing, do you understand?"

"Do I strike you as a man with a low intelligence?"

Typical Hamas contempt. "No. But if you move prematurely, it will be *your* men who die. We will act only when we know their intentions. Then we act quickly."

"Of course," Du'ad said. He sounded nonchalant, but Abu heard the heaviness of his breathing.

"Be careful, my friend. It isn't likely that you will be needed. We cannot overstep ourselves. This is only a precaution."

"Of course."

"God be praised," Abu said.

The line went dead.

Abu swore and dropped his phone in its cradle.

40

R EBECCA AND CALEB REACHED THE BEACH fifteen kilometers north of Al Birk in just over forty minutes, with no sign of pursuit. If Ismael had survived the Eritreans, he either hadn't made it off the ground, or was too far behind to make a difference. But either way the Saudis were surely alerted by now, and Rebecca insisted that they avoid something so obvious as an airfield. For all they knew, Al Birk was already crawling with the Saudi National Guard, looking for a Jew and a man in a tunic.

The pilot set them down on a deserted wash of sand with less than a hundred liters of fuel to spare before lifting off and angling south.

"Now what?" Rebecca said. "We're thirteen hundred kilometers south of my country, in hostile territory, stranded on a beach. But the plan has come to you, right?"

"Yes," he said. "We should make for the road." He untied a white cotton scarf he'd wrapped around his midsection. "Cover your head and face. It's the custom for Muslim women here to wear an *abaaya*."

"I'm not Muslim," she said, but wrapped the cloth around her head anyway. She had no intention of standing out in this hostile land.

"You look marvelous," he said with a wink.

"You prefer my face covered up?"

"No. I like your face."

He stared at her for an awkward moment, and then turned on his heel and walked away from the beach.

"What about the trough?" she asked, indicating their fake Ark.

"Leave it."

Rebecca hurried after him, securing the last of the scarf. "Do you even know where the road is?" Her voice was muted by the cloth over her mouth.

"No," he said. "But you do. Where is it?"

She pointed in the direction they were walking. "That way."

The coastal plain along the kingdom's western coast was a narrow one which led to the Tihama Range and the mountainous Hejaz region before dipping back into the deserts Saudi Arabia was so well known for. A single road snaked north along the coast through mostly deserted land, but the large city of Jidda waited in their path, five hundred kilometers north. They might be able to find a way around the dozen other small towns spotting the coast, but not like this—not on foot.

Rebecca swallowed. "So . . . Caleb. What *is* the plan?"

He surprised her by answering in plain terms. "To go to Jerusalem. The plan has always been to go to where the Ark is going. We should hurry. Come on." He began to jog and she caught up quickly. They ran over a small hill and saw the road two hundred meters off, slightly below them.

"We don't know if the Ark's even going to Jerusalem," she said. "Avraham has it."

"Yes. But even a rumor of the Ark will bring out the armies, isn't that what you told me? So at least in reputation, the Ark is already in Jerusalem."

He was right. "Which is why I have to get there," she said. "Which is why we should have gone into Massawa instead of flying here."

"Which is why *I* have to go to Jerusalem," he said. "The Ark was hidden in the Debra Damarro for a purpose before I was born."

"You didn't find the Ark—Zakkai did," she said. "The Ark has to do with the nation of Israel, not you. Without us, you would still be picking weeds in your garden."

He turned to her, bright-eyed with excitement. "Exactly! Without you I wouldn't have found Father Hadane! Without you I wouldn't have found *you!* Or the Ark!"

She ignored him and jogged down the hill. He ran past her, tunic flapping in the wind. "Like Elijah, Rebecca!" he said, laughing. "We are running like Elijah! Just like Hadane said we would!"

He did look somewhat like her image of the ancient prophet, but he possessed far too much levity to complete the image.

The road looked freshly paved on the white sand, like a strip of licorice on a bed of cotton. She ran for it on his heels, wondering what in the world he intended to accomplish with a deserted stretch of road.

And then suddenly it wasn't a deserted stretch of road, because there was a Jeep roaring around the bend.

Rebecca pulled up, but Caleb raced out to the middle of the road, straddled the yellow line with wide legs and faced the oncoming Jeep. "Elijah, Rebecca!" he yelled, wearing a mischievous grin. "Like Elijah! Do you want to jump off a cliff?"

A lone soldier drove for Caleb, pell-mell, less than fifty meters off now. Caleb did not move.

The soldier suddenly cried out in alarm and stood on the brakes. The Jeep laid down a strip of rubber and squealed to a stop, three meters from Caleb. The Saudi soldier stood, furious.

"Get out of the road, you imbecile! You almost got yourself killed!"

"Hello, my friend," Caleb said. "We would like to use your Jeep. We have an important engagement awaiting us."

The soldier looked at Rebecca. The shock left his face and he reached for his gun. "Who are you? What are you doing here?"

"We are trying to go north and we need your Jeep," Caleb said.

"Don't be absurd! I am with the Saudi National Guard. You can't just take . . ." He didn't bother finishing. "I should have you shot for endangering my life. You westerners think you own our country?"

The man wasn't backing down. Rebecca looked at Caleb and she thought she saw a flicker of doubt in his eyes.

Caleb lifted his right hand, majestically. "No, you shouldn't have us shot. You should give us your Jeep."

The man was unfazed. "I don't have time for this. I will give you a count of three to get off the road."

"I don't think you understand, my friend—"

"One!"

Caleb glanced at Rebecca, and she saw the confusion run through his eyes.

"Two!"

"Caleb?"

"Three!"

Caleb stepped aside.

The soldier humphed. "You nearly died, you fool." He sat and started the Jeep.

"Could you give us a lift?" Rebecca asked.

The man looked from one to the other. "Who is your employer? Shell Oil?"

Rebecca stepped forward. Thank God Caleb had thought of the head wrap. "Yes. We went on a sightseeing trip with some friends and got lost. If you could take us north towards Jidda, we would be grateful."

The soldier studied Caleb for a moment, clearly wary. "Jidda? Why didn't you say so? Step in."

Rebecca hopped in and scooted over on the back bench. Caleb just looked at her, bewildered. "Caleb? You coming?"

He finally broke out of his stupor, pulled himself in, and sat beside her. "It wasn't the will of God," he said to himself.

"Thank you," Rebecca said to the soldier.

The driver nodded and dropped the clutch. The Jeep jerked forward. Caleb blinked beside her, somewhere between crushed and lost, she thought. She swallowed, patted his knee, and then smiled at him awkwardly.

———

It took Avraham three hours to persuade Captain Moses Stern to surface long enough for him to make contact with Israel. The captain insisted that he already had his orders—which were directly from the admiral himself—and that activity in the area was three times what it should be. Surfacing exceeded protocol.

There was no protocol for retrieving the Ark, Avraham argued. He had to get through. To whom? To the people who had sent him. They finally surfaced to clear waters and allowed him to use a satellite phone.

Stephen Goldstein answered on the third ring.

"Hello?"

"Good day, sir. I trust all is well in Jerusalem."

"Avraham? Good heavens . . . where are you, man?"

"I'm in the Red Sea at the moment."

"Do you know what's happening up here? Why haven't you made contact? Never mind! There are some people who are saying that the Ark has actually been discovered and is on the way to Jerusalem."

"Really?"

Goldstein had always been a pretentious fool, Avraham thought. But he was a wealthy pretentious fool, willing to pay surprising sums of money to block David Ben Solomon, and that had made the last two years manageable. This business of stealing the Ark, were it ever actually found, had started as nothing more than an afterthought. It was Goldstein's way of covering his bases.

"Then they would be right," Avraham said.

The line was silent. "You . . . you actually *have* the Ark?"

"Yes. Yes, I do."

Another silence.

"I'm sorry, Stephen, but I don't have all day," Avraham said, enjoying the moment. "We're on a submarine, and the captain is a bit testy."

"What does it look like?"

"The Ark? It looks like a gold box. A gold box that's worth a billion dollars if it's worth a penny. I've been thinking that we should renegotiate. The rest are dead, you know. I left no witnesses. How much is that worth?"

"You're also on a state submarine, for heaven's sake!"

"I've gotten this far, haven't I? I want double."

"You can*not* allow that relic to enter Israel! They're losing their minds here already."

"Double."

"We can't actually sell the thing, you fool! If the world even discovers that it exists, we will have problems."

"Then someone will pay for its disposal. Either way I want double. Four million U.S. dollars, my friend."

"I can't believe we're even having this conversation."

"We're having it because I actually have the Ark."

"Just get it to Eilat, as we talked about. You'll get your money."

"I will expect you to remember our agreement."

"And I expect you to remember that if the Ark shows up in Jerusalem, there will be problems. Many people will die. Among them, they will find your body. That is also part of my agreement."

"You're threatening me, Stephen?"

"I am rounding out our deal. It's the price for your increased payment."

Avraham spit overboard. "Your people are ready in Eilat?"

"Of course. They're ready."

"Good."

"Do not fail me," Goldstein said.

Avraham hung up on him.

41

THE DRIVER HAD A NAME, AND he was eager to give it. Ahmed. He was a talker, but Caleb didn't seem so eager to chat, so Ahmed settled for talking to Rebecca. So he said after carefully eyeing Caleb for the fifth time.

It was Ahmed's first year in the army, and he was eager to show the world that the kingdom could fight like any other superpower. Saudi Arabia might only have seventeen million people—okay, fourteen without the foreigners—but it owned much oil and great wealth and would one day be seen for its true power. He was one of a new breed of soldiers, ready to fight with modern weapons and a new courage. And so on and on with Rebecca's encouragement. As long as he was boasting, his mind would remain occupied.

He was actually going past Jidda and, as it turned out, so were they. They rambled through three checkpoints without even stopping.

Rebecca couldn't help wondering if Caleb's God hadn't come through after all. One look at the military Jeep, and the guards would merely wave a hand, evidence of the fact that this territory had not seen a proper military conflict in over a hundred years. If, on the other hand, Caleb had succeeded in commandeering the Jeep, they would have been stopped at the first checkpoint.

The ride lasted eight long awkward hours, the latter half of which Caleb slept through. It ended in a town called Wejh where Rebecca learned that Ahmed was on his way to a special military exercise near the border.

What kind of exercise?

A security exercise, he said. No civilian would make it anywhere near the border with Jordan without being thoroughly interrogated. In fact, the first post was set up just beyond this very town.

When she asked him why they were running the exercise, he took an indignant tone. That was military business. Way over her head. Over her head or not, Rebecca knew then that their ride with Ahmed had outlived its usefulness.

She reached over and shook Caleb only to discover that he had already woken. He'd heard as well. But instead of looking concerned, he wore a coy smile. She felt a small shaft of alarm rise through her chest.

"You may let us off here, Ahmed," Caleb said.

"Here? I thought you were going all the way to *Dhaba?*"

"We are. But we need to rest and eat."

"It's only two more hours."

Rebecca leaned forward and spoke quickly. "Actually, my friend has a condition which must be treated when it flares up," she said apologetically. "I'm sure you can understand."

Ahmed glanced at Caleb in the mirror. "Condition? What kind of condition?"

"It's something I'd rather not talk about." The buildings were thinning as they approached the end of the town. "But we need to stop now. Don't worry, we'll be fine. You go on. Just let us off at this street."

He pulled over, let them climb out, and sped off after they'd thanked him again.

They stood on the side of the empty street, watching the Jeep disappear to the north. "Well, that was a close call," Rebecca said. "I can't believe we got this far."

"Condition?" Caleb said.

"Well, you do have a condition, don't you? You're obsessed with jumping off cliffs. Are you okay?"

"Yes." A mischievous glint crossed his eyes. He turned and began to walk towards the north.

"Where are you going?" Rebecca asked.

"To cure my condition," he said.

She ran after him, pulling the wrap from her face. Without the breeze from the Jeep, it was suffocating.

"What are you talking about? You heard what he said. There's a post ahead!"

"Exactly."

"Caleb, listen to me. I know you were embarrassed back there, but we can't do this!"

"Do what? Never mind, *I'll* tell you what I'm doing. I'm going to Jerusalem." He winked at her and kept walking. "I'm going to Jerusalem because I can feel it drawing me like the tide. Nothing tells the tide to stop halfway in, and nothing is telling me to stop now. If you would like to find us a car, that's fine, I'll ride. But either way I'm going that way." He pointed north.

They were walking around a bend, and suddenly the first soldiers came into view, a hundred meters off. Rebecca stopped.

"Caleb!"

"Yes, I see them."

"Please, this is insane! You failed back at the Jeep. Your tricks didn't work. Now for God's sake, you don't have to do this!"

"Yes, Rebecca. Actually, I do have to do this. For God's sake."

"No, you don't!" The road ahead was thick with soldiers. Two tanks sat on each side of the post, their guns pointing ominously. "Don't be so bull-headed! We walk in there and we might as well be dead."

"I'm going."

She felt panic rip through her spine. "Why? You don't have to do this!"

He spun to her and hit his forehead with an open palm. "Yes, I *do* have to do this!" He stared at her fiercely. "And I think that you have to do it as well."

His shoulders relaxed and he took a deep breath. "I can't explain what happened at the Jeep, but then I'm not supposed to know how these things happen either. I'm only supposed to do them." He pointed behind him at the soldiers, some of whom had noticed them and were watching them curiously. "I *am* supposed to do this. The world hangs in the balance, and you want me to question now?"

"But—"

"We don't have time, Rebecca." He lowered his arm and walked back for her. "Please, you aren't here by mistake. While we were in the desert, did you ever think you'd be here, so far north, with me? No, but you are, Rebecca. And you're alive. Please, come. You'll see. I promise you'll see."

She looked into his eyes, and for the hundredth time since first meeting him, she wanted to curse him. To curse this mad grip he seemed to have on her. To curse the impossible situation he seemed to have worked her into. He was determined to help her jump off one of his cliffs.

"We will die," she said.

"We'll die if we go back."

The sweat on the back of her neck felt chilled. Every fiber in her legs screamed for her to spin and run south, away from the hundreds of armed soldiers waiting seventy meters away. Soldiers who were undoubtedly looking for a man and a woman, foreigners, traveling together.

"This is crazy!" she whispered through clenched teeth.

"Madness," he said.

The world seemed to slow around her. She became aware of her steady breathing.

"It's ridiculous," she said.

"It's freedom," he said and she blinked at the twinkle in his eye.

She took her first step towards the soldiers before she had consciously made up her mind to go with him. Caleb turned and walked by her side in the direction of the tanks.

There were at least three dozen guards on the road itself, leaning on the tanks. They wore the familiar tan desert garb of the Saudi army. Slowly they ceased their talking and turned to face Caleb and Rebecca.

"You will remember this, Rebecca," Caleb said in a very soft voice. "Watch carefully."

It occurred to her that she had left the wrap off her face. Maybe that's what the soldiers were staring at. They'd turned and stood squarely, with crossed arms, like a firing squad. She was marching to her death.

Rebecca swallowed. *Dear God, have mercy on me. I beg you, have mercy on me!*

Beside her, Caleb lifted both arms out to them, as if he wanted to bless them. She glanced at his face—his eyes might as well have been on fire. The corners of his mouth twitched to a crazy thin grin. He kept a steady pace, and she forced herself to keep stride with him against her will.

Several of the soldiers shifted their weapons. They clearly weren't wait-ing with open arms.

"I want to tell you something, Rebecca," Caleb said without turning. "The power of God is not in the Ark. It's not in the Ark of the Covenant because there's a New Covenant between God and man, and that Covenant is Christ's promise to send the Holy Spirit. He wants you to know that. It's his power, not mine."

Rebecca felt a lump of desperation rise through her throat, and her vision suddenly blurred with tears. *Dear God, have mercy on me.*

"Stop!"

Caleb did not stop.

She matched his stride. They were thirty meters away. Several rifle bar-rels lifted.

"Stop! I said, stop!" The cry was tighter and higher pitched.

A murmur rippled over the waiting soldiers—but Caleb walked on. Rebecca could feel her hands shaking at her sides.

"It's them. It's them!" someone cried in Arabic.

With those words, two things happened simultaneously in a way Rebecca never could have imagined. The first was a clanking sound of three dozen rifles snatched up to aim in their direction. That she understood clearly enough, like a bullet between the eyes.

But the second came on the heels of the first: an impossible sense of peace—almost as if it were a material substance she'd walked into—settling around her mind. Or perhaps she had indeed stepped off a cliff, and instead of falling, she was floating on this cloud of simple assurance. It was the kind of peace she thought might arrive the moment before death.

Caleb stopped immediately ahead and to the left of her. She followed his lead, coming abreast. He suddenly lifted his chin to the sky, threw his fists up to God, and screamed.

Rebecca jerked, surprised. A heavy weight suddenly pressed against her chest, and she immediately began to cry. Her mind scrambled for orienta-tion. Her first instinct was to think she'd been shot. The shock she felt was the result of a bullet to her chest.

She turned to face Caleb. He stood there with an open jaw, screaming, like Hadane had in the desert. Only this time she could hear it. This time she was somehow in that scream.

She faced the soldiers. They stood exactly as they had been standing a second ago, looking wide-eyed, breathing steadily. But they were not shooting. The scene seemed frozen in time, with this latter-day Elijah screaming at the sky.

One of the soldiers suddenly lowered his rifle and looked around, absently. He scratched behind his ear and swatted at a fly. Others began to shift and look around, as if also distracted. Two of them began to talk beneath the scream that filled the air beside her.

Rebecca gawked at them, stunned. The soldier right in front of her, the one who had called for them to stop, glanced at her casually. He said something she imagined might be a greeting.

The air suddenly fell quiet. She looked slowly over at Caleb, afraid to break the spell. He gazed about, awed.

"Where are you going, miss?" It was the soldier in front of her.

Rebecca just looked at him.

"We are going to Jerusalem," Caleb answered, putting his hand on her shoulder.

"Jerusalem. The holy city." He nodded, satisfied.

"Thank you," Caleb said to him. He nodded at Rebecca nonchalantly, as if this sort of thing were an everyday occurrence. "We should hurry."

Caleb walked down the blacktop, between the two tanks and their mob of soldiers, nodding at one and then another. She followed quickly. Her bones seemed to be vibrating with a silent energy that hung in the air. Her legs felt wobbly, but she walked on, past nothing more than bored soldiers who hardly seemed to notice their passing.

Caleb stopped and turned in the road, just past the tanks. "You see, Rebecca? Do you see this?"

"Yes! Yes, I see! What—"

"Then you are seeing the hand of God."

She glanced back. "Do . . . do they see us?"

"They seem to."

"Then why aren't they attacking us?"

"I don't know. You could ask the same of Shadrach or Meshach or Daniel or Jonah. We are alive." He continued walking and she strode beside him, heart beating like a tom-tom. They rounded a bend and the soldiers were gone.

Rebecca kept looking back, to make sure.

"This . . . this is hard to believe."

"Believe it."

"I'm not sure I have a choice anymore."

They walked in silence except for the dull sound of their shoes striking asphalt. Caleb kept smiling at her, but he didn't seem interested in explaining more. She wasn't sure he knew more than he'd said. This had been God. Period.

"What now?" she finally asked.

"Now we go to show the world what we've seen."

"I'm . . . I'm not sure anyone would believe . . ."

He was three steps ahead of her and he suddenly tripped.

But it wasn't really a trip. He was hurled forward, midstride. He tried to catch himself with his right hand, but it buckled and he sprawled to his face on the blacktop's yellow dotted line.

Rebecca's heart slammed into her throat like a fist. She saw the blood immediately, seeping from the side of his head. For an impossibly long moment she stood, immobilized.

Caleb had been shot!

A bullet tugged at her tunic, just below her armpit. Panic swallowed her and she dove for the side of the road. The faint *pfft, pfft* of a silenced rifle reached her ear, and she knew in that instant, rolling to roadside boulders for cover, that Ismael was not dead. She'd heard this rifle before.

A dozen years of honed instinct screamed to the surface. She scrambled for a large boulder to the right of an outcropping. They had just been ambushed; this was a fact. Caleb had been shot in the head; this was also a fact. They had walked nonchalantly through the soldiers, and then Caleb had taken a bullet in his head.

But she didn't know if he was dead. It could be a surface wound—head wounds tended to bleed more than most.

She stopped herself and closed her eyes. *Dear God, listen to me . . . Caleb. Oh, dear Caleb! Caleb . . .*

A bullet cut through the air centimeters from her ear and she ducked. She had to survive. Her heart was aching, as if one of those bullets had lodged itself at its core, but she forced herself to shove the emotion from her mind. Her eyes blurred with tears, and she grunted.

Rebecca ground her teeth, counted to three, and lunged to her left. She dropped to the sand, rolled backward, back behind the boulder, and sprang to the right, into a full sprint. This she did without hesitation, knowing that very few marksmen could possibly follow such an abrupt change in direction with any accuracy.

Ismael came close. His slugs whined past her furiously. But she reached the large clump of boulders she'd angled for. She sprinted around them and ran for the hills in the cover of the boulders.

She already knew what she had to do. The sun was setting in the west, and she would soon have the dark with her.

Dear God, help me.

She ran away from Ismael, her eyes blurred with emotion, desperately pushing back the panic. Twice she stopped and started back, but she knew that was what he wanted, and she forced herself to run on. Every step felt like a small death to her. She was leaving a part of herself back there on the road.

Caleb lying there.

42

THE DOLPHIN CLASS SUBMARINE SAT ON the surface in the Eilat docks, quiet except for the grinding of an electric crane that slowly hoisted a make-shift crate through its loading bay. A full moon shone from a dark sky, casting an eerie light over the sub's black hull.

Of the dozen men who worked around the sub, most of them knew nothing about the contents of the crate. In fact, only the captain, Moses Stern, the first officer, a burly man whom they called Dan, and Avraham himself seemed to have any idea at all.

It was more than Avraham could have hoped for.

He watched the box swing towards the dock in its canvas sling. Water lapped gently against the steel hull three meters under the suspended sling.

Avraham was mildly surprised that half the members of the Knesset were not crowding the dock. David Ben Solomon at least. There were the six guards who waited with the army truck parked on the dock to take the Ark to Jerusalem, but they would hardly present any challenge. Goldstein's ambush waited ten kilometers ahead, twenty men who would be attacking in the narrowest part of the road. These six would be easily overwhelmed.

Avraham's greatest concern was avoiding the attackers' bullets himself. If Goldstein's men could follow simple orders and keep their fire away from the cab, he would be fine.

Captain Moses Stern strolled up beside him, arms behind his back, staring at the crate as it thumped softly to the concrete. Avraham had seen the man only once after his phone call to Goldstein, an hour earlier when they had first surfaced.

"Amazing, isn't it?" the captain said.

"Yes. Hard to believe."

"David Ben Solomon finally has his day."

Avraham froze. Solomon? What did Moses Stern know about Solomon's involvement?

Easy, Avraham. Everyone in Israel knows about Solomon's obsessions.

"He has," Avraham said. "I'm surprised he's not here."

"Believe me, if there was any way for him to be here without drawing unwanted attention, he would be. It'll be hard enough to get it to him without half the Knesset pouncing." Stern chuckled.

"Do you know him?"

"Solomon? Who doesn't?"

Avraham forced a nod. His firearm hung at his hip, and he briefly considered taking control of the situation by force now. But that was ridiculous, of course. He hadn't lost control of the situation.

"Actually, I know Solomon quite well," the captain said. "I've sympathized with his ideas for twenty years. He's a good man."

Avraham swallowed. Waves of heat washed over his skull. Something was not right. "Yes. Yes, he is."

"In fact, I talked to him just an hour ago," the captain said. "He wanted me to tell you that there has been a slight change in plans."

Avraham knew then that he'd been made. Solomon would have learned from the captain that Rebecca was dead, contrary to what he'd been told.

He eased nonchalantly to his right and nodded. A thousand voices screamed in his head. Two of them surfaced as options. The first was to accept the consequences of defeat. The second was to take the captain hostage and force the situation. He immediately opted for the latter.

Avraham jerked his pistol from his belt and whipped it around to face the captain. From the corner of his eyes he saw the three sailors behind him with rifles at their shoulders. The muzzles flashed simultaneously, like three rockets detonating at once.

The slugs took him in his right side, like a huge battering ram. In one instant he was thinking that he could at least kill the captain, and in the next the lead slammed into his arm and hurled him violently to the side. It occurred to him in midair that his shoulder was gone.

His world went black before he hit the water.

Rebecca had eluded Ismael and she was alive; that much was good. The Arabs had scoured the hills in search for her as night settled. She'd heard Ismael's call to her—screaming that she was a witch and that he was going to kill Caleb slowly, like a pig. They were nine and she was one, he screamed, and sooner or later he would kill her as well. Like a pig. And then about four hours ago their sounds had faded to the north.

So then, Caleb was alive.

Or Caleb was dead and Ismael only wanted her to think he was alive to lure her in. Even if he was alive, he might be terribly wounded. Either way, Ismael was baiting her, daring her to come out.

It was there, huddled in the small crevice she'd found, that Rebecca first embraced the fact that she felt things for Caleb that she'd never felt for another man. It would have been one thing to feel sorrow at losing such a unique man of God. But to feel the impossible ache that gripped her heart and slowed her breathing—she knew that she loved him.

She was in love. With a crazy man who'd been shot in the head.

Although to be honest she had never loved a man, so she had nothing to compare it to. But this desperation that raged through her at the thought of losing him definitely felt like something you would call true love.

She grunted, clenched her eyes, and shook her head. She was in an impossible situation. The first thing she'd learned in the army was that the mind does strange things in impossible situations. It was natural for her to feel this compulsion to bring Caleb back.

She was about 250 kilometers south of the border, a border that was lined with tanks, if Ahmed had been right. Ismael waited with Caleb somewhere between her and that border. And three days had passed since Avraham had taken the Ark. She had to get to Jerusalem. Nothing else mattered now.

Except Caleb.

Dear God, except the one man who might have been able to get her past the tanks. Except the one man that made her heart hurt and her head spin.

She grunted again and stood. *Caleb, Caleb. You'll be the death of us all.* She took a deep breath and glanced at the bright moon. *Dear God, save us. This was your doing, not mine.* For a fleeting moment she wondered about praying to the Nazarene. Only for a moment.

Rebecca jogged in the direction the Arabs had gone, keeping low and in the shadows of the boulders. With each footfall a small piece of her courage returned. She had been trained for this by the best. She had *been* the best. Killing was still in her blood.

Do you want to step off a cliff, Rebecca?

I've been in free fall since mother died, she thought.

Ismael's camp was three kilometers north, in a group of rocks west of the road. She heard them before she saw them, which meant that they meant for her to hear them. Ismael wasn't a stupid man. And if they meant to be heard, they had set a trap.

Rebecca ducked behind a boulder and stilled her breathing. She had to get a weapon. There were two ways to do this: the smart way—the way she'd been taught, the way Ismael would obviously expect—or the mad way. The smart way was smart because it actually stood a chance of working. The mad way was mad because it didn't. Which was why Ismael would not expect it.

Rebecca was getting used to madness.

By the carrying voices, the camp was fifty meters ahead, just beyond a group of tall boulders. A fire crackled, and she could see the smoke rising gray against the black sky. She isolated at least five unique voices, which meant that there had to be double that. Nine Ismael had said. Nine to one. And Caleb.

She picked up a rock the size of her fist and hurled it over the boulders into the camp.

It clattered noisily and the voices quieted immediately. She'd done this once in the Golan, behind enemy lines, but not alone. She had two other prisoners with her. However ugly, the strategy had paid off.

Rebecca waited one last desperate moment and then bolted out of her cover to the west. She screamed—a long chilling scream that tore through the air like a gargoyle's howl. Ten long, screaming strides, nine more than she knew was sane, and she threw herself back the way she'd come. She rolled on the ground quickly and then scrambled on all fours to the same rock she'd come from.

A shot boomed somewhere behind her, lighting the night like a flash-cube. They were shooting for the sound. She lurched to her feet, ran to the east, towards the road, and then cut north in a full sprint. Before they had the time to reorient themselves from the scream she was past the camp, on its northeast.

She screamed again, running west, and then reversed her direction as she had before, back to the road. But this time she cut for the camp instead of running past it. Her breathing came hard, in burning pants, but she had to approach them as quietly as possible, so she ran without taking deep breaths.

She palmed the bowie knife from her waist and rushed the camp, hunched low to the ground, praying that the Arabs were still fixated on the north and the south.

Rebecca sprinted around a boulder and saw the camp in a flash. They had built a fire and now stood with their backs to it, six of them. A body lay curled up on the perimeter, under a small rock ledge. Caleb.

Rebecca hurled her knife in a full run and took the last ten meters screaming at the top of her lungs. The knife struck a startled soldier in his sternum and he grabbed crazily for it. His rifle thumped to the ground.

Half of them spun and began firing wildly in her direction, but by then she was even with them. She snatched up the fallen rifle, leapt right over the fire, past the two men on the far side and into the boulders beyond. One of them yelled out in pain, shot by one of his companions.

Rebecca ran to her right. Guns were still firing, chasing the sound of her echoing cry, but the boulders covered her retreat. She immediately doubled back. Back towards the camp, still in a fast run.

This time she dropped to her knees behind a large rock and brought the AK-47 to bear on the exposed camp. She was too winded to aim properly but at this range it would be difficult to miss. Her first shot ripped through them less than ten seconds after her first attack.

She killed four of them before they got off a single shot in her direction. The fifth was turning for her when she shot him through the chest.

Immediately, slugs smashed the rock around her. She heard the telltale puff from Ismael's rifle to the south. Rebecca ducked and retreated into the night. She slid behind a group of low shrubs and lay on her back, panting as quietly as she could manage. Her lungs burned, and her heart felt like it was tearing itself loose, but she had survived without a scratch.

Ismael had not been in the camp.

A crouched form suddenly ran past her, straight for two Jeeps that she now saw for the first time. She rolled on her side and shot him in the back.

That was seven. Two more.

One of the Jeeps suddenly roared to life. She scrambled to acquire a target, but she couldn't make out the driver. The vehicle spun out in a U-turn. Its tires squealed on the pavement and it tore south. The eighth soldier had gone for reinforcements. That left Ismael.

"Rebeccaaa!" Ismael's voice echoed in the night. "Rebeccaaaa! Do you know what I see, Rebeccaaa?"

The sound of his voice made her skin crawl.

"No? I see a man in my scope, lying like a baby. Is this your man?"

He was talking about Caleb. Rebecca pushed herself to her knees.

"I am going to shoot him, Jew. I'm going to put a bullet through his skull. Unless you step out by the fire."

She ran towards the sound of his voice and slid to her knees behind a boulder, frantic. He would do it! He had nothing to lose.

"You can't face me like a man?" Rebecca yelled. "You've allowed a woman to beat you, and now you have to kill an innocent monk to force my hand?" The fire crackled. "Is this the Palestinian way?"

"You're taunting me, Jew! You take me for a fool?"

"I'll throw my gun out to the fire," Rebecca said quickly. "I'll come out unarmed if you come as well. I want to meet Hamil's brother."

He didn't respond right away. The reference to his brother was an afterthought, but it worked.

"Throw your gun out."

She inched around the boulder. "You'll come out?"

"Just throw your rifle out, Jew."

"Not until you agree."

"I don't need to agree. I have your monk an ounce away from death."

"Yes, but you want to agree. You want to meet me face to face. You want to look in the eyes of the person who killed your brother and fooled you into thinking you were in pursuit of the Ark while the real Ark sailed safely to Jerusalem."

That stopped him.

"You lie!"

"I don't have the Ark, Ismael. Kill me and you achieve revenge, but you won't stop the Ark."

"Throw your gun out!"

"You'll come out?"

"Yes."

She heaved her gun into the camp and it landed on the sand with a dull thump.

"Step out," he said.

"After you. I'm unarmed."

"Step out or I shoot Caleb."

Even as Rebecca stepped out, she knew it was suicide. Caleb might already be dead. And if he wasn't, she couldn't save him now.

She walked out slowly and spread her arms, anticipating the slap of a bullet. But there was no bullet. Ismael waited ten seconds and then came out of the rocks, holding a pistol on her. His dark wavy hair was short, and he wore a scruffy black beard.

His lips twitched. "Where's the Ark?"

"I told you, I don't have it."

"I saw it."

"You saw a wooden feeding box with a blanket over it."

He stared at her for a long time. "Then we will go to war. This time the Arab nations are ready."

The way he said it sent a chill down her spine. He at least believed it. The Arab nations knew at the very least. And he was right, it would be war, unless Avraham had done something else with the Ark.

"We don't want war," she said.

"Of course you don't. Israel will be destroyed. *We*, however, do want war. You have butchered our people long enough. It's time for you to leave Palestine."

The form to her right suddenly moved. Caleb groaned and then lay still.

"Don't move," Ismael said, waving his gun at her. "Don't worry, your monk won't awaken. If he wasn't such a perfect lure, I would have finished him off on the road," Ismael said. "Instead I've drugged him. But now he's no longer useful, is he?"

"Drugged him?" She took a step towards him.

Ismael casually fired a shot into the sand by her feet. "I thought I told you not to move."

"Why should I care? You're going to kill me anyway."

"Yes. I'm going to kill you."

"Then at least let me die with some dignity. My whole life love has evaded me—you know how that is. But now I've found that love. In this man."

The words sounded funny coming from her. It was an awkward moment. Her focus shifted from Ismael to Caleb. He'd rolled on his back so that his face shone in the moonlight. Blood had dried on his forehead. His hair lay in tangles, and his chest moved with his breathing. Suddenly she wanted desperately to be with him. To care for him. If there was only one thing she would do in this life, it would be to make sure that he lived.

What a fool she had been to deny her love! Her eyes filled with tears and she blinked.

Ismael slipped a knife from his belt and walked over to Caleb. "You want to die with dignity? Like my brother died?" He stood over Caleb wearing a wicked grin. "He has a pretty face, this one."

The blood in Rebecca's head throbbed hot.

Ismael began to kneel, and she began to panic. His gun was trained on her, unwavering, and his finger was already tense on the trigger, but in that moment she lost the ability to care what any of that meant. Her world simply exploded.

"Hamil told me who your real father was," she said.

His eyes momentarily narrowed in confusion.

Rebecca dove forward in that moment, while he was distracted by her absurd claim.

Ismael's gun boomed. Pain ripped through her right shoulder. She staggered to the right and launched herself at him. Ignoring the gun, which boomed again, missing clean, she went for his head with a blind fury she hadn't felt since first understanding that her mother had been murdered. Her palm slammed against something soft and Ismael went limp.

She pulled her arm back and smashed his face again with every ounce of her strength before he could fall. His face had changed shape. He collapsed in a heap, lifeless. She stood over him, panting. Her vision returned and she saw that his nose had been shoved back into his head.

Rebecca dropped to her knees and brought trembling hands to Caleb's face. "Oh, Caleb. Dear Caleb, I am so sorry." She shoved her hands under his back and pulled at him. But her arms felt like rubber, and she only managed to fall back down on him.

She lay her cheek on his chest and began to weep. Deep in her belly a dam seemed to break. Two weeks of sorrow and desperation rushed from her eyes. And love. Yes, and love.

She sobbed uncontrollably, letting her tears wet his tunic. She felt dirty and wicked next to his heaving chest. But his gentle breathing worked through her like a salve, easing the pain. He was alive.

She lifted her head and kissed his chin and then his cheek. "I love you, Caleb. I love you!" The bullet had only nicked his head; she saw that now. She felt her shoulder, relieved to find only a surface wound.

A gentle rumble floated on the air, and she thought he might be groaning again. It came again, from the south.

The soldiers!

Rebecca scrambled to her knees, grabbed him behind his neck and his knees, and hoisted him from the ground. He was heavy, but her military training had given her the strength of most men. She heaved to get her arms under him.

Carrying him like a sack of potatoes, she stumbled across the camp and struck for the Jeep beyond the rocks. The rumbling grew louder, and she ran as best she could, staggering, lugging his weight.

She reached the military Jeep, eased Caleb into the seat, fired it up, and bounced onto the road just as the first headlights poked over the hill. But they hadn't seen her. She knew that because they stopped behind her at the camp, just as she took the first corner.

She blazed into the night with Caleb slumped next to her. Alive, for the moment. But far from home.

She began to cry again. It was hopeless.

43

"PUT IT THERE." SOLOMON LIFTED A trembling finger to the conference table in the Speakers Bureau. Four soldiers lifted the crate and eased it onto the dark wood surface, using the canvas-wrapped poles along its base. It settled with a clump that sounded obscenely loud in the stillness.

"You may leave," Solomon said.

Jerusalem slept in the early morning hours outside.

Behind and to the right of Solomon, Prime Minister Ben Gurion stood stock still. To his left, Speaker Moshe Aron stood by his desk, in front of mahogany wall units filled with black books. The room was richly decorated with classical paintings and exquisite trim, but their eyes were not on the décor. They were on the crate.

The prime minister stepped forward. "So. This is it?" His voice sounded breathy.

Solomon stared at the crudely constructed crate. His daughter had given her life for this crate, and he wasn't sure how he felt about that. The news had thrown him into a tailspin. Of the team that went into Ethiopia, only Zakkai had survived. He'd managed to climb back aboard the expedition ship, but a Saudi warship had detained him half way up the Red Sea. Solomon had learned the ugly truth when they'd finally let him make contact. Rebecca was dead. He had cried his eyes dry.

Now there was this crate, and it occurred to him looking at it that his own blood had purchased it.

"Are we going to open it?" Moshe Aron asked, stepping up. It was as if they were kids, staring at a forbidden box in the attic.

"Lock the door," Solomon said.

The prime minister walked for the door, and Solomon picked up a crowbar that rested on the couch. They stood around the table for one long, last minute. Solomon looked into their eyes and then gazed at Zakkai's crate.

"The fate of Israel is in that box, my friends," he said slowly.

"You're sure this is the Ark?" Ben Gurion asked.

"We will find out soon enough."

He jammed the claws around a rustic-looking nail. The room filled with the screech of iron pulling past wood.

"I would be careful," Ben Gurion said. "Touching it might not be a good idea."

Solomon shook the nail free and dug at another. The first cross brace came off and he attacked another. The thumping of blood filled his ears. *Dear Rebecca, your life will not be in vain.* He pulled on the crowbar, working faster now.

"Be careful, David."

Solomon ignored him. A tremor betrayed his excitement. *Dear God, redeem your name.* The second cross brace clattered to the table and then toppled to the carpet.

Solomon stood back, breathing steady through his nostrils. A single nail held the boards on this side. "Pray to God, my friends." He placed the tip of the crowbar between two boards and twisted hard. The brace popped and a single board slid down at an angle, revealing a dark interior.

Solomon peered inside, mouth open, hand quivering. The fabric of a gray blanket stared back at him. "It's covered!" He could hardly contain himself now. He dug furiously at the braces on the other side. The blanket would protect them and whatever it covered, he thought. For most of his life he had patiently begged God for a moment like this, and now he had lost his patience entirely.

The Speaker and Ben Gurion helped him now, carefully pulling boards off as he freed them. Quickly they bared a dusty, gray wool blanket wrapped around an object Solomon eyed to be roughly one-and-a-half cubits by two-and-a-half cubits, with twin peaks on top. The blanket smelled musty—like something wet taken from a deep hole.

They pulled off the last board and stood back. Sweat beaded Solomon's forehead and he wiped at it. He reached a hand for a loose corner and touched the wool.

"Careful, Solomon."

He barely heard the prime minister. When he tugged, the whole blanket came loose, and he yanked it off with a powerful jerk.

Brilliant gold filled his sight. Solomon saw the chest, gleaming under the ceiling lights, and for a moment he thought he was going to fall from the quiver that shook his legs. He stood with the wool blanket in one fist, gawking at the rectangular chest he knew without a shred of doubt to be the Ark of the Covenant. Two cherubim, bowing with outstretched wings, knelt over the Mercy Seat. It was so bright that for a moment Solomon thought it might actually be glowing. He took a step back.

Silence, tempered only by the pulling of ragged breath, held the room in an endless embrace. They were too stunned to speak.

Ben Gurion walked slowly to his right, eyes peeled with shock. Behind him, the Speaker didn't move, but he kept blinking and was breathing heavy through his nose.

A fist of emotion rose through Solomon's chest and he began to weep. Three thousand years of history seemed to boil up within him and spill out in an anguish that made his knees weak. He wanted to rush forward and kiss it, but he knew it would mean his death. The power of God Almighty surely dwelled within this Ark.

"May God forgive our sins," he said.

"May God let his face shine upon us," Ben Gurion said softly. A tear leaked from the prime minister's eye and rolled down his right cheek. "My God, my God. I cannot believe what I'm seeing."

Moshe Aron found it in himself to move. He circled the Ark opposite the prime minister, still blinking.

"'And they shall make an ark of acacia wood; two and a half cubits shall be its length, a cubit and a half its width, and a cubit and a half its height,'" Solomon quoted. "'And you shall overlay it with pure gold, inside and out you shall overlay it, and shall make on it a molding of gold all around.'"

He paused, gathering himself. "'And there I will meet with you, and I will speak with you from above the mercy seat, from between the two cherubim which are on the ark of the Testimony, about everything which I will give you in commandment to the children of Israel.'"

"And inside?" Ben Gurion asked. "Do you think . . ."

"The stone tablets and the scroll of the Torah," Solomon finished. "All that is Judaism is contained here."

Solomon wiped at his eyes and walked around it slowly now, shaking his head and studying every centimeter. It was almost exactly as he'd imagined, although slightly more decorative. Concentric circular etchings ran around the lid. The cherubim were faceless, but their wings looked as if they'd been cast with a mold taken from a real bird. The space between them—the Mercy Seat—if he used his imagination, he could almost see God's power hovering there. Israel would never be the same again. The Ark of the Covenant was in Jerusalem.

"We have to rebuild the Temple," Speaker Aron said in a low voice. "We have no choice."

Solomon exchanged a knowing look with the prime minister. They both knew that the Knesset would overwhelmingly agree, once they laid their eyes on what stood before them now.

"God still speaks from this Ark, Solomon?" Ben Gurion asked.

"Yes. Don't be ridiculous."

"Then he will tell us what to do."

A rap sounded on the door and they exchanged glances.

"David?" The muted voice belonged to Stephen Goldstein. "David, please open this door. Immediately!"

Ben Gurion nodded at Aron who walked over and opened the door.

Stephen Goldstein entered with Defense Minister Benjamin Yishai. "What is the meaning . . ."

Goldstein saw the Ark and pulled up.

Aron shut the door and locked it again. The room fell deathly still.

It took a full five minutes for the initial shock to wear off—enough so that Goldstein could muster his old self anyway.

"We can't know if this is the original Ark," Goldstein said.

"It is the original," the prime minister returned.

"Have you opened it?"

"No. Be my guest."

"This is ridiculous. We can't throw our nation into war over this."

"Go ahead, Stephen," Solomon said. "Touch it. Open it. See for yourself."

Goldstein collapsed in a chair and wiped his forehead.

The prime minister turned to the minister of defense. "What's your assessment, Benjamin?"

"My assessment is that we are headed for war," he said.

"Then we will head for war," Ben Gurion said. "We can't ignore our history any longer."

"A war may not be easily won."

"You're telling me something new?"

"No." The defense minister walked towards a Re'uven painting of olive trees and pomegranates and gripped his hands behind his back. "But this war will be a war with four fronts. We've never faced anything similar."

"You're talking about the Palestinians within our borders. That would require some preparation. They haven't had the time."

"Maybe. But forty thousand armed Palestinians could tip the balance in the favor of an upgraded enemy." He turned around. "Either way, we can't allow them to make the first move. We should activate our reserves now."

"Don't be reactionary!" Goldstein snapped. "You activate the reserves and you will only escalate the situation. Can't you see that?"

"Escalate to what? An inevitable war?" the prime minister said. "It's time to get this over with."

"If our air force were caught off guard, and the Palestinians launched a coordinated attack . . . it could get ugly," the defense minister said.

"You're forgetting the Ark," Solomon said. "We have the Ark. We have God on our side, and therefore we have no choice."

"You don't know *what* you have, Solomon," Goldstein said. "You have a gold box."

Solomon stared at him and fought the impulse to walk over and slap him. "Blasphemy comes too easily to your lips, my friend."

The room quieted and they stared at the Ark.

"Activate the reserves, Benjamin," the prime minister said. "Bring the military to full alert. Twenty-four hours?"

"Yes. Twenty-four hours."

"And deploy a level-one armament of tactical nuclear weapons."

"I must object—"

"Yes, Goldstein, I know that you object." He faced the Speaker. "Call an emergency session of the full Knesset. When can we have them all here?"

"By tonight, I would think."

"Sooner. We will meet at noon. Put the word out immediately."

"It's three o'clock in the morning."

"The phones don't work at three in the morning?"

"What about the Americans?"

Ben Gurion hesitated. "In the morning. We don't need them shutting us down before we get started." He eyed the Ark. "May God have mercy on his people."

44

THE SUN WAS COMING UP ON Rebecca's right, and the border was approaching dead ahead. Caleb had not budged.

Rebecca had piloted the Jeep north, her nerves stretched to the snapping point. She'd tried to wake Caleb, but whatever drug Ismael had administered refused to release him. The use of various drugs was not uncommon in both camps, and apparently Ismael had used them before. Caleb was nearly comatose.

She had stopped the Jeep once and considered turning east, crossing into Jordan, and heading north the back way. But there was no reason for the detour—if anything it would only increase her risk, if such a thing were possible. The only way to reduce her risk was to head back the way she had come, and that hardly seemed like a reasonable alternative.

She'd headed north again, driving slowly, anticipating a checkpoint at every corner. None came. Her mind had considered every possible outcome of this drive north and every one of them ended very badly. She was headed into the mouth of the lion and Daniel slept like a baby beside her. She was Isaac, and the ram had been drugged to a stupor an hour before it was to make its lifesaving entrance.

Her tunic was damp with sweat, despite the cool night air. But two things kept her crawling north. Three things.

First, the simple fact that Jerusalem lay directly to the north. Second, going south or any other direction gave her no more nor less hope than going north. And third, Caleb had insisted they go north. True enough, he was no longer giving directions. But she knew that her only hope was somehow in him, if not in the waving of his wand like Moses over the Red Sea, then as the man she loved.

She had spent a good part of the last hour muttering prayers to God. Silly little prayers that sounded foolish in the face of her predicament. For all practical purposes, God had put her in this situation himself! She was heading north, and every turn of the tires on the blacktop groaned her insanity. And as far as she could figure, it was all God's doing. The Nazarene's doing.

A Muslim prayer call echoed over the hills, and Rebecca moved her foot to the brake. Where had that come from? There shouldn't be any town anywhere near here if her geography was correct. She eased the Jeep forward at about thirty kilometers per hour. To her right, the eastern sky was orange over the Midia range. Another sound reached her ears—the clanking of metal against metal.

Tank tracks!

Rebecca slammed on the brakes and stopped in the middle of the road. A ring lingered in her ears. She held her breath and listened.

There it was again, the unmistakable sound of steel tank tracks. And beyond that, the Muslim prayer call. She spun around.

Nothing. The road was deserted.

"Caleb?" She shook him. "Please, Caleb." His head lolled gently.

A deep-seated desperation swept through her chest. She sat immobilized behind the wheel, unable to think. The border was just ahead; she could feel it more than anything. It had taken her four hours to travel 250 kilometers, and she'd done it without meeting a single patrol. But her luck had run out. The inevitable waited.

Rebecca eased the clutch out and started the Jeep forward. She rolled another kilometer. The sound of the tank tracks hadn't returned. Maybe, just maybe, the checkpoints were on a parallel road nearby or . . .

She'd come around a corner and the sight ahead made her jerk. Heat washed over her skull and spread down her back. The desert opened up to a wide basin. As far as she could see in either direction, hundreds of tanks lined the basin, facing north, like a huge herd of beasts. Division strength, at the very least.

She swerved on the road and then quickly pulled off, less than a hundred meters from the first tank. As many APCs and half-tracks were scattered among the M-60 tanks. Egyptian and Saudi. Thousands of soldiers crawled over the machines and leaned on their tracks. The road wound between them, without obstruction except for a single machine gun post facing Rebecca.

The Arabs had seen her already. They were staring in her direction.

Rebecca felt the first waves of panic lapping at her mind and she closed her eyes. *Hold on, Rebecca. Hold on.*

She opened her eyes. She'd been here before, only the last time it had been with Caleb, facing a ragtag outfit of soldiers. Now she was alone, facing a division of M-60 tanks.

One of the guards was waving her forward. He yelled something she couldn't make out and a hundred soldiers faced her.

Her muscles refused to move. This was it. She was finally facing her death. She had found love and death in the same day.

Rebecca looked over at Caleb and swallowed. Now, facing death, she felt desperate for his power. Sorrow washed over her, and she thought she might start to cry again. Her mind skipped absurdly to a story she'd read about Jews walking innocently over a canyon cliff at Nazi gunpoint. She had wept when she'd read it, and the same sorrow filled her chest now.

"I was wrong about your God, Caleb," she whispered. "I was wrong about the Nazarene." The words sounded impossible on her lips.

Would you like to step off a cliff, Rebecca?

She looked up at the soldier who had his rifle pointed skyward now. A shot rang into the air and he yelled again, demanding she come forward.

A thought struck her. *If Caleb had been protected by God in the desert, was it so that he could die today?*

She sniffed and jammed the shifter into gear. The Jeep bounced back onto the blacktop and rolled for the tanks. Rebecca steeled herself with a set jaw.

"If your God shows up, I will follow him, Caleb," she said through clenched teeth. "You hear me? I will follow your Christ."

Another tear slipped from the corner of her eye. She slowed the Jeep to a crawl and continued forward. Fifty meters. Forty.

A gunshot split the air. The Jeep sagged to the right. Someone had shot her tire out.

For a brief moment Rebecca stared at the line of tanks without really seeing them. She set her jaw and climbed out without looking up. The soldier was yelling again, in a high pitch now, as if he were about to shoot her. She ignored him and rounded the vehicle. She pulled the passenger door open, shoved her arms under Caleb's back and legs, and hauled him from the Jeep.

She faced them, with Caleb in her arms. He was too heavy to carry forty meters, despite her strength, but she no longer cared. It was a fitting end to the mad journey that had delivered her here. Caleb's journey. They wanted her to stop, but she couldn't stop. She had to get to Jerusalem, and Jerusalem lay beyond this line of soldiers.

Rebecca walked forward, towards the division of tanks.

The absurdity of it all struck her fullface and she had to force one leg before the other. She covered a third of the distance, and the valley seemed to have hushed for her journey. Her shoulders began to shake with a sob. She tried to hold the emotion back for a second, and then she surrendered herself to it. The tears flowed silently from her eyes like streams, dropping on the man in her arms.

She looked down into Caleb's peaceful face and the sight made her cry harder. She lifted his head and kissed his cheek.

"Messiah, show your power to me," she said aloud. "Jesus of Nazareth, have mercy upon me, a sinner."

The heavens might have opened in that moment for all she knew, but to her it felt like a bucket of anguish had suddenly been dumped into her mind. It spread down her spine and into her chest and she threw her head back in a silent cry. She was facing death here with Caleb in her arms, but really she was dead already. Dead because she had rejected truth. The simple, unalterable truth that she'd denied the Messiah already. He was the Nazarene, wasn't he?

She was suddenly crying aloud, slogging forward with this man in her arms. It was too much. She nearly lost her footing, but she hung on, wading against this sea of sorrow that flowed through her. The soldiers and tanks became a mere backdrop to her own drama.

"Dear God, forgive me," she sobbed quietly.

Waves of warmth washed over her skin and she sobbed open-mouthed and unabashed, eyes still clenched. "Oh God! Oh Gaawwwd! Forgive me!"

It occurred to her that she might be headed in the wrong direction now, but the thought was lost to this overpowering emotion surging through her chest. This raw love. This passion born out of God's heart. Out of the Nazarene's heart.

The sound of sorrow swallowed her, and she thought that heaven itself was weeping with her. She leaned over and kissed Caleb's cheek again. "I love you, Caleb. Oh, how I love you." Perhaps she had been shot and *was* in heaven. Perhaps . . .

Rebecca stopped, swallowed. She looked past blurry eyes to her right. A large soldier dressed in tan desert garb was on his knees beside the road, head bent over, weeping.

Beyond him a tank stood with its huge gun aimed at the sky. The commander stared at her with long trails of tears down his cheeks.

The sound of weeping came from all sides. Rebecca turned slowly around, stunned by the sight that greeted her. By the hundreds men were lying slumped over their tanks, or kneeling on the ground, or lying in the sand, gripped by a sorrow that twisted their faces. Not a single man stood unaffected. The army of tanks had become a field of anguish. To a man the soldiers wept bitterly.

It was the Tower of Babel. It was a sea of tears, and God was parting that sea.

Rebecca turned north and walked forward as if on a cloud. This was real. She was not dead. If anything, she had come alive. She'd found a new world with new rules, and at its center was this man she had once despised. The Nazarene.

She began to cry again, and she cried for a long time, walking right past a division of tanks. With Caleb in her arms. Which might have seemed impossible because of his weight, but was clearly not impossible. The huge weapons had armor of hardened steel, but the men who commanded them had become butter. It was as if anyone who looked her way felt what she felt and ended in a puddle of tears.

Rebecca didn't know how long she managed to walk, but the army fell behind until only her own sobbing surrounded her. Three times she staggered and set Caleb down, exhausted and numb. Three times she picked him back up and walked on, dazed and disorientated. The army was back there, beyond a bend in the road. She could hear them still, a gentle sound of sorrow. She wanted to leave the sound, find some solitude. She wanted to be alone with her new revelation and with Caleb.

Her strength finally left her altogether, and she stumbled to the side of the road only to drop Caleb in the sand at a crossroads.

He grunted and she dropped down beside him, horrified that she might have hurt him.

"Caleb? Caleb, are you okay?"

She stroked his hair and fresh tears blurred her vision.

"Oh, Caleb . . ."

His eyes fluttered open.

45

GENERAL NASSER OF THE SYRIAN air force slammed the phone down in its cradle. "The Israelis are calling up their reserves!"

"You're absolutely positive?" Abu Ismael demanded. "One report doesn't necessarily—"

"Not one report. Five reports. The call has gone out. Every hour that goes by now we lose our advantage."

Abu stalked across the war room, furious that it had come to this. Ismael hadn't checked in for nearly two days. The last he'd heard, his son was tracking the Ark into Saudi Arabia. For all he knew he was dead. The thought sat like lead in his gut.

"Colonel Muhammed Du'ad's men are in place around almost every target we outlined," he said.

"It's too early," Nasser said. "We don't have independent verification that the Ark is even in Jerusalem, much less that they have any mandate to retake their Temple Mount. I don't think we would have the support from Egypt to attack without confirmation."

"No, we wouldn't. But we do have this mobilization of theirs—that's confirmation that they're concerned enough to risk war. They know that they can't keep mobilization on this scale secret. We have far too many operatives throughout Israel. And still they do it. Why? Because they have the Ark, and they know that Ismael knew they had the Ark. They can only assume we know as well. So we do have our confirmation."

The logic wasn't ironclad, but the information on which wars were based rarely was. *Where are you, Ismael? What do you know, my son?*

"We can't attack their air bases, Abu. What if we're wrong?"

"Then we are wrong! Perhaps it doesn't matter. We've looked for an excuse for fifty years, and now we have one. Does it really matter if the excuse is based on mistaken information? Israel can't coexist with the Arab states. That is what matters."

"Now you sound like your son. We're not the Hamas. The last time we went into Israel, we came out with our tail between our legs. And they didn't have nuclear weapons then."

"And we didn't have an air force to speak of then."

"Without Egypt, we still don't."

Abu glanced at the man. "Don't let the king hear you say that. Besides, we have Egypt. And we also have forty thousand armed men inside Israel's borders, around their towns."

"You're forgetting that it was I who drew up this plan in the beginning. But it's dependent on complete surprise. Something we've evidently lost."

"And if we *have* lost it, can't we still win?"

They had discussed it many times before, but never with true intent on the table. General Nasser sighed. "If . . . if we are absolutely sure about Egypt's total commitment, and if . . . if the PLO proves to be more than a scattered band of poorly trained civilians, then yes, I think so. But it would require a full assault without compromise from any of our friends."

"Exactly! And if we don't mobilize immediately, then we will remove the option of a full assault from the table. We have to at least put our forces in a position to attack. The Israelis are doing nothing less."

"If we mobilize, they will see it."

"They will, but they still need time to gear up their military machine. Twenty-four hours, at least. And even then we stand a chance at a face-off. We have no choice, Nasser. We must mobilize."

They stared at each other for a few long seconds. "Egypt will agree?"

"Yes," Abu said. "Absolutely."

"And Colonel Du'ad will refrain from attacking?"

"Unless we give the word," Abu assured him.

"The plan was flawless the way I drew it up," Nasser said, closing his eyes. "Now this. Every time an Arab belches, the Jews seem to know." He swore. "Okay. Okay. Then we mobilize. I'll inform the king."

"Immediately," Abu said.

"Immediately."

Abu snatched up his phone and punched in a number. He waited for the answer, trying his best to ignore the surge in his pulse. A voice filled his ear.

"Yes?"

"President Al-Zeid, this is—"

"I know who you are."

"Yes, of course. They've called in their reserves. We believe that we should mobilize immediately."

Silence followed.

"Sir?"

"And Jordan?"

"They have agreed to follow our lead."

"Then we mobilize."

"I thought you would agree."

The president of Egypt kept the line silent for a moment. "They have it then?"

"We think so. It's the only reason for their action."

"May Allah grant us mercy," the president said and hung up.

Rebecca wiped her eyes quickly and looked at him again. Caleb was staring up at her with wide green eyes.

"Caleb?"

He blinked but didn't answer.

She gently pushed his hair from his forehead. "Are . . . are you all right? Can you hear me?"

"Rebecca," he said softly.

She couldn't help what she did next. He was alive and he had just spoken her name tenderly, and for some reason this simple fact flooded her with the desire to kiss him.

So she did. On the forehead.

"Caleb, I thought I might have lost you." She pulled back. "You scared me to death."

Caleb smiled. "Hello, Rebecca. Did I miss something?"

She laughed, short and full of relief. "Yes. Yes, I suppose you did. You missed my heroic rescue." The grin faded from her mouth and she looked back to the south. "You missed the Nazarene's rescue. I think you would have been impressed." She looked at him again.

"And you missed . . ." How could she just tell him that she had fallen madly in love with him? What if he couldn't return that kind of love? After all, he was a Christian from the deserts of Ethiopia and she was a Jew from Jerusalem. What if she had just imagined . . .

"I love you, Rebecca."

Her heart wanted to burst. She looked deep into his eyes. "You do?"

"I have loved you from the first time you stomped off in the desert."

They were holding their gaze, and Rebecca could hardly stand the warmth running through her chest.

"When I tried to kiss you?"

He grinned wide. "Yes, I think that did it."

She stared at him. Was he serious? A giggle rose to her lips and she let it out in a burst.

He laughed in a way she'd never heard from him, more of a snort than a real laugh. It only made her giggle more. This was love, wasn't it? This embrace of silliness. She impulsively kissed him again, this time lightly and on the lips.

He turned red and she knew that she had swept him off his feet.

"Ohhh, my head," Caleb said, touching his wound.

She quickly removed his hand. "No, it's okay; leave it alone. It's just a graze. We have to get some water."

Caleb sat up and looked around.

"I felt the Nazarene's power, Caleb," she said.

He turned back. "You did?"

"Yes. I did."

Caleb scrambled to his feet. "You did." He covered his face with his hands. "Thank you, Father."

Caleb suddenly froze. He pulled his hands down and spun to face the north. "We have to get to Jerusalem!"

The sound of cowbells reached faintly to them. Rebecca looked up the dirt road that intersected the highway. A cart was clip-clopping towards them, piloted by a man in rags.

She exchanged a glance with Caleb. "Yes, we have to get to Jerusalem."

The cart pulled closer, and then stopped abreast of them. "Shalom," the man said in an old crackling voice. He was a hundred if he was a day.

"Shalom," Rebecca returned. "Do you know that there's an Egyptian army gathered around the corner?"

The man looked to the south. "No. Is there?"

"Yes, there is. You shouldn't be here."

"And you? Why are you here?" The man spoke Hebrew.

Rebecca hesitated. "Where *are* we?"

"You are five kilometers from Eilat," the man said and looked to the south again. "The Egyptian army, eh? Are we at war with the Egyptians?"

"No. No, I don't think so. We're in Israel?"

"Do I look like an Egyptian to you? Yes, we are just over the border which is around the bend where your army is gathered."

Rebecca looked at Caleb, surprised. She must have crossed into Jordan before meeting the tank division! That's why the drive had seemed so long. But what were Egyptian tanks doing in Jordan?

"Can you take us to Eilat, my friend?" Caleb asked.

"I just came from Eilat," the man said.

Caleb smiled. That smile of his. The one that reached into the heart.

"But I would be happy to take you there," the old man said, casting a last look south. "Very happy, despite losing a day's wage."

"You may save far more than you lose," Rebecca said.

"As I said. Very happy," the man replied.

———

An American satellite had already seen the tanks roll into Jordan, three hours before Rebecca saw them, in the dead of night. It was a little unusual, but they had been tracking the joint Saudi-Egyptian exercise for three days now, and this latest push north didn't receive the attention it otherwise would have.

But the landscape began to change during the midmorning hours.

The movement began in the Sinai Peninsula, south of Israel—long rows of tanks rolling towards the fifty-kilometer ribbon of land known as the Gaza Strip. Thirteen hundred M-60 and M-1A1 tanks approached the border, dragging enough self-propelled artillery to flatten Tel Aviv at the push of a few buttons.

The Saudi mechanized division Rebecca had encountered pushed further north, through Jordan, along Israel's eastern border, and was joined by a Jordanian armored division south of the Dead Sea.

Jordan had the weakest military among Israel's neighbors, but what it lost in brute strength, it gained in geography, with the longest common border, nearly a third of which ran along the Palestinian controlled West Bank. Two hundred upgraded M-60A1 tanks rolled for this border along the West Bank. All twenty-four of Jordan's AH-IS attack helicopters put down on three bases west of Amman, a twenty-minute flight from Jerusalem.

Syria sent three bloated mechanized divisions south into Jordan. Syria had the land power among the Arab nations, and it began to flex its muscles now. Fifteen hundred tanks, eight hundred of which were T-72s rolled south of the Golan towards Ma'ad. Two more divisions lined along the Golan itself, just beyond the border. A sixth division headed into Lebanon, towards the northern tip of Israel.

In all over six thousand tanks and twice as many APCs and launchers converged on Israel's borders, like ants scrambling to feed at the edge of a splotch of honey. From a twenty-thousand-foot reconnaissance shot, the region looked like a ring of fire. Plumes of dust rose in the still morning air, trailing thousands of tanks, as if the desert surrounding Israel were venting like a volcano, preparing to erupt.

The Atlantic phone lines began to burn midmorning. The president of the United States canceled an appearance at the Kennedy Space Center and boarded a plane for Washington. Something was up. Something major. By all appearances the Middle East had begun to melt down without warning.

He was a new president who'd based his candidacy on domestic policy. When he was finally told by Israel's prime minister that they had retrieved the Ark of the Covenant, and that the Arabs were taking issue, the president asked how a gold box could bring the Middle East to its knees. What, in God's name, did a relic have to do with the Temple Mount, and for that matter how could a single plot of land the size of the White House lawn bring grown men to blows?

Ben Gurion hung up on him.

The news spread like wildfire through the IDF, and the reserves clogged all the arteries flocking to their assigned posts. Very few knew that the Arabs were gathering, and even fewer knew why. They were calling it an exercise, but the rumors were already flying through the streets. Israel raced to arm herself nonetheless, like an ant unknowingly preparing to take on an elephant.

A few isolated groups of Palestinians were discovered and arrested, but the bulk of Colonel Du'ad's men remained hidden, watching with wide eyes, waiting for the order.

By noon the land of Israel and her neighbors had armed themselves with enough destructive power to flatten every building in all of their respective lands a hundred times over with the single strike of a match. The situation gave the term *powder keg* new meaning.

But the matches weren't lighting.

Not yet.

46

Of the 116 seats facing the podium in the Knesset Plenum, all but one was filled. Isaac Mendal was in the hospital and couldn't make the emergency session, but he had arranged for a closed circuit through one of the cameras in the Plenum.

Each chair sat behind one of a dozen long continuous desks that wrapped around the room, like landscaped tiers. A giant horseshoe-shaped table known as the government table, reserved for the prime minister and the ministers, sat facing the podium, where the secretary general, the sergeant at arms, and the Speaker sat stoically. David Ben Solomon stood in the middle of this empty horseshoe, beside the table that held the Ark of the Covenant, hidden under a black velvet cloth.

A television camera and its lone operator looked down from the second-story gallery above them, filming as it normally did, but this time only for Isaac Mendal, as requested. For obvious reasons, broadcasting an image of the Ark could prove catastrophic.

The gavel sounded and Solomon looked up at a sea of questioning faces. The emergency session wasn't an everyday occasion.

"Ladies and gentlemen, a point of order before we begin. I have asked the Speaker for permission to examine an old question with you, and I beg your indulgence for just a few minutes."

Several objections rumbled from the seats—comments about wasting time that referred to some of his past performances in the Plenum.

Solomon ignored them and turned to the table. "I want you to imagine, for the sake of argument, that the Ark of the Covenant is under this black cloth."

A silence settled over them.

"And I want to know whether you would vote for the rebuilding of the Temple, on the Temple Mount, if we had indeed uncovered the Ark of the Covenant and put it before you today."

They stared at him as if he must be mad—as if they didn't understand what he could possibly be saying. The notion that the Ark sat under that black cloth was absurd. And the idea of being called here to discuss this idiotic notion was clearly beyond most of their comprehension.

But that was precisely what Solomon wanted. Let them get their philosophical quibbles out of the way before they understood what was happening. The prime minister, the Speaker, and, with some coaxing, Stephen Goldstein had all agreed that to uncover the Ark before the arguments had been cast would throw the group into an emotional quandary that would only lengthen the overall arguments and extend the meeting. Time was the last thing they had now. The Arabs were gathering, their own military was screaming murder, and the world was demanding answers.

"I don't know about the Ark, my dear old friend," Shmuel Weiss of the Labor Party said, "but surely my phone didn't ring off its hook at five this morning because of some wives' tale you would like to discuss." A few members chuckled. "Maybe it would make more sense to talk about why our reservists are being called out on an exercise without it being scheduled. The country is a mess this morning, or didn't you notice?"

"I'm sure you have many questions, Shmuel, and I'm sure someone who's qualified will answer them," Solomon returned. "But for now please try to concentrate on mine."

"Why should we discuss an absurd abstraction in an emergency session?" Shmuel demanded.

"Because, however absurd, the issue of the Temple Mount and the *Waqf*'s current excavations around Solomon's Stables do play a part in this session." They all knew about the Muslims' "archaeological dig" to make room for yet another mosque, and Solomon counted on his mention of it to throw them off track for the moment. "So indulge me for a few minutes. I've done the same for you a dozen times."

Several of them immediately objected and demanded to know about the reserves being called as well. But a member of the Labor Party took up Solomon's question.

"We don't even know precisely where the original Temple was built! Risking a war over a fifteen-hundred-square-meter piece of real estate that may or may not have any historical significance is not clear thinking."

"Nonsense!" A Likud Party member returned immediately. "Only the most politically motivated archaeologist even suggests such a thing! Among the serious scholars there is no doubt. And among the people there is no doubt."

The debate had launched itself as Solomon knew it would.

The Speaker banged his gavel. "We will follow proper protocol here."

Another stood and received a nod. It was Chaim Peled, an Orthodox scholar, and they all knew what he was going to say before he said it. "As you know, the Muslim claim to the Al-Aqsa Mosque as the mosque from which Mohammed supposedly rose to heaven is absurd. Mohammed died in A.D. 632. The Dome of the Rock was a Byzantine church until and the Al-Aqsa was built even later. Twenty years later. Neither even existed during Mohammed's life. But we let the world of Islam pretend anyway? The evidence for King Solomon's Temple, on the other hand, is incontrovertible. The whole thing is an embarrassment. We should take the Temple Mount, with or without this hypothetical Ark."

"And this from the Orthodox?" Shmuel shot back. "Would not God strike you dead if you went to take the Mount?"

"I do not agree with some of my brothers that we must wait for the Messiah to rebuild," Chaim returned. "But the Temple *will* be rebuilt—our prophets have made that clear. Perhaps you are standing in the *way* of the Messiah's coming by refusing to build."

That set off a dozen protests at once.

Solomon let them argue for twenty minutes—old arguments from a dozen perspectives, peppered by strenuous objections to spending so much time on a conundrum based on a hypothetical abstraction. Someone even had the gall to bring up the American Christians who were clearly looking for the rebuilding of the Temple as predicted by their own prophecy.

Every point thrown out by the skeptics was quickly countered by the more faithful. And every argument cast by the faithful was quickly trashed by the skeptics. And then the objections were repeated in slightly different language, testing Solomon, who mostly listened now, to his limit.

The soft conversation of those in the background built to a steady dull roar. The demands that they get on with whatever had brought them here began to increase.

Solomon looked up and caught the eye of the prime minister who was talking into a red phone with quiet urgency. He nodded and tapped his watch. Whatever was happening on the other end of that line could not be good. Solomon nodded.

He held up his arms. "May I have your attention, please!"

A member from the United Arab List was in midspeech—the timing could have been better. The man ignored him and continued.

The prime minister hung up the phone, pushed himself back from the government table, and stood.

"Ladies and gentlemen . . ."

The room quieted. "Ladies and gentlemen, it is my duty to inform you that as we speak forces for Egypt, Jordan, and Syria have gathered on our borders and are threatening a fully coordinated assault on Israel."

Now the silence was complete.

Every head in the room jerked to face the prime minister. Somewhere a sheaf of papers slipped from a desk and slapped to the floor.

And then, as if a switch had been thrown, the members broke into questions of alarm as one. Above them boomed the outraged voice of the Deputy Speaker, Rafael Dayan, who hadn't been told and clearly thought he should have been told.

"What *is* the meaning of this?"

Solomon decided it would be now. He grabbed the corner of the velvet cloth covering the Ark and yanked it. The sheet flapped through the air like a huge, black batwing and then settled slowly to the ground, revealing the brilliant gold chest with its two cherubim bowed in reverence.

"This!" Solomon yelled above them all. "This, my friends, is the meaning of this!"

A singular gasp seemed to evacuate the room of its air. They stared, stunned and blinking, at the large chest of glimmering gold.

"The Ark of the Covenant has been found, oh Israel! And it stands before you today." Solomon's voice echoed in the room. His heart pounded in the silence.

Somewhere a single wail broke out softly. And then the truth seemed to hit them all at once. The Ark of the Testimony, the Ark of God's Covenant, the same Ark that had brought their ancestors into the Promised Land, stood on the floor of the Knesset, wrapped in gold so bright that it appeared luminescent.

Shouts of alarm mixed with cries to God as bedlam swept through the auditorium. Haim Edri, an Orthodox Jew from the Likud, vaulted his desk and rushed for the front, locks flying. Dozens of members began to move for the aisles; some stood immobilized; still others began to shout in outrage. It all joined into a strange roar that could just as easily have been a choir of angels as far as Solomon was concerned. Only in his wildest dreams had he imagined such a response.

"Silence!" The Speaker slammed his gavel. "Silence! Silence!"

But they did not silence. In fact, the volume seemed to surge. Someone grabbed Haim Edri before he got to the government table and hauled him down, yelling something about touching the Ark.

A gunshot suddenly thundered over their heads. Silence engulfed them. A guard lowered his rifle and looked tentatively at the prime minister.

"Thank you, Samuel," Ben Gurion said. "Everyone return to your seats immediately. We will do this in an orderly fashion or we won't do it at all. Our nation is facing a terrible crisis, and we must act quickly! Sit down!"

They hesitated and then moved back to their seats. Most of them sat. Haim Edri stood to one side, bobbing at the Ark and weeping softly as he had done a thousand times at the Wailing Wall. Four others joined him, and no one could dare to object. Part of Solomon wanted to join them as well.

The prime minister walked out to the Ark.

"Now, I know this is out of the ordinary, but given the circumstances we face, I'm sure you'll understand," he said. "I won't go into all the details, but last night the Ark you see before you crossed into our borders from

Ethiopia where it has evidently been hidden for at least fifteen hundred years. It arrived in Jerusalem at about three this morning. We have had our best archaeologists study it within the confines of the Law, and there is a unanimous consensus. What you see is the same Ark carried by our forefather David many years ago."

They began to talk in hushed tones again, and the prime minister quieted them with another stern warning. Three more joined the group nodding and praying with Haim Edri.

"Our neighbors know that we have the Ark. They believe that we'll now demand the Temple Mount back. Evidently they have taken advantage of the situation to force our hand. As we speak, our own forces are building to full strength. We currently have a squadron in the air, and our own mechanized divisions are already rolling into position. Within twelve hours we will be at full military strength."

The Plenum had calmed to a deathly quiet, broken only by a single soft wail from the lips of Haim Edri.

"All because of the Ark?" someone asked.

A dozen members erupted to silence the member. "Of course for the Ark! Are you not a Jew?"

Solomon knew then he would have his way. He glanced at Goldstein who stared at him with angry eyes.

"How can we be sure this is the Ark?" Shmuel demanded. "Does it contain the tablets?"

"You know that we can't even touch it, much less open it. But the poles are a different story. They are at least three thousand years old. This we have verified. The goldwork dates back to our best understanding of the age. The rabbi has examined it—there can be no doubt, my friends."

"And does the rabbi say that God's presence dwells there?" The question rang from the back and sent a hush over them.

Solomon stepped forward. A tremble had taken to his legs. "To doubt this would be to doubt Judaism," he said softly. "Everything which makes us Jews is held in this chest, my dear friends. Without it, there would be no Jew today. Let no one be mistaken, the Creator of the heavens and the earth has granted us favor today. It is time for his people to claim their inheritance once again."

For long seconds, no one spoke. They only stared, as if frozen by the weight of the moment.

"Then we have to build our Temple," Shmuel Weiss said. He stood slowly and then turned to face his peers. "I know this is not what you would expect from me, my friends." His voice was tight with emotion. "But the world of the Jew has just changed. We cannot allow the mockery of God any longer."

"You're making a mistake!"

They spun to Goldstein who stood across the room. "Maybe you didn't hear the prime minister." He shoved a finger towards the east. "There are over six thousand tanks lining our borders as we speak. We are outnumbered three to one on the ground. The Arabs will crush us!"

"Joshua was outnumbered a hundred to one!" someone cried.

"Joshua wasn't up against chemical weapons!"

"How *dare* you question the power of God!"

"I don't question his power. I question how many Jews will die in the next twenty-four hours."

Solomon stretched his hand out. "Perhaps you live in the wrong country, Stephen. We are Jews who exist because of God. And now we must exist for God. Without him we are not Jews. Deny this Ark, and you are not a Jew."

He faced the rest. "The military balance is even, but the spiritual balance is not. They have camped in our throne room too long. Today God has sent us an imperative." He pointed at the Ark without looking its way. "An imperative no Jew can deny."

The room erupted again, but now mostly with those in agreement. Someone yelled for the prime minister to speak.

Ben Gurion eyed Solomon. "I see it quite plainly," he said when they had quieted. "If we have the Ark, we must have the Temple. Our history is very clear."

"But our history does not have to be written here today," Goldstein said. "We *must* talk to the Arabs. Surely—"

"You are wrong, Stephen. We talked to General Abu Ismael of the Syrian forces half an hour ago. They are demanding that we deliver the Ark to them by nightfall. Nothing less will satisfy them. They see this as their opportunity, and I believe they will take it. The Ark is as much a convenience as a problem for them. I think our hand has been forced. Forced by God, himself, perhaps."

"Then give them the Ark!" Goldstein shouted, red faced.

Now the Plenum exploded, mostly by those outraged. The tide was unstoppable, Solomon thought. The Temple would be rebuilt. Unless the Arabs were bluffing.

He dismissed the thought.

The Speaker banged the podium, but no one was listening now. He was banging the podium and calling for a vote, and Solomon was thinking they would have to fire another gunshot when the door to his right suddenly slammed open.

At first the sight of the two people in the doorway had no effect on him. He wondered who had let the visitors in. But then he saw the woman's face, and he caught his breath.

Rebecca?

She stood still for a moment, scanning the room, her long hair flowing over her shoulders. Then her eyes met his, and he knew that his daughter lived. Tears flooded his eyes.

"Rebecca!?" he cried.

The Plenum quieted and followed his eyes.

"Rebecca! You . . . you're alive!" He stretched out his arms and stepped towards her.

"Father." She walked towards him quickly, around the government table. The man at her side followed. He stood tall, dressed in a dirty tunic. Tangled dark hair fell to his shoulders. His eyes were bright and they had fixed on the Ark, and Solomon knew that this man was Caleb.

But walking beside his daughter, the man looked more like Elijah.

47

THE MOMENT REBECCA SAW THE Ark in the Plenum, she knew Israel would never be the same again. And it wasn't because the Ark had come to Jerusalem; it was because Caleb had come to the Ark.

They had taken a ride from Eilat with a reservist headed to Jerusalem, and the further north they drove, the more enigmatic Caleb had become. He had stopped talking altogether as they entered the city. But it wasn't until she'd been told that her father was here, at the Knesset, that she really began to understand the significance of Caleb's coming.

He was a Christian from the desert, unknowing curator of the Ark, and he had been practically dragged north by a strange, undeniable power that she now knew came from the Nazarene.

It was as if her father was really the Roman governor, Pilate, and Caleb had come to reopen a two-thousand-year-old case. The Jews versus the Nazarene. The old Ark versus the new ark, the one that was now in man. A spike of dread nudged her heart as she walked towards her father.

Rebecca embraced him.

"I was told you were dead," he said.

"I was," she said. She smiled. "But no more. Do I look dead to you?"

"No. No, thank God!"

Her father turned to Caleb. "And this must be . . ."

"Caleb." She turned to him. "This is my father."

But Caleb might not have even heard her. He was staring at the gold Ark and a glint lit his eyes. A glint she'd seen before.

"What is the meaning of this?" A member she recognized only by sight called from the fourth row back. "Please, we don't have time for this!"

Caleb turned his head and looked at him, stupefied. The man settled to his seat, as if reprimanded. Rebecca glanced at her father. He was watching Caleb intently. She backed up, struggling with an uncertain emotion that rose through her throat.

Her worlds were meeting. The old and the new. Old wineskin, new wine.

Caleb turned back to the Ark and walked towards it.

"Stop!" Solomon ordered.

Caleb stopped, one meter from the Ark.

"Who is this man, David?" the prime minister demanded. "What is the meaning of this?"

Solomon answered without removing his eyes from Caleb. "This is Caleb. He's from the monastery where we found the Ark."

"And what's he doing here?" the prime minister asked in a low urgent voice. "We don't have time for this!"

Solomon hesitated. "I don't know." He glanced at Rebecca, brows arched. "Rebecca?"

Rebecca looked at Caleb and their eyes met. She might as well have been looking into pools of bottomless love, she thought. Because she did love this man, more than anything she had ever loved. Her knees felt weak. He was here for a definite reason, and the love that had grown between them somehow fed that reason. He had lost his first love and then found it—and she had played a part in that. She had inadvertently forced him to face his faith, and now his reborn faith would be tested here, before this court.

"I think he wants to tell you something," Rebecca said. "You should listen. He is a prophet from God."

A few protests rippled through the auditorium.

"We don't need a prophet," Solomon said. "We have the Ark."

Caleb turned and faced the camera in the gallery. He looked at it for a few seconds.

"The world must see what I have to show you," he said. "Is this camera broadcasting?"

Immediately an objection was raised, but the prime minister raised his hand. "No. But it is recording."

"I must object," Solomon said.

"Let him speak, David."

The cameraman bent behind the camera, face glued to the eyepiece.

Caleb turned then walked slowly around the government table, blinking, like a lost child examining a strange breed of aliens. He tapped his fingers on the wood as he walked its length. It was unreal. The Knesset just watched him, stunned.

"You are the Jews?" he asked. *What was he asking?* Of course they were Jews—he knew that.

No one answered.

"When I was a child, I sang and a thousand people fell down. Did you hear about that?"

A low murmur said that some of them had.

"Then I somehow misplaced my love for God. It can happen to anyone. But I have found it again. And I've come to tell you that his love is now in the hearts of his children. It's no longer in the Ark."

"You have no right to come in here and tell us about God's love!" Solomon bit off, furious. "You are a Christian! Your people have killed more of us than the Arabs."

"You mean the Nazis? They weren't my people, and they weren't God's children. God's power now lives in his children, through the Holy Spirit, not in this Ark."

Shouts of protest boomed across the auditorium.

"Blasphemy!" someone shouted. The call pushed others into open argument, and the noise rose to a dull roar.

Caleb looked around, as if perplexed by the scene. He turned and walked to the Ark and then spun around so that his dirty white tunic swept around his ankles. He planted his feet wide and shoved both arms over his head.

Rebecca held her breath.

Caleb tilted his head back and screamed at the ceiling. A long, chilling *Ahhhhh!* sound that ripped through the room and silenced every last man and woman with their mouths still open.

Rebecca felt her heart melt. She lowered her forehead into her right hand and stifled a sob.

Caleb's cry echoed to silence and he looked around. Tears slipped down the prime minister's cheeks. Others in his cabinet blinked at their own tears. Confused, they looked down, avoiding Caleb's eyes.

"The power of the Messiah fills my bones," Caleb cried. Now several began to weep openly.

"But *I* am not the Messiah. I am only like a voice crying in the wilderness. The Messiah has already come and he was the Nazarene. He was Christ."

It was all too much for the Orthodox Jew, Haim Edri. He jumped to his feet. "You are speaking blasphemy! How dare you defile this holy place of God!"

A dozen others jumped to their feet and joined in the protest, red faced. Rebecca watched them and felt her heart bleed.

Caleb suddenly threw his hands skyward and yelled again, the same long, chilling *Ahhhh* sound that had stilled them before.

The effect was immediate. Those standing, including Haim Edri, collapsed to their seats. Weeping broke out like an epidemic, and suddenly Caleb was weeping with them. Standing with his feet spread and his hands lifted, weeping at the ceiling. Tears rolled off his cheeks and fell on his tunic. The room swelled with the terrible sound.

Solomon stood to Rebecca's right, staring angrily at Caleb, fighting his own tears. She wanted to rush over and tell him that it was all going to be just fine. That all of his dreams were not being dashed by this seemingly impossible moment. But she knew that it wasn't true. Whatever it was, encountering the Nazarene's power could not be characterized as *just fine*.

Above them the camera continued to blink green. The prime minister sat with his head in his hands, crying like a baby.

Caleb suddenly stopped, looked around as though dazed, and then walked for the Ark. He reached out and touched it before anyone could stop him.

Silence slammed into the room.

He shoved the lid sideways with a scraping sound that grated across the Plenum. The members were too stunned to respond. They only gaped with horror.

Caleb reached into the Ark and pulled out first an ancient looking scroll and then a flat tablet of stone. From where she stood, Rebecca could clearly see the black markings on the slate. She was looking at the fingerprint of God, and the realization made her dizzy.

He held them up, one in each hand. "Yes, real. The Ark of the Covenant. Stone, paper, gold, and wood."

He tossed the relics back in the chest and they landed with a loud clunk. "But powerless!" he yelled. "Powerless!" He walked away from the Ark.

"The same power that once flowed through the prophet Elijah is now upon me." His eyes flashed eagerly. He walked to the government table and back, staring out at the people.

Still no one spoke.

"And if God gives you a sign today, will you then believe? How many times must he speak before you listen? Not the Jew only, but the world!" He pointed into the camera. "The Muslim and the Christian and the Hindu—all of you!"

Caleb lifted a hand. He looked over at Rebecca, eyes on fire. "Do you believe, Rebecca?"

"Yes," she whispered.

"Do you believe?"

"Yes! Yes, I believe!" she yelled.

He closed his eyes and immediately she felt the energy tickle her skin. The hair on her neck stood on end. It was as though an electric current were passing through the room.

"If you cannot believe what he has said, then at least believe in the evidence of his power," Caleb said in a loud voice. "'As men gather silver, bronze, iron, lead, and tin into the midst of a furnace, to blow fire on it, to melt it; so I will gather you in My anger and in My fury, and I will leave you there and melt you.'" He was quoting a prophet.

His hair moved in a breeze that inexplicably swept across the room. His arm lowered slowly, eerily, with a single curved forefinger pointing towards the Ark, as if Michelangelo himself had painted him on the stage. The wind continued to blow softly across the room, sweeping at his tunic and hair. His arm stopped level with the Ark and hung there lazily.

The wings on the cherubim closest to Rebecca began to sag, and she felt her heart jump in her chest. The angels bowed together, until their heads touched. The rim about the lid began to fold out slowly.

The Ark of the Covenant was melting!

A shriek of alarm shattered the silence. Haim Edri stood pointing at the Ark. Those seated closest, around the horseshoe table, shoved back in alarm from a sudden heat radiating out from the Ark.

Like lead in a furnace, the Ark withered. The two angels melted flat into the lid, and now the ancient acacia wood under the gold bared itself and burst into flame.

Caleb stood with eyes closed, hand suspended, smiling. Scores of members had fallen to their knees and wept bitterly. But whether they were weeping for the Ark, or for the presence of God carried on the wind, Rebecca did not know.

Scores of others were too stunned to move.

Solomon sank slowly to his knees, weeping. *Father, I beg you to reveal yourself to him,* Rebecca prayed. Her father lowered his head and shook with sobs.

It was over in two minutes. The burning ashes of the wood sat on top of gold that had melted to the table and dripped like icicles to the floor. Only then did Caleb lower his arm, still smiling wide like a child.

The camera still blinked green.

48

REBECCA STOOD IN THE DIM light of the candles in her father's home and smiled at Caleb who sat at the wood table. Solomon looked out the window as he had on a thousand nights, gazing at the Temple Mount to the east.

The Dome of the Rock glowed gold by the moon's light, just as it had each of those nights. The *Waqf* guards marched its perimeter as they always had, and if you looked long enough, you would see one of them walk to the Western Wall and look down on the courtyard, empty now in the moonlight. Nothing at all had changed.

It had been two days since the meeting of the Knesset.

Solomon turned from the window. "Then do you believe it will one day be rebuilt?" he asked.

Caleb grinned. He hadn't lost his enigmatic flare, but Rebecca had decided it was part of what attracted her to him. "Many do. I don't know. The New Testament seems to suggest it, but in reality the Temple is here." He pounded his chest twice with a fist.

"Yes, I think you've made your point with bells and whistles," Solomon said.

Solomon had run from the Knesset that day, and they hadn't found him until late in the night. He'd been thrown into an abyss of confusion. But if Rebecca was not mistaken, he was beginning to emerge.

The camera footage of Caleb's finger pointing at the Ark while it slowly melted into a puddle on the floor had been played and replayed on nearly every television station around the globe. The Arabs had watched in disbelief as the reason for their war dissolved before their eyes. It had taken them twenty-four hours to begin their withdrawal, mostly because of the confusion left in the wake of the footage. Not that the footage itself was confusing, but the implication of this undeniable supernatural intervention of God clearly was confusing. What did this mean to Islam? Or to Judaism? Or to Christianity, for that matter? Abu Ismael, at least, had seen the hand of God and had called the prime minister personally. He had actually asked to speak with Caleb. It was hardly imaginable!

The talking heads were just now placing their spin control on footage that had made it to the street level already. The rabbis were beginning to line up with some nonsense about illusions and the Islamic imams were saying something similar using different words. Even Christians, in substantial numbers, were voicing dissent, decrying the destruction of the Ark, which would have hastened the end of days.

No matter how you looked at it, one thing was clear: there was no Ark and therefore no need for war. The U.S. brokered the pullback, but it would have happened on its own, Rebecca thought.

Caleb glanced at her nervously.

Ask him, she mouthed. And then she winked.

Caleb faced Solomon. "Actually, I have come to ask you something, sir."

"Yes? Then ask. I doubt you can do any more harm than you already have."

"Yes. Well then I would like to ask you for the hand of your daughter," he said and glanced at Rebecca again. She dipped her head and smiled in support.

Solomon's face lightened a shade. "Ask for her hand? You're not suggesting . . . marriage!"

Caleb cleared his throat. "Yes. Yes, her hand in marriage."

"She's a Jew! You're a Christian, for God's sake!"

"I'm an Ethiopian and she's an Israeli!"

Solomon stared at Caleb, and then at Rebecca. He finally let out a long sigh and turned back to the window. Rebecca hadn't expected his immediate approval and, all things considered, this was actually a good start.

"So you think you love my daughter; is that it, boy?"

Caleb looked at Rebecca. "I love her deeply. She is beautiful beyond my imagination. She is wise and she is kind and she is tender. She is—"

"I know my own daughter, Caleb. No need to fill me in." Solomon turned back. "Tender? Are you sure you know her? The rest I'll grant you, but killing isn't done with a tender hand."

"I think she's done with killing. Her hands have become too tender for killing," Caleb said.

Her father raised an eyebrow. "You have taken one treasure from me already this week, and now you ask for the other? All my life I have done little but dream of rebuilding God's holy Temple."

He couldn't let it go, and Rebecca hardly blamed him.

"Then build his Temple," Caleb said. "But build it in here." He placed his hand on his chest again.

Solomon nodded. "Yes, yes. In *here*. How silly of me. And what about you, Rebecca?"

"Father?"

"What do you think of this ludicrous suggestion?"

"I have felt his power in my veins, Father. I have given him my life."

"Whose power?"

She hesitated. "The Nazarene's."

"I'm talking about your marriage to Caleb!" he said.

"Oh." She looked at Caleb and smiled. "Then I don't think the suggestion is ludicrous at all. I can't imagine a man I'd rather marry. He's won my heart already; why shouldn't I give him my hand?"

Solomon glared at her for a full three seconds. Then his face softened and he closed his eyes. "My, my, you have taken the other treasure from me, haven't you?"

Caleb spoke softly. "My treasure is Christ—"

"I'm talking about Rebecca!"

"Yes, I know. But I would like your blessing."

"And now you want my blessing as well as my treasures. Then take it." For a moment, Rebecca thought he was speaking out of spite. But then a soft smile lit his face. "Winning my daughter's heart is no small task. God knows you have earned it."

"Then you agree?" Rebecca asked, slightly surprised.

"But you will live in Jerusalem."

"My home has been destroyed," Caleb said. "Your government has been good enough to promise funding the restoration of the Debra Damarro—the least I can do for my parents is to rebuild it."

The flap with Ethiopia over the Ark had been short but heated. The Ethiopian Orthodox Church insisted that they still had the original Ark at Saint Mary's in Axum, and they were demanding an apology. Israel's first gesture was this rebuilding effort.

"Then go to Ethiopia and return to Jerusalem when you're ready," Solomon said.

"But I am ready now."

"You want to take my daughter to Ethiopia?"

"Just while we rebuild. I would also like to visit Father Hadane."

"We can marry here, Father," Rebecca said. "A Jewish wedding."

He frowned and faced the Temple Mount again. "You have made a mess of my life, Caleb. Do you realize this?"

"Yes. Yes, sir." Caleb stood and stepped towards Rebecca. "But what gets torn down may be rebuilt. I am confident you will rebuild your faith, as I have mine."

Caleb smiled and took Rebecca's hand. "I think it's time to begin building, don't you?" he said.

Solomon turned around and looked at his daughter. For a long time none of them spoke. When Solomon finally did, his voice was soft and introspective.

"Perhaps you are right, my friend. Perhaps you are right."

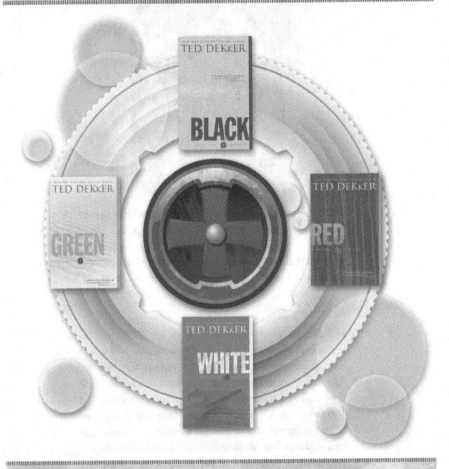

ABOUT THE AUTHORS

Cheryl Mahr

Ted Dekker is a *New York Times* best-selling author with more than five million books in print. He is known for stories that combine adrenaline-laced plots with incredible confrontations between unforgettable characters. He lives with his wife in Austin, Texas.

Bill Bright went home to heaven in 2003, but his legacy endures through his family and ministry. He was best known as the founder of Campus Crusade for Christ, an organization that now has over 26,000 full-time staff and more than 553,000 trained volunteers in 196 countries. Dr. Bright was the recipient of six honorary doctorates and numerous achievement awards, as well as the author of more than one hundred books and thousands of pamphlets that have been distributed by the millions in most major languages.